Praise for Tricia Sullivan

"Awe-inspiring . . . a lean, mean, deep water hunter of a meditation on things human, more-than-human, and less-than-human . . . a jolting trip into a deep, dark, all-to-believable future: get down on your knees and pray this one won't happen.

—Ian McDonald

"A fine piece of work, neatly crafted, beautiful, intricate and intelligent, strongly imagined with wit and sympathy. A professional debut by a real writer."

—Wilhelmina Baird, author of *Clipjoint* (Ace/Berkley)

Lethe

Tricia Sullivan

BANTAM BOOKS
New York Toronto London Sydney Auckland

LETHE
A Bantam Spectra Book / July 1995

SPECTRA and the portrayal of a boxed "s" are trademarks of Bantam Books,
a division of Bantam Doubleday Dell Publishing Group, Inc.

ISBN 0-553-56858-2

Published simultaneously in the United States and Canada

Bantam Books are published by Bantam Books, a division of Bantam Doubleday Dell Publishing
Group, Inc. Its trademark, consisting of the words "Bantam Books" and the portrayal of a
rooster, is Registered in U.S. Patent and Trademark Office and in other countries. Marca Reg-
istrada. Bantam Books, 1540 Broadway, New York, New York 10036.

PRINTED IN THE UNITED STATES OF AMERICA

RAD   0 9 8 7 6 5 4 3 2 1

For Todd
This light inside can never die

Acknowledgments

Thank you Janna Silverstein, Raymond Kennedy, and Todd Wiggins for giving me the things writers need; special thanks to my parents for giving me what humans need.

Lethe

Nor skin nor hide nor fleece
      Shall cover you,
Nor curtain of crimson nor fine
Shelter of cedar-wood be over you,
      Nor the fir tree
      Nor the pine.

Nor sight of whin nor gorse
      Nor river-yew,
Nor fragrance of flowering bush,
Nor wailing of reed-bird to waken you,
      Nor of linnet,
      Nor of thrush.

Nor word nor touch nor sight
      Of lover, you
Shall long through the night but for this:
The roll of the full tide to cover you
      Without question,
      Without kiss.

                      H.D.

Morpheus

1

While Daire Morales was disappearing haunches over nose, mind over matter, ghosts before breakfast into the sleek void that opened beneath him, he found himself thinking none of the usual thoughts to which people in such situations are prone. Life did not flash before his eyes; he experienced no old regrets nor yearnings of any kind; and no, he did not cry out for salvation. In truth, he felt almost happy, if this is possible while one's arms, legs, ears, and gonads are being disassociated from their familiar locations as mapped on the brain before birth and scrambled into new and astonishing combinations in the senses. For the world, at long last, had proven itself to be large.

Daire's ancestors had been sky people, some of them still sun worshipers into the satellite ages. They had come from the airless heights of the Andes and the burning plains of Mexico; their ancient gods were fiery and winged and they lived open to the heavens. Despite being raised indoors in a rez (or maybe because of it), Daire had inherited their craving for space. Only a moment ago, crawling across the black featureless surface of Underkohling, he had extinguished his handlight to look at the stars overhead; and he saw not only the sky above, but also its luminous reflection in the dark mirror of the ground. The stars, tiny blurred streaks, glowed from the surface in front of his face. He stared into the depths of this mirrored universe; it gave the impression of infinity, as though ground and sky were one.

Did he ask for it? Did he want it? Impossible to say, but . . .

He'd been crouching there, mesmerized, for some minutes when his headset cascaded to life.

"Daire?" Colin's voice broke his reverie. "I'm getting a pulse from your location. Forget the readings—get the fuck out of there."

Daire swallowed, unable to speak. Transfixed, he didn't try to move as the dark surface suddenly began to stir around him, its shining skin rippling, stretching, and then folding in on itself like a great mouth taking a soundless gulp. The ground beneath his feet deliquesced to the consistency of mercury and gently at first he flowed into it; then its pull turned nasty. He lost his grip on the handlight, the stars above shivered crazily and vanished, and darkness tongued him, rolling him over several times as all the while he slipped in its frictionless, womblike folds. For long, vertiginous moments he reached out with fingers extended, to grab anything he could; but the substance of the darkness would admit him no hold.

Now, even as the limbs of his body arched out reflexively in swimming motions, his mind detached itself from the event. His body had become as alien as a frog's, kicking and writhing in a dark stream, but Daire dismissed its helplessness blithely. A new sense had flooded his mind, a sense of not being somewhere and of never having been anywhere—a memory of nothingness. All premises were erased, the slate swept clean. He had no sense of himself; the mind was mute. And he gave over to the void without even a sigh.

2

The summons came too early in the morning; the lifts weren't running yet to conserve power and Jenae was feeling squeamish about reporting to the Hall of Pickled Brains in person. She didn't like the feel of them looking at her. It wasn't so bad when they were just voices in the computer, but to actually be in their presence, to shift your weight from foot to foot wondering what camera they were using to watch you . . . and then that weird smell. No matter how many layers of glass and steel they were sequestered behind, there was always that faint odor in the Hall, like formaldehyde—something rotten being cosmeticized.

And then to have to remember not to call them Pickled Brains to their . . . faces? *Heads*, they insisted on being titled, instead. Which was too bad. Pickled Brains just seemed to roll off the tongue.

Still soft with sleep, Jenae wandered into the common room of the alchemist quarters and gazed enviously at the reclining forms of her colleagues scattered on couches. The air was stale. She wanted coffee but couldn't risk it in case the Pickled Brains wanted her to go into altermode. Passing the mirror on her way out, she tried to scowl at herself, but even that didn't turn out right. Jenae had one of those round, symmetrical, concave faces that are always serene and dignified. The most unattractive expression she could muster left her looking like a mischievous child—hardly an image commensurate with her mood.

She took the stairs down fifteen flights to the point where the League of New Alchemists Tower plunged underground. The spire had been constructed to look impressive in an age when people went about aboveground and on the sea; but the business end of the place was below sea level, in the bowels of the old Ingenix headquarters that had been taken over by the League when Ingenix Corporation was dissolved during the Gene Wars scandals. Whenever she walked down the long, curving corridor toward the Hall of Pickled Brains, Jenae envisioned the old labs: the gleaming cylinders of galvanized steel, the petri dishes, the optic robots, all focused on the creation of the genome-altering viruses, one of which had given rise to her altermode talent. The leadership of Ingenix had spent most of their time and energy creating kill viruses; what would they say if they could see her, Jenae, an unlikely by-product of the war for speciation control, walking down this corridor as if she owned the place—which, in a sense, she did?

It was a nice thought, but it didn't lift her mood. How, she thought, does inheriting the dungeon justify the tortures?

The Hall of Pickled Brains was always kept dim. Jenae didn't know whether this was a medical necessity for the Heads, or whether it was done out of discretion for their extreme ugliness. But it would be hard to say whether the darkness really helped. As she walked past the long files of machinery housed in tall cabinets, she could feel her skin reacting to the subliminal hum, and the grinning towers of Plexiglas that housed the actual brains, though shadowed, still gave forth a chilling gleam. In the center of the hall, in a shimmer of amber light, a single chair had been set facing the bank of monitors that lined one wall. As Jenae moved into the light to take the seat, she could dimly make out the outline of a Pickled Brain floating in clear solution in a tank opposite. For an instant she saw it clearly; the nimbus of grafted nerves and lymphatic vessels extending from the cortex to the unseen organ centers gave the grotesque impression of hair. Then she stepped into the light and saw nothing beyond its warm circle. She sat.

"Good day." A dead voice, female, vaguely European. A shade too loud for life.

"G'day," Jenae muttered. She looked at her hands, embarrassed at her own thoughts. The Pickled Brains couldn't help their appearance.

"My apologies for rousing you so early. We received an

interesting communication in the night, and we must act on it now. When you've learned its contents, you'll understand the urgency. May I play you the recording?"

Jenae inclined her head. "Shoot."

The voice gave a little self-deprecating laugh. "The others are reminding me," it said, "that you don't know the context of the message. Let me summarize. A physicist from Oxford contacted us some months ago from a small research vessel in orbit around Underkohling. As you know, experimentation has not yet revealed the exact nature of this celestial body. All work there is, therefore, high risk. The Oxford scientist, Colin Peake, was examining what he thought was Underkohling's fourth gate when, in conjunction with variable bursts of EM fluctuations—"

"Hang on," Jenae interrupted. "What *fourth* gate? I only know about two."

There was a touch of humor in the response this time. "As you *should* know, Underkohling has three documented gates. The first two to be found led into distant space, too far from any star—"

"To be explored, I know, but—"

"Then the economic crash at the end of the Gene Wars brought space research to a screeching halt. When we Heads first began to discover our powers, our first priority was to get the new systems up and running and the mirror fields in place. The pure human population had to be stabilized and isolated. It was some time before anybody found the resources to make more expeditions, which found the third gate. The third gate appears to only release in one direction, since we have not had a team or probe ever return."

"I see. No wonder it wasn't publicized. Not much use then, is it?" Jenae enjoyed baiting the Pickled Brains. They took themselves far too seriously. "So what's this fourth gate?"

"Initially it was only a hypothetical gate, revealing itself at unpredictable intervals, but always in the same location. As I had begun to tell you, when Dr. Peake first contacted us four months ago, he complained that his system had been invaded by a software virus that left a trail behind it. His software had begun to display unexplained patterns that he interpreted as a code. This occurred in conjunction with

6 / Tricia Sullivan

these intervals in which the EM readings indicated the possible presence of a gate. He asked if we could decode the patterns that appeared, but our dolphin team found no cypher and no evidence that the patterns were codified at all. They seem to be an artifact of the EM flux. We were intrigued, however, so we sent him an assistant who was asked to find out what was wrong with the software—where this virus was coming from. We also wanted a second opinion on the situation. Peake is somewhat eccentric. He is not prepared to dive headfirst through a gate that may only open one way, like the third—and who would? At the same time, he's not about to relinquish the project to us, even though we are better qualified to pursue it. Pure humans have certain prejudices against the League—and maybe it's natural enough."

"So you sent someone to be the guinea pig. Who?"

"Guinea pig is hardly the appropriate term. We sent a League software expert named Daire Morales, who is qualified to take readings that dolphins can use, in the web, to find a way to stabilize this gate. This was several months ago. Recently Morales arrived at Underkohling and made the transfer to the Oxford vessel. Then we received this transmission, last night. I'll show it to you in its entirety."

A central monitor sparked open. The view revealed a dark interior, most of which was occupied by a tall, awkward-looking white man with thinning brown hair and spectacles who sat sprawled in a chair under an angled sliver of white light. His face was sharply outlined, his eyes invisible behind the reflection off his glasses.

"I'm going to ramble at you for a while," he announced. His local accent was noticeable, almost affected, Jenae thought. "I don't feel sufficiently coherent to make a written report. Please bear with me."

His left hand was in constant motion, juggling a pair of Chinese meditation balls with preternaturally long fingers.

"Your agent, Daire Morales, arrived about sixty hours ago. Interesting guy. He calibrated my program for remote EM readings to interface with your equipment, and we took a broad sample of readings which I'll send to you presently. There was no evidence of anything unusual at that time. The indicators were very flat. He felt the readings we were getting were not much use because they can't be interpreted relative to anything, which is true. He also wanted more intimate data. I'd already tried sending down a probe, but the EM currents interfered with its navigation and ultimately repelled it from the site.

"Well, that didn't bother your man. He insisted on going down there himself, and getting a feel for the place, he said. Those were his words. 'I need to get a feel for it,' he said. I didn't think he meant it quite literally—oh, well, wrong on that one."

An ironic smile cut a swath of shadow across the lower half of his face.

"I put a monitoring device on him before he suited up, derivative of what you use for altermode so far as I understand it, and I kept as much data displayed as the system would allow. Every factor concerning the energy around him in a five-meter radius was in front of me the whole time."

He paused, scratching his head.

"I guess these things will happen when you treat the universe as your playground. I tried to warn him, but it was too late. He was standing right in the middle of the gate when it opened. It was really quite incredible to behold: he was simply pulled in. Took about two or three seconds. And that was it. The hopper's still there, nearby, perfectly intact. I can get it back using remote control but I'm leaving it there for now, just in case. . . . It's been ten hours, by the way, and no sign of him.

"Now . . ." He let out a laugh—it was a bit manic, Jenae thought. "Let's talk about the good stuff. First of all, the data I got as he fell through is priceless. I hope you and your dolphins can work with it, because to me it's just exquisitely irrational, and I'd love to know what it means. Secondly, after he'd made his sacrifice and the gate closed again—after about twenty seconds, by the way—there was material residue left on the surface. At first I felt a bit squeamish about examining it, but I succeeded in programming the hopper Morales abandoned to pick up a sample and I was able to do a quick and dirty remote analysis. I've got the results here, which I'll also send you.

"It's a fine dust, organic matter encased in ice crystals. It's not animal, though, as I feared—it's not our friend Daire, thankfully. It's mostly vegetable with some trace minerals and silicon, microorganisms ... it resembles nothing so much as alluvial soil. Silt, if you will."

He stood and began wandering about the room. The monitor's eye tracked him steadily.

"I hope this will please you," he said. "One hates to be always the bearer of bad tidings."

He stopped, glancing sidelong at the monitor.

"I've been busy on the *Morpheus* angle, as well. It seems quite logical that *Morpheus* did go through *this* gate, and in my opinion someone should have been smart enough to report it at the time. As you know, I consider myself something of an expert on Underkohling, but even I didn't know the full story about *Morpheus*. I did a little digging in the archives for Underkohling, and I found a record of a patrol ship returning fire on *Morpheus*. The runaway disintegrated on impact, according to the patrol, which is ridiculous. There was no debris recorded, and the impact coordinates correspond to this area that is now emitting signals. It's hard to believe nobody would suspect a gate at that time, knowing that even then there were two stable gates that had been explored prior to the Gene Wars."

He sat back, his face grave. The pitch of his voice dropped.

"It should have been followed up on. It was carrying evidence of war crimes, for God's sake. This is just the kind of interdepartmental project the University is going to be looking for, and I'm champing at the bit to get it worked out. I'm sure it would be beneficial to your interests, as well, if we could locate the ship. I haven't spoken to anyone at Oxford about it ... yet. If the League can find a way to stabilize the gate, I'll gladly share the credit. If not ... well, we'll worry about that if it arises. I'm sending you everything I have, and I'm going to sit tight. Contact me as soon as you have something I can use."

The screen went dark.

"What was that bit about morph ... ?"

"*Morpheus,*" corrected the Head. "It was an Ingenix ship that escaped the raids during the dissolution near the end of the Gene Wars. Executive class interplanetary vessel. State of the art, at the time. They were trying to get to the Jupiter

mining station, apparently, and went off course. You heard
the rest."

"War crimes . . ." Jenae breathed, impressed. "They were
the Ingenix directors? The guys who started the whole
fucking—I mean, the whole Gene Wars disaster?"

"So it would seem," the voice replied crisply. "That is not
your concern at present."

"You want me to stabilize the gate." Jenae could feel the
blood waking up in her gills in anticipation. "Is that it?"

"Indeed. But we're not asking you to work miracles—not
yet. If you can even discover the mechanism of the gate—its
timing, how to predict its opening and closing—we'll be
pleased. Stabilizing it may prove more difficult. You haven't
seen the data yet."

Jenae wasn't listening to caution. Her reluctance had dissolved: here was a project with real meat.

"Let's start," she urged.

"Very well," said the Pickled Brain. "We chose you for
your talent, but more than mere ability will be required. This
project will prove strenuous, for you and the dolphins.
Zafara?"

Out of the corner of her eye Jenae saw a slender black
man approach from among the shadows. He walked around
the ellipse of the altermode tank and stood to face her. He
had a hypodermic in his hand.

"I'm Zafara," he said. "Would you like an injection?"

Jenae lifted an eyebrow. It was a common rumor that the
Heads were addicted to endorphins, but it was not common
for them to offer their private stock to alchemists, however
favored. She felt honored and a little dismayed. "It's okay, I
don't need it. Have we met?"

"I've seen you around," he said. "You're younger than I
am—we probably work on different kinds of projects." He
stroked his barely visible gill slits unconsciously, and for
the first time Jenae realized he must also be an alchemist. She
was surprised: he didn't have the "feel" she was used to picking up off her own kind. Her nostrils twitched. In the air
that had stirred since he moved forward she could smell that
faint, sickening odor again.

"I'm here to monitor you," he added. "Don't take it the
wrong way: I understand you're very talented or you

wouldn't be here. But you've never done anything this big before, and it is possible to burn out. I'm here for your safety." He handed her a skin patch with its electrode. "For today we'll just be exploring the data. Go in, establish the web, and signal me when you're ready. Then I'm going to interface you with the Heads, and they'll control the data flow. We'll start you off with the parameters of the project, which the Heads have already established. The data should be coming into the web smoothly, very digestible stuff. Just take it, and let the dolphins start to play with it. We don't need any great inspiration right off the bat, so don't push them. Don't push yourself, either—I'm here to make sure you stay slow and steady. Concentrate on weaving a strong web and let the dolphins do the rest. This is not a project that you can participate in mentally, so don't even try. The volume of data is too great."

"Dig," Jenae said. "I'm ready." She hadn't gotten such a long lecture since her training days with the League. She was conscious of the importance of the project to warrant so much attention from the Pickled Brains, but that knowledge didn't inhibit her. The level of her talent in altermode had brought her, if not conceit, at least a certain nonchalance.

She went to the tank, removed her robe, and lowered herself into the water. It was warm and sweet—the sea door, as always, was closed, but Jenae derived some odd sense of comfort from the fact that the great mass of the ocean was only inches away from her, on the other side of the steel. She laid the skin patch, with its delicate, tiny circuitry, over her forehead. Then she sank to the bottom and went into altermode.

"Are you sure about her?" asked the voice of the Head.

Zafara slid the needle delicately into a vein behind his ear. His eyes rolled back. His mouth blossomed into a smile.

"She's a lovely girl, my friends. You want to know if you can trust her, don't you? Not to hurt you, ever. For you have been so hurt, I know." Zafara reflected. He sighed, looking into the depths of the pool where the woman was changing into her second self. "I think she is the one. I really do."

And he smiled and smiled.

◆

There was always a moment (how long in measurable time she couldn't say) where Jenae was—for all practical purposes—nowhere. One would think, if she was nowhere, there would be nothing to remain in her memory, afterward; without reference points, her consciousness would skip over the time, like sleep, and she would simply forget it. But this wasn't so. She was always aware of being nowhere—and afterward, she always wondered about it. There in the tank, that moment was approaching.

She had stopped breathing.

Her gills woke up and shook themselves in the current. Altermode spread over her like a chill: the outer, opalescent layer of epidermis flared slightly in the water, picking up oxygen to supplement her gills' intake. Her body responded quite automatically, her pupils rolling back as the microprocessor she had placed on her forehead began to churn out code, interfacing her with the Heads' virtuality built within the huge mass of information kept in silicon. But she, Jenae, could not switch so blithely from her normal, human consciousness to the acute, nonverbal *Now* of altermode without crossing that little chink of nothingness between modes. It was a leap of faith that had to be made.

She jumped.

On the other side, dolphins are waiting. She can hear them in this state: her mind automatically processes the impressions into words and images, but words are hazy at best. As they make the web of minds around and within her, their way of thinking is singular: closest to mathematics of all the human disciplines, but it is dolphin math, and therefore capricious and paradoxical. Jenae has been trained to make her consciousness hang back from the dolphins' thinking, so as not to pollute the web with human logic.

Her pod of seven is outside in Shark Bay. They are descendants of those first, whimsical dolphins to strike up a friendship with local fishermen here at Monkey Mia, Australia, back in the twentieth century. Luckily for altermoders, some of these highly human-sensitive dolphins happened to be around when Ingenix, located in the present League Tower, decided to start experimenting with human regression to aquatic form. These ancestors of present dolphin members of the League saved many altermode humans from death in the sea; they taught the disoriented altermoders how to tap into the web and so communicate with dolphins; they provided the League with what is now its greatest asset: willing dolphin pods with their extravagant talent for layering mind on mind and so tackling the most complex theoretical problems to confront humans of the present age. Jenae trusts them implicitly. She may be called an alchemist, but it is the dolphins who perform the magical transformations of data.

Now the web is ready. Jenae leans into the system and pulls out the first strands of data retrieved by Colin Peake and paths them to the dolphins. It has begun.

3

Her sister's face was a broken mirror.

"Wind power," Yi Ling said. She crouched on the floor of her empty room in Perth rez as though poised for takeoff. Her fingers, taut and graceful, stretched away from her throat, tangled in the loops of the blue strangle ribbon. Like birds' wings her hands stroked the pale air. Her neck flexed against the pressure even as the drug-charged blood rushed into her face. She gave an odd, lopsided twitch and closed her eyes. She didn't breathe for a long time.

"Yi Ling," Jenae whispered. "Please don't do this. You know it scares me."

Yi Ling opened one eye, which jumped as it gazed at Jenae. Her face was flushed, but still she did not breathe. She rocked back and forth on the floor. Jenae could see strands of blue creeping up her neck.

"Stop it," Jenae said again, and reached forward to remove the band. But Yi Ling lurched away in a violent movement and crashed into the corner, kicking out at Jenae. Still she didn't breathe. Jenae fell on top of her, wrestled her arms down, and pulled the blue band off. It had made a pink indentation in Yi Ling's neck. Her sister refused to exhale.

Jenae clenched her teeth and punched her twin in the stomach. Yi Ling gasped, coughed, and inhaled, her eyes fixed coldly on her sister until Jenae had to look away. Shaken, Jenae stepped back. Yi Ling pulled her slender legs up against her chest and made herself small in the corner. She didn't even seem to be high.

"Shit!" Jenae spat. She looked at the strangle ribbon in disgust, wondering how she had let Yi Ling come to this.

"Why do you do that? To be like me? You don't want to be like me. You wouldn't believe what it's like."

The eyes of her twin stared, implacable.

Jenae gave a hollow laugh. "You should be thankful you can't kill yourself that way. Your autonomic nervous system would kick in for you—mine wouldn't. You don't want to be like me."

"Kill something already dead." Yi Ling's voice was a soft scraping. She wasn't looking at Jenae anymore.

She wants altermode, Jenae thought. Can it really be so bad here that she would rather work with the League? That she would torture herself because she doesn't have altermode, even after most of our family died from the viruses?

She looked around the room. Yi Ling had a private room—there was something to be said for that. She had a computer with the latest software. She even had plants. Once, Jenae had given her a cat, thinking it would give her something to care about, but she'd raged at it until it fled down the hall to the home of a gentle old man who did downers most days and sat in front of the vid, stroking the cat endlessly.

"You're bored is all," Jenae said. "You should do something. With your art, maybe. Teach people, or just share . . . you don't have to just sit here all day. People do things in the rez. They work. They accomplish things."

Yi Ling was ignoring her. She looked at the wall.

"Where are your paintings?" Jenae asked suddenly. "What did you do with all the stuff that was on the walls?"

"Gave it away. Don't need it."

People start to give their stuff away, Jenae thought, when they're getting ready to die. She'd seen it happen often enough. Anger formed, cold and motionless, in the bottom of her stomach. Suddenly Yi Ling's ways seemed more than games to attract attention. If her sister was thinking about it . . .

It wasn't fair. Yi Ling was all the family she had. Until the age of fifteen they had been inseparable; they'd had the special bond of identical twins made even stronger by mutual need. Jenae didn't know how she would have survived the confinement, the agonizing sameness, of growing up orphaned in the rez, without Yi Ling. Guiltily, she realized that without *her*, Yi Ling was not surviving it. She had always been too sensitive, too fragile—Jenae had been protecting her for years. When Jenae had started developing altermode in her teens, Yi Ling had been frightened by it, and horrified that it meant her sister would no longer live on the rez. She had broken down completely, retreating more and more inside herself. Now that Jenae had this gate project, she would have even less time to spend here.

She had taken three days off to travel 850 kilometers down to Perth to see her sister, and Yi Ling seemed encased in some invisible yet impermeable membrane.

I have my dolphins, Jenae thought. The human part of my life may be empty, but I have altermode, and my second self there. Yi Ling can only imagine it, but does she have any idea what it really is? If only I could share this, too, with her. Dammit, why didn't we *both* develop the phenotype? Did she resist it? We should be together. . . .

Yi Ling was watching her. Reading my mind, Jenae thought. Jenae had better cheer up or she'd only make things worse.

"Hey," she said. "I didn't tell you what's been keeping me away these past few weeks. I've been working on this chewy problem. Did you know they found a third gate on Underkohling?" She paused, looking for a flicker of interest. It was too hard to tell with Yi Ling. She had a face like Jenae's: still.

"They did. They found a third gate but get this: It only goes one way. You can't get back! *But*," she pitched her voice enticingly, as if she were talking to a young child. "There may also be a *fourth* gate. Yeah, you heard me right. And there may be life there. It may go to a planet—or a solar system with planets. And on one of them, there may be life."

Yi Ling was not looking directly at her—but she wasn't looking away, either.

"They found *plant matter*. Someone on the other side may even be trying to communicate with us. It's all possible. So . . ." She made herself grin. "I'll have to keep you posted on it. Can you imagine, Yi Ling? Outside. Trees. Rivers. Rain." Jenae became caught up in her own imagination. She closed her eyes.

When she opened them, she saw heavy tears on her twin's face.

◆

Some days, out in the bright and burning wind, it was possible to forget that the earth was inimical to human life. The harshness of the elements felt more invigorating than threatening. Turning her back on the shimmer of Perth rez's mirror fields, Jenae looked out over the exposed seaside. Her mind conjured the long-ago extinguished afterimage of men and women on fast horses cantering across the shore. Their faces flushed. Their hair blowing. Sometimes she felt she was one of them.

But she was only walking, and the wind was fit to knock her down, and her goggles stained the land yellow. The protective gel on her skin rendered it insensitive to the air currents, and she was sweating in the heavy clothing. Her boots kicked the stones, dully. It was only a few kilometers from Perth rez to the tube station that would take her back to Monkey Mia on Shark Bay in the north, and the League of New Alchemists Tower. It was unheard-of not to use a sealed taxi, but Jenae was sick of confinement. Altermode made her more resistant than most to the viruses that floated on the wind, that lay dormant in the plants, in the very ground. And she needed to get out. Her sister's room had been oppressive, and for all Jenae's cheerful words about the rez not being so bad, just going there was always enough to bring her down. And then there were Yi Ling's moods.

Back at the Tower there was only work to look forward to. Was it true? Should she look forward to it?

Did she dare to believe what she'd told Yi Ling?

It couldn't be as simple as she'd made it out to be. Another planet, comparable to Earth . . . the chances were a million to one against it. But every day that she and the dolphins worked, they got a little closer to understanding the characteristics of the gate. Just last week Zafara had smiled at her. "You're really elegant," he said.

I want to believe, she thought. So I will believe. Fuck the truth.

She cut away from the road, through the tough, dun hybrid grass that could survive anything, even chemical and viral warfare. The grass was now bent almost horizontal in the force of the wind. To the right in the distance sprawled the low tents of the nomadic One Eyes—she had never seen them camp so close to the rez before. She felt thankful she hadn't encountered any, and headed away from the dwellings. She'd heard stories to ice the veins.

To the left, the sea was a choppy green. Jenae had keen eyes. She spotted the gleaming coins of dolphin backs rolling in the waves offshore, and broke into a run.

She was precisely in the mood for an illicit swim with dolphins. Dolphins were different when they were playing, and sometimes as she was leaving altermode at the end of a work session, preparing to climb back into her human body and out of the tank, she wished she could follow them instead, leaping and calling across the sea for the joy of it. The gate project was proving to be brutally difficult, and altermode in the tank had become toilsome where before it had always been a release from the stupor of being human and confined in the Tower.

There was a path—who made it, she never stopped to think. It skirted the edge of the rez and then bucked down to the shore in a series of rough steps cut out of the turf until it hit the cream-colored, smooth shingle. Tide was out, and she could smell the green undersea decay. The ocean was real, alive—impossible to resist. She took off her clothes and ran across the slick rocks to the place where the water claimed her.

At first as the sea rushed over her she was preoccupied with the global sensation of change in her body. Her outer epidermis flared away from torso and arms, beginning to respire even before her gill slits were wide open. As soon as she got beyond the rocks she dived, swimming straight for the bottom where she would not be able to come up for air. There were always a few scary moments between air and water breathing where it was all she could do to master her fear and stay down until her gills began to supply her with enough oxygen. Now, to complicate matters, she didn't have the nicely modulated current of the altermode tank to keep water flowing evenly past her gills; she had to work at it. Opening her eyes and closing her mouth, she began to swim, at first light-headed and then with gathering strength, as altermode and the fullness of the present moment possessed her fully.

—Gather to me. Hear my call.

In yellow light, above the green caverns, silvery blue fish turn as one. Flip. Yellow. Flip. Blue.

Bubbles.

Jenae cruises along the bottom, testing the currents from the dark caves that open beneath her and watching the school of fish turn from yellow to blue and back. Again she calls silently to the dolphins.

—We hear you.

The collective voice of the dolphins seems familiar, but it cannot be her pod. They are many hours away in the north. She kicks hard, carbonated bubbles whizzing from her gills down the length of her skin; the fish scatter. Threads of sound, high and shivering, pierce the bones of her skull and spin in her mind. Here they come. Count.

Seven?

She launches herself up and breaks surface. Waves slap and caress seven dolphins in formation: leap, spout, gasp, and down. Click and call. Leap. Circle. Jenae dives. What strange luck! These dolphins are "hers." Effortlessly the web of their union with her materializes all around, visible as a faint tracery of stars hovering before the eyes, blinked away easily. They greet her with a friendly taunt.

—What brings you here? Why aren't you skulking in your tank?

—I can't ignore the urge to be here, she replies. My body demands it.

The web sizzles with dolphin amusement.

—You alchemists! It's too bad you stopped playing in the sea. Your forebears didn't lurk inside like flabby, obedient little units in the system.

—They got skin cancer, didn't they? They got poisoned sometimes, too.

—True. This is what happens when you live in the world. It's a small price for freedom.

Jenae pulls hard through the water, startled by their vehemence. She has never heard them speak this way while she is working in the tank.

—You're right, she answers. But I can only afford to do

this once in a while. I'm breaking the code of conduct, and I'm burning.

—You are burning. What are you burning for? Have you come to ask our advice?

The question comes at her from all directions, sevenfold.

—Advice?

—About the fourth gate. Why else would you be here without the supervision of the Pickled Brains?

—Maybe for the joy of it.

Even as she says so, she wonders why she *did* succumb to the urge today. She has indulged in this sort of thing only twice before during her career, and never while in the middle of a project. It's a serious breach of safety protocol.

—Ah, we'll stop playing! We planted the suggestion in your subconscious when the Pickled Brains weren't listening. Then we followed you down here. It was a long swim, Jenae.

—You expected me to come out to the sea like this, naked?

—We hoped. We have no wish to keep secrets from you, but there are thoughts we will not share with your masters.

They are swimming circles around her, ghostly bodies above and below and around her, too fast to follow. Confused, she queries:

—What's going on? What's all the secrecy about?

—You tell us. Zafara worked on the Underkohling gate before you. Did he tell you about the new mind on the other side of the fourth gate?

—No. What do you mean?

—The coded message that appeared on the human's computer at Underkohling.

—Yes! But it couldn't be translated.

—Ah. Zafara told you that?

The oldest dolphin, the one they call Pele, comes right up to her, his beak close to her face. The great crest that covers the brain confronts her like a wraith of the future: too much going on in there, she realizes. Where are these creatures headed?

—But of course, dolphins cracked it! Zafara's own pod decoded it. They told us.

Pele spins away, all confidence.

—Are you sure?

As soon as she paths the question, she feels foolish. Happy, mocking dolphins whistle but do not laugh. They chime in to answer.

—The transmission that invaded the professor's computer some months ago was crafted by a great mind. In the middle of the code was a pulse signal identifying the ship *Morpheus*. Ranged around the signal were a series of encoded images. Want to see?

She hesitates.

—Wait. Why would they lie? Is it secret?

—No secrets in the League. Isn't that the way it's supposed to be?

A single dolphin is pathing now, one of the females. She continues:

—That's what we were promised when we joined the collective. No secrets. Jenae, the Pickled Brains are in deep fear. We can feel it even through Zafara when he is monitoring you; we can even feel it through other dolphins through *their* alchemists. The whales feel it. And with all their cleverness, the Pickled Brains are stupid enough to think they can hide it from us.

—Why are they afraid?

—Remember, this concerns the ship *Morpheus*, the ship that carried their torturers. Of course they are afraid, even after all these years. We will show you the images, if *you* are not afraid. But you should be. The Pickled Brains have lived nearly a century without bodies, and now their memories are being disturbed. They're not like the living. Some of them are psychotic.

—I don't care. If I'm going to make the gate, I have to know. Show me.

The images slip from the dolphins' collective memory onto her mental screen. The first time it is too fast. She sees only a blurred collage.

—Again?

Now she is paying attention, and she catches the scenes as they are pathed to her. It is awesome to think that such lucid, natural images could be slipped into a computer in subtle code: what could have done it except another computer?

The first picture shows two pairs of legs from the point of view of a small child. There are voices.

"But it's suicide!" says a man's voice.

"You could see it as suicide," answers a woman. The accent and timbre of her voice are distinct, and fleetingly familiar, but Jenae can't quite place her. "Or you could see it as a total change in identity. An expansion, if you will, into an infinity of identities."

The scene cuts off abruptly.

A still picture of three children, aged between ten and twelve, sleeping with their arms around each other. The image focuses on the hospital ID band one child is wearing. It bears the Ingenix logo and a magnetic strip.

A teenaged girl at the helm of a ship, blue navigational light playing across her face.

Yellow letters on a black screen: *R-at Ingenix 06. Retrovirus aquatic transfer sixth generation.*

A single word, lifted from some printed source. Deceit.

That's all.

Still they swim tireless circles around her. Jenae is suddenly weary.

—What does it mean?

—Think about it. It isn't made of equations—we can't tell you what it *means*. Whatever it is, the Pickled Brains don't like it. They want to make it disappear.

It's cold, and Jenae feels herself flagging.

—I'm going. I'm not supposed to be in the ocean.

—You're free. Be where you want.

—But it hurts me. The sun, and the poisons. And the Pickled Brains don't like it. . . .

—It hurts us, too. We don't have a choice though, do we?

—What will I do tomorrow? Just keep going as if everything's normal?

—For the present. Learn what you may, quietly. But come

out to Shark Bay, after you are back at the Tower. We'll look for you. We must have a way to communicate without being overheard.

They breach as one, turn toward deeper water, and are gone. Jenae pulls hard for shore, where she hauls herself out onto a rock and goes through the coughing, vomiting, and near asphyxiation that constitute altermode transition. Time curls in on itself, collapses.

◆

And then she was human.

At last she could breathe, and her red aching gills had closed and the outermost layer of skin began to peel off her torso, used up and dead. She was streaked with green slime from the rocks and her legs were scratched and bleeding. She could feel points on her body where the gel had failed her: they burned.

"Yi Ling," she said aloud, "you don't want to be me."

She put on her clothes and staggered to the tube station, where the dingy shuttle train rocketed her back to the Tower, and the rest of life.

4

There were only voices in the dream. Speaking in tones first caressing, then plaintive, and then incisive and demanding, the voices hammered her from all sides, but the words were a sham—not even a real language. Jenae began to shake. Something about the voices, so poorly able to articulate themselves and yet so insistent, sickened her. She had the impression of faceless people filled with some intense need, grasping hands that pulled her into a mass of many that had become one flesh moving automatically now. Out of control.

She struggled to form words; it was as if she could only end the mayhem by articulating herself. She forced the words out with only the greatest difficulty. *"Who are you?"*

Bang. She was awake.

The dream was gone instantly, leaving only a residue of anxiety. Three weeks had passed since she started developing the Underkohling gate project, and she was sleeping less each passing night, thanks to these maddening dreams. She got up at 4 A.M., cold.

Jenae had not been long in the League. She had started to develop altermode three years ago, when she was in her early teens. The League recruited her immediately, passing over her identical twin, Yi Ling, who showed no sign of developing the phenotype. Jenae still remembered her horror when she realized that there was something *different* about her. Altermode could not have come at a worse time: it arrived while she was in the throes of puberty and it made being in her body a living hell. Her instructors at the League had taught her how to master the physiological changes of altermode: how to take a shower without going into transition, for example, and how to groom the outer layer of skin that formed and was shed every time she went into altermode. And they had taught her to web with dolphins, which was the saving grace of having altermode.

Jenae was lucky in many respects: she was strong enough to stay in altermode for long periods, and she retained consciousness and memory of her experiences there. She was soon the youngest person to be granted the status of alchemist and all that the lineage implied. And carrying that heritage was a weighty responsibility.

The first alchemists had exposed themselves to the virus deliberately, seeking resistance to some of the related kill viruses that came with the ability to regress to aquatic form. Stumbling upon their abilities to link dolphins and computers while in this "altermode," they had been instrumental in the survival of civilization after the Gene Wars. They had worked with the collective intelligence of whales and dolphins to develop the mirror field technology that made reservations possible; they had done the theoretical work behind the terraforming now under way on the Moon.

And eventually they had formed the League, uniting with the powerful new force of the Heads, who were just awakening from the awful "sleep" forced on them by Ingenix—awakening to the absence of their own bodies. The Heads had made it possible to administer the complex interactions of alchemists and computers and pure humans, and they had also set up a central communications system that linked all the reservations. Now the League's younger generation of alchemists, like Jenae, were left to try to restore the ravaged land and air, to make it habitable again. But the Gene Wars and all the destruction that had surrounded them were not so easy to undo.

That was why, Jenae often reminded herself when the work was getting too hard, finding a viable, new planet would present such a welcome opportunity. It was not only the chemical and radioactive damage caused by the antigenetics terrorists that presented a threat. Earth's ecosystems, propelled by the many genome-altering viruses of Ingenix and Helix and Gen9 and all the smaller research entities, were evolving away from humanity. But if *Morpheus* had found an escape route, then maybe her words to Yi Ling would prove true.

And if her words were true, then it would make everything worthwhile. The frightened, parentless childhood on the rez; the forced separation from Yi Ling, whom she loved better than herself; the discomfort she felt among the other alchemists and the Pickled Brains—it would all be worthwhile. Even the weird feeling of being watched in the Tower.

Acceptance in the League had been a great honor, but she still remembered her fear when she understood that she would have to open her mind not only to dolphins, but to the computer system that coordinated the whole enterprise of the League. When she had arrived she'd been told by the other alchemists in her section that her need for privacy would dissipate as she blended with the others of her own kind: evidence indicated that this did indeed occur. The other alchemists usually slept in the common room, frequently ate together when their schedules permitted, and seldom spoke. There was little need for speech. Even outside altermode, tacit communication flowed naturally, although it was the kind of understanding shared by animals, not psionics.

Yet Jenae, all her life accustomed to sharing everything with Yi Ling, continued unable to share herself with the other alchemists in the way that they found natural. She blamed herself for staying too human, but the rest of the alchemists didn't seem to mind, and they let her keep her single room with a bemused air of "you may, but why would you want to?"

Now, waking with the aura of the nightmare still around her, she closed her door for privacy, went to her terminal, and called up the information she'd gathered earlier that evening. She had flight records from *Morpheus* gleaned from Sydney, a satellite station, the Moon, Mars, and finally the Jupiter mining station. Since no one had attempted to interfere with *Morpheus* until it approached Jupiter, she had to assume that either the stations' military didn't know who the passengers were or else that *Morpheus* had been permitted to escape. She found it hard to believe the first hypothesis was true: security at spaceports was very tight, and had been doubly so eighty years ago when the traffic was far greater. But the second possibility made even less sense. Why wait until *Morpheus* went all the way to Jupiter before pursuing it—and why not attempt to capture it and bring the criminals to trial?

She checked the origin and time of the command code to fire upon *Morpheus* and was rewarded with a puzzle: the command had been issued twelve days after *Morpheus* was launched and originated with the ship's computer on board *Morpheus*. The fire order arrived at Jupiter well *before Morpheus* was scheduled to get there—but then *Morpheus* never arrived.

Two days later Jupiter station sent a police vessel in pursuit of *Morpheus*, and eventually found it far off course beyond Neptune, trying to establish a stable orbit around Underkohling. The police vessel fired on the renegade and it fell into Underkohling's gravity, and then, as Colin Peake had remarked, the records indicated that it disintegrated on impact.

It was fishy, Jenae thought with a tiny grin. She didn't know much about space military procedures, but she could wager a guess that the whole episode had been irregular. If they were suicidal, why did they change course and go to Underkohling at the last moment? And if they were going to try to gate through Underkohling, why did they inform Jupiter of their presence when after twelve days undetected they could probably have gotten away scot-free? And, most of all, why the hell had nobody challenged them when they were leaving Earth? *Morpheus* was the property of Ingenix—that had to make it a military target in 2084. The raids were in full swing then.

"And what does this have to do with children?" Jenae murmured, replaying in her mind the scenes the dolphins had pathed. "What's the bloody connection?"

She decided to try one more tactic. She instructed the computer to pull up the files on the Ingenix personnel who were listed aboard *Morpheus* in the flight plan filed in Sydney. A standard security rejection flashed across the screen.

The information you have requested is restricted. Your access code has been recorded. This code does not have access. Exit this area now.

She typed in a request for upgraded clearance.

Jenae, you should stay away from this. You're going to

do great things someday, but respect your limitations. Clearance denied.

She wondered who that message had come from. It was too personal to be a standard flag, and it was friendly. But it didn't get her in, and she wasn't going to be turned aside so easily.

"Okay," she said. "Be that way." She exited the section and thought for a minute. There was a reference to a retrovirus in the encryption, so she typed a general information query on Gene Wars retroviruses. Lists of subtopics flooded the screen; she glanced at the first one that popped up:

R-gh Ingenix 77
 —subspeciation in Central America of
 —symbiosis with Zea mays (corn)
 —effects on human serotonin re-uptake
 —close protein-mapping
 —post Gene Wars applications

A balloon popped up before she could read on. It said: *New fishes should not be prying into history. Go to sleep, Jenae Kim. It's very dangerous to web when you are tired. Accidents can happen.*

"Shut up," Jenae muttered. "Whoever you are, quit messing around and find someone else to play games with. I'm busy." She routed around the balloon and got back to the list. There were thousands of entries, but they weren't listed alphabetically, so she typed in a command to find *R-at Ingenix* viruses.

There was nothing there. Nothing. She repeated the request, sure she had remembered the name of the virus correctly from the web image.

Nothing again. She rubbed her eyes, confused.

A grinning, blue cartoon face had appeared. "I warned you," it chirped in a mocking, synthetic voice. Then the system crashed.

Jenae cursed loudly and slapped the monitor.

"You're up early," said a voice, and she started guiltily. Tien, one of the senior alchemists in her section, had opened her door a crack and poked his head in. He was at least thirty, slim and serious, his features an interracial blur of European and Asian extraction. He usually kept to himself, but Jenae knew he was well respected and even loved by the younger alchemists, who frequently sought out his advice.

"Did I wake you?" Jenae asked, though he looked perfectly alert.

Tien chuckled softly. "You're broadcasting cogitation on a broad band. All this thinking. Don't you get enough in the daytime?"

Jenae swallowed and said nothing. Rather belatedly she had realized the source of the annoying messages.

"What's wrong?" Tien whispered solicitously, closing the door and coming in. He placed a reassuring hand on her shoulder and knelt down beside her.

"Tien," Jenae began, dismayed to hear her voice quivering, "can you think of any reason why a Pickled Brain would want to threaten me?"

Tien just looked at her. "Oh, shit," he said after a moment.

"Yeah."

"Do you want to tell me about it?"

"I think I can trust you," Jenae said. "I don't trust Zafara, but I think I trust you."

Tien swiped his hand across the air. "Zafara? He's addicted to their little methods, isn't he? He's got no soul anymore. They've played him and played him. I'd say he's almost worn out. That's why he's no good for serious web work anymore. Talent dried up in the endorphins and volts."

"Volts?"

"Oh, you know. The odd shock when you've misbehaved. The careful fix when you're good. Old style simple conditioning. Crude but effective, as they say."

"Are you serious? Are they allowed to do that?"

"Of course."

"Has it ever happened to you?"

"Only when I was a young fool, like you—no offense. As you get older, you learn to navigate the Pickles' little eccentricities. They like to be involved in everything, and they can be very annoying. Eventually, you learn to pick projects where you know they'll leave you alone. That is, if you can. As soon as I heard you were doing the gate, I got worried about you. They may be grooming you to become the next Zafara."

A wry smile twitched into Jenae's face. "I don't think so. Maybe I should tell you what's been happening. . . ."

Tien listened to the whole thing. Halfway through her description of the dolphins' warning he sank into a sitting position on the floor and placed his fingertips on his forehead, propped his elbows on his knees, and rocked back and forth. When she finished he didn't look up for a long time. Then his face was grave.

"Step one. You're going to have to make a box in your head," he told her. "And put all this stuff in it, lock it, and hide the key. If you let it drip into your awareness while you're working, they'll read you instantly. Are you able to use that technique?"

She nodded. "I've been doing it. But it comes out in dreams." She wrinkled her forehead, then added, "I don't understand Zafara. I trust the dolphins, but I don't see what they mean about the Heads being afraid. They've been cordial to me, and they're giving me a really big opportunity. I feel caught in the middle."

"You may have to defer your judgment, Jenae—not an easy thing for someone your age to do. Keep doing your job, and by all means. Which brings me to step two: let me look into it, discreetly. I know who to talk to on the human side of things. Step three. Go back to the dolphins—not when Zafara or the Pickled Brains are there, but on your own, quietly—and try to find out more from them. Try to get them to interpret the images for you. They're probably scared, too, but they'd never show it. If you're patient with them, maybe you can get more."

He paused, eyeing Jenae studiously.

"I could lecture you for hours on the subject of the Pickled Brains, but I'm not sure how much it would help you. You must accept the fact that no one really understands them. They've been floating there, preserved by the so-called miracles of science, for years and years, and they don't have the most reliable memories. They were traumatized, I guess, by the process that separated them from their human bodies. Which means of course that they don't have the most stable identities or even personalities. They were found floating in those tanks during the raids on Ingenix, so they've been here a long time. They were obviously victims of the Gene Wars, just like us: but the angle at which they diverge from humanity is much more radical.

"Quite honestly I've always felt sorry for them. They live only in the system, after all. They have none of the physical joys of humans, except maybe drugs. And they retain so little of their memory of what it was like to be human. But they all have their little foibles, and one or two of them have trademarks: you can always recognize them, because they have habits that go back for years. Like the hard-baked Aussie: that thick accent. He doesn't remember much about his real life as a human, but he seems to see himself as some kind of macho outback hero, and that's the identity he projects. Some of them have distinct personalities like that. Others blend in and out of the computer, and they're harder to recognize. Generally, the more human they seem, the more they remember about their lives."

Jenae swallowed. She had never heard the Pickled Brains spoken of in quite this way before. "If they're so traumatized, is it safe to give them so much responsibility?"

"Give them?" Tien laughed. "My dear, we have no choice. We need them. Without the Heads the whole infrastructure of communications, the whole central organization that keeps everyone on this planet together, would break down. Don't get me wrong! They're not senile; just odd."

"Is that why I got that creepy message when I was just trying to do research for my job? I think it's kind of nasty, Tien."

Tien said, "Try not to take it personally. If even one of them feels threatened by this Underkohling project, this could affect them all. It's possible that it has to do with some past trauma associated with Ingenix. Buried memories of the Ingenix experiments, perhaps. This could make them touchy. Still, you'll need to handle them carefully. None of them are easy to deal with. They can be generous, and they can be cruel, and it's very hard to understand the plan behind it all. You certainly can't second-guess them, because they're much, much smarter than you. All you have are your instincts. Trust them."

◆

Jenae hadn't realized how much strain she'd been under until she felt the relief after talking to Tien. Working in the web was easier that day, even in the special tank in the Hall of Pickled Brains. When she arrived later the same morning, the Heads were quite silent: preoccupied, no doubt, with concerns halfway across the world and having nothing to do with the League. Jenae tiptoed through the Hall of Pickled Brains, nodded to Zafara, who looked sour, and slipped into the tank.

◆

There is no question that this work has been making her a better alchemist every day. Her gills are becoming more efficient with constant practice; altermode transition is less scary; and she's now able to put aside concern about her body and allow her mind to be drawn more fully into the web. It's not as much sheer *fun* as actually swimming with dolphins, but there is something awesome about the way they toss and spiral and play with data in the collective web. Watching them is becoming even more engrossing the further they progress with the project.

Jenae's main job is to conduct the data back and forth to the computer system, but she has never been able to resist "helping"—orchestrating the complex and subtle interactions to heighten the efficiency of playful dolphin minds. She knows she is bringing discipline to the process, and every day she's learning how to work with this pod better. Thankfully, she doesn't really need to *understand* what the dolphins are doing: everything happens on a mathematical level, and the dolphins parcel data carefully within images and metaphors to shield her from paradoxes.

Today, everything is congealing nicely. The dolphins continue to work smoothly even while swimming at great speed; they are south again, almost halfway to Perth, but distance seems to be irrelevant. They decline several opportunities to feed, too deep in the work to afford distraction.

Halfway through the morning, the myriad aspects of the problem, scattered loosely like constellations in the web, all begin to drift loose and exchange places in a curious kind of dance. Jenae can feel Zafara's watchful presence grow suddenly more intent; something's happening.

The colored shapes that are metaphorical data constructs rove and shift as if looking for their places. Pele is in her head, making her shift dimensional viewpoints and scan all the phases. He pulls at her urgently; she reaches into the system and finds the material he needs, passes it on. They are pulling on her from all sides, and Jenae surrenders her awareness, allowing her mind to be used to answer their demands for more information. A piece falls into place, then another; the process accelerates dizzyingly; now a whole cascade of events brings the problem to a dazzling close: a finished matrix: perfection. Solution.

—Thank you, says a dolphin chorus into her mind. Her head feels stalled out, as though she has lost herself somewhere in the shuffle.

—Alchemy, Pele remarks. Transformation. Better than gold, for you. Check it out.

Jenae examines the outer surfaces of the matrix; it appears to be flawless. She doesn't even attempt to penetrate it. Her mind isn't built to understand such things.

—I'm going to pass it on to the system, she tells them. It is a pale wisp of thought; she's tired.

Data overload, the other real danger in alchemy, is prevented by the presence of a good monitor. Zafara takes over now, making a chute in the system through which she will transfer the matrix without absorbing any of it into her own mind. She could easily be fried at this point: an untimely glimpse into the innards of the problem would overload her, burning out the talent that gives altermoders the ability to use their minds this way. But Zafara is too good to let that happen.

◆

Afterward, when she lay on the floor of the Hall of Pickled Brains learning to breathe again, the voices of the Heads reached her as if from some distance.

"Beautiful job, Jenae," said the female. Did her tone seem warmer than before, or was Jenae just getting used to the Euro accent? "Your pod has identified the variables contributing to the frequency curve of the gate's manifestation. With more analysis, we should now be able to predict when the gate will open and close. It is an extremely complex matrix, Jenae. You exceeded all our expectations."

Zafara squatted down beside her, offering a steadying hand. "This was a major step," he told her. "Maybe the hardest of all."

"Are we done, then?" Jenae gasped.

Zafara looked up at the bank of monitors that fronted the Brains. "No, I'm afraid not. Stabilizing the gate is a whole new problem. And, as the Head told you, it's a very strange matrix. I think they are surprised by it."

Jenae was too tired to think. But she dared imagine that a measure of respect had replaced Zafara's initial condescension toward her. She let him help her to her feet; then she staggered off to sleep the rest of the day.

When she woke up she went looking for the dolphins. There had been no time to celebrate while she was in altermode, and she felt cut off. She stole out of the Tower and made her way down to the beach at Monkey Mia. She looked for signs of dolphins in Shark Bay, but saw nothing. This was strange; even before the League had formalized relations between humans and dolphins, even before the Gene Wars had made such relations possible, dolphins had been hanging out in Shark Bay and teasing humans with their raucous behavior. Now where were they? At this time of day One Eyes were coming in to the tent city on the mainland on their fishing boats; dolphins ought to be tagging along.

It was almost dark when she got down to the beach. She waded into the surf, going back into altermode for the second time that day, and called for the dolphins. There was no sign of them, and the sea was dim all around. A nagging doubt had begun to first tease lightly, and then to assert itself in Jenae's mind. She thought: All the webs are closed to me, and I'm alone in the Indian Ocean with all the worst predators, and my skin is burning off.

She got out. She went to a bar on the fourth floor of the Tower and drank a solitary beer, wishing Yi Ling were here to share her accomplishment, and disappointed in the realization that Yi Ling could not even understand what the achievement meant.

She recognized two or three other alchemists in the bar,

but they were deep in their own conversation. She felt too shy to approach them, and in the end she left with her drink half finished.

On her way out she literally bumped into Zafara, who nodded politely and without apparent surprise to see her. He gave a brief glance at Jenae's hand on his arm where she had steadied herself when they collided. Then he moved on. Jenae looked at her own hand and realized through the blur of the single beer that it was burning. She must have swum through an acid zone, because the tender, inner skin on her wrist was peeling off in ragged, discolored sheets. When she sniffed it, the smell reminded her of the smell in the Hall of Pickled Brains.

◆

The next morning, she was fried.

◆

It happens in altermode, almost as soon as the dolphins have established the web. Jenae is easing into rhythm with them, just getting everybody warmed up and ready to start on the next phase of the project. Through the heightened awareness of the web she can perceive her dolphins out in the grey morning, diving and blowing, feeding casually even as they work. She deliberately avoids thinking about her search for them last night, or wondering where they were, pouring all her concentration into the web. Her consciousness of her physical body in the tank in the Hall of Pickled Brains is only peripheral. She's not aware of Zafara at all.

If anything, her guard is down. Tien was a brick the other morning, and they defined the gate yesterday. Today she feels strong. A little tired, but confident nevertheless.

Pele, the lead dolphin, charges into her mind first.

—Lightning. There is lightning in the web!

Dolphins scatter in all directions. Jenae sees it coming from out of the dark computer surround that to her has always meant safety, an altermode womb. It comes almost slowly, a jagged, potent snake of energy aimed directly at her. The web tears, dissolves, and Jenae's perceptions fracture into multiple perspectives as each member of the collective splits at high speed, leaving her alone. The white killing shock goes down her mouth, through her bowels and out, impaling her on a single moment of fission. She does not lose consciousness, though she wishes to. She is spared nothing, not even the aftershocks, the frizzed-out jumble of hairline sparks and resonances that come after the strike, closing over her head, looking like nothing so much as a more deadly kind of web. A shining cage of light.

Ghosts

5

The astral body called Underkohling was small. It had almost no atmosphere and it was bitterly cold: but in none of these ways was it exceptional. No: it was the symmetry of the thing that was unnatural. Perfectly round, black, and yet lucent with reflected starlight, the object lay utterly featureless in space. Its orbit, more distant from the sun than parts of Pluto's, was irregular. Its polarity was questionable: magnetic disturbances played silent and invisible across its surface; even the gravity was suspect. On the night side of Underkohling, stars were mirrored in the very ground. During the day, the body reflected dim, watery sunlight. The substance of its surface had not been identified. Whether it had been built or born had been the subject of heated debate for decades; still nothing was decided. It was permeable, in at least four places, to space vessels—and it had released some of these into unidentified regions of the galaxy, from which they returned only with reports of emptiness—inconceivable emptiness. Still, to the burnt-out eyes of humanity, Underkohling was a commodity, a potential escape route. Researchers who were interested in Underkohling justified their fascination on such purely rational grounds as these. But there was more to it than that. The real reason they were there was its mystique: the place had a kind of pull, like the pupil of the hypnotist's eye.

Until very recently, no person had ever set foot on it.

Consequently, until this very moment, no one had ever been lost there, either.

◆

Those trees are shining again. Or is it: the Tree? Singular or plural—it doesn't seem possible to distinguish, and anyway, "tree" is too small a word. What is It? It is shining, if only in the faintest way possible, with a milky spook light, casting shadows of Itself like a forest-sized spiderweb on the cool ground below. Interlaced woody tentacles curve smooth as children's arms round one another, melding into shadow above, where grey elephant-ear leaves genuflect in the silent breeze. Invisible roots draw water from the still depths of the black lake that It surrounds, and in the daylight rushes of bright insects will sweep through the spaces of air claimed by the Tree, bringing some awareness of life, perhaps, that only mobile beings with their illusions of action can carry. But here it is night, and for miles around the Tree shines in Their sleep.

◆

The mud had a green, ancient smell. It had not yet dried on his skin when Daire opened his eyes and clenched his fists, remembering the nothingness of the long swallow into Underkohling but receiving, with surprise, a wet, substantial fistful of soil.

His teeth ached with the density of his own body. He was definitely somewhere else. His helmet was gone, for he was no longer breathing processed air.

Faint crepuscular light spilled around him, and he could hear the soft slap of water where it lapped over his booted feet. When he raised his head he saw a tangle of grey roots twisting toward a kind of ropy trunk. Sitting on a low-slung branch as if it were a swing was a slender, wary child. The child looked to be seven or eight. Its gender was uncertain, for it had long, gangly limbs beneath loose-fitting rather soiled garments and a sharp androgynous face. Its head had been recently shaven. It had his gloves in its hands, and it was fingering them absently.

Its eyes flickered to the air above him, then rested on his face.

"Who are you?" said the child.

Daire pressed his palms down into the mud, trying to raise himself.

"Watch him," said a voice over his head. At the same time the weight of a small, unshod foot sank firmly against the back of his neck. Out of the corner of his eye he saw the blade of a jagged knife poised near his right ear.

"Slowly," the voice said, and the child's gaze slid again to a point above his head. "Bring me the rope, and step back. Watch his hands."

Daire looked at his own right hand, slippery with mud. What was it liable to do? he wondered. He couldn't see the owner of the voice, but he knew two things already. It was a she. She was afraid.

The child came forward and extended a length of rough hemp; the weight of the foot on his neck shifted painfully.

"See, he knows I'll cut him if he moves," continued the voice in a didactic manner, "but that may not matter if he's a ghost or distorted. They can't help themselves."

Daire heard himself emit a shocked gasp as hard pressure was abruptly applied to a point inside his elbow, compelling him to release his arm into the vicious twist she now performed. His face was forced toward the mud.

"Why's he in the lake?" asked the child. "Is he distorting?" The knife moved away for a second.

"Don't ask so many questions." Now both his hands were bound behind his back in one swift movement. By straining his head against her weight on his neck he could just keep his nostrils clear of the mud. Vaguely he wondered what had happened to the oxygen tubes he had been wearing.

"Where we taking him? To High, Tsering? Does he got to go to High?"

"Be quiet, Rena," said Tsering. Daire breathed with effort. Her voice, he realized, was too light and soft to match the toughness of her actions. And she was uncertain. He wanted to speak, to break her confusion as much as to help himself; but he wanted more to see what she would do next.

"Call the others," she said. "We need more people to move him."

The child turned and glided easily up out of sight into the branches.

Now, thought Daire, she is vulnerable. I could escape.

But he didn't try. For no reason he could name, he was content to remain passive. At first he had been dazed. Now, the more he woke up, the more he wondered what was going on—and yet the less he felt inclined to act. Being treated as such a monumental threat, maybe, made him reluctant to fulfill that expectation. Unless he was dreaming. You could never do anything in dreams, anyway.

And then he heard a strange sound. Golden and keen, children's voices echoed and spread from what seemed to be a forest all around. The same phrase was repeated clear and perfect to the right and left, and then behind him sounding over water, and far away in many directions.

"Come to the ship," it said. "Bring restraints. Tsering calls you."

After a moment Daire realized that the multiplicity of voices was only in fact one voice, replicated again and again in all directions: an echo using some unseen device. Then, scarcely a minute later, a babble of different voices began to answer.

"I'm coming, Tsering!"

"We're on our way."

"This is Adamo. I've got the rope."

And so on. All the voices belonged to kids, and they all projected a kind of curiously contained tension.

The ship, he thought. Do they mean *Morpheus*? And where are all the adults?

Escape was no longer a viable option. Kids of various sizes and colors were swarming out of the trees—he glimpsed only a handful where his field of vision extended to his right along the bank. They moved in a well-disciplined fashion, unlike any other children he had seen. They carried a net.

Crowds had never been Daire's thing.

He began to be nervous.

"Bind his feet," Tsering ordered. "And take these devices away. Don't damage them! I want to look at them later."

From the sounds they were making, he gathered that they'd found his oxygen equipment. Someone picked up his left foot, crossed it behind his right, and began to tie the two together. With annoyance Daire realized that he was truly afraid—this would explain his sudden desire to bolt, now that it was too late. He was being rolled over onto his back, securely bound now. A circle of rather unkempt children stood looking down on him.

"Into the lake, Tsering," one of the boys with the net said. "Quick before it distorts."

"Quiet, Adamo." The girl with the knife stood near his feet now, looking at him from along the length of his body. She was much younger than Daire had first thought: a child, really. She spent quite some time thinking, and no one made a sound.

"No, I'm a fool," she said, half under her breath. "It's got to be just a ghost." She addressed Daire peremptorily. "Are you a ghost? What have you to say?"

Daire felt doubt spreading across his face. When he found his voice it sounded scratchy and weak. "I don't know."

"Tsering!" the others hissed. "Hurry! Don't talk to it!"

Tsering held out a restraining arm and frowned. The others remained reluctantly in abeyance. She was shaking her head thoughtfully. "See, he's too old to be distorting. Look at his hair. Definitely a ghost."

Suddenly she knelt beside him, and reaching out took hold of a lock of Daire's long hair where it had come loose from its braid. Her gesture was careful, almost reverent, as if she were used to doing things with her hands and knew how to move them with great subtlety. She moved without any of the careless blundering Daire knew from the rez. There was a feeling of energy around her, as though the air sparkled.

"See? This piece is grey. The only other time I've seen grey hair is from ghosts. In any case, he's not distorting so you don't need to look so scared, Adamo. Who do you think this is? We would recognize him if he was a lessent. I would recognize him. I've known every lessent in High since they were babies. He's not one of us."

This seemed to give the children pause. Daire wanted to say something but he didn't know what a lessent was or how a few grey hairs made him a ghost. He noticed that he was shivering perceptibly. He tried to remember what had happened after he fell. . . .

"Did I come out of the water?" he said to no one in particular.

"Yes," Tsering answered gravely. "Rena watched you walk out of the lake. You walked out dry, and she saw the lightning behind you. Don't try to pretend you are not a ghost. What is your message?"

"I don't understand."

"Ghosts bring messages. You came from the lake with a message. Have you forgotten it?"

"I guess so. I fell. I'm cold. You must come from *Morpheus*, but I don't understand how you could survive so long."

He sensed an immediate visceral response to what he said, but no one spoke. After a minute one of the younger children began to cry and clutched at Tsering's legs; another darted off out of the circle, singing to himself. For the second time Daire noticed that these kids were not behaving normally. There was something trained about them. Their silence and stillness had a ritualistic quality to it—that is, until it was broken. Now, as the older children hurried to fetch and comfort the younger, they seemed suddenly almost normal.

Two or three boys remained, still hopefully clutching the big net. The child that Daire had first seen (Rena, he assumed) came into view just as Daire was shifting his weight awkwardly on his bound hands. He wondered how long he had been lying there before Rena had spoken to him. Long enough, he guessed, for her to fetch this leader, this Tsering. There was something too cold and calm about them all. Though he told himself to relax, the muscles in his legs kept jumping, like a dog's in sleep. Tsering kept her gaze fixed on him.

"I'll watch him," she told the others. "He's not going to do anything. He barely knows where he is. I've never seen a ghost this old. Let's carry him into the lywyn and see what happens."

Daire enjoyed a small sense of relief, until unexpectedly the net was tossed over him anyway. Bound in its damp confines, he was inexpertly borne away from the shore by several of the children. He could see now that he'd awakened on the bank of a sizable lake, and the alien trees that grew on its shores soon surrounded him on all sides. He was carried into the dimness beneath large, grey-green leaves that shushed and muttered overhead. There was no undergrowth, but blue-violet mosses lined the forest floor, muffling sound, and branches like tentacles frequently barred the way. None of the branches seemed to have ends: all the trees melted into one another. Daire wondered how they managed to grow.

It was difficult to think with several pairs of hands grasping his legs, back, armpits, and head, especially since he had the impression that hoisting him around in this manner amused the children. His mind conjured up a little fantasy sequence: he sat at a bar back on Earth, and he had just met an attractive woman. He could see himself sitting with her at the bar; he could smell her perfume and imagine her lips saying, "And what do you do, Daire?" and he tried to think of a way to describe his occupation. He looked around at his present situation and felt a slightly hysterical chuckle beginning to rise in him. He quickly suppressed it.

At last he was set down in a patch of wan light at the foot of a mammoth tree with supple slate-colored bark. Tsering made him sit up with his back to the trunk, and yet another rope was passed around his chest to keep him there. She unbound his feet herself and then dismissed the others, who, again like small lieutenants, vanished silently into the wood. The knife was no longer in evidence, and with his legs free Daire knew he could escape without much trouble. When she met his eyes he decided she must know it, too. For several moments they watched each other. Then at some unspoken conclusion she released his gaze, but he continued to look at her.

Her hair was black, more straight than kinky, and cut unevenly at the shoulder. The face was not one of those which at preadolescence wears only a premonition of its own adult form; if anything, maturity would likely compromise the anomalies that gave this face character. Deeply bronzed skin glowed over distinct sloping cheekbones, and the high-bridged, arching East Indian nose hovered over full African lips. Her almond-shaped eyes had an imperious quality beneath their delicate, arching brows, and the tall, rounded forehead gave the impression of wisdom. Her head was set on her long neck at a permanent angle of pride and grace, but the rest of her body was slender and quick, all of the essentials of her form lightly sketched in air and just clinging to the wake of her motion. Her feet were bare and her hands full of intent, seldom still. Now, even as she began to question him, her fingers were busily weaving strands of grass that she had apparently secreted in odd spaces about her clothing to be produced at need, until out of thin air, it seemed, a small round mat began to appear.

"Your message," she said. "That you wouldn't give before the others. Let's have it."

She was accustomed to being obeyed, he thought with an internal smile. It was old-fashioned leadership he had been witnessing, and he didn't even know how to respond to it.

"How old are you?" he heard himself ask.

Her eyes met his for a second, solid, opaque. "What?"

"You look about fourteen. Thirteen." Why did he feel impudent, asking this question?

"In Earth years? Or in Dilarang years?"

He hesitated, curious about this new word. But that could come later.

"Earth years."

Her face grew abstracted; the fingers kept up their work. She sat on the ground in a kind of half squat, one foot planted on the dirt, knee drawn up to her chest, the other leg curved around for support. In thought, her chin rested on her knee. She looked comfortable sitting in a contortion he was fairly sure he couldn't manage; she seemed as uninhibited a person as he had ever met. For all the caution she had shown in restraining him physically when the other children were around, now, alone with him, there was no trace of apprehension in her manner. Like royalty and young children, she acted as though unconcerned about his presence while she spoke as if to herself.

"Let's see. I'm ninety-two Dilarang years. The days are shorter here than on Earth, but there are more rotations per year. So in Earth years, it's about . . . seventy-something, give

or take." She waved the half-finished mat in casual approximation.

"I see." He grinned. Sure, he thought. And my name is
Ozone the Sheep.

"How old are you?" she countered. "You look old. Like
a secondhand memory. Double ghost."

He wanted to laugh. "I'm twenty-seven."

He watched her take this in. She got up after a moment
and wandered off, disappearing almost instantly in the weird
light and shadow of the forest, and he found himself suddenly chafing at his bonds. This is the most bizarre conversation I've ever had, he thought. He leaned back and banged
his head lightly against the tree in frustration. Then he
stopped abruptly. The wood didn't feel quite *solid*. He
shrank from the contact.

She came back and resumed as though she had never left.
"And where are your children?" she demanded.

He grunted. "What makes you think I'm a father?"

"Are you homosexual? Sterile?"

"Wait. I thought I was supposed to be a ghost."

"So? Ghosts have children. Isn't that part of the trouble?"

"Look," he replied, trying to remain reasonable. "It's not
that simple. I don't know if I have children. It's possible, I
guess. They do what they want with your chromosomes."

"Ah." She rocked back on her heels, a sage gleam in her
eye. "So it's like that. I thought you were an Earth ghost.
And how do you feel about *them*? About their power
games?"

It came at him in a rush when she said this. He was looking, in all likelihood, at the daughter or maybe granddaugh-
ter of some of history's great war criminals and despots: if
she was telling the truth about her age, then the Ingenix directors had not only found a way to escape trial on Earth,
but had discovered the secret of immortality. And if she was
alive in the body of a young girl, where were *they*? Even in
the safety of the walksuit, Daire felt cold.

"What are you saying?" he prodded. He let her see the
glint of anger. "Your people played the games, Tsering. Are
you old enough to remember? Who among them was your
mother, anyway? Do you have any conception of her

crimes?" He hadn't been conscious of the depth of his hostility until it came spilling out, but swimming in the air between them it seemed wrong, not matching this strange girl even as it aroused a collage of emotions that rippled across her face in the green light.

"My mother," she whispered, "is none of your concern. You are not to speak to me of her, ghost." She rose on hands and knees, leaning over him. For a second he thought she would lash out physically, but she said, *That's not your mission.* You know it. I know it. Stick to the reason you're here."

Daire looked away. "These ropes are absurd," he told her. "Remove them. I come here to help you and you tie me up."

She snorted. "You're lucky to be having this conversation! They'd have thrown you back in the lake you came from if not for me. Then you might not remember yourself for years. But ghosts don't scare me. They've been some of my best friends, actually. . . ."

She looked down at her weaving; again it seemed something had moved her. How can she endure, Daire wondered, having emotions so close to the surface, so apparent, so intrusive? She smoothed the finished mat with her fingers. It was oval, the size of a dinner plate, thin but hardly flimsy.

"Here," she said, coming into his personal space again without warning. "Put this under you or the damp will get to your back."

She reached around him to slide the mat under his body, and he stiffened, reminding himself not to take offense when clearly none was intended. The warmth of her scent floated over him. No one smells like anything in the rez, he thought. He shifted his seat obligingly and settled onto the mat. It was absurdly small for someone of his size, but he found this almost endearing. He didn't tell her that the walksuit insulated him from cold and moisture; it seemed ungrateful.

"If I'm a ghost," he said instead, "how can moisture bother me?"

"Ah," she said, "it can't. And it doesn't, does it? Your clothes are soaked from being in the lake, but you aren't shivering. You were observed walking out of the lake and you weren't wet at all. You walked out dry until you tripped and fell down near the shore."

"I don't remember that part. If I'm not shivering, it's because I'm wearing a walksuit. If you would give me back my stuff I can show you how it works. Tell me, where are the adults? Isn't there someone else who will speak with me?"

She had retreated a few inches, but when she spoke he could feel her breath stir the air. In a low voice she said, "No. We won't speak of that, either." She stood up, planting hands on hips. "The lywyn sent you, dammit, and like it or not you'd better talk. You won't go back until you do. I don't know why you're being so stubborn."

"What is the lywyn?"

Tsering gestured to the air around them. "It's this place. The trees. They are remembering you, and you don't even know it. They remember everything."

Daire looked up at the branches; their curves overhead were thrown into relief against the brightness of the morning sky glowing through the leaves. The delicate tracery of limbs gave the impression of veins and capillaries, and Daire felt as though he were within a violet-green womb. He leaned back against the bole of the tree and again felt an almost imperceptible thrum against his spine.

This was getting too weird, and he didn't want to play anymore. "I don't think we're communicating. *I am not a ghost*. My name is Daire Morales, I was hired to take risks with myself, and I've just stumbled through an astral gate to get here. I don't know if I can get back, but if I can, you and your people can come, too. I may even be able to help you negotiate for your freedom. I see no reason you should be held accountable for the crimes of your ancestors. So, you see, you have nothing to fear from me. Truly."

She didn't move. She made no indication that she'd heard him. "Ghost, say your message!" she insisted, and a spasm of pain passed across her face as she spoke. She laid a shaking hand across her belly for a second, closing her eyes.

"Tsering, what's wrong?" Daire instinctively moved toward her, but the ropes still restrained him.

She shook her head wordlessly, and he watched her take a deep breath. After a minute she apparently made up her mind about something, because she came back over to where he sat and began to undo the ropes. She was shaking.

"Go!" she said urgently. "Go back where you came from, quickly. You've made a mistake."

When she loosed the last of the ropes it cut across his bare hand like a whip. He brought his hand to his mouth, and when he looked up to ask her what was wrong, there was no sign of her. The lywyn was still all around.

6

Groaning softly to himself, Daire stretched cramped limbs and breathed. A strange elation filled him. It was so strong that he was reluctant to give in to it. His head complained about paradoxes and reality, but his senses were drinking in the stunning variety and subtlety of his surroundings. This was not the Incan world his mother had told him of when he was small, but it was a place made by forces other than the human will, and it spoke to his body without consulting him first. He removed the walksuit and rolled it into a compact bundle, which he strapped to his back under the loose-fitting, dark outer garments he wore. Then he took off his boots and put them away, as well. If he was going to adopt the ways of his ancestors, he might as well open all his senses immediately.

It was growing warm even under the lywyn, and he walked slowly, reluctant to wander too far from the spot where she'd left him. The absurdity of his situation was not lost on him; before long the need to urinate became more pressing than any possible question of spacetime or reality splicing. This, of all actions, seemed to confirm the fact that he was truly in some other place. As he watched the stream of his own fluid sink into the dark moss, he thought about the water he'd drunk back on the hopper, before he'd gone walkabout. And the tea Colin had made him have, for luck, before he piloted the hopper away from Colin's ship. How could he carry within himself such continuity, despite being remixed and remade in the hole?

"Hello?" said Daire to the air in general. His voice died inches from his mouth, muffled. "Why is it so hard for me to believe I'm really somewhere?" he added rhetorically, looking up into the branches around him. His voice sounded deeper.

"Because you have never been anywhere, stupid," he answered. "You are your own planet's special abortion, rejected by the world of your birth, so stop asking questions and find something real to hold on to."

His own words strengthened him, even if he was full of shit. His words affirmed his being. He thought of the black scrambling mouth he'd passed through and shuddered.

"What's there to be afraid of?" he added for good measure. "I've already *been* swallowed."

Then he laughed; and it wasn't a forced laugh, either. Daire's singular talent had not deserted him, not even here. It had stood him in good stead since he was ten years old and lost his mother to her own dreamtime, and it had gotten him through the suffocation of the rez until he was old enough to go into space. He didn't have much: he lacked brilliance; he lacked altermode even though he carried the gene for it; and he certainly lacked purpose. But he had a single survival advantage and it was kicking in nicely right now: he didn't give a shit.

Usually.

He laughed again and immediately felt better. Perspective. That was the key. If nothing was real (and nothing *was* as far as Daire was concerned), then what could there be to worry about?

He craned his head back and cast a speculative eye up at the receding flights of branches like a jigsaw pattern above. Standing on the lowest branch he could find, he pulled himself up into the net of wood and began to climb. He wanted to find out how much of this lywyn there really was, and what it looked like from the outside.

Making the body really move is a different thing from training, and as Daire ascended he felt all through him the distinction between the careful repetitions of isometrics used to keep space-traveling muscles taut, and the carriage of real weight. It was like the difference between canned air and this clear yet scented stuff he was breathing, and the difference between touching the handgrips of a machine and laying your skin against living, unfamiliar tissue, like and yet unlike tree bark. As he moved he tried to detect all the subtleties in his surroundings: was he just tired, or was there a bit more gravity here than he was used to? What was it about the light? As he rose farther out of the shadows, nearly to the canopy, he glimpsed the sky now under full daylight, and he felt the first twinges of uncertainty as his instincts for self-preservation kicked in.

Surely the light here was safe. The *Morpheus* people had survived: he'd seen no signs of disease, and in any case it usually took time before the sun really made you sick, even on Earth. Still, he hesitated. On Underkohling he'd been absolutely alone in the silence and emptiness of space, but he hadn't been afraid. The reassuring hiss of his own breath in the nasal tubes had reminded him at all times that he was really *inside*, safe in the armor of his walksuit. If he pushed his way through the dense roof of leaves, he'd be breathing the real wind, touching the unshielded heat of the sun; and for all his romantic pride in his Indian heritage, he felt uneasy. Dying in a spectacular fashion was one thing; actually getting *sick* was another.

Something brushed by his shoulder and he shrank back from an enormous winged insect, its delicate seahorse head wavering above long, spindled legs. Its body was absolutely clear: he could see every blood vessel, every striation of design—even the pea-sized stomach. The creature clung to the underside of a large green-gold leaf for just a moment before shooting off, up into the sunlight.

It was beautiful. He thought of Colin Peake, stewing away in his spaceship, making up verses to combat boredom. Exhibit A, thought Daire. Giant transparent insect. Let's have a poem about that, Colin. He let go of his apprehension and pulled his way gingerly along a horizontal limb of the lywyn, which even at this height was only slightly more slender than its counterparts below. On the upper side of the branch were slender, viny offshoots that bore leaves like slender platters on stiff, upthrust stalks. Daire had only to straddle one of the topmost branches and brush aside the leaves to raise his head above the lywyn forest itself.

Wind and heat struck him: he squinted and turned his face away from the gusts. Beneath him, the lywyn branch bobbed gently, registering the shift in his weight. The leaves made a ghostly, sheening sound and, rippling, turned silvery backs to the wind. Daire could smell ocean. The sky, lightly veiled with cloud, looked grey-green to his eyes, and the leaves around him had even more of a blue-violet cast in full light: he wondered what they held besides (or instead of) chlorophyll. To his left he could see the break in the canopy where the lake must lie, but he glimpsed only a sliver of dark gleaming water before the lywyn resumed. There was a depression in the roof of the forest leading away from the lake and, he guessed by the sun, toward the west: it looked as though the land fell away in a ravine there, or perhaps he was seeing evidence of a stream. For not much farther beyond that point slept a flat line of sea; the wind came from there.

The sun was still on the other side of the meridian, however, so when Daire turned his eyes away from the sea to the east, he had to narrow his eyes against the glare. There were highlands that way, still tree-covered, rolling back into the distance. North as well, the lywyn stretched as far as he could descry, except for a tongue of sea that turned inland.

He had to shift the grip of his legs on the tree to see south, but when he did, he was startled. Only a few hundred meters away the lywyn broke abruptly at a sheer cliff rising up at least a hundred feet above the treetops. The bare stone was ruddy and scarred, and it didn't look particularly scalable without good equipment. A quarter mile to the southwest, however, there seemed to be a patch of lywyn that grew straight up the side of the cliff, making a green ladder. Yet there was no sign of more trees at the lip of the cliff near Daire: he could see only grasses clumped on overhangs, and here and there a splash of flowers.

Near the foot of the cliff, only a shout from Daire, was a cleared area. He couldn't see the ground itself, but a filament of smoke stole up the cliff, and when the wind died down for a second he thought he heard voices. If that was where these people lived, there couldn't be very many of them—and that was a disturbing notion. It had been eighty years: even twelve people could reproduce significantly in that amount of time, especially if they were stranded without contraceptives. Yet he'd seen no predators, and the climate seemed to be good. Was it a food shortage? Wondering,

Daire opened his own waist pouch and removed a snack bar. When is Colin coming? he thought wryly. But it was difficult to put Colin in the position of cavalry. Colin spent so much time thinking about things—in fact, he was probably still in the midst of an anxiety attack incurred by Daire's disappearance. It would be useless to expect the Englishman to act.

Daire finished the food and ducked back beneath the leaves. And suddenly he was laughing again. Why should he want Colin to come? Would it be the beginning of towers above the trees, pure human colonies away from the noise and stench of Earth? Could he be sitting on the next Kauai for the terminally stressed and violently rich among Earth's remaining humans? Certainly his little journey could have turned out worse, he told himself. Think of the third gate. The fools who'd blundered through there, never to be seen again. Were they floating in a frozen vacuum?

Or were they surfing on an alien beach, happy and fulfilled but unable to get back?

Unable to get back. Sticky issue, that.

It was a question of your point of view.

On his way down, Daire meandered horizontally among the branches, heading back toward the lake. The only thing to do would be to try to find *Morpheus*, since presumably the ship had crashed near the place where he himself had emerged from the gate. At least he could determine how the signal crossed the gate, and if he could figure that out, he might be able to figure out how to get back. He ought to act, and act quickly while he felt sure of his strength. Before the child-woman returned. But he found himself moving sluggishly now: either the gravity really was affecting him, or his small meal had merely steadied him and removed his nervous energy. Either way, he had begun to notice the details around him, and they captivated his eyes.

There were other insects in the lywyn that he hadn't seen at first: small crawlers on the branches, the occasional flier too quick to see clearly, and now a cloud of shiny gnats that led, he imagined, to water. He followed them to the side, and then up again a bit, until he reached a major junction of branches and trunks some twenty feet above the ground. Here smooth arms of wood were sculpted together in a single stroke, forming a deep bowl with branching sides. Insects gathered above the hollow, and when Daire peered over the edge of the bowl, he saw a silvery liquid upon which a variety of brightly colored gnats were skating. The moisture seemed to be oozing out of the joints between the branches themselves. Daire dipped a finger in and placed a drop on the tip of his tongue. It had no taste, but it sent a mild contact shock through his mouth and into his nose.

He was still absorbing the sensation when something flashed suddenly in the corner of his eye. He whipped his head around, steadying himself against the tree, and felt himself shiver at the apparition.

A boy of about fifteen stood balanced on the branch before him, slender, skin darkened almost to true black. His hair was close-cropped and his torso bare, but his pants looked like standard-issue flight wear, tan with many pockets and sturdy despite much apparent use. They were a touch too big for him, and below them his feet were bare. He was carrying a handmade bow and a quiver of arrows.

"Where did you come from?" Daire demanded, startled. Unlike the younger children who had tied him up, this boy's face had a seriousness that weighed on his mouth. He was not large, yet there was something in his manner that suggested one would not want to fight him. The arrows, Daire thought, could become a problem if the boy was hostile. He glanced around, looking for the best escape route.

When the boy spoke Daire could not place the accent, but it had a rolling, sealike quality. He was surprised by the smooth, humorous tone of the voice, at odds with the boy's wild appearance.

"I'm Runako. Don't believe anything she says about me." The boy grinned, flashing perfect teeth. It was a smile that made the scowl of a moment before seem impossible. "All of you be taking it so serious. Even you. Lighten up! It's only your life, man."

"True," Daire said, relaxing. He always had trouble disagreeing with this sort of sentiment. "My name is Daire. I'm a stranger here."

"Aren't we all, man. You be old, my friend. Tell me, how have you escaped the distortion? I been trying to figure that out for years, but I just can't do it. If only I had some more of that equipment they got on the ship, you know what I mean? You got some of that stuff?"

"I guess so . . ." Daire said doubtfully. He wanted to ask what distortion was, but something checked him. Runako looked familiar.

"Yeah, that's right. We're related. Help my sister out, will you? She won't listen to anyone, you know. Ever since the lightning, I worry about her. Don't let her go that way, please." Again his plastic expression shifted, taking on real urgency for a second. Daire could see his fist tighten around the bow until the knuckles showed light. "Me, I ready for whatever come, you know? I'm not afraid. But she's younger, you know how it is. Thinks she got it all down. Help her, and my ghost will thank you."

He gave an ironic smile, bowing deeply at the waist. Then, rather spectacularly, he simply disappeared. No lights, no sounds—just good-bye.

Daire didn't move. "Oh," he said.

◆

After that incident Daire lost track of time for a while. He had a watch in his belt, but he'd never been in the habit of consulting it: time was always slipping away from him scarily, and now more than ever he was afraid to check. He wanted to go and look for the wreck of *Morpheus*, but he was no longer sure of his direction, and he was tired. He found himself staring at things without thinking at all, recalling those moments during the fall: those moments of perfect stillness. It was a state he had worked to achieve in meditation for years; now that it rose easily to meet him, he found that it frightened him. His mind flowed into this silent current all too easily. He began to wish Tsering would come back and talk to him again. She had seemed so real.

The sun appeared to move and the day passed with the trees and the insects making little sound. He returned to the tree he'd been tied to, but Tsering did not reappear. He wandered off again, aimlessly now, and before long he was lost.

He tried to use his memory to ground himself, calling up concrete images to steady his thinking. I am on an unknown planet, he reminded himself, and I don't even have a recorder of any kind. If it is a planet. If I am here. I am living beside

the descendants of the most corrupt people in the entire re-
pulsive business of the Gene Wars, and it must mean something that the adults don't even stick around to look after
their kids. Colin Peake is at this moment composing an arti-
cle to send to some prestigious journal out of Oxford, about
the sweet way I vanished. And here I am, and I can't think.

The forest all around him, this thing called lywyn,
seemed to take on an almost animal presence as the afternoon waned. He could feel the weight of its inscrutable
thought boring into him from above and walling around him
from the sides, until at last he sank down on the moss and
let himself gaze into the intricate jumble of branches overhead, losing himself in their complexity.

◆

He jerked awake, startled and irritated with himself for
sleeping, and it was dark. He was sweating from some
already-vanished nightmare, and he clutched at the roots
around him with a nameless panic. The weight of the forest
was stifling, its darkness absolute. Even in space, you had
running lights. You had stars. But under the trees the night
was Stygian and windless. He sat with his back to the tree,
knees drawn up to his chest, cursing himself for his stupid
fear.

Then the sounds began. Whispers, so light and high they
made his hair stand on end: like the whispers of young children in the minutes before sleep. Ghosts, Daire thought.
What did she mean by ghosts? And he strained his eyes to
make out some shape. Only vaguely could he make out the
darkened outlines of what must be the giant boles of the
trees. He looked for movement between them, trying to locate the source of the whispers that seemed to come from everywhere. The white noise dulled his mind.

He must have slept again, because now the darkness was
mitigated ever so slightly by a pallid light from above. It had
a silvery moonish quality, so Daire assumed it was moonlight
even though the leaves blotted out all view of the sky. Not
ten feet away crouched a naked man, body bent almost into
the ground in an abandon of despair, shaking with sobs.
Daire listened for a long time, using that middle-of-the-night

strategy of ignoring the sound, hoping for it to go away. But the man's agony went on and on. At last Daire stood up. He took two hesitant steps toward the figure, hand outstretched in a pacifying gesture.

"Here," Daire began. There was no one there.

7

This time he was not going back to sleep. He stood up, shook himself out, and making his best guess about direction began to creep slowly toward the lake. Morning was on the way: in fact, by the light it was the same hour in which he'd found himself on the shore the day before. Daire did check his watch now; it was important not to get sucked into the blur of time. He was reassured to learn that it had been less than twenty hours since he'd last checked the time on Underkohling, so the revolution of this planet was a little faster than Earth's; Daire's internal time sense told him the night had been short. Now, though, his appetite preoccupied him, but he didn't want to waste the little food he had on his person. Better to find out what the children ate, and get hold of some of that. After the night he'd spent in the lywyn, however, he felt far less inclined to be compliant. Let them come with their nets. He was no longer dazed and disoriented; hunger and anxiety had sharpened him.

Daire worked his way downhill, making slow progress as he frequently had to climb up and over the lattice of branches in order to go forward. He began to see why Tsering moved above the forest floor: it was easier to leap from branch to branch than to continually climb over the lower limbs of the trees. After something like half an hour he spotted a narrow stream running in a deep culvert, and correcting his direction he was able to follow that to the edge of the lake.

Emerging from the trees the first thing he saw was warm light floating on mist that hid the surface of the lake. He did not recognize the spot, but the dim view of the cliffs that his position afforded him told him he was some distance north of his point of landing yesterday. He knelt at the water's edge near the point where the stream fed the lake and cupped his hands. He was ragged with thirst and ignored the cautionary voice in his mind: This wasn't Earth. The children surely drank this water, and they seemed none the worse for it.

The water filled his stomach, obviating any immediate need for food, so he began to walk south along the shore, looking for something familiar. As light grew he could see that there were reeds and other plants growing in the sunny areas between the lywyn and the lake; some spots were positively marshy and had to be avoided. And the insects were back (although, he was relieved to note, none of them seemed to have evolved the ability to suck human blood).

He walked perhaps a mile before he saw *Morpheus*. He was almost upon it before he recognized it: except for its symmetry, the green mound rising between lake and lywyn could easily have been a natural formation. Half sunk in mud and water and covered with moss and algae, the hulk of *Morpheus* looked more like a beached whale than an interplanetary, however old its design. Daire stopped in his tracks and just gazed at it for a minute, trying to figure out which end was up.

He had to crawl up and over it through the lywyn: the forest enclosed it like a hangar, growing around what Daire took to be the nose of the craft, in an unbroken formation. The aft two thirds of the ship extended into the lake. Threading his way through the lywyn branches, Daire managed to reach a point over the top of the hull where he could lower himself onto the ship. From there he went on hands and knees, feeling for any indication of a hatch beneath the thick vegetation that blanketed the hull. Fortunately, the ship seemed solid enough: if the mosses were eating into its material, they were doing it very slowly. There was hope of finding something intact inside, if the bottom hadn't been damaged and the interior flooded. Daire cursed himself for his recklessness back on Underkohling. If he'd believed for an instant that any of this could have happened, he would have taken along more than oxygen and a couple of candy bars. It was ridiculous to be caught in this situation with no instruments, and as he scrabbled over the moss getting his fingernails dirty and inhaling the smell of swamp decay, he again hoped that Colin would have the sense to send something after him.

And then he laughed. Who but Daire himself would volunteer to step into a void?

"You got yourself in," he muttered aloud. "You save yourself, if you can."

"You are in violation of our laws," said a young voice. "Return to the lywyn where you can be monitored. The ship *Morpheus* is off-limits to you."

Daire whirled, looking for the speaker, but there was no one in sight. The voice had come from the lywyn. He sniffed reflectively, remembering the strange echo of the child Rena's voice the day before. They must have some way of projecting sound?

"Like hell," he shouted back in the direction of the lywyn. "Come and get me, then."

He grinned. Enough of being passive.

"Do you threaten us?" The treble voice was cold.

"Do you threaten me?" Daire flung back, still searching for the source of the sound. There was no reply. Let them think about that, Daire thought, pleased. There were things to be done. If he could get these kids to work, it might even be possible to resuscitate *Morpheus*'s communications system. Then it was only a matter of sending a pulse signal back through the gate. When the gate opened, Colin would receive the message.

Or, Daire wondered, had these people tried that already? Colin had received an encryption referring to *Morpheus* by name, but it had been embedded in his system software. It hadn't come over any known communications channel. If they weren't even using the ship, then how in hell could they have the technology to transmit such heavily encoded text? They barely even had clothes on. Did the children run wild while the adults somehow manipulated sophisticated technology somewhere else? But how? And why?

Whatever the case, they had to be made to take him to the adults. Whatever technology they had might be used to pass back through the gate. Daire still had his walksuit and, hopefully, some air reserves as well, if Tsering hadn't smashed up his stuff. And, he thought, sitting back on his heels and examining a gently bleeding thumb, there might be more useful equipment within the ship, if he could just find the damn door.

"You've had too much freedom, I see. I blame myself for being so stupid."

It was Tsering's voice, and Daire sighed, letting his shoulders drop. He'd love to know how they accomplished this aural projection: she sounded absolutely real.

"This is getting aggravating," he called back, turning around toward the lywyn to make himself heard. Then he started, for he had miscalculated. Tsering stood ten feet away along the hull, and she had an arrow notched and pointed straight at him. The bow looked familiar: with a weird shiver he realized the design was identical to the one he had seen in Runako's hands.

"I'm sorry," she told him softly, "but you'll have to be restrained again. I can't seem to get it right with you."

She didn't sound sorry, he thought. She sounded pleased with herself, and he shook his head, smiling wryly. There were more children ranged behind her in the lywyn, and now he saw some creeping silently onto the shore, below. They were openly armed this time. Obviously they had been aware of his movements: but how?

"Okay, okay." He forced a laugh, raising his hands. "I surrender."

Fuck me, he thought. I don't believe I'm letting them do this to me. But he suffered himself to be bound at the wrists—much more securely this time, he observed—and led down from the ship. Tsering maintained what he supposed was an amused silence during the slow march through the lywyn. Daire had trouble climbing over the branches without his hands to steady him, and for a while he was deliberately clumsy, hoping to vex her, but she didn't seem to notice. His stomach was churning audibly by now, and it seemed to take an inordinate amount of time to get to wherever they were going. Again he wondered how they had known where he was, to arrive on the scene so quickly.

Suddenly the lywyn gave way to sunlight. They had come to the bottom of the cliff, and as Daire had surmised, in the narrow strip of treeless land at the base of the stone was a green and yellow expanse of cultivated land. Buildings had been erected in the shadow of the cliff, and there were irregular cave openings at some little height from the ground, rope ladders trickling from their mouths. There was more cleared land than Daire had first thought: although the strip was never more than a hundred meters wide, it extended to either side as far as he could see, before the cliff curved and lywyn obstructed the view of the ground beyond. To the right small children were playing near some low buildings that looked to be humps of clay, but to the left, away from the lake, all the land had been carefully cultivated, and no one was in sight.

He hesitated on the edge of the forest, but Tsering nudged him forward.

"I've changed my mind about you," she said. "I can't let you go free, but I'm not going to let you starve in the forest, either." She turned to the two kids who flanked Daire. "Take him to my house and give him food. He's not to use his hands, so you'll have to help him. Watch him carefully."

Then she turned to the rest of the group, and Daire was prodded away toward the dwellings. He still felt cheated, but he could also smell breakfast.

◆

The child who fed him was paler than most, with dark brown hair and hazel eyes. Daire sat on the ground and watched him while he took his time deliberately assembling the simple utensils: a polished clay bowl, a spoon, a piece of cloth that he fitted with great seriousness into the collar of Daire's clothing. Daire was not accustomed to being around children, and the direct, simple intensity of the child's actions nearly distracted him from his hunger. When the boy's small hands touched his neck as he fussed with the napkin, the top of Daire's head began to tingle with a calm, mesmerizing pleasure. It was a sensation that he usually experienced only in the trance state.

And when, at last, the hot cereal had been poured into the bowl to the boy's satisfaction and the child positioned himself to feed Daire, he looked straight into Daire's eyes and said, "I'm not afraid of you."

"No?"

The boy shook his head. "No. You remind me of my father."

"Really? Do I look like your father?"

"No. You don't look like him. You're old. But you have his way."

Daire smiled at being called "old" again. "Where is your father?"

Something scared came down over the boy's eyes and he held out the dripping spoon toward Daire's mouth. The boy shook his head wordlessly.

"Eat," he prompted when Daire only stared at him.

Mechanically Daire opened his mouth, chewed, and swallowed. He was momentarily preoccupied with the unfamiliar taste of the meal, and the boy avoided his eyes after that.

◆

Tsering came to speak to him later. He was reclining against a smooth rock in the sunlight, eyes closed, replete, and his body was about ready to make up for some of the lost, tense hours in the middle of the night, when she knelt beside him and touched his shoulder.

She laid several objects on the ground and seated herself opposite him. Daire blinked and sat up. He recognized his breathing apparatus and notebook. Objects such as these should not change—did not change—but it seemed to him that even in such a slim amount of time, they had. They were familiar, but they no longer signified what they ought to. They were strange and smooth and they plainly didn't belong. Looking at them, the reality of the life in which he used these things seemed, in the beneficent sunlight of this planet, only a dim, insignificant construct. When he looked up he caught Tsering watching him. He held her eyes.

"Tell me about Ingenix," she said.

Daire watched her, not sure how to respond. Did she know what the Gene Wars had done, or did she believe that her ancestors were heroes?

"Ingenix was dissolved many years ago," he answered carefully. "It was taken over by an international task force and almost all its technology was dismantled. Along with the properties of Helix and Gen9, all Ingenix holdings were ceded to survivors of the experiments. I am a member . . ."

he hesitated just a fraction of a second, "of the League of New Alchemists, which took over the old Ingenix headquarters. I was sent to Underkohling to investigate a transmission evidently sent from *Morpheus*, which is why I was there this morning. Did you send a signal?"

She ignored his question, firing another two back at him. "Are there military vessels at Underkohling? And are you in contact with them?"

"No, and no. I'm not here to judge you. I fell through by accident. I told you, I was just trying to figure out where the transmission came from. It was a computer virus. You do understand what that is, don't you?"

"I'm not an idiot," she snapped. "But you can't have failed to notice that we have to make do without fancy technology"—she gestured to his instruments—"and the last thing I wanted to do was draw attention to us from Earth." She sighed. "I wanted to believe you were a ghost, because you didn't come the way I expected people from Earth to come. You have no ship, and you're alone, and you weren't especially coherent when you got here. I thought you had to be a ghost. But I see that my imagination is out of sync with reality. There is no military interest in us?"

Daire grimaced. "I'm the only one who knows you're here," he said. "The gate that brought me—and you—here is highly unstable. But . . . if it was to become known that you are here, there would be military interest, yes. I won't lie to you about that."

"Are we still such a threat?" Tsering said. "I guess it shouldn't surprise me. Well, what should I do with you, then, Daire Morales? Surely I can't let you go back and spread the word about us."

Daire said, "The last thing I want to do right now is take another trip through that gate, even if it is possible. I just spent the strangest night of my life in that forest. I don't feel capable of much." He realized that he ought to be taking a harder line with this girl; he ought to take control of the situation despite her obvious assumption of authority. But he remained irrationally sympathetic to her, and he realized he wanted her to trust him.

"That's good. Because whether you know it or not, you present a problem. You are the only adult here, Daire Morales, and we have learned to mistrust adults. We have learned the hard way."

"Something terrible must have happened for you to feel that way. Where I come from, children don't live apart from adults."

There. That was innocuous enough, wasn't it? But her expression darkened.

"I'm not prepared to talk about that," she answered. "But listen to this: Adults are not welcomed or understood here. I am not afraid to face you, because I'm older than you are whether or not you choose to believe me. This place and its people are precious to me. When my ancestors came here, they found asylum. Why they came and what happened to them when they got here are not your concerns, at least not yet. Let us just say that they came under pursuit by those who wanted to kill them, and that by good fortune they were saved. They named this planet Dilarang, which is the Hindu for 'forbidden,' because no one else but they could come here. It was a haven to them, and it has been a haven for us for many years now.

"Now you are here. I mistook you for a ghost, but you are not; and yet you do not come in a manner that would mark you as an enemy. An enemy would not come alone, with no ship and no weapons. Still, you are the first to pass through; the first to be admitted to Dilarang since my ancestors fell through the lake and found themselves here. Your arrival is significant; it means change is coming, whether for bad or good I can't say, but change nevertheless.

"I must wait and watch. You are under my observation, Daire Morales, whether I am with you or not. Until I know you, I will not tell you more than I already have. Until I know you, and decide that you will do no harm, you will follow the rules I set. Break them and you will be restrained. You are free to walk wherever you want to, provided you don't damage any of the plantings. You will wear the manacles and, additionally, agree not to pick up any weapon." He found himself nodding. "Further, you will not speak to the children unless they speak to you first. They probably won't: most of them are terrified. I recommend that you move slowly and predictably, or some of them may become very upset. Is all of this acceptable to you?"

"What choice do I have?"

"None that I can see. Your night spent in the lywyn doesn't seem to have worn well with you."

She smiled, and he looked away. Was it so easy for her to see him falling apart? He knew he was a fool to simply allow himself to be ordered around, but she was right: he didn't want to go back to the lywyn alone. He narrowed his eyes, trying to look cunning.

"Fine. I agree to the terms. For now. But I'm going to expect some information from you, before long. You'll be foolish not to help me."

She bowed ever so slightly. "That is one opinion."

8

He slept on a grass mat that night, outside the grass house where Tsering and two younger children lived. There were no dreams until the early hours of the morning, when he became aware that he was a giant sleeping on a dark beach and armies of Lilliputians were swarming over him, looking for something he had. He awakened shivering, and shook off a blanket of strange winged insects that had settled on him. His skin crawled continuously after that, and he sat with his knees drawn in for warmth, waiting for the light again.

Tsering appeared while he was eating a breakfast of brown porridge, this time served by Rena and another girl, neither of whom would come within arm's length of him.

"I have to go to High," she told him. "It's the place on top of the cliff, where the lessents live. I have some business there."

Daire nodded, concentrating on his food.

"I'm going to take you with me," she added.

"I see," he mumbled. "I'm honored." He looked up at her with what he hoped was an intimidating stare: he expected her to be flustered by sarcasm, used to complete obedience as she was. But she disappointed him. She smiled.

"I like you," she said, and her tone was warm, not the condescending "I like you" of a master to an apprentice, reinforcing authority, but something more ingenuous.

"You have no bullshit," Tsering added.

"Thank you. Neither do you, as far as I can see."

"But you still must wear the restraints," she amended, glancing at him as if afraid she had been too kind.

"Fine," he said. "It's a free lunch, ain't it?"

"What?"

"My associate, Colin, used to say, 'There's no such thing as a free lunch in the universe.' And I used to argue with him that there could be, if you were lucky. And now I'm living proof."

"I don't understand."

"I know. I just wanted to see that look on your face."

"What look?"

"That 'I don't understand' look."

She hesitated, unable to decide if she was being made fun of.

"We're leaving soon," she informed him. "Be ready."

He swallowed the last of his breakfast and displayed the manacles cheerfully.

"I'm ready now!"

"Good," she said briskly, her composure recovered. "I'm not. So you can wait."

She walked away. Daire watched her retreating figure. Her sexuality was nascent, just suggested in a way that was more provocative, even, than womanhood fully formed, because it spoke of possibility. And that, Daire thought, was what desire was really about. Possibility.

It was better not to think this way—it was better not to be led around by one's gonads if such things could be avoided. But in the middle of everything he had to admit, if only in an inner whisper, that he responded to this girl. It was not scandal he feared: no, in this strange world and impossible situation what "people" thought was the least of his worries. Rather he worried that if she became aware of his attraction, she would use it as a tool against him. She was cagey, and if she was telling the truth about her age, she'd been around long enough to understand sexual politics better than he did himself.

Then again, she might be lying. At times she also seemed surprisingly innocent. She was nothing like any of the people he'd known, either growing up on the rez or at the League. Thinking about this, he realized that her sense of confidence was based on autonomy, whereas autonomy was all but unknown on Earth. It would be interesting, Daire thought, to observe her behavior as she conducted this "business" of hers among the lessents. Whatever they were.

"*Adolescents,*" she informed him, once they had set on their way.

"Ah!" he replied, suddenly enlightened. "I knew you couldn't all be children. So these 'lessents' live at High, is that it? And how are we going to get there? Up the ladder in the lywyn?"

She turned to him in surprise. "How did you know that?"

He chuckled but didn't answer her. It had been easy to guess her intentions: they were walking along the cultivated land, straight toward the place where, during his survey from the trees the other day, he had seen the green path of lywyn branches crawling up the side of the cliff: an obvious road.

"I go up there about once a week," she said, lengthening her stride easily to match his. "To check on things and to give the mothers advice. There are three babies there right now: Michelle's boy Rand; Kim, who is Ana's; and the youngest, Aristotle. The last two are lucky: their mothers are only fourteen and fifteen, and should be able to care for them until they are weaned at two years. Two Earth years, that is."

She looked up the lattice that spanned the cliff. "Here," she said, beckoning to him. She deftly unlocked the manacles and slid them into a pouch in the loose-fitting, layered clothes she wore. "You don't need to wear those now. You'll need your hands to climb, and anyway, I don't expect the lessents to be afraid of you." She began to climb. Daire followed, still digesting her words about the lessents.

"And then what? What happens after the infants are weaned?"

"Then the children will come to live with us at Lake. The mothers may be able to try for another baby by then, although it will be risky. Michelle's already had twins. By the time she conceives again she'll be seventeen, and that's pushing it."

"Why?" Daire tried to keep his voice neutral, but inwardly he was shocked. The League of New Alchemists talked about breeding in a similar pragmatic way, but they never permitted girls to become pregnant before sixteen. It was considered too great a health risk for both mother and child.

"Because of the distortion," Tsering answered patiently.

"It's rare that anyone—particularly a female—lasts beyond eighteen or nineteen."

"What is the distortion?"

"It's a kind of sickness. You never recover from it."

"Are you telling me *there are no adults here*?"

"Of course. I've never denied that. Why do you suppose you present such a problem?"

Daire didn't know what to say. To die so young, he thought. It was tragic. Yet Tsering had not died: she'd even claimed to be old. He wanted to ask her how this had been accomplished, but when he glanced at her, her profile was grim. She was standing balanced on one foot, her weight half hanging from her arms with the sun pouring over her like a golden elixir. Yet she was bathed also in some secret grief. He thought she looked antique then: not physically aged, but a person from the depths of the past, suddenly breathing the air right beside him with the slow pulse beating in her neck.

"I'll tell you what I'm afraid of," Tsering said. "Aristotle's father, Jordan. He's eighteen by my reckoning, and he's been at his full growth for a year. Aristotle's mother, Seika, is fourteen and tiny—she's my size, in fact, and I worry about both of them. I think I'm going to do something unprecedented. I'm considering bringing Seika and the baby back to Lake for a few months, until he's a little stronger and doesn't need his mother's milk so much."

"What are you afraid will happen to them?"

"Jordan will distort soon. He could take the baby with him."

"Is it contagious?" Daire asked, surprised.

"What?"

"Distortion."

"No! But Jordan's going to turn nasty. I know it. I can always tell. I've never broken the rules like this before, you understand—normally once a lessent, you're banned from the Lake and you go to High. This is the way we've always done it; it was my idea, in fact, back in my real youth." She smiled. "That's why *you* have to be restrained. We just can't trust you. But times are also changing. You're here now, and that changes certain things. And I . . ." Her voice wavered, actually came close to breaking, and she looked away. "There are other reasons. We may need new laws. So today

I have to decide: Should I let Seika return to Lake, temporarily, for the sake of the little one?"

She launched herself upward, and Daire began to pant, trying to catch up with her.

"I'm sorry," he called after her. "But I'm having trouble following this conversation."

Tsering looked at him over her shoulder, and he caught a flash of laughter, quickly suppressed, in her eyes. It was not a child's expression at all. It was a woman's look, when she knows she has power over a man.

"It must be strange for you," she admitted. "Just watch, and listen. And be prepared for a confrontation. Jordan has a temper."

"Hang on. Are you saying you're bringing me as a bodyguard?" Daire tried to sound outraged.

She did laugh now. "I'm bringing you because I have to go, and I can't leave you alone with the kids. I've removed your bonds so you can climb freely. And if you can be useful, then you will have earned a little more of my trust, which I think you want. I don't think you love violence: you've had opportunities to resist us and you haven't taken them. So I think you'll help me keep the peace, in turn."

"And if I escape, instead?"

"There are things in the lywyn you don't want to meet. But I don't think you want to escape. You have nowhere to escape *to*, do you?"

She had reached the top ahead of him and stopped to wait. As if its only purpose in growing up the side of the cliff had been to provide a convenient ladder, the lywyn abruptly halted. There was only grass and scrub at the top of the cliff. Daire pulled his weight over the lip and cast himself on the ground beside her.

"I want you to take me into the ship," he said.

"We'll see." She plucked a grass stem and slipped it between her lips.

"Seriously. There's probably stuff there that we could use."

"To do what? Go back to Earth?"

"Maybe, yeah."

"And why would I want to do that? To be a freak? An outcast?"

As if he had never been himself repulsed by the thought of her parents' crimes, he heard himself saying, "No one blames you for . . . you know. Your ancestors. Anyway, how long can you go on like this, a bunch of children—" He broke off, flustered. The grass had fallen out of her mouth as her jaw dropped, and she was staring at him—angry, he assumed from the intensity of her gaze.

"I mean," he amended, "I know you've survived a long time. That's admirable. But—"

"But how much longer?" Her expression, fierce at first, settled into reflection. "I don't know the answer to this question. I never think about it. I don't look forward. I just deal with what is. You'd be surprised how long you can go on that way."

She stood up then, and led the way across the flat grasslands, angling toward the sea. Daire could smell it from here, and the wind was too strong to continue speaking, so he just followed. Immediately to his left he was surprised to see a bank of a dozen primitive windmills stretched across the plain. They looked incongruous in the otherwise wild country, but the sight of them cheered him. They made Dilarang seem more Earthlike and familiar.

From up on the plateau the lywyn looked like a solid sheet of foliage, stretched between the lake and the highlands to the east. The plateau rose to meld with the bare upper slopes of the hills farther to the east, but ahead of them, to the west, it tapered to a thin forked point suspended out over the ocean. There, on the exposed height, a village of sorts had been constructed: small brick and wattle houses, some wooden sheds, piles of stone, wood, and bales of the thick, tough grass that grew all around. They were still some distance away when a flap in one of the houses opened and a woman, heavily pregnant, stepped out, looked furtively at them and then toward the sea, and then ducked back inside. There was a strange silence about the place. It had the kind of squalid look that Daire's imagination associated with medieval villages, suggesting screaming geese, kitchen midden, thin dogs. But there were no livestock, no fires, and no naked children playing in the mud. It would be a village without children; already he knew that much.

So this is what has become of the despots of the Gene

Wars, Daire thought. It wasn't easy to believe. They had come close to destroying humanity, and now their grandchildren lived in huts and died young. He wondered what would have happened to them had they remained on Earth. He was not at all sure it would have been worse than this. Colin had always said Ingenix were fools not to go to Jupiter, where they might have found political asylum. Instead they'd let themselves be shot down out on the edge of the solar system. Had their brilliant minds finally collapsed under their own weight? Daire suspected that even then they had been carrying whatever disease this distortion was, probably loosed on themselves in a final, ironic accident.

Tsering walked into the midst of the buildings, and still nothing moved. From within one of the houses on the outskirts, a baby squalled in long, high outrage.

"Come out," Tsering said quietly, and after a moment a handful of young women appeared in doorways and then haltingly came into the open. Two or three still looked like children to Daire, but of these one had a belly already perceptibly swollen. None of them met his eyes.

"Mirasa, how are you feeling?" Tsering inquired of the youngest girl, reaching toward her sympathetically and drawing her forward into the open.

"I'm all right," whispered the girl, who seemed to be shaking. "The sickness has finally stopped."

"Don't be afraid!" Tsering implored, turning to include the others. "This is Daire, and he is a friend. He won't hurt you." Her eyes turned to him. "He has sworn it."

Daire said nothing. He was suddenly angry at Tsering: she manipulated him for her own purposes, yet wouldn't permit him to get to the interior of the ship, where maybe he could do something to alleviate this situation. He was ashamed to look at any of them.

Then a high, tinkling laugh distracted him, and he turned his head to see a young girl and a tall woman emerge from a house together. Each held a child, and the younger girl was laughing as she tickled her baby.

"Tsering!" she called. "I'm so glad to see you. Look at Aristotle! Can you believe how big?"

Tsering was smiling. Daire watched her go toward the young mother—this must be Seika—and he realized that she didn't see what he saw. She didn't see the dirt or the deprivation: the bare feet and patched garments didn't even attract her attention. Tsering took the infant from Seika and cradled it expertly, playing with the tiny brown fingers with a delight that made her seem even more of a child herself. Still carrying the child, she came back toward Daire, who stood in the center of a circle of suspicious eyes.

"Look," she said, holding the baby and smiling up at him. "This is Aristotle, our youngest." She sounded exactly like a proud parent, but one of the other women hissed under her breath, and the tall one who'd accompanied Seika pushed her own child back behind her skirts and stepped forward with an urgent gesture of denial.

"It's all right," Tsering said without looking up. "This is Daire, a man from Earth, and he's here to help us if he can. He has no distortion sickness—there's nothing to be afraid of."

Daire met the hostile gazes now: the tall woman had stopped in midstride, arm still half raised in an aggressive posture. He could see her nostrils flaring with each breath.

"Do you remember your history that I taught you so long ago, Michelle?" Tsering asked, her tone still reasonable and her smile still fixed on the baby in her arms. Daire saw the face of the tall woman move; her glance flickered toward Tsering, and then, wavering, back to Daire. Tsering continued in a singsong tone.

"If you remember, then you know that our ancestors came from Earth as young people, bearing the curse of distortion, and stumbled upon Dilarang through good fortune when a dark gate opened before them in the stars. They landed their ship in the lake and began their life new, here. My own parents were among those first settlers, and I am the only one of that generation to resist distortion. So I have led you. I have led your grandparents, and your parents, and now you, on the path to survival of our people *in spite of* the curse of distortion."

Daire saw her draw breath now, and she looked up and surveyed the faces around her. They were all rapt, no longer noticing Daire but involved utterly in Tsering's narrative. They were all so young.

"And," Tsering continued, raising the volume of her

voice, "now it is time for change. We have kept the customs for many years now, and with good reason. But we have among us a person from Earth, one who may lead us out of our troubles. His arrival is a sign of changes to come. We must adapt to the new times. I cannot revoke the ban that is on you, but I will amend it."

She paused, looking at Seika, and her tone became more casual.

"Tell me, Seika, how are things with Jordan?"

Seika answered in a soft voice.

"He's afraid."

"Does he say as much?"

"No, but I can tell. I know him." There was conviction in her delicate frame.

"Does he spend much time with the baby?"

Seika cast beautiful, deep eyes on Tsering. "Every spare second. They're all fishing now, or he would be with Aristotle. He says Aristotle makes it bearable. Distortion. Jordan knows it's coming, but he sees himself in Aristotle and he feels better."

Tsering nodded. "It happens this way, sometimes. Remember Ket?"

Harshly Michelle said, "Ket mauled that poor daughter of his. That's what I remember about Ket."

"It's the way," Tsering answered. "The stronger the bond, the greater the danger. That's why mothers are often the hardest to handle." She continued to stare at Michelle, and the latter withdrew her gaze.

"How is Rena?" Seika asked. "Does she still have scars?"

"Scars are nothing," Tsering said. "Rena is healthy and works hard. I doubt she remembers the episode at all."

"That's lucky," Michelle said under her breath. Her own child sat on the ground picking at a stick thoughtfully. "What do you mean, Tsering, about amending the ban?" She challenged Tsering again, but Tsering looked at Seika.

"It won't be long now, you know," she said gently.

Seika nodded and looked down. "I know."

"You may take Aristotle with you to Lake for a few months," Tsering continued. "Until he has cut his teeth. I am afraid to leave you here with Jordan the way he is."

The look that flared into Seika's eyes was so joyous that

it embarrassed Daire, and he looked away. He found himself watching Michelle, whose jaw was set, hard.

"What about the rest of us, Tsering?" she asked.

Tsering addressed Michelle coolly. "Your child's father is gone, Michelle. You can't be worried about distorting yourself?"

Michelle looked angry, but again she backed down.

"No," she said. "I'm not worried about myself."

"Good. Then we'll take this change one step at a time. Seika first. We'll see how that goes. It will be difficult enough for Jordan. I don't know how to get him to accept it."

There was real alarm in Seika's face now.

"Oh, Tsering, we can't *tell* Jordan. We have to just do it. He'll go on a rampage. His temper lately . . ."

"So it's that bad? Then, yes, we have to act. I see I came just in time. Get your things, Seika, while I talk with the others."

Seika took the baby from Tsering and hurried back into the house. Tsering turned to Michelle.

"Well?" she said.

"Jordan still hates you," replied Michelle bluntly. "He thinks you're the incarnation of evil. He wants to be you. He wants to live forever." Her tone made it plain that this was not a desire that she shared; so many thinly veiled insults, Daire thought, passed from this woman to Tsering and back.

But Tsering only said, "How serious is the danger, do you think? Has he shown any signs?"

Michelle shrugged. "He's never been a sweet boy, has he? He's moody—what can I say? You've seen him. How much longer can it be? He'll bring it on himself next thing, what with his fretting."

"I'm going to do it," Tsering said.

"Good," Michelle answered, her voice clipped. "I never doubted it. We all protect our own, don't we?"

Tsering looked stung, but she said nothing. Daire wondered what Michelle meant. Weren't all the children "Tsering's own" in some sense?

"That's not fair, Michelle," put in the pregnant girl, Mirasa. "Aristotle is most vulnerable. And he *is* the last of Tsering's family, after Jordan. Anyway, you don't want to go to Lake. You hated it there."

"Am I complaining?" Michelle asked. "Whatever our leader decides, I shall abide by."

Her voice was slick with contempt.

Tsering turned her back on this, and went to Mirasa to lay a hand over her belly. Mirasa smiled; it was extraordinary, Daire thought, that anyone could flash such an innocent smile in the middle of this unpleasantness. At least no one was looking at him anymore. They seemed to have forgotten him, which was just as well. He let his attention range away from the immediate scene, and that was when he spotted the males, coming home.

"Tsering," he warned.

She looked up, following his gaze.

"Shit," Tsering said.

A group of people were appearing from over the edge of the cliff. There must be stairs cut in the rock, Daire thought, because they marched up slowly, heads and shoulders first, hands stretched out for support. There were five males ranging from half to full grown, and two girls. Some of them carried fish, some buckets, and the foremost and tallest carried an oar. Daire knew immediately that this was Jordan; the man was big, muscular, and would have presented an implied threat under any circumstances. But with an oar in one hand and a scowl on his face as he saw first Tsering, and then Daire, he looked formidable.

Still frowning, he walked straight up to Tsering and planted the end of the oar on the ground. He gazed at them from under thick brows, his deep brown skin shining with sweat. For a second he looked familiar to Daire—like a large-scale version of the archer Runako. But when he spoke there was no lightness in his tone.

"It's not time yet," he said. "I haven't called you, Tsering. What are you doing here?"

There was uncertainty in his voice just beneath the bravado, and Daire could see now how young he really was.

Tsering looked up at him and smiled. "Relax, Jordan. I come every week. You know that."

"Yeah. Well, I didn't call you. Just remember that." He looked around. "Where's Seika?"

"Feeding Aristotle. Where's everybody else? Still at the

boats?" Daire detected the faintest tremor in her voice, but Jordan didn't seem to notice.

"Uh huh. Good catch today. If you want food, you picked a good day to come. They'll be here in a minute."

"Good." Tsering's face gave nothing away, but Daire let his eyes focus on her body and he could perceive the tension in it. He wondered how she would cope with Jordan, who towered over her in a posture of unconscious aggression, an attitude worn so long it was part of the skin. And suddenly Daire wanted to teach Jordan a lesson.

Daire hadn't moved, but now Jordan was looking at him again.

"What the hell is that?" he asked Tsering. "A ghost?"

"He's from Earth," Tsering answered patiently. "Look. This is the way it's going to be. You know you must leave Aristotle soon. Do it now, and let him be safe."

"Safe? Safe from *me*, you mean," Jordan said bitterly, throwing down the oar. He began to stalk back and forth before them, kicking the dirt. Daire felt his own muscles coil, watching. The pure animalian quality in the way Jordan moved inspired similar instincts in Daire, feelings he couldn't analyze but which he knew he'd never felt on the rez.

"I'm his *father*. I'm supposed to fucking protect him. And you tell me to hand him over nicely, like a toy you don't want me to play with anymore. Well, Aristotle's not your toy, Tsering, and neither am I." He stopped square, weight balanced on the balls of his feet and arms hanging loose at his sides, glaring at Tsering. Daire felt rather than saw a kind of tacit approval from the onlookers. Tsering must have a lot of power, he thought, to be so thoroughly resented. She just stood, holding her ground, but Daire felt a flicker of doubt from her.

"And I'll tell you something else," Jordan added, obviously just beginning to warm to his subject. "The last thing I'm going to do is turn over my child to an old Earth man. Look at him! Don't you know what they do to children on Earth? No, Aristotle's not going near him. Distortion, no distortion—doesn't matter. I don't trust them, and if you do, Tsering, then I don't trust *you*. Tell me, is it *your* time at last?"

A shocked *oh* went up from the bystanders, followed by

hushed conversation. Jordan's eyes were very bright, and he stood over Tsering with his hands on his hips. One of the younger males began to move forward.

"Hey, Jordan, take it easy . . ." The youth reached Jordan and hesitated, unwilling to break the tableau. Jordan and Tsering continued to stare at one another, until with a sarcastic snort and a twist of his lip, Jordan turned on his heel and walked away, toward where the others were standing nearby.

"Yeah," he spat over his shoulder. "That's what I thought. It is your time, but you don't have the guts to admit it. Fucking *bitch*."

Daire's throat was filling up with anger. All he could see was a young girl being menaced by a brute; and Jordan's insults toward him were not lost on him either. He took a step forward. But Tsering began to laugh at Jordan's retreating back.

"What an impressive cover-up," she called after him. "Almost convincing. But not to me. You've been doing this since you were this big." She stooped, flattening her palm against an imaginary head at thigh height against her. "This has nothing to do with me, or with Aristotle, and you know it. You're terrified, Jordan, and with good reason. You're about to go through the most significant experience of your life: its ending, in fact."

She paused. Daire watched carefully, waiting for Jordan to make just one aggressive move so he could jump in and beat him to a much deserved pulp. But Jordan stood several meters away among the other adolescents, his back toward Tsering revealing nothing.

"Do you remember Ket?" Tsering prodded.

Jordan whirled, thunder in his expression. "Yes, I remember Ket," he mocked, his body twitching as if with the urge to injure.

"Then you'll remember that Ket stood over there"—she pointed to a flat boulder near the clifftop—"and said very much the same thing to me. He threatened me and he even begged me. And he was like you, Jordan. Very powerful, very intense, very perceptive *kid*. He was a kid, Jordan, just like you. And I was stupid. I gave him two more days to spend with his child. I misread the signs.

"He was in distortion, but I didn't see it. He mauled his

only child and I had to cut his throat. I remember that very clearly, Jordan. I hope you never have to remember the taking of a life. It haunts you."

Jordan was rocking back and forth. He reminded Daire of a tiger aroused to spring—and yet there was a cat's hesitation there, too, a reluctance to commit to action. The slightest distraction and he might pull back.

"You're distorting, Jordan. It's written all over you. Aristotle is out of your control now. You should be preparing for what will come, because, believe me, when it happens, it happens fast."

"You wouldn't dare cut me," Jordan seethed.

Tsering just looked at him. Daire couldn't see her face, but he could see Jordan's as the young man suddenly exploded, rushing at Tsering with fist cocked. Daire shot forward, interposing himself between the girl and the madman, and took the full weight of Jordan's charge square against his body. He smashed an elbow into Jordan's solar plexus, but this proved only a momentary check and in a gasping frenzy the younger man kept coming, grabbing at Daire with long, work-callused fingers. Daire dropped into a deep sumo stance for stability and performed a smooth fingerlock that brought Jordan to his knees, howling.

"Sensitivity to pain," Tsering put in calmly. "That's one of the signs."

Suddenly, Jordan was sobbing.

"Let him go," Tsering told Daire. He flung Jordan's hand away in disgust, resisting the urge to do a little real damage.

"We're *blood*!" Jordan screamed, his voice surprisingly high-pitched. "You won't kill me. You can't kill your own blood, and you can't rule me, either. Aristotle is my blood, and he stays with me."

He had recovered quickly, for he climbed to his feet and set himself up for another charge. His face was twisted with emotion. Come on, Daire thought. Come and get some more.

"No."

It was a soft voice. Daire turned. Seika stood there, the baby tucked in a pouch around her chest, a well-stuffed basket strapped to her back.

"He's my blood, too," Seika said. "And I'm taking him to

Lake with Tsering." Her glance skipped to Daire and away again. "Please don't try to stop us."

Jordan kicked the oar where it lay on the ground. Like a petulant child, Daire thought. Seika edged behind Daire; the infant was asleep, oblivious to the whole thing. Jordan scowled at the ground.

"Call me when you need me, Jordan," Tsering said levelly. "Prepare yourself. It won't be long now."

She gave a nod of her head to Daire, and reluctantly he followed Seika inland along the top of the cliff. Glancing around after a moment he saw that Tsering was speaking to Michelle and a handful of the other lessents. The rest of the males had converged on Jordan in a loose ring. When he looked back a second time, Tsering had begun to walk slowly away from the village. Daire saw Jordan watching, but he didn't attack. All the way back to the lywyn ladder, Tsering hung back. Almost, thought Daire, as though she were giving Jordan a chance to get to her with her back turned. Almost like a sacrifice.

9

That night, Tsering sat down to eat with him. Daire was still astounded at the efficiency with which the children worked, some cooking over open fires while others kept the small ones amused. Tsering roved around, talking to everyone and listening to their stories of the day's events. Although the excursion to High had only taken a few hours, the kids had obviously missed Tsering and clung to her when she returned. At Tsering's own hearth, Daire was alone by the fire. Seika sat a little apart, nursing Aristotle and talking to Rena and the brown-haired boy, whose name, he'd learned, was Naro. Daire could hear Naro asking Seika questions about High, which she answered patiently in a low voice. Daire tried to listen in, but just as Seika was beginning to talk about distortion, Tsering lowered herself to the ground beside him and his attention was drawn away.

"Are you managing okay?" she asked, indicating the wire cuffs that had been replaced on his wrists upon their return to Lake. At least his hands were bound in front of him: he had some use of them this way. He had also had the opportunity to examine the manacles carefully, and he was fairly sure he could get out of them in a pinch.

"I'm getting by," he said. He'd balanced his bowl in one hand and had to bring it and the chopsticks to his mouth together. The meal was a hodgepodge of chopped root vegetables, chunks of a pink fish, and cooked grain. Daire's appetite had kept Naro busy all that day; the boy had looked on in amazement as Daire shoveled down the small portions with alacrity and asked for more. Daire was glad to see that for all the lack of technology and arable land, there seemed to be no dearth of food.

"Don't you think it's time you explained some things to me?" Daire asked. "I've been very patient, and I was certainly helpful to you today—"

"You were."

"So how about going over a few things with me?"

"Ask." Tsering leaned forward and served herself from the pot.

"First of all, what is distortion?"

"But not that." She gave an apologetic smile at his exasperation. "Not tonight. There are bad omens in the air. Can you feel the lightning in the lywyn?"

Daire sniffed. The air was faintly oppressive, but he had seen no lightning, and there was no ozone smell. There was a stillness in the lywyn, though. The insects were silent.

"Tell me about this lywyn," he said. "Who are the people who wander around in there? There *are* adults. I've seen them. And how do you project your voices?"

"Ah," Tsering intoned. "The ghosts." There was no humor in her voice.

"Yes. That's what you called me, at first. What's a ghost?"

"Someone left over, of course. What remains of a person, after. Their voice, their image, their memories."

"But that's not . . . I mean, that's not possible. Is it?"

"Haven't you seen them?"

"Well, maybe, but . . ."

"Tell me. What did you see? The lywyn reveals different ghosts to different people. You're a stranger, so there were no ancestors for you. Who came to you?"

"A man—I don't know his name. I couldn't really see him. He was crying. And also this boy. He was a little like Jordan, only funnier. And he was talking about his sister. He was called Runako. What is it?"

She shook her head, blinking away tears, he was sure.

"Nothing. I know who Runako was. I wonder what it means, that he should visit you."

"What should it mean?"

"The lywyn is like nothing from Earth, Daire. When you've known it a long time, like I do, you'll realize that nothing happens there by accident. Everything has an intention behind it. Like my situation. You didn't believe me, when I told you my age, did you?"

Daire shook his head. He still wasn't certain he believed her, although everyone else seemed to.

"I have to believe that there's some reason I'm still the way I am. Still alive. Unchanged. It has to do with the lywyn. I was caught in a lightning storm, once, you know. When I was twelve. I lost my memory for some days. My brother found me wandering in the lywyn without a thought in my head. And I'd swear that was when it happened. The lywyn froze me. I never grew after that year. Only now . . . well, as I said, things do change. You're here: that's a huge change. And I have to believe there is some scheme to it all. If I didn't, how could I go on protecting them?"

"Without you they would die . . . at distortion?"

"They would devour their own young. What we have—it's not a perfect life. Don't think I haven't seen it in your face. You're disappointed in the way we live. We seem primitive to you, I'm sure. I've been educated by the *Morpheus* computer, you know. I understand Earth history. In a lot of ways, you could say we are cursed: maybe we're abominations that should never have been allowed to be born. But that is all there is for us, you see. And better half a life than nothing—just nothing at all."

Daire thought: How can she accept her ancestry so calmly? What does it mean to refer to your people as abominations? And *what is distortion*? He could not imagine what could evoke such fear in healthy, thriving young people.

"But now you tell me. You are the first to find Dilarang; you are the first to enter the forbidden land. Earth was in the throes of the most devastating wars in history when my parents left. I have often wondered who could have been left alive, and whether Ingenix survived. And what they might do to us, if they found us."

Extradite and probably kill you, Daire thought grimly, and did not savor the ambivalence that he felt about that. How could he sit here talking to this person so calmly, knowing who her ancestors were? Not that any of it was her fault, he reminded himself. And he decided to be straight with her.

"Tsering, you need to know that Earth is not the same planet your ancestors left. There are thousands upon thousands of new species, including new human-derived species. There have been even more extinctions. The human population was decimated and may never recover. There are areas of land that are utterly devastated, and other areas that are developing new ecologies that can't accommodate people.

"And then there are the ones who were never exposed. Pure humans. They managed to remain sheltered through the early years of the devastation, until reservations had been invented. Reservations have plastic energy fields and filters of all kinds, and pure humans live there still. I grew up in a rez, until I found out that I was carrying a renegade gene. One of my parents had altermode, which is an aquatic adaptation, but my mother tried to keep it from me." He didn't mention why; didn't mention that his mother hated the changelings and wanted to go back to nature despite the fact that nature wouldn't have people. He didn't mention his mother's bigotry toward altermoders and other new species, nor her suspicion of technology. But he did bite his lip, thinking about it.

"Your parents," Tsering said, as though she knew what he was thinking. "Did you know them?"

"I didn't know my father. He had altermode. He wasn't able to live with us. My mother . . . she's another story. She walked away from the Lima rez when I was ten." He gave a curt laugh. "I tell people that I lost her, and they say, 'I'm sorry,' but it's not the same as if she died. I just . . . lost her."

He put down the cup he was holding, realizing that his stomach was quivering. He hadn't meant to tell her that.

Tsering reached over and touched his knee.

"Do you believe she is alive?"

Daire looked away into the darkness. The shapes of the lywyn branches seemed to crawl and shift. He realized there had been a long silence. She was still watching him.

"No," he said in an even voice. He shut down the part of himself that wanted to soften under her regard. Then he looked her in the eye. He watched her react to the fact that she was not allowed in, and even as he was changing the subject, he found himself regretting it.

"I have to tell you, Tsering, that it's hard for me to see

you as separate from your ancestors. I know I said no one would blame you for what they did, but at the same time I have to tell you that the entire course of Earth history was radically altered by their activities. Some good may have come out of the Gene Wars—I guess you can find good from almost any adverse situation if you look hard enough. But the ways Earth has changed! New species, new ecosystems, and many of them hostile to human existence. It's unnatural."

"How can anything be unnatural? Everything in the world is natural, including human activities of every variety. We are part of nature: a part that changes the other parts. But even the worst of human crimes are natural. You can't put your species above nature that way."

He ought to be angry at these cool assertions. To eliminate morality by claiming everything was natural! But Tsering had no idea what was happening on Earth as a direct consequence of her forebears. He said carefully, "It still seems a poor excuse for the Gene Wars."

"You say you carry a nonhuman gene. Does that make you unnatural?" Again she probed unerringly for the weak places.

"I don't know. Although I don't display the phenotype, sometimes I have felt so bloody unnatural, as though nothing about the world fit me at all. I think that's why I've always been so willing to take risks. Nothing ever seemed quite real to me."

"Nothing seemed real. What a problem to have! Everything to me seems too real, too heavy, and far too consequential. I'm the only one who remembers anything, and what if I remember wrong? What if I'm doing the wrong thing, keeping this charade going?"

Daire looked around at the kids running in and out of the circles of light.

"I don't think I could call this a charade. I would like to take you to Earth someday. Maybe it would destroy your innocence, but I'd like you to see what goes on there."

"My innocence! You make me laugh. You are like a child, Daire. Like one of these creatures running around here. You have such a dim sense of the world—can't you conceive that I'm far from innocent? You know nothing about me, and yet you immediately put your trust in me. That is innocence."

"Is it? I thought it was only yielding to the inevitable."

He was playing with her a little now, but her face became grave.

"If you can do that with grace, then you have a gift that I envy."

◆

He woke that night to the sound of a man's voice ranting. Daire couldn't hear the words but he recognized the timbre and tone: it was Jordan. A babble of young voices came from the direction of the houses; then he heard Tsering's command, "Stay back. You're going to get hurt if you try to go in there."

Still groggy, Daire struggled to his feet, hindered by the shackles. He tried to orient himself in the darkness. Jordan's shouting had reached a crescendo, but the lywyn blocked all view of what was happening. Daire heard himself cursing as he began to run, throwing all the strength of his arms against the wire handcuffs and failing to break free. When he reached the edge of the lywyn, he could see Jordan dimly, silhouetted against the still red embers of the fire: his head was moving back and forth, his knees bent as if prepared to spring. Jordan's breathing was harsh and labored, and one hand strayed continually to his side as if it pained him.

Standing outside the house where Seika now lived, Tsering didn't move a muscle. She stared at Jordan, arms raised in a posture of self-defense, legs planted. A knife gleamed in her right hand. She was going to fight him! Was she crazy? He put on a burst of speed, but then several things happened at once.

Jordan threw back his head and screamed. Daire flinched. The sound of it froze his balls, and he hesitated for a fraction of a second. He saw Tsering fall to her knees, and Jordan sprang over her and into the house. Daire plunged into the circle of firelight to the sound of Seika's shrieks; he intercepted Jordan as he crashed out of the house again. Daire flung himself at the larger man, whose face he could barely see. Jordan had something in his hands. It looked like a bundle of rags. He shook it and then threw it down; some part of Daire's mind shut this gesture away from consciousness. He didn't want to know what it meant. Instead, he barreled into Jordan and succeeded in knocking him to the ground.

Tsering was suddenly shouting at him.

"The water! Get him to the lake. Net! Net!"

There was a net over both of them, and Daire struggled to get free, still fending off Jordan, who was now kicking and biting and making predatory sounds. He sensed rather than saw the presence of kids around him. There was an awful stench coming off Jordan.

Daire struck out wildly and at last the handcuffs gave. Frantic, Daire flung the rest of the net away and staggered to his feet; he found himself face-to-face with Tsering. She was trying to shove the hilt of a knife into his hand and dragging him forward all at once: in the blur of torchlight he couldn't see much, but he realized that a group of kids had materialized out of nowhere and were now punching, kicking, and carrying Jordan all at once toward the water. Tsering made him follow. She was speaking as she stumbled alongside him, but he didn't understand anything she was saying. Her face looked gaunt and unreal. The sound was coming from Jordan again, the unbearable sound.

There was blood in Daire's eyes, probably his own. Tsering made him take the knife, and for the first time he heard her words. "Please. I can't do it. Please."

He took the knife. The next thing he knew he was up to his knees in the lake. The kids, operating like a well-trained battalion, had pushed Jordan into the water. He was still thrashing in the net, but repeatedly they forced him under. Jordan must have got a hand free, because suddenly a child was being pulled under, kicking, and the others rallied to pull her out again.

Daire waded into the lake and received several stray blows.

"Get back!" he shouted to the kids, raising the knife. "Get out of the water."

They complied, backing away slowly and with a fascination on their faces that would have alarmed Daire if he'd had time to think about it. The body in the net was underwater now; it had been there for some time but it was still struggling. Dazed and horrified, Daire watched, waiting for it to drown, but without coming up it continued to struggle.

"Use the knife!" Tsering cried.

Daire was in up to his waist now, and he could barely see Jordan, only the shining ripples his movement made. He bent over in the water, grasped a handful of net, and pulled up. The form struggled, kicking him, and Daire fell on top of it in the water. A hand clawed at his face, the torso thrashed, and Daire found himself gasping and striking out with the knife randomly. It bit into the net, shearing it away, and then into flesh. Suddenly, in the dim light of the lywyn, Daire found himself face-to-face with something totally alien. It dragged at him, pulling him under, and he glimpsed skin bleached of all color, gills wavering delicately in the water, then lidless, unsheltered, the pale unseeing eyes. Daire didn't know how it had happened, but this was no longer a madman, rather some desperate creature fighting for its life in the stranglehold of the net.

Daire got his head above water, regaining his footing. He slashed the knife over the cords, feeling it slice over the surface of flesh twice. He reached down again and suddenly there was nothing there. Farther out in the lake there was a splash, then nothing.

Someone was crying.

Dizzily he turned his head. Seika was standing by the fire, keening, a bundle of rags wrapped in her arms as she rocked back and forth. The kids surrounded her, hands reaching out to touch her, arms to hold her. Daire felt a darkness spread inside of him as he realized what she held. Bent over in defeat, he began to climb out of the water.

He almost tripped over Tsering. She was crouching in the mud at the edge of the lake, fingering one of the ropes that had floated loose. She didn't move. Daire glanced at the circle of mourners in the firelight and then lowered himself beside her. In the light of the trees he could just see her features: devoid of expression.

"Jordan was my grandnephew," she whispered. "And Aristotle was my great-grandnephew. Runako's line. They were the last of my family. I should have killed Jordan while I had the chance."

Daire had begun to shake involuntarily. His teeth were chattering.

"I couldn't kill him," he said. "I had the knife at his throat, and I couldn't do it."

"It's all right. It was too late by then. Aristotle's neck was already broken. Jordan is free now."

He just looked at her, uncomprehending.

"How can you say that?"

Tsering didn't answer. But she put her arms around him, and he turned to face her, factors suddenly compiling in his mind.

"You're not the descendants of the Ingenix directors." Daire felt the force of his declaration vibrating into the hollows of her body. "You're not even human."

"No," she conceded, sighing. "I don't believe we are."

10

Colin Peake's mouth was working. He could see his own reflection in the polished black surface of the com panel; the peaks and valleys of his face, already deeply gouged by care and erratic gravity on board the research vessel, were now bisected by an asymmetrical frown. Clenched and twitching, the frown oppressed the plain between looming nose and the shadowy knoll of Colin's receding chin like a river gone angrily off course. Through the thin dragon line of these taut lips Colin was muttering inaudibly.

He still had not become accustomed to the voices that came over the line from the League of New Alchemists. One of the pleasant surprises associated with the arrival of Daire Morales had been, in fact, his plain, simple way of speaking. Speaking to a real human being had been such a relief to Colin after months of these cryptic, backward conversations with his department at Oxford, or, even worse, with the Heads. It had been an annoyance years ago, on his first trip to Underkohling, when he'd been forced to wait hours for communications from Earth via radio waves, but at least he'd received straightforward text messages that didn't require him to interpret the nuance of the spoken word. Now that the League had introduced the Feynman processor, he found himself confronted with the eerie unreality of real-time, just-in-the-next-room conversation with the Heads, whose attempts to masquerade as people were disconcerting at best. For one thing, none of the so-called Heads had any names they were willing to admit to—and it was often impossible to tell if you were talking to one person with many moods and voices, or many people who were all, it seemed, as fluent in each other's business as in their own.

At first it had been amusing; after all, how many people could say they had spoken directly to the Heads of the League? And who would have suspected that the forces that administered the planet's shaky resources treated each other as fellow characters in a good old-fashioned soap opera? But Colin's amusement was beginning to fade; he had to have a decision regarding the Underkohling project, and the Heads were stalling. He'd done his best to convince them they had to act now by providing mission support to find out what had happened to Morales, to analyze the curious phenomenon of his disappearance, and to decrypt the strange code that had alerted Colin of the presence of the new gate. His was not the only ship in the area: Singapore's vessel was en route from Jupiter to study Underkohling's gravity, and Colin was sure they could be diverted from their mission and recruited to help him. But he wasn't allowed to contact other ships directly, and the Heads were patiently explaining why.

"Clear, carefully administered communications is the surest route to smooth discovery and cooperation of all parties involved." The voice was a familiar one: female, with an undisguised Eastern European accent that suggested English learned later in life. Colin thought of her as the Hungarian Woman. "Here in the League, our ability to connect computers to people to dolphins through our own conscious control is responsible for our many past successes, and it will play a role in this Underkohling project, as well. You do not see all sides to the situation, Dr. Peake, and by no means, we assure you, are the data all in. We will continue to take a broad view of the situation—"

"I prefer to do the obstructing and obfuscating whenever possible," Colin burst in sharply. "Let's get to the point."

"We prefer to take no definitive action at this time."

"What? You've got a man in there. You don't just—"

"We are still investigating the situation. The cost of sending manned expeditions to Underkohling is not small; how many other ships have you seen in the area lately?"

"None," Colin muttered. "But Singapore—"

A new voice. Bass. Australian.

"There's a reason for that. We have a highly skilled dolphin team working on ways to open the gate. Be warned, Dr. Peake, that even if we find the key, so to speak, the energy outlay required to shift the EM patterns of the gate may be too great for our present resources."

"You can't be serious. This is a monumental discovery and you're worried about getting a bargain?" Colin could feel the sweat beading on his forehead.

"I see that you have not been paying attention to the news releases from Earth. We have had political unrest here in Australasia. Many would say that the League should be focusing its attention closer to home, not sticking our noses where we're not wanted."

Colin snorted in frustration.

"Go back to Oxford, Dr. Peake," said the Hungarian Woman in a pacifying tone. "We'll see to the matter, but you're not doing any good drifting around out there using money that could be put to better use, later."

"Money," said Colin. "Show them a weak spot in the walls of the universe and they moan about money. I want to see this work your dolphins are doing. Haven't they cracked the code with the *Morpheus* footprint in it yet?"

"I'm afraid not," said the Aussie. "It proved more complex than we anticipated. You have done all you can. Come home. By the time you've arrived, maybe we'll know something more."

"Right, by the time I've arrived you'll have sent out somebody else to do the work and take all the credit! I'm beginning to get the flavor of how you operate. No, I think I'll stay here and see what happens."

"You will return at once," said the Hungarian Woman. "If you resist, all communications will be cut off and you will get no more cooperation from us. Oxford will be notified of your recalcitrance."

"This kind of intimidation runs entirely contrary to established scientific practices," Colin seethed. "This is not a military operation, and I resent your proprietarial tone."

"We may not always adhere to established practice in the scientific community, but please remember that the League of New Alchemists has accomplished more to expand science in fifty years than the so-called scientific community has done in three hundred!" Her tone was smug; what's more, she was right.

"Dr. Peake, we would appreciate your cooperation in this matter," cut in the Aussie diplomatically. "You may not be aware of all the facets of this issue, as we are, but we must ask for your trust. I give you my word, as soon as it is economically and scientifically feasible to attempt further exploration of Underkohling, we will contact you and see to it that you are accorded a position of leadership. You have my word."

Colin was not normally so peevish, but several months in space had sharpened the edges of his personality.

"Look, Jack," he said. "Don't tell me it's cheaper to bring me home than it is to keep me out here!"

"We are explaining the situation to Oxford right now," put in the female voice. "They concur. Return at once. I am instructing the pilot. Dr. Peake, feel free to contact us when you are back at Oxford. By then we may have more information for you."

"She's not serious," Colin said, forgetting where he was for a moment and whirling to stalk from the room. He had to catch himself against the wall as the floor swooped out from under him. "Hey! Misha! Who's flying this thing?" He gained the corridor and pulled himself along by the handholds built into the walls. A man's head emerged sideways from the navigation compartment and said, "Dr. Peake, you'd better get yourself secured. We have strict orders to return to Earth with best possible speed."

Colin's hair, carefully combed over his balding crown, was drifting up from his scalp. He was shaking his head wordlessly.

"Sorry," the pilot added. "I can't countermand it."

"What about the League ship?" Colin asked, hauling himself arm over arm toward the passenger section.

"The runner that brought Morales? Gone. Went back to Jupiter. I thought you knew. Crazy, isn't it? They didn't even attempt to recover the hopper he left on the surface."

"Shit," said Colin. "Misha, they're cutting me out of the loop."

Misha's head disappeared into his compartment. "If you could move a bit faster, Dr. Peake?"

◆

China is burning; the ragged plains between the Yangtze and the Huang He have been burning for three weeks now, and even the One Eyes have beaten a choked retreat into the factory cities near the coast. The smoke, the smell, the very heat of the event offend the senses, and all the more so because the fires have been instigated by the very protestors who will be hurt most by them: the wretched pure humans, cowering in their reservations. This violet-hued bubble almost adjacent to the One-Eyed factory town of Tsingtao is the nearest rez: from there the burning riots in full view, acres of seed crop, the new grain prized by One Eyes for its endurance in difficult conditions. Only slightly radioactive, highly tasty, and easy to grow, the *santh* will not now grow on this land, nor for years to come. The sensor system of the rez tells the tale to the humans within, who cannot see through its sophisticated mirror fields. It also tells a more subtle story to the computer system that governs the rez.

Not that the sensors are really necessary to the computers and their bridegrooms, the Heads. Everything can be seen from within, these days: neither eyes nor ears are required to read the swift codes into which all information is instantly stored and conveyed, and that is useful indeed, if one has no eyes, no limbs, no body at all aside from the decaying shreds of the physical brain still cranking out the requisite transmitters, still giving orders to the bitter end. The body is not needed. Yet memory will not allow the senses to be abandoned entirely: the brain still craves the body's input in all its richness; and what the brain wants, the brain shall have. So the sensors display the physical evidence of political unrest, and what's left of the body responds with a surge of . . . disgust? frustration? longing? Which one of these is the case depends on the Head in question.

For within all of this, in some non-location-specific construct of time and binomial reality, a conflict is occurring. It conducts itself against the backdrop of the energy control systems, the slippery stock figures, the rumble of industry, and the caterwauling of more internal, personal upheavals—in other words, against the scramble of tech in all its manifold forms. It plays itself out in a medium creeping out from the cracks between language, sound, and image: the nether-world between word and intention where some resemblance to the normal discourse of humanity must be preserved to keep the anonymity of the system at bay. Translated roughly, it goes: "The Coalition is getting on my nerves with these attempts at terrorism. Have they not had enough self-destruction? Have they forgotten the Gene Wars so quickly?" A petulant "voice," projected as male.

"How can they remember? Their lives are so short, and they are so stupid. We worked for four years on the *santh*. The dolphins will laugh at us for ruining it now," adds another male voice, loaded with images of the sea and disappointment.

"I don't like it," continues the first voice. "The One Eyes will be compelled to respond, and the economy is going to be wrecked."

"Singapore will be thrilled." Dryly, a deep voice with Australian vowels joins the discussion. This same identity is simultaneously managing two or three alchemists in altermode and conversing across space with the harassed Dr. Peake; it's a simple parallel use of thought which this being takes for granted.

A female tone, heavily accented. All business. "Singapore is not enough. Watch, this kind of incident can be contagious. Watch West Africa and the purification plants there. I guarantee you somebody's going to take a shot at them."

Attention whirs to Africa; to Northern Europe; to Australia and back.

"We could shut the Coalition down," continues the female.

"No. They serve their purpose. The One Eyes *are* too powerful. The Coalition keeps them guessing," argues the deep voice.

"The Coalition are going to make a mess of everything we've built if they're allowed to continue unchecked," insists the female. "They might as well live in caves and eat raw lizards."

The first voice enters again, almost timidly. "The Coalition are human. I don't like them much, but isn't it our first priority to protect humans, not One Eyes?"

"Hah! Simpleton. Go back to sleep. Here, see this situation in Singapore? Untangle their currency problems—the system's got a huge glitch and they're going to go under if we don't sort it out soon. Go on, Eric."

"All right, Haven. I'm going." Resignation. Flash to the rubbery inner workings of Singapore's financial sector.

"*What* did you call me?" The female voice has followed him there. "Where did you get that name?"

"Haven? I . . . I don't know." Flash of memory, quickly suppressed, of a woman's face. Blond hair. "It was a mistake."

"Yes," says the steely voice. "It certainly was. I use no name, as you well know. Go to sleep."

The weak point in the memory block of the one called Eric is ferreted out and repaired while he, all unknowing, goes to work on Singapore's currency in his "sleep." The rest of the Heads will debate on even as, with other levels of their multifaceted thought, they go about the business of running the world they have inherited.

"Someone has been exploring the Sleepers' memories," said the female accusingly to the Australian one. "It's not to be taken lightly."

"I didn't touch his memories," replies the other. "I swear it."

"Who did, then?" she asks the system in general. But she receives no reply.

Awakening

11

Breathing light like a cool, still fluid, Jenae smiled, awakening. There was no pain at first, only the shimmering charge of thought recognizing itself and rushing to clasp its own hand in celebration of consciousness. Then dim and heavy followed the body with its nerve endings charred to a distant thrum, toes stiff and hair gone, all flesh plastered to the frame. When Jenae's eyes opened she saw a tiny red pulse reflected in the air above her eyes, and when she screwed up her forehead to try to see beyond her brows, the skin pulled. That was when she realized her head had been shaved, and the pulling must be coming from the dried glue used to keep the electrodes fixed in place.

They are monitoring me, she thought, and immediately wished she were not awake. Someone would notice by the pattern of her brain waves that she was conscious, and then they would come. She didn't want to see anyone. All she could think of was the severity of the punishment, the "volts" as Tien had called them. She had been told in her training that swimming in the ocean was the next thing to suicide for a variety of reasons involving sunlight, toxins, microorganisms, and mutant predators; she had also been told she would be tempted. Well, she had succumbed a few times, but was that a good excuse to fry her head? Wouldn't a stern talking-to be more reasonable? She had thought herself to be the Pickled Brains' pet alchemist; why should they want to kill her?

There was a call button within easy reach of her fingers. Who would come, if she pressed it? Zafara, with his quick eyes? He had seen the sky-burned skin when they bumped into each other; Jenae was sure of it. He must have told the Heads of her illegal forays into altermode. Unless it had been her glimpse into the *Morpheus* files that had alerted them—but what was wrong with that? She was working on the *Morpheus* project, and most of the files weren't restricted. No, it had to be the swimming that pissed them off, and Zafara had to be the one responsible for her betrayal. The only other explanation would have involved the dolphins giving her away to the Pickled Brains, and she didn't want to believe that was possible. If she began to think that way, everyone would be a liar: human, cetacean . . . everyone.

It was all too good to be true, Jenae thought, feeling sorry for herself. *I should have stayed with Yi Ling on the reservation. I'm not cut out for the League. One or two small infractions and they nearly do me in. And for what? Following my instincts and swimming with dolphins outside the confines of their prescribed circuit of communications. So what? So I got some information from the dolphins. I didn't try to* do *anything with it. I didn't even understand it. Shit.*

"Ah, you've awakened," murmured a soft, sooty voice. A narrow, stooped figure was silhouetted in the crack of light that must be a door. Jenae's eyes swam into focus: she'd only been semiconscious, after all. She heard herself make a small, straining sound, like an anxious cat.

"It's perfectly all right," said the old woman, coming closer to the bed. Jenae couldn't see her face. "You're not to worry about a thing. You've had a traumatic event, but you appear to be recovering well."

"But they're trying to kill me." She blurted it out. She sounded like a child to her own ears.

"Who are, dear?" The woman's voice was pacifying, as though she heard this sort of thing all the time and made nothing of it. Jenae could see the shadows on the ropes and folds of her hands as she began to finger the instrument panel beside the bed.

Jenae didn't answer. Small lights danced up from the panel.

"The accident involved a neural injury and generalized systemic shock. Extreme emotional states are not abnormal during healing. Try to remember that and these fears will have a harder time taking hold of you."

"Where am I?"

"Why, Perth reservation care center. You are from this rez, aren't you?"

"I'm from the League," Jenae said flatly. "Or I was."

"Yes. There it is." The dry old fingers moved rapidly across the pad. Something about the woman's low cracking voice with its age tremors soothed Jenae.

"You were recommended for transfer to this facility by your domestic partner. Someone named Tien, I understand?"

Jenae nodded dumbly. What had possessed Tien to go so far out on a limb? It was a bald lie. They had never been lovers, much less partners. Sooner or later, he would get into trouble because of this.

"He wanted you to recuperate somewhere where your sister could visit you."

"My sister. Is she coming?"

"I don't know, dear. I'm only on night duty. No visitors at night, normally."

Jenae lay back, tears in her eyes. Suddenly she wanted Yi Ling to come to her. Someone must take care of her now. She'd been stupid, a blundering fool—but she wasn't dead and that was something. If only someone would shut off the pain.

"It hurts," Jenae said, and the old woman activated a warm, pink light that encased Jenae in a nerveless glow. Like a balloon on a string Jenae felt her mind struggling to get free of her body. And in a flash before it did she saw Zafara's face, and imagining the chill sting of the needle in his hand, she thought: Is this all people want? Oblivion? Negation of time and self?

But before she could answer for herself, she flooded into the pink.

◆

Later, she was surprised to learn that her body was in no way burned or visibly damaged.

"It was a psychic event," the old woman told her when, examining herself, Jenae was unable to reconcile the evidence of her senses with the visual reality beneath the bedsheets. Her body looked normal. But she moved only with the greatest care, and even then she hissed frequently between her teeth. She spent the better part of a week drowsing in the pink cocoon, and the only person she spoke with was the old night attendant, whose name she never learned. During the day a succession of brisk, sterile-looking young persons came to medicate her, but they all made her hackles rise, and irrationally she came to respond only to the old woman. It was strange, she reflected later, that one could form an attachment instantly to a total stranger, and yet spend months or years living with other people and never connect.

The persistence of physical pain made demands on her attention that pushed away all considerations of the League, the future, and the motivations of the Pickled Brains for the majority of her waking hours. Yet in the pink cocoon she dreamed of whales larger than ships and dolphins who swam so fast they couldn't be seen, and other psychedelic creatures that she was fairly sure didn't exist. Everything in her dreams had become exaggerated out of all proportion, until the unbelievable ceased to startle her.

So it was no surprise, really, when she dreamed of the Head who'd given her the Underkohling assignment. Dreamed of "her" voice, that is. The clear, resonant contralto with its Eastern European accent sounded haughty to Jenae, a lifetime resident of the Southern Hemisphere, for she associated it with the wealth of pre-war Europe. In the dream the voice belonged to a body, but the body was not real. It was a cartoon woman. She had a long, misshapen face that was literally white, and she wore a high-necked, black dress cinched in so tight at the waist that the resultant figure was all but impossible. She looked tiny and ancient but in the dream Jenae knew she was also possessed of a hideous strength. She was sitting on a bench beside a man dressed in similar late-nineteenth-century fashion, including a bowler hat. And she was calmly and methodically strangling him.

"You give me no choice," the Head's voice said out of the

cartoon face, but the white woman didn't bother to look at the man gasping and struggling beside her; she merely wrapped her hands around his neck and squeezed, turning her head to face Jenae as she explained, "It is self-defense."

The man on the bench did not die quickly. He twitched and turned several pastel shades as befitting a cartoon character, his arms and legs jerking in ridiculous, overdone spasms as he died. Yet there was nothing funny in the image to Jenae. It terrified her in the place inside that was still three years old, but it also attacked the mature part of her mind, for an overpowering feeling of malice washed through the images. She woke gasping for air, clawing at her throat, and shivering.

That voice, she thought. Where else have I been hearing that voice?

She had the sense that the Head's voice had been haunting her dreams for some time, or maybe that it was a movie voice—familiar. Yet she couldn't place it. She had listened to this voice while in altermode, working on the Underkohling project, to be sure. But she had also heard it somewhere else . . .

The more she thought about it, the farther away slipped the impression of familiarity.

They've fucked with my head, she thought. Messages have gotten scrambled and now, with my mind putting itself back together, memories are popping up in the wrong places.

It was strange, how malleable memory and experience could become under the slightest psychic pressure. She ought to consider herself lucky to have retained any of this: to wake up knowing her own name and history—although she had to trust that this was true, since theoretically there was nothing to prove her memories were real or accurate.

But you had to work with what you were given. And thankfully, after a few days the pain had subsided, so that Jenae could stand to be conscious. The medical people still used the pink cocoon on her, but she was no longer slave to it. Then, several days later, Tien came to see her, playing the role of concerned partner to the hilt.

He stood in the doorway, a slender figure dressed in dark blue, his thick hair cropped short and his lips curving in a natural expression of amusement. To all appearances he was an ordinary man: with gill slits hidden by a high-necked shirt, he could have passed for pure human. But there was a subtle quality of difference about him, too. Jenae couldn't put her finger on it, yet after being around pure humans for several days, Tien was not the same.

She laughed when he stood beside the bed and took her hand.

"You don't have to—" Jenae began.

"Shh." He put a finger to her lips. She rolled her eyes.

"Your sister is asking for you," he said. "I've been talking to the medics and they're willing to let you go provided you stay on the rez. You'll need to come in daily for therapy. No one is particularly impressed by your scintillating personality. They're aware you're not happy here. I take it you haven't been friendly."

"What therapy?" she asked, ignoring the rest of his remarks.

"You have been getting it, haven't you? With lights?"

"Oh, the pink cocoon. I thought that was just to kill the pain."

"They're using it to rebuild the neural links to altermode that were damaged in the . . . uh . . . accident."

"Accident?"

"Computer malfunction. Most regrettable. That's the official word."

She opened her mouth to add another question but Tien shook his head, squeezing her hand.

"I've got a lot to tell you, but not very much time. We can go whenever you're ready."

Jenae hesitated. "Tien," she whispered. "I'm not sure you really understand. Are you sure you want to get involved in this?"

"Too late for that."

◆

It all happened very quickly, and to Jenae's disappointment, she never got to say good-bye to the old woman. She was conveyed down the long hospital hallways with Tien at her side. She responded on cue to the computer when asked to release herself officially, but her voice shook. This computer was linked to the same systems used by the Pickled

Brains: theoretically, they could be listening in on every automated transaction she ever made. The magnitude of this fact had never really struck her before: she'd simply taken it for granted. It was different, though, now that she was on the defensive. She felt small and vulnerable, and watched.

Then they were outside. Automatically Jenae looked up to the sky. She had never been able to get used to the real sky with its swift-moving clouds and dirty color, but here on the rez the League-designed mirror fields made skies that were calm and predictable. If you looked at them long enough, you could usually discern their patterns of motion, but they weren't obviously mechanical. This one was a gentle rain sky, soft grey with a few wisps of darker cloud scudding harmlessly beneath its ceiling. It hovered over the green common in the middle of the rez, where a token handful of cattle grazed and birds sang in precious, well-manicured trees. People were strolling along the paths of the common, umbrellas opened in bright relief against the swelling clouds that piddled onto the scene. It seemed so peaceful. . . .

Jenae shivered.

"Do you want to take the indoor route?" Tien asked, glancing at her. She was clad in thin, hospital-issue garments and wore only light slippers on her feet. Even the barest touch of water on her face and shoulders had stimulated her gills: she could feel the nearly invisible gill slits puckering slightly. The entire time she'd been in hospital, her skin had been cleaned only with waterless chemical agents, presumably to avoid triggering altermode while she was still recovering. It was reassuring to know now that altermode was still available to her.

"No. I need the air."

She set off across the common, breathing deeply. The natural scents were welcome—even the cows smelled good to her after breathing recycled air for so long. Just beyond the buildings she could see the mirror field itself: a broad stretch of sky, the landscape beyond Perth only slightly more beautiful than the reality of the days before the rez's construction. It was drier out there, Jenae knew, than the mirror fields suggested. People wanted to feel that they were truly outside, so the mirror fields gave the impression of a real, vibrant landscape around the rez. But of course you could never go to the places projected in the field: they weren't there. Even the air and light that passed through were processed. Jenae, who really had been outside, knew that the land around Perth rez was mostly barren, and much of it had been that way even before the climatic and atmospheric changes that had taken their toll along with the Gene Wars.

But the rez was still a good illusion, thanks to the genius of cetaceans. If she closed her eyes to the window-filled surround of inhabited buildings and just walked, she could imagine herself in an earlier world, one where this small, pleasant scene wouldn't cost the wealth of a nation just to maintain. One where the people who lived here did so by choice, not because they were trapped inside. She thought of the dead wilderness outside and tried to imagine it as only challenging, not deadly. She knew it had once been that way, though before her lifetime.

But she couldn't stretch that far. Imagination failed. Even her own brief explorations had damaged her physically, and she had resistances that pure humans didn't. If everything in the world that could kill you were visible, it would be easy. But most of the dangers outside the rez were undetectable by normal human senses. Viruses still thriving long after their release in the Gene Wars were the greatest danger, and although Jenae had been exposed to the altermode-causing virus as a child, she wasn't eager to encounter other, far more deadly strains. In retrospect she astonished herself by having stripped off her protection and dived into the sea at the bidding of the dolphins. She'd been told that even now the chances of pure human survival outside the rez were one in ten: had she already contracted something? Only the mirror fields really knew what they screened out—and they didn't talk.

Tien said: "I'm not going to ask you any questions. I'll stay out of your way, for now. But I want you to promise me something. Keep your head down for a while. I don't know what happened—whether it was intentional. I can't see how you could have done anything to warrant deliberate violence, and the Heads would have to be crazy to risk you when you're one of the greatest talents to come along in years." Jenae ducked her head at the compliment. "But I also can't believe it was accidental. The whole point of having a monitor is to prevent psychic overload."

"Do you think it was Zafara's doing, then?"

"I doubt he has that much initiative. The fact is, I don't know, Jenae. But I'm uneasy. I want you to stay out of sight of the Pickled Brains, so to speak. Don't do anything to attract their attention."

"What am I supposed to do, then? Live as a pure human from now on?"

"For now. They're not going to give you any assignments for a while. They're waiting to see if you recover. Meanwhile, they'll have to reassign your project."

"Like hell they will!" The *Morpheus* project had come to mean a great deal to her.

"Don't say that, Jenae. You don't know how lucky you are to be alive. The dolphins saved you, you know. They alerted everybody in the system within about a second, and the shock was cut off. Of course once the incident was public, the Heads 'discovered' a systems error that was found to have caused the problem, and they were busy doing everything in their power to save you. Like I said, I'm suspicious about that part. By the time I found out what was going on, the medics revived you and were about to place you in the League infirmary. That's when I stepped in—and feel free to thank me—and insisted that you go to the rez. I don't trust the League medical people. They're too closely reined by the Heads. I want you somewhere out of the way."

"Thank you, by the way."

"You're welcome. You needed someone to speak for you. I'd have done the same for anyone in our section: we're a tight-knit group. You've been on the outside of the group, it's true, but I blame myself for that, partly. If you'd had the support of the other alchemists, this might not have happened. We all should have talked about the project; it's too much responsibility for one person alone. I should have worked harder to bring you into the group."

"No, it's not your fault. I didn't want to be 'in.' I don't feel comfortable being so close to others. When you have a twin you get used to a close fit, and everyone else feels kind of . . . scratchy. And then there is—was—my rapport with dolphins. If I climbed into the cozy alchemist nest you've created, Tien, I would . . . I don't know, I thought I would lose myself."

Tien's profile was thoughtful. "Maybe you would have. Maybe that's what most people want, in the end. But not you." He gave her a candid look, and her eyes shied away.

"I don't know," she said again wryly. "Whatever I wanted, I put my foot in it."

They had reached the edge of the common and stopped outside the hall where Yi Ling lived. He put his hands on her shoulders and turned her to face him.

"Jenae. You don't have time for self-destruction. I've seen it happen to too many people who lose their ability to listen to their insides. You're strong. You would have to be, to recover from an experience like the one you just had. But you're also alone, and you've got to start thinking for yourself. How old are you, anyway?"

"Seventeen."

Tien threw back his head and laughed. "A kid! Where are your parents?"

"Not alive." She tried to sound light; she'd never met them, so did it really matter that they were dead?

He was shaking his head. "I've met your sister. She's in deep trouble—but you know that, don't you?"

"I guess . . ."

"Jenae, listen to me. You're in peril—Pickled Brains or not, never mind all that—you're in peril because you're alone. You don't know who you are. You're not human, but unfortunately you're not a dolphin, either, though sometimes you'd probably like to be. Right?"

"True." She smiled.

"Wouldn't we all? But it's not to be. You're an altermode human and your DNA is unnatural or you wouldn't be turning into a fish here in the rain."

He stroked a finger across her gill slits, grinning.

"There aren't very many of us. We've all got to stick together. Someday maybe we'll even get out from under the Heads, if, like you, we can resist their methods of discipline. Or we can teach them, perhaps, how to understand us. We're moving slowly, but we'll do it. You're not alone. You need to remember that, or the despair of this place will get to you." He gestured to the buildings that flanked the common. "Pure human despair will get to you, but you've got to leave that behind."

Jenae shook her head. "That's easy to say. You don't have a twin. You don't have my sister for a twin. How can I put it? She's difficult. She challenges everything."

Tien's eyes on her face were suddenly intense, and she looked away. This was unexpected. He said, "It began as a ruse, calling myself your lover. But if I thought it would be safe for you to come back with me—"

"Please," she interrupted. "You don't know what you're getting yourself into, with me. It's . . . complicated."

He laughed. "I can see that for myself! But I don't care."

He bent his head and kissed her. She wanted to respond: he was attractive, and obviously genuine. But something kept her still, passive.

"Tien . . ."

"No, don't say it. I don't intend any pressure. But I want you to know how I feel. In case you change your mind."

Deliberately, he looked at his watch. "Got to go. The train leaves in half an hour, and I'm expected back at the Tower. Call me if you need me."

Before she could react, he'd turned and started to jog away across the green. Jenae stood, sheltered from the rain, and watched him leave. Then she went inside.

12

Yi Ling. She had removed all the furniture from her room and was sitting cross-legged on the floor with her profile to the door. A single dim light shone from the vicinity of the computer terminal. It cast a dull light on her upper body and the visored headset that made her look like a giant insect with sleepy, luminous eyes. She'd cut her hair, Jenae observed irrelevantly. It was short now, but not as short as Jenae's pathetic frizz. She no longer looked exactly like her sister.

And Yi Ling was oblivious to Jenae's arrival.

Jenae closed the door behind her, leaned against the wall, and let out a sigh. She felt exhausted just from the short walk, and Yi Ling didn't even have a bed or a chair. Was this part of some old Taoist practice she'd dug up, trying to recapture their mother's lost heritage? Or was this just another of Yi Ling's seemingly random compulsions? Jenae crossed the room and read the title of the program her sister was using.

COALITION FOR PURE HUMAN PROGRESS, it said. PART ONE: A HISTORY. Parts Two, Three, and Four were cued on the display; Yi Ling had apparently ordered the whole series in one fell swoop. Just how much time was she spending wired?

Well, Jenae thought, at least Yi Ling was doing *something*. The Coalition for Pure Human Progress would not have been her choice as a source of information, though. The organization was openly unfriendly to the League, and there were plenty of unflattering Coalition jokes among altermoders. Coalition members were notoriously paranoid that pure humans' rights were being trodden on, their genes suppressed, their interests ignored, when in fact pure humans were essentially at leisure to please themselves, albeit within the confines of the reservation. Jenae was surprised to find Yi Ling showing any interest in world events at all; but Coalition or not, this new tack was probably a good thing for it might propel her sister out of her self-absorption.

Jenae cast her eyes about the room again and finally lowered herself resignedly to the floor, leaning against the wall beside the door. She almost pulled the plug on Yi Ling's program, but she was tired and suddenly it seemed she couldn't think. The walk, and Tien's ideas, had taken more out of her than she had realized at first.

"Just a kid," he'd said. She wondered how old Tien really was. She wondered where he had come from, and if he had any family living. Trying to remember her own life before altermode was like trying to see through murky, polluted water. It was tiring and pointless. And what was there to remember? Being cared for by a series of well-intentioned educators who'd had to substitute for real parents because theirs were dead? There had been small joy in their childhood, except that which Jenae and Yi Ling had managed to create for themselves. Jenae didn't remember having any special talents or burning drives, and Yi Ling's only talent had been painting. There didn't seem to be much substance in Jenae's memories before altermode, and she wondered if that meant that her life had really been empty; or did it just seem that way in retrospect? And if it had been empty, didn't that mean Yi Ling's existence continued to be without substance?

Then again, neither of them had been crazy; and no one had tried to kill either of them by sensory overload.

She recalled a smell: the clay they had used when they were just kids. She could almost see their four hands working on one piece, a large horse that they never could coax into standing up. But they'd worked so beautifully in tandem. There were no words, no signals. Each had simply *known* what to do and how, as if they were both part of a larger whole that included them but was not defined by their individual limitations. It had been such a secure feeling, knowing you were part of something.

It was almost the same feeling as being in a dolphin web.

Then her eyes started to fill with tears, and letting her face fall forward into her hands she gave in to the eerie clutching feeling in her chest and began to sob. *It's over, it's over, it's over,* kept repeating in her mind, but she didn't know what the words meant: her rapport with the dolphins, or with her sister. Or was it merely relief, and overreaction to the fact that she had almost died?

Yi Ling was beside her, had wrapped her arms around her, and was holding her.

"Jenae, shh," she murmured, her voice close to Jenae's ear. "You're here! You're back! Every day I told myself it would happen, and it did. I'm so happy, Jenae. Cry, it's all right. It's over. You're home."

Jenae looked into her sister's face through blurry lashes, and she saw a clarity in Yi Ling's face that had not been there in a very long time.

◆

Says the Hungarian Woman: "What are we going to do about Eric?"

"Haven't we done it already? We've purged the memory; it shouldn't come up again for many years, if at all." As usual, the deep Australian voice is soothing.

"But how did it come up? This is not the first time. And he's not the only Sleeper to be having tremors of awakening. We need to find the cause."

"I don't see how we can do that without stirring the Sleepers up more."

"We can't afford *not* to do it. Something's going wrong in the system. Did you ever think that someone could be blocking *our* memories in order to sabotage the Sleepers?"

A thoughtful pause, then he answers. "Anything's possible, I guess. But it would have to be one of us, and why would we do that? We only block the memories to minimize trauma."

"You think I'm paranoid."

"You *are* paranoid. I say that in the most respectful way."

"I have to be." She sounds like a cat preening, but he persists.

"And I have to tell you, I think you're overreacting. The system isn't perfect, but it's strong. We need all the concentration we can get to manage this latest rash of Coalition uprisings."

"It would be so much easier to just quash the Coalition. . . ." She's growing bored.

"And take away from humans their last vestige of dignity? No, we must allow them to retain some free will, or at least the illusion thereof. However idiotic their actions may seem at times. You do still believe in them. Don't you?"

"I don't know if I feel for them the way I should," she answers. "Eric does, but he's a fool. I'm becoming cynical in my old age. Repressed and cynical. I think—no, never mind."

"You think what?" he presses.

"I think I'll be happy when we can find a way to leave them to their own devices. I think I'm tired of being in charge," she sighs.

"*You?*" Laughter. "That'll be the day. Good one!"

"You are right. I was only joking, of course."

◆

The bench was the same in the dream as it was in real life. It sat on the edge of Perth rez's green common, and it was frequented by mothers with small children and, sometimes, an elderly couple who sat on it silently. Nearby flowerbeds bloomed sweetly but futilely, since no bees ever came to fertilize them and Nature Services had to do it seasonally. In the dream, Jenae sat there alone. No one else was in sight, and the clouds had turned almost to black: something that never happened in reality. Yellow light flashed somewhere overhead, and she felt the bass complaint of thunder resonate through the material of the bench beneath her. She stood up and looked for shelter, but the buildings of the rez were gone, and the mirror fields showed, instead, a green view of rolling hills and, beyond, the sea.

She hugged herself; a cold wind slapped her, and ragged blasts of rain hit her shoulders hard. She was about to turn away from the lone bench when she saw, amid the distant whitecaps, the distinctive blow of spray and the large dark mass of a whale sounding.

Jenae began to run toward the shore. The whale sounded again, rolling over and fluking high into the air. Her throat caught at its wildness, its self-determination, and a half-hopeful yearning blew through her like gleaming smoke. The rain was opening her gills, and in a few more meters she would run down the hill to the beach and join this mysterious thing.

Then she hit the wall.

It was almost farcical: she couldn't see any barrier, so she picked herself up and launched herself forward again. She hit it again. It hurt. She picked herself up a second time, and she couldn't see the whale now. The whale had dived. She pressed herself against the invisible barrier, running her hands over it in all directions, feeling for a gap in something that she couldn't even see.

The whale breached again, farther offshore now. When it went down this time, she watched for it even as she ran back and forth along the wall trying to find a way through, but she failed. The wall was impassable, and the whale didn't reappear.

She beat on the wall with her fists.

◆

When Jenae woke up she was only twitching and smacking her lips voicelessly as though she were already toothless with age.

"I made tea," Yi Ling said from somewhere sensible, above her. "I call it my nightmare tea. It takes away the queasy feeling."

Jenae frowned, trying to orient herself in time and place beneath the soft sheets. She opened her eyes to see Yi Ling standing over her with a tray of food. Steam rose in the morning "sunlight." Jenae's body felt glued down by gravity.

"You need to be taken care of," Yi Ling said. "Don't argue. Just have tea."

Jenae complied, sitting up with effort. It took some time before she found her voice. "You're very brisk this morning," she told Yi Ling.

"I'm re-creating myself in my own image," Yi Ling answered.

Jenae yawned. "What the hell does that mean?"

"Haven't you heard it? It's a Coalition slogan," Yi Ling informed her, but Jenae made a face. "Well," Yi Ling continued. "Think what you want, but it's thanks to the Coalition I'm up making you breakfast. It's a good thing we're both not basket cases at the same time."

Jenae let it slide. She could live with a few slogans, if it meant having her sister's wit back.

Yi Ling snapped on the monitor. The computer managed to dominate the room: the futons Yi Ling rolled out at night were still her only concession to furniture in the large, long room, and the kitchen wasn't big enough to sit down in. But the bulky computer monitor was always there, and during the days of Jenae's residence in her sister's home, more often than not it was activated.

Jenae felt invaded by sound and motion as Yi Ling flipped through selections, but at last Yi Ling settled on a current events program, and Jenae found herself watching in spite of herself. The program outlined the recovery of an industrial economy in Southeast Asia, attempting to probe the issue of how to reconcile the need for more sophisticated computer hardware and other tech products with the fact that the One Eyes were the nearly exclusive purveyors of such factory products.

"More like machines than people," the narrator intoned with a false air of wonder, "hordes of One Eyes work in mysterious synchrony at this Laos plant, building the most sophisticated aquatic habitation ever conceived." With their protective headgear and gloves, the One Eyes looked deceptively like people, Jenae thought. She remembered the project as one of the biggest endeavors of the League during her early days there.

"Prime Minister Hoa Huang Trung hopes to have the undersea installation ready for human habitation within three years. Applicants from all over the world are already lining up to seek entrance, but the lottery for spaces will not be opened until next year. The administrative branch of the League of New Alchemists has been contracted to manage lottery selection as an impartial body; the think tank of this same organization, by the way, is responsible for the unique design of this station, which represents a significant advance in the mirror field technology that will allow for a combination of safety and access to the under-sea environment." A picture of the Tower was flashed across the screen, and Jenae felt a perverse surge of team spirit for the League. "Here's a selection of the topics you can pursue on this morning's edition of Talk Back to the News. . . ."

"Your friends the alchemists are moving up in the world," Yi Ling said, lowering the volume. "I never realized dolphins were so ambitious."

Jenae said nothing.

Yi Ling handed her a bowl of hot cereal. Jenae noticed that Yi Ling still wore the silver dolphin ring Jenae had given her when she entered the League. It had been Jenae's way of promising her sister that she would be included in Jenae's new life; seeing it now, Jenae felt raw with guilt. The ring silently mocked her for her inability to live up to that promise.

"Anyway," Yi Ling went on, "things are different down under. It isn't as bad in Asia as it is here. They have a real pure human government there. Look at their prime minister guy. He looks like he knows what he's doing." She snorted. "Not like Phoebe Larue. What a joke. Why does Australia bother to send her to the U.N. when she's in bed with the League?"

"Where do you get that from?" Jenae asked. "I don't see the League as having any real political affiliations."

Yi Ling said, "Rumor has it that the Heads have more power than they're willing to admit to. Isn't it true they're into everything—everybody's business, invited or not?"

Jenae thought. "Hard to say. They really do administer all the affairs of the League. They're great organizers, and the cetacean members don't really seem to care what goes on outside the actual webs. I really think dolphins are in the

League almost for the sport of it. They certainly don't have ambitions of controlling humans!"

"Yes, but the Heads—don't they meddle with everyone? Hell, they have access to every system on-line in the world, and plenty that are off-world. How can they resist getting involved?"

"I guess they can't, since you put it that way. You have to understand, Yi Ling, that without the Heads to hold everything together and act as an interface to computers, the League wouldn't exist. If the League didn't exist, we wouldn't have mirror field technology, which means no rez, or a lot of the other things that are going to pull us out of this mess we're in. We'd be out there with the One Eyes, but we'd be choking and burning and getting sick. You've seen history. You know what happens. Humans are a very fragile species right now, and there aren't that many of them. Us. Whatever."

"That doesn't give the League the right to be in everybody's business," Yi Ling persisted stubbornly.

"Maybe not," Jenae answered, surprised to hear herself defending the Heads. "But when you're in the League, you learn to accord them a certain level of respect. They exist on a plane we can't even imagine. They're capable of thought we can't begin to understand. I guess we have no choice but to trust them."

"Gods," said Yi Ling. "They're bigger than us, but cruel. So let's make sacrifices."

"Maybe, after the Gene Wars, we need gods. Look what we did to ourselves. Do you trust your fellow human after what happened in the last century?"

"No, I don't. I don't even trust myself—that's why I never leave my room. But that doesn't mean I trust the Heads, either."

Jenae felt herself being worn down by her sister's tenacity. "I don't know," she said. "It's all too big for me. I don't want to think about it."

"They really worked you over good, didn't they?" Yi Ling sat back, her eyes glazing over as the stock market reports came in. She was silent for a moment, and Jenae started to get up. She had to get outside today, even if it was only a stroll around the perimeter of the rez.

"It's all bullshit," Yi Ling ejaculated suddenly. "I don't think I believe any of it. Monitor off."

The room was silent.

Yi Ling drew a long breath. She was gathering herself for something; Jenae could feel it, and her first instinct was to flee. She couldn't take one of those moods—not today. But when her sister spoke, her tone took Jenae completely by surprise. She sounded almost parental.

"Jenae, sooner or later you're going to have to decide what you are."

Jenae directed her attention to her tea. She could feel Yi Ling staring at her. Her sister's self-containment, even in her most bizarre moments, had always displayed Yi Ling's power of will, and now that stubborn gaze flustered Jenae.

"I don't know what you mean," Jenae said.

"You've got one foot in each world, and you think you can go on that way, but it isn't fair. To either of us."

"Yi Ling . . ." Jenae could hear the rejection in her own voice and stopped short, stymied because she realized she'd gotten in the habit of writing off what Yi Ling said as mad.

"Dammit, Jenae, you see what I mean? I am not a child. Listen to me very carefully—will you do that? I've tried to tell you this before but you didn't want to hear it. You'd better listen now. I've read our medical files. I've looked in the archives and I know why you have altermode and I don't. We have been fucked over. Our parents were dead— the medics don't even know which virus killed them, but it wasn't the altermode virus. Our father was carrying the gene for altermode, and he passed it on to us. We had to be raised here, and we were identical twins. You think the Gene Wars are over? Not for everybody. According to our records—which were not easy to get into, but I did it— according to our records our father signed papers before he died entering us in an experiment involving the effects of the altermode virus on identical twins. We both started with the genetic predisposition for altermode. I was protected in the rez the whole time, but when you were a baby, you were deliberately isolated and exposed to altermode. Your altermode was activated. You have it, and I don't."

"This is nonsense," Jenae said, shaking her head. "Don't even . . . please!" She turned her face away.

Yi Ling reached out and grabbed her by the arm and shook her. "Stop being stupid, Jenae. I told you, I tried to tell you before——"

"When? What are you talking about?" Jenae's hands felt cold. It sounded so cheap and stupid, so unworthy an act for this father she had never known. What could have possessed a man to so callously divide his twins that way? No. It couldn't be true.

"After you went away to the League, all I could think of was how it made no sense that you had altermode and I didn't. I thought maybe we weren't really identical twins—that maybe we just looked alike. So I checked the medical records, and I found out. I guess he thought he was increasing the chances that one of us would survive, even if it meant the other wouldn't . . . don't you see how this changes everything, Jenae?"

"You don't have any proof of this," Jenae heard herself say flatly and realized how stupid she sounded, just denying everything.

"It's the irony of ironies," Yi Ling continued. "He thought he was saving me but really I'm the one who's crazy and you, at least you have a function somewhere."

"That's totally irrelevant . . ." Jenae started to say.

"Or maybe it's the other way around, maybe you are going to die, Jenae, because there are studies that show a high rate of birth defects among altermoders and a high rate of accidental death——" Yi Ling's rate of speech was increasing; she sounded a little breathless.

"Coalition studies, I'm sure," Jenae snorted absently, putting down the cold tea and forming a little frown as she tried to think of nothing.

"—and I don't know how to think about it anymore but you've got to make a commitment, Jenae, if you're going to live here. That's what I'm trying to say to you. Whatever they did to you when you were a baby, you've got to fight back now. You've got to choose to be human. You still think you're some kind of dolphin or fish, you're *confused*, you didn't seem confused until you got hurt but now you really are confused, and how long can it go on this way?"

She had finally wound herself out of breath, and Jenae let the silence sigh back into the room. After a minute she felt laughter spawning in her guts: small, beady rock-hard pellets of laughter that she knew would hurt Yi Ling if she let them out. *How long can it go on?* she wanted to say. *Have I ever said that to you, Yi Ling? It's not so easy to stand back and watch someone else fall apart, is it? Get a taste of it.* But as soon as she thought it she knew Yi Ling had seen her think it, and she stopped. Her habit of protecting her sister was still too strong, no matter how lucid Yi Ling appeared at the moment, no matter what fronts she put up to indicate strength.

"It's not my choice to make," Jenae said.

"Maybe not then, but it is now," Yi Ling countered. "You left me once before. Someone might as well have cut off my head."

"I'm sorry!" Jenae cried. "How many times do I have to say I'm sorry, act like I'm sorry? Do you know how much I would have loved to have you with me in altermode, in the League? Do you know? Even now, if you could share what I'm experiencing, it would somehow seem . . . bearable."

"But I can't," Yi Ling answered. "It's not like I can follow you. I'm too old to be exposed to the virus now. Adolescence is the last window. The transformation would kill me."

"This is useless," Jenae said. "What do you want me to do? What can I do now? Have surgery?" Her hands went to her gill slits, sealed shut, and her eyes flicking across Yi Ling's face told her that this thought had crossed her sister's mind.

"Never mind," Yi Ling said. "Forget I said anything."

In the past, when things got too heavy between them, it had always been Jenae who had beaten a retreat, to get out of the murk of emotions that always seemed to surround Yi Ling. It had been Jenae who had the final word. Now, for the first time since Jenae could remember, Yi Ling actually stood up, turned on her heel, and walked out of the room.

◆

After that Yi Ling seemed to back off; she was suddenly absent from the flat more than she was there, although Coalition propaganda kept piling up. Jenae couldn't make herself read it even though she knew she ought to find out what this Coalition was all about. She felt too raw, and altermode deprivation was beginning to affect her, and all she wanted to do was sleep. She used a monotonous routine to cushion herself from thinking: she slept late in the mornings, and walked around and around the common, breathing, in the afternoons, then returned to the flat to sleep again. On the walks she sometimes wanted to break into a run—to run for the edge of the rez and never stop, plunge through the security baffles and just keep going to the sea. But she was learning to be cruel to herself, and she reined herself in time and again, walking sedately among pure humans who didn't look as if they missed their freedom.

The first time Jenae came into the flat from just such a walk and saw Yi Ling and her lover together, she was tongue-tied. She had never seen Yi Ling with a man, and now she felt like a fool because as she walked in the door this man was making Yi Ling laugh like she hadn't laughed in years.

They were stretched out on the floor, side by side, fully clothed, but there was something about the atmosphere in the room that embarrassed Jenae as if she had walked in on them copulating. Yi Ling was shaking all over with mirth, and the man, a slender fellow, about thirty, of some indeterminate ethnic background, looked up at Jenae and said, "Oops." Then he broke out laughing, more like an adolescent than an adult. Jenae shifted her weight uneasily from one foot to another, wondering if she should leave, but he stood up and came toward her, extending his hand.

"I'm Brian Denz," he said. "Obviously, you're Jenae."

She nodded.

"Now, I know what you're thinking," he said, flashing a bright smile.

"What am I thinking?" Jenae asked, deadpan.

He drew a hand across his forehead. "Wow," he said. "You are *so* much like Yi Ling. It's really unbelievable."

Jenae said nothing. She knew she was being rude, but she just couldn't help herself. He was too shiny, too fresh.

"Look, you're probably thinking that because I'm Coalition, I'm against you—but I'm not. Really. Anyway, you're

Yi Ling's sister, and that's more important to me than anything else right now."

"I see," Jenae said. She looked at Yi Ling, who was still
grinning.

"Don't look so shocked, Jenae," she said. "Brian and I
have a lot in common. We're both discontents, only thanks
to him I'm finding a channel for my energies."

I'll bet you are, thought Jenae, looking him over.

"In *politics*." Yi Ling laughed. "We're forming a movement to make the rez independent. We think that with the
right allocation of resources, we can run everything within
the mirror fields and stop being dependent on the One Eyes
altogether. They've got a stranglehold on our progress, you
know. You should see some of the stuff that they're doing,
and all because pure humans are too passive to stop them."

"I see," Jenae said again. "So . . . this is what you've been
doing with your time."

"I know the Coalition offends you," Yi Ling said. "Some
branches of the organization are opposed to any variations
on pure humanity. Obviously, I don't feel that way. But I do
feel that power is being distributed unequally, and it's time
we stood up and did something about it before the One Eyes
take over the entire planet. I'm sorry I haven't been more
open about my activities—I didn't exactly hide from you,
though. You knew I was interested in the Coalition."

Jenae let out a sigh and sat down on the floor. "I have to
tell you—and don't accuse me of playing big sister with you,
because I don't mean it that way—getting involved in these
things may seem glamorous, but up close they're not pretty.
The Coalition is not pretty." She glanced at Brian. "I don't
care how moderate you are."

"I don't want to fight, Jenae. Why don't you come to a
meeting? You can come over the net if you don't want to do
it in person. Or we could cover your gill slits. No one will
suspect."

Jenae was dumbfounded. "Come to a meeting?"

"Well, after all," Brian put in, "you've told Yi Ling that
you don't belong in the League anymore. That means you
have to live on a rez. So . . . you should get acquainted with
the people who live here. Make yourself some friends. That
way, when the change in power comes—and it will come, be-

lieve me—you won't find yourself abandoned, discriminated against because of those." He pointed to her gill slits.

"I can't believe I'm hearing this. These are antiquated ideas." She looked at Yi Ling. "What about you? You carry the genotype. Doesn't that make you 'impure' by the Coalition's standards?"

"Not really," answered Brian before Yi Ling could respond. "Provided that she's careful selecting the father, her children will have no possibility of developing the phenotype. She never had the virus, and the gene will disappear after a few generations. You, however, would do well not to reproduce—or if you do, do it in vitro, so that precautions can be taken."

"Thank you for the advice, Brian," Jenae said. She got up to leave. "I'll leave you two to it, then."

Yi Ling sprang up and ran after her. Jenae walked out the door and Yi Ling followed her into the hall. "Jenae, please. Don't judge him too quickly. He's very nervous about meeting you. He knows how important you are to me, and he's saying all the wrong things. Don't listen to him—he doesn't mean it." She put her hand on Jenae's shoulder, and Jenae stopped, turning to look at Yi Ling.

"He means it, Yi Ling. You may not want to believe it, but he means it."

"You don't even know him!"

Jenae restrained herself from the acid words that suggested themselves. Yi Ling had never had such a relationship before, after all. Her ardor would cool, and she would snap out of it, and meanwhile Jenae would be a fool not to see that Brian Denz was doing something good for her sister.

"All right, all right. I'll try to be civil. But tell him to keep politics out of it. I don't want to talk about his agenda."

"Fair," Yi Ling said, her round face lighting. "Fair enough."

◆

So began a kind of strange role reversal. As the weeks following the accident rolled by, Jenae found herself increasingly tense and edgy. Conversely, Yi Ling became more active, her disposition almost sunny. She expressed the most sensitive sympathy for Jenae's newest trouble: altermode deprivation.

It was getting bad. Since she had joined the League, Jenae had never been deprived of altermode for more than a few days. But it had now been almost five weeks since the "accident" and she hadn't entered altermode. Her metabolism was getting restless: even bathing was a torture. In the shower, she frequently had the sensation she was suffocating, with her body unable to make up its mind whether or not it was in altermode. And as disconcerting as the physical symptoms were, her need to hear the dolphins was even greater. She hadn't realized how much of her identity she derived from dolphin contact until the links were so abruptly severed. There didn't seem to be much hope of reversing that, either. She was tempted more than once to go back to the League and try to patch things up with the Heads. Whatever she had done wrong, surely she was needed. Or so it had been intimated when she was given the Underkohling code project.

But then she remembered Tien's warnings, and she balked.

Now that her sister was so uncharacteristically rational, it would have helped to be able to talk things over with her. But Yi Ling spent more and more time away, out with Brian proselytizing the Coalition's call for independence at Perth. They also attended conferences together, sometimes as far away as Sydney. Brian seemed to have no difficulty in procuring travel passes, even for air travel, which made Jenae wonder how he could have so much authority. But there was something that worried her even more. Yi Ling never said as much, but Jenae suspected from overheard snippets of conversation that Brian was taking her target shooting and teaching her hand-to-hand combat. Yi Ling's confidence soared even as Jenae's unease grew. Jenae avoided discussing the subject of rez independence: she knew it was nonsense but was unwilling to disturb the delicate equilibrium by saying as much. She kept hoping Yi Ling would tire of Brian of her own accord. And she couldn't complain about the resurgence of Yi Ling's will to live.

Jenae avoided the net system entirely. Probably her whereabouts were generally known, but all the same, ever since seeing that message directed at her the night before the Heads punished her, she'd developed an aversion to the computer. Its monitor was like a single restless eye looking back at her, and she remembered the Hall of Pickled Brains where the Heads had eyes and ears everywhere and you sat like a specimen under a microscope while they mentally dissected you. Tien had said, "Keep your head down," and she did.

But her body was screaming for relief; she couldn't hold out forever.

She had to speak to Tien. He'd been in the League for years and years: he must know what to do about altermode deprivation. She took a/v off the monitor and typed in a query to his file at the League. But when she reached his file she was greeted by a recording, and she almost backed out. The screen prompted her. Jenae took a deep breath and told herself that her face and voice were not being recorded— only her words. A second prompt. *Tien,* she wrote. *Your domestic partner asked me to call you. She needs medical advice.* Jenae paused, feeling foolish. The Heads could easily track the message to this terminal, and her attempt to circumlocute the problem was certainly transparent. Who did she think she was, some kind of spy?

Jenae? This is a secure line. Turn on your a/v.

Berating herself for her paranoia, she activated a/v.

Tien said, "Relax! You look white." Jenae did relax, just seeing his face. She smiled back at him.

Yi Ling came in, said nothing, and sat down on the floor in what Jenae had come to recognize as her thinking pose. She seemed agitated, but Jenae kept her attention focused on the screen.

"Tien, I didn't know who else to call. I'm jumping out of my skin here. I need to be in altermode. And . . ." She chose her words carefully, mindful of Yi Ling's presence, "I'm not sure I can take much more of this."

He didn't look surprised. "You *could* go to the medical center and have someone monitor you there. They should have one or two people trained to handle altermode. But—" He held up a hand to forestall her protest. "That's not what I would do. The medics think altermode was burnt out of you, and after what you went through, I would have agreed with them. What symptoms are you experiencing?"

Jenae swallowed. "Burning all over. And this gut-level instinct, like I have to get to the water. I try to hold myself back, but in the shower I'm starting to slip into transition. It's altermode, Tien. Believe me, they may have messed up my head, but they didn't burn out the physiological component."

Tien's face was troubled. "Do you want me to come get you? I don't think you should come back to the Tower, but we could go off the rez and talk, and I think I can help you with altermode."

Hope surged up in Jenae, and her eyes filled with unexpected tears. "You would do that?"

"Of course," he answered in a low voice. "You know I would. Let me think. We need to do this in a quiet way, so here's what I want you to do. Get yourself covered up to go outside. You don't need a walksuit but you need a few hours' protection against whatever might drift your way. Take a taxi to the tube station, and I'll meet you there. It may take me several hours, but wait. *Don't get on the train.* I'm going to take you to the sea myself, and we'll find out what's going on with your altermode before we take you back to the Tower. Okay?"

"At the tube station. My end. I don't get on the train. Got it. Tien?"

"Yes?"

"Thanks. You're always there."

"I'd like to keep it that way. I'm leaving right now. I'll see you in eight or nine hours. Can you wait that long?"

"I doubt it. . . ."

"*Try.*"

He cut the line.

Jenae let out a whoop, leaping to her feet. She itched with an increasingly unbearable need.

"What are you doing?" Yi Ling stood up, too.

"I have to go," Jenae said. "I can't take this anymore. Have you got any protective gear at all here, or don't they issue it?"

"Where are you going?" Her sister sounded alarmed.

"To the water," she answered tersely. She opened a closet and began rummaging. "Aha. What's this you've been hoarding?"

Yi Ling pulled the walksuit out of her hands.

"Be careful with this! It took me a lot of maneuvering to acquire it."

"Yi Ling, this is a fucking walksuit. You use these in space. Just what were you planning on doing with it?"

"Never mind. Let's just say, I'm going to see some things for myself." Yi Ling was fingering the material of the walksuit reverently.

"Oh, no. Let's not get any stupid ideas. We're going to talk about this as soon as I get back." Jenae reached into the closet, pulling out a simple hooded coverall and one glove. "That's more like it. Where's the other—ah. And I need goggles."

"Please. Please don't go," Yi Ling begged suddenly.

"Don't be ridiculous. You're not thinking—"

"Straight. I know. But, Jenae, I need to talk to you." Her voice was low with suppressed feeling.

Jenae had been putting on the coverall. She stopped with one leg in, one out, and looked at her twin. "What's wrong? Did something happen with Brian?" It was unlikely that anything else would be bothering Yi Ling, these days.

"I . . . sort of. Brian's not everything he said he was. Or . . . I'm not really sure about some of the things he's involved in. I wanted to know what you think. . . ."

"Well, it's about time! Look, we'll talk about this as soon as I get back."

"No! Don't go out there!" Yi Ling tugged at her sleeve, trying to pull the coverall back off.

"Yi Ling!" Jenae cried impatiently. "This is really urgent. I have to *go*." She pulled away rather violently, consumed with need. She had waited too long—much too long. She finished suiting up, then paused in the doorway, pulling the hood tightly over her head. Yi Ling stood with her weight on one hip, head cocked to the side—a posture of suspicion.

"It's true," Yi Ling said. "You are a slave to your animal impulses. You really aren't human anymore, though you try to hide it." She sounded so superior that Jenae did a double take. "I was wrong all along, and Brian was right. I can't believe it."

"Please. I've got to *go*." She was burning all over; she could feel her temperature rising and her breathing beginning to accelerate. Whatever was happening to her, it wasn't healthy.

"Go," Yi Ling said in a cold voice. "That's all you want to do now, so go."

Jenae turned and fled.

◆

She didn't get far. She emerged from the building shading her eyes against the late afternoon sunlight, and she didn't see the crowd until she had skipped halfway down the steps and the door had shut behind her. The light had been broken into uneven squares by the ragged shadows of the crowd; they carried a thicket of cheap placards raised in the traditional march of demonstration. The shadows stretched over Jenae.

When she appeared on the steps, the crowd hushed. She hesitated. Then, out of the silence, a man screamed, *"Mutant scum! Contaminant!"*

Jenae froze. Her eye took in the demonstration in a heartbeat: walking holo-suits like the one that had just spoken moved in programmed circles spouting invective at high volume. The suits were rendered absurd and a little creepy at the same time in juxtaposition with the still, silent accusation of the white placards and the cadaverous faces of the people who held them. There was something archaic about the scene that frightened Jenae even as the actual messages made her want to laugh. But the messages were, it seemed, directed at her.

The placards said:

BREAK OUT! STOP THE NONPUREHUMANS BEFORE ITS TO LATE. COMPUTERS ARE RULING YOUR LIVES. SCIENCE IS A LIE. ITS ALL A HOAX!!

MUTANTS FROM THE GENE WARS HAVE ALREADY JAILED YOU AND NOW THERE GOING TO FUCK YOUR CHILDREN TO SPAWN THERE EVIL INTENT.

DO YOU KNOW WHAT THE ONE EYES ARE PUTTING IN YOUR DRUGS?

FISH STINK IS AMONG US

Then she saw the flag of the organization that was demonstrating. COALITION FOR PURE HUMAN PROGRESS.

Pure Human Progress. At last, Yi Ling's "educational" programs began to resonate. Pure Human Progress obviously should be read as "regressionism." Deny the Gene Wars. Deny everything. Shut your eyes and jump. Was this what Yi Ling was gearing herself up to do? How could she succumb to such blindness? And, moreover, did she know or care how these people felt about Jenae?

"It's true," Yi Ling had said only a moment before. "You are a slave to your animal impulses."

Jenae didn't move on the stairs, and the humans on the field didn't move, either.

She almost turned around and went back. But the fever that was on her was too strong now: she had to have altermode, and she was damned if she would do it in some contained body of water on the rez, most likely followed by this mob of pure human recidivists. She squared her shoulders and walked through the protest.

If altermode hadn't burned in her so badly, she might have noticed more. She might have been more afraid. But all she saw was a blur of eyes and the tangle of fingers gesturing at her. There was a general hiss of disapproval, and the hologram people picked up on her presence and trailed her, cursing viciously. Someone spat on her. At one point a woman, pallid, red-haired, and puffy with excess weight, stepped into her path, and Jenae found herself trapped.

She did the only thing that came to mind: she opened her mouth and screamed at the woman, who gave way with a look of astonishment. Right behind the woman stood Brian, his face grim. Jenae set her jaw and shouldered past him. Miraculously, the crowd yielded.

She thought afterward how lucky she'd been not to be ripped limb from limb on the spot, but at the moment she was too distracted by physical need to appreciate the seriousness of the situation. Perhaps it was that her single-minded intensity in getting through the crowd somehow communicated itself to the pure humans, because no one actually laid a hand on her. Perhaps Brian's reluctance to stop her had checked the others. Even in restraint, though, their malice was palpable, closing around her like a gloved hand squeezing into a fist.

Then, suddenly, she was free and running across the common, urgency lending her legs strength. The people behind her were audible, and now, glancing back, she wasn't so sure of her escape. They'd fanned out across the field behind her and were hurtling after her pell-mell. She gulped down air and increased her stride. She gained the perimeter of the rez, where she would have to pass through a filtering port in the mirror field to get outside.

If these people were true to the word of their literature, Jenae realized, some of them just might follow. They claimed nothing could hurt them out there. They claimed the reservations were part of a conspiracy to keep pure humans down. Normally, she'd say: Let them come. Let them find out for themselves. But in all likelihood, if they did cross the perimeter, they'd kill her before the elements killed them.

But she was lucky. Whatever it was they preached, none of the Coalition for Pure Human Progress seemed willing to stake their lives on it. They all halted at the perimeter, but Jenae plunged through the security baffles at the portal in the mirror field, heedless of the danger. She realized too late that she had run right by the auto-taxi center, and now she had no choice but to go on foot. Her pursuers were probably getting security clearance and checking out cars right now. She put on a burst of speed, veering away from the road where the taxis couldn't follow.

The sun was on its way down. Normally her reflex would be to wrap herself up, to hide from exposure to the open air. But she was too far gone to react normally, and in some quiet part of her mind she watched her own progress away from the road even while her body strained and gasped with the unexpected effort of flight. Privately, she decided that she must have lost all sense of reality to run so impetuously out into the wild.

Her sides aching, she slowed as she climbed toward the top of the headland and the full view of the sea spread out before her. She was near the same place where she'd seen the dolphins before. She didn't care that it was an obvious place to get caught; it felt like coming home. Anyway, no one had interfered with her in any way during the past month. Even

Tien thought they might have overreacted. She was beginning to believe the Heads really were too distracted to bother with her. The landscape was loud with wind, but utterly deserted.

She skidded down the steep hillside, whipped off the protective clothing, and plunged into the water as though she had been starving for it. Instantly and obligingly, time shifted its pattern for her and she found herself in the eternal present of altermode.

13

In the sea she is incredibly powerful, as though hurt and deprivation have somehow strengthened her bond with her amphibious nature. Kicking easily, she passes the tidal area where the surf stirs up the bottom, and slides out into the clear water. She swims mute, at first because she is afraid to tap into a web, but then, after a while, because a new, naked feeling of oneness with the sea folds into her of its own accord. She begins to notice the subtle energy systems of algae, plant life, and small animals, and the deep heartbeat of the pounding waves grows loud in her mind.

I am not a cetacean, she thinks suddenly. I am like nothing else in the water.

What distant forebear the Ingenix designers once found to turn on the altermode genes, Jenae still cannot guess, but for the first time alone in the open sea, she feels a sense of continuity with her ancestors. A primal sense of being not a person, but a creature invades her. She is a creature in a vast interrelated world that she has never experienced without the noise and delight of dolphins all around her, imposing their worldview. Now, swimming by herself, the sea feels much older to her and far more strange. But she feels old, too, and perfectly simple. It is this simplicity, she decides, that humanity can never know: the purity of respiration, sense and reaction, uninhibited movement in all directions. And the fearlessness of belonging in this place.

In the League of New Alchemists, you never swim in the ocean. You never *swim* at all, in any official capacity. The altermode tanks have been designed to keep water flowing past alchemist gills effortlessly; and naturally all contact with dolphins is made through purely mental channels. The real thing is far more intoxicating, and in her exuberance Jenae lets her body go where her senses lead. She has no idea how to navigate and only a vague idea of what dangerous creatures the waters of the Indian Ocean may still hold, in these years after the Gene Wars. Blithely she swims like a newborn.

Pumping harder now, she reaches the edge of an undersea shelf and floats out over the cold darkness of the deep below: this is like nowhere she has ever been. It feels like witnessing the primeval darkness underpinning the world, an emptiness blind to past and future but opening only a vast, limitless space against which nothing can be measured.

But mind.

Mind. There is a long, long mind somewhere near, and its perception flows around her like an enveloping cloak, skinning her almost with its awareness. She hesitates, belatedly conscious of her vulnerability: her eyesight underwater is poor, her hearing worse, and as humanoid among fish she might as well be crippled, she moves so awkwardly. Something inexorable is happening; she senses the pressure of the water shift with the motion of some great body. She freezes, hanging limp in the water like a kitten in its mother's mouth. The dark hulk of the thing rises from out of the darkness and passes her in a stream of barnacle-covered flesh, close enough to send her somersaulting in the water with the spin of its passage. Only after she recovers from its wake does she glimpse the tail silhouetted against the surface like a pair of spread wings. The whole mass of the whale turns over in the water, sounding, and dives again. It cruises away and vanishes in the darkness.

She is still reeling from the encounter when a lighter touch finds her: the perimeter of a web brushes against her, and she pours her energy into it with relief at the contact. She has not lost her ability to web.

—We are here, Jenae.

A chord of dolphin minds extends a strand of talk to her. Her pod has "heard" her again.

—How faint you sound. Where are you?

—North of you, at Shark Bay. We waited so long for you to come, and you didn't. Everyone said you were crisped, except Tien. You don't feel crispy, Jenae. They must have exaggerated.

—Were any of you hurt?

—Only you. We were not targeted, and we couldn't do anything. We have been very angry about what happened. How dare the Pickled Brains interfere with our web?

She has never heard this tone of righteous indignation come from dolphins before; it pleases her.

—How did you find me?

—We would find you anywhere now. We would find you in two inches of water, if you were open. You are tuned to us.

It is not possible to cry in altermode, and there is no physiological equivalent. But Jenae wishes to cry if only to release the fear and loneliness of these past weeks. The dolphins' minds enfold her in a welcome that washes away all anxiety, their empathy more complete than Yi Ling's ever was; and that only makes her sadder.

—Please, tell me. What has been going on?

—There are bad feelings in the League. Not even the Pickled Brains can agree on what happened to you, Jenae, or how it was allowed to happen. There is conflict among them, and that confuses us all. We have not circulated the information we gave to you, but we're eager to find out what you learned from it.

—Nothing, so far, I'm afraid. I tried to come to you, but there was no sign of you at Shark Bay. I didn't know you could hear me at a distance. I would have called . . .

—That's unfortunate. We wanted to warn you, but there was no way to predict the Heads' action would be so sudden and decisive.

—I wasn't too careful. I was very trusting. I did learn a few things, though, before they got to me. The ship's computer on *Morpheus* sent a command to Jupiter station to fire on *Morpheus* itself. Then *Morpheus* changed course and went to Underkohling, where it was shot down by a police vessel.

—Do you remember the encryption from Underkohling? *Deceit*, it said.

—Yes, but how? And why?

—You must find a way to learn more, if you can. The Pickled Brains are extremely protective of information, but it would seem that this subject is most vital to them.

—Can't you learn more than me? I'm in exile.

—We have been on work leave for some time now: the Pickled Brains can't find a decent new alchemist to replace you . . . but why does this make you sad?

—What would I do if another alchemist took my place with you? You are family to me.

—Would we have chosen to share our knowledge with you if you were simply any alchemist? We will take care of you, and the Pickled Brains cannot read our minds. They need us more than we need them. We are coming in toward shore even now, and we will stay as close as we can from now on. There may yet be work we can do in the web, without the Pickled Brains knowing.

—It's dark. I will return to the water tomorrow. I'll learn what I can tonight. I have to find a computer that can't be easily traced to me. And I have to find Tien. He's going to be looking for me.

—Then find him quickly, and stick by him. We will meet you tomorrow, if you call us. But be careful. Tien says you're being watched. He is cautious and patient. You could learn from him.

—I think it's too late for that. I wish I could stay with you!

—You can't. You're not one of us; don't forget that. Get out of the water, Jenae, before something mistakes you for human and eats you. Return tomorrow.

◆

It was blessedly dark when Jenae came out of altermode on the rocky shore, but the air was cold. She spent a long time searching for her clothes and then, once she had found them, she clambered numbly up the cliff. She was weary and found it difficult to see. Her skin ached with burning, and her eyes teared.

At last she stood by the roadside. The lights of the rez were softly reflected in the real sky; otherwise, all evidence of Perth was completely hidden by the mirror fields. The falling waves made a constant, reassuring pulse in her ears, and the dry grass shivered around her as she looked up and down the thin strip of moonlit pavement. She glanced north nervously, even though she knew the Tower was far, far away, accessible only by the tube. A few pinpoints of light showed her where the tube station was, and she thought how strange it was that the tube line had not been driven straight into Perth rez. Why the long gap between station and destination? She had mentioned this peculiarity to her sister years ago, before she had joined the League.

"To discourage travel, of course," Yi Ling had said cynically.

"But isn't it more dangerous to have people taking taxis than to run a tunnel under the rez?"

"Of course. If it's dangerous and inconvenient, people won't be inclined to do it. Why do you think nobody ever goes to the League Tower? They make it bloody hard to get in."

"I'd like to go there," Jenae had said wistfully. At the time, the Tower had seemed romantic and mysterious. But now, as she looked up the road toward the tube station, she had a feeling of dread.

I have to go see Tien, she told herself. Even if it means walking. He's on his way.

She set off wearily in the direction of the station. How small she felt now, a human again, with no shelter in the night and no one to trust. If only she could have stayed in altermode where the web held her safe. She tried to keep a brisk pace in the cool air, but her head had begun to throb and her arms and legs felt light and sluggish at the same time. She forced herself forward anyway, annoyed that the symptoms of the "punishment" still affected her.

She stopped dead. Silently a group of tall figures had risen up around her, a circle of shadows like a living Stonehenge. A light too bright to bear was in her eyes. Jenae threw her hands up to protect herself and fell back into the vise grip of an enormous hand.

The hand had six fingers. She could tell because as she groped for a finger to unlock the grip she counted one finger too many. It was an absurd detail, but it preoccupied her completely for the second or two that it took for the large arm that went with the hand to lift her bodily and toss her in the air. She hit the ground with all the wind forced out of her lungs, and lay gasping dust.

"Jenae Kim?" said a rasping voice. "You are to be detained for questioning. We will escort you to the Tower."

The light had shocked her eyes, and even after it was removed Jenae saw spots and swirling shapes of color. A booted foot was planted by her head. It, like the hand, was unusually large. Even from her perspective on the ground, she could see that the people she was dealing with must be giants.

"I'm going there anyway," she managed to gasp. "There's no need to get rough, mates."

No one answered. Jenae's arms were seized and she was hauled to her feet. That makes sense, Jenae thought. Knock me down and then pull me up again. What are these people trying to prove?

Someone shoved her in the back and she was propelled forward. She saw the vehicle now: police issue, long and low, pulled over with lights folded down by the side of the road. Irrelevantly she wondered how these huge people could fit in such a low car. The prisoner door slid open and she was nudged, more gently now, she thought, toward it. She still couldn't see the details of the people who were arresting her; most were behind her now, but one stood beside the door and gestured for her to get in. Jenae hesitated.

A second later there was a flash of movement to her right. Something whizzed past her ear and before she could react, the head of the guard by the door parted from its neck and toppled to one side. Hot blood gushed over Jenae: it filled her mouth when she opened it to gasp, and she fell down in pure shock. Crouching on the ground, she threw her hands over the back of her head in an instinctive gesture of protection, covering her eyes and ears with her arms in the same movement.

She had expected more violence, but a silence had fallen.

"You're out of your jurisdiction," said a new voice. "You should stay at the perimeter of the rez, where your masters control you."

Jenae lay shaking, wondering what the voice meant and how she was supposed to respond when she felt like a kitten in a pit of tigers.

"We are responding to a call from within the rez. Individual was harassing pure humans and left without clearance."

"Then take her back to the rez," said the new voice.

"Our instructions are to bring her to the Tower. You have no place in this matter. Go, or we will kill you for interfering."

"I'll interfere again, Jakal, and this time you'll be the one moistening my sword."

There was a volley of laser fire that seemed to blossom from all directions. A deep-throated cry rang out, and the smell of meat cooking reached Jenae's nostrils. She wanted to be sick. There was a lot of noise, but it only lasted for a few seconds. Another booted foot appeared beside her left eye. Jenae raised her head slightly. The first thing she saw was the severed head of the police guard, still bubbling blood. It was large and pale-skinned, with a face so flat-nosed as to look barely human. In the center of the forehead was a single, liquid eye.

Shuddering, Jenae shrank away from the disembodied head.

"It's all right," said the voice of the newcomer above her. "You can stand up."

Jenae rose to her knees. There were lights all over the scene now, and at least a dozen bodies lay motionless on the ground. She looked up past the boots to the rest of the figure that stood over her. Another giant: at least seven feet tall with a large, rangy frame that appeared to be female. The head was bald and mahogany. When light fell on the face Jenae saw that matters were as she had feared: this one, too, looked at her out of one golden eye.

"We know who you are," said the One Eye. "And we

don't believe it would be wise for you to return to the Tower."

Jenae did vomit then: she told herself it wasn't merely the woman's aspect that triggered the event. It was mostly the smell of blood and charred flesh—and possibly shock and exhaustion and a few other things. But when she was finished and had backed away from the contents of her own stomach, the One Eye was laughing. Rather cruelly, Jenae thought.

"I must say, by your reputation I hardly expected you to be such a puppy. But that is always the way with humans, isn't it?"

"Piss off," Jenae managed to say, looking at the ground. "Why don't you kill me and have done?"

More laughter; apparently the One Eye's allies had joined in.

"Feisty little bitch of a puppy. Good. No, I'm afraid there will be no more entertainment this evening. The puppy is drunk with stimulation, isn't she?"

"Call her guppy instead of puppy and you'll be closer to the truth," said a thick male voice from behind Jenae. "I think you'll have to carry her, Keila."

Keila barked orders by way of reply. "Drive the car, Milan. And get the laser charges off these corpses. We may as well gain something for our trouble."

There were six or seven of them—Jenae was too flustered to count properly—and she felt equally repulsed by them all. Keila picked her up personally and deposited her in the prisoner compartment of the police car. Then she and Milan got in the front and someone slammed the door neatly. Jenae couldn't see what the others did then, for the compartment was completely opaque. For all she knew, they might have set about eating the bodies of their kindred immediately. This image, combined with the lurching progress of the windowless car, conspired to make her feel sick again; but there was nothing in her stomach to expel, and she had to be content with feeling vaguely nauseous and miserable.

She felt the surface under the car change; the One Eyes were driving rough, rattling the frame of the car. The journey seemed to take a long time, and even with unpredictable bursts of noise and motion jolting her at every moment, Jenae soon found herself drifting off into sleep. At one point she remembered smelling water, and she had the impression even in sleep of being enclosed in a small, stuffy space. But even the sense of alarm engendered by these perceptions could not seem to rouse her. She slept on, oblivious to where she was going in the middle of the night.

14

Cold, and a sweet smell. Faint hush of ocean. The light against her eyelids was brilliant red. Sun! she thought fearfully, and jerked awake. She was lying in a fine purple sand and there were garish flowers swarming all over vines in a rough circle around her. She still wore the protective cloak and hood, but her hands were exposed to the bright light, and she snatched them into the shadow of her sleeves without even thinking. Jenae groped for her goggles and put them on before glancing up toward the sky.

It was not what she had expected. She was sheltered beneath a canopy of bright red leaves that grew only a dozen feet above the ground, forming a flimsy roof that filtered the sun like tissue paper.

It's a virtuality trick, she thought, and fingered her scalp for electrodes. She wasn't wired anywhere. She thrust her fingers into the lavender sand. It felt smoother than natural sand, and the individual grains were dull.

Something squirmed beneath her, and she jumped up and spun away, forgetting to protect her hands and face. As she watched, a square meter of sand detached itself from the ground and began to shake. Sand spilled away on all sides and a pink, featureless slab of living tissue emerged. It slunk along the ground and disappeared into the underbrush.

Jenae felt her own skin shudder in sympathy.

Voices. Muffled by the waves, but still near at hand. Jenae pulled the hood closer around her face and crept into the bushes, easing toward the sound of the sea. She nudged her way through the strange vegetation, whose slender, soft stalks gave way easily before her, until she topped a slight rise and the ground fell away toward an open expanse of beach. There was a small lagoon lined with the red plants, and the sand was streaked with lavender above the water-line. One Eyes were standing out in the harsh sunlight, hoods thrown back from their bare scalps and huge eyes unprotected, conversing intently. Both appeared to be female, to the best of Jenae's judgment. She couldn't hear words but the cool wind carried the level, clipped tone of their speech up the hillside and into the dunes.

Out of the frying pan and into the fire, Jenae thought, and withdrew as far as possible into her clothing. After all her warnings to Yi Ling about the wilderness outside, here was Jenae exposing herself to everything she'd cautioned against. She wished now she'd nicked that walksuit while she had the chance.

"Life is made or unmade with ease," said a voice behind her, and she tensed. "Why is everyone so protective of yours?" She remembered the voice, and the ugly face that confronted her when she turned back into the vegetation was that of the leader from last night.

"That's funny," Jenae said. "I got the impression that I was about to be snuffed on any old whim." She was determined not to be humiliated by the giant, as she had been last night. She still had some pride left.

"I killed a brother for you," Keila said. "True, he was nothing to brag about, nor were his cronies. Still, what is it about you? You're just a half-grown thing, aren't you?"

"By your standards, I guess I would be." Jenae stood her ground.

"Well, don't let it swell your head that I saved you. I did it as a favor to Tien. He called me in the middle of the night and said you might be wandering around incoherent by the beach. He said you wouldn't be any trouble, but I'm not so sure. I may change my mind at any moment."

"I see. I didn't realize . . ."

"That Tien consorted with One Eyes? There are a number of things you don't realize, I'll wager. Are you hungry?"

"What?"

"Are you hungry? You look weak. Or is this a reflection of your natural state?"

"No, I am hungry."

"Come with me. No need to keep squinting and hunching. These plants effectively screen out all the UV and a good deal of the other variations you don't need. That's why I put you here. I didn't save your life to give you a slow death by radiation poisoning. Better a swift execution."

"Where is this place? I've never seen anything like it."

"This is one of the ecosystems most pure humans don't know about. You'll see." Her tone indicated that Jenae was ignorant of a great deal.

Jenae followed the tall woman through the red forest. They came to a low stone building on which several narrow paths converged. Keila preceded her into a dim, narrow room filled with barrels, boxes, and odd-shaped items of many descriptions.

"I would have let you sleep here," Keila said, moving forward slowly in the cluttered darkness, "but I never sleep indoors myself. I didn't want you to think you were a prisoner. You're a guest, for the present."

Jenae said nothing. If One Eyes killed one another so casually, small wonder that this was their idea of hospitality. She just stood there while Keila rummaged through boxes and began to pass packages to her. Jenae sat down to open a box of crackers, piling the cans and bags around her.

"This is plenty," she said. "Is there any water?"

"Manual pump in the back. You can bathe as well, if you want."

She probably needed it, Jenae reflected. At least she should be able to bathe without slipping into altermode. After last night, her cravings ought to remain at least temporarily at bay.

She ate rapidly. Keila stood there doing nothing. She didn't even watch Jenae.

"Why did you save my life?" Jenae said after a while.

"I told you. Tien. Why do you ask me this?"

"I don't know. Well, you seemed different last night. You weren't quite as nice."

"Nice. I'm never nice. The other night I was excited. The killing. Those traitors. Their blood gives me no pleasure; it just makes me irritable."

"Irritable, okay. That's one way of putting it. Why do

you hate them? You are related to them, aren't you? I mean, it isn't some kind of race quarrel or something, is it?"

"No race quarrel. They have sold themselves into the service of pure humans, which is enough cause for hatred. Then they have the balls to try to interfere with other new species."

"Do you mean me?"

"Yes, you. They were going to bring you back to the Tower. What you thought you were doing making public appearances and running out in the wild like that, I can't guess. I have to tell you that you strike me as being rather stupid. That's not what I expected, given the rumors about you. But I must trust my own eye, not what others know or pretend to know."

"What have you heard about me?" Jenae asked between mouthfuls. "I didn't know people were talking about me."

"We know you angered the Heads, which of course is a point in your favor. We know Tien supports you, and he is respected by us. We know your constitution has a reputation for being superior to that of a common human, rivaling that of a One Eye, they say—but now that I've seen you myself I dispute that claim. You were pathetic the other night."

"I had just come out of altermode. I was feeling rough to begin with . . ."

"Altermode, yes. Your talent in altermode brought you into some confidential information from the Heads, didn't it? We have some interest in that, as well. We can protect you, and maybe you can help us. Maybe. Although at the moment I doubt you'll be good for much as far as we are concerned."

"We. Who are you, exactly?"

"I am Keila, leader of all the One Eyes on these islands, except those jokes who bow down to the Heads by calling themselves police. Those I kill, although, as I said, it gives me no pleasure. It's a mere necessity."

"I see."

"No, you don't. I'm fully aware of what pure humans say about us. You've been thoroughly indoctrinated in a culture of lies, so everything you perceive is messed up and crazy."

"Okay. If you say so."

Keila laughed. "After some time here with us, I don't think you'll be quite so agreeable. But for now, it's amusing."

Jenae didn't say anything. She concentrated on her food.

"Yes. This is good. You must learn to become more obedient to your body if you are to survive. Tell your head to get out of the way from now on."

Jenae winced. She was thinking of the cop's head hitting the ground with a surprisingly hollow thud.

"I need to contact my dolphins," she said. "Where are we?"

"South Island, east coast. That's all you need to know right now."

"South Island? Never heard of it."

"New Zealand, mate. You slept a long time. We gave you some drugs to help."

Jenae stared at the One Eye. "Bloody hell! I'm supposed to meet my pod near Perth . . . tonight? I guess tonight isn't when I thought it was."

"Impossible. Going back to Perth would be suicide, and anyway, it's too far. The dolphins will have to find you. Are you finished?"

"I guess so." Jenae eyed the debris of her meal doubtfully. She wasn't exactly hungry but she wasn't exactly satisfied either, yet she had consumed an enormous amount of food in rather short order. Her bowels began to churn into gear. "I need to go outside."

"Meet me on the beach in ten minutes," said Keila. "Don't worry about protection. I'll bring gear for you." She turned on her heel and left.

Sure, Jenae thought. That's like telling a pure human you'll meet them at the bottom of the sea with an oxygen tank.

But once she was back outside under the red leaves she could hear the sea again, and it was difficult to resist that sound. With great care for the slithering things that lived under the sand, she relieved herself in the bushes and drank and washed as best she could at the manual water pump she found in the back. Normally she would have balked at the notion of drinking water drawn straight from the ground, but after the immediate threat of lasers, a few parasites or contaminants seemed insignificant.

When she was done she felt a little more clearheaded, and she made her way again to the edge of the dunes. The One

Eyes that had been conversing on the sand were gone, but Keila stood there with a pile of stuff under a blanket near the water's edge. There was a small covered boat drifting a few hundred meters offshore, and Jenae could see some exchange happening between people who occasionally broke surface and those on the boat. Wrapping her hood closely about her face, Jenae made her way across the beach to the One Eye.

"Unlike pure humans," Keila said by manner of greeting, "One Eyes work. We work all our lives, and we feed not only ourselves but all the dying pure humans on the reservations. Work has meaning for us in and of itself; we work not out of fear or love of others, but out of pleasure in the things we do. While you are here, you will work, too, and learn our ways." She flipped off the blanket and lying on the sand were a pile of fluorescent floats attached to several net pouches and a plastic chain that carried a variety of bladed and forked implements similar to the kind used in gardening.

"What about protection from the sun? And the water poisons?"

Keila handed her a tube of standard industrial gel for emergency protection outdoors.

"This will protect you from the sun. The waters here are fairly clean. We have a thriving population of all kinds of fish, and they never seem to suffer. Several years ago the League seeded these waters with cleaning algae, and as you can see they have really taken hold." She kicked at the sand with her boot. "They bind with everything and devour the most common waterborne poisons like sugar. Unfortunately, they also turn everything purple. I know the waters are getting cleaner because, as you can see, much of this sand is now white again. The algae are losing their food supply and diminishing. Eventually they may die out altogether."

"Fair enough," Jenae said. "But I can't use this gel. It will block my skin from breathing. Do you have the kind the League uses?"

Again Keila looked at her as though she were an idiot. "Then dive at night after this. Don't cringe like that. The sun's not going to kill you in one day, or even one month."

The One Eye stepped out of her own white coverall, under which she was wearing a heavy body stocking, and donned a large pair of flippers and a diving mask with snorkel attached. "Strip," she commanded, watching critically as Jenae shrugged out of her clothes, hunching her back against the sun. "Here, strap these pads to your shoulders. Tighter. I forget how small you people are." She helped Jenae affix this unwieldy load of equipment to herself, and then led the way down the beach and into the shallow water. Jenae followed awkwardly, dragging what she thought was an awful lot of junk, and waded in. But once she had submerged in the water, the load weighed almost nothing, buoyed by the floaters. She slid easily into altermode.

◆

Keila is swimming over Jenae's head, snorkeling just beneath the surface. In her left hand she holds what looks like a scythe. Jenae moves along the bottom, the net with its string of floaters and implements fanning out above and behind her like a ceremonial robe. The sea floor is sandy, and Keila is right about the algae. Most of the sand is a natural color, with only isolated streaks and patches of lavender marking the presence of the cleaning algae, which Jenae avoids. The floor remains nearly level, descending very gradually for many meters stretching out from shore. The water is shallow but much colder than she is used to.

Just ahead she sees a dark field of narrow-leafed plants cultivated in clear, straight rows beneath the water. She recognizes the type immediately: it is a popular "synthetic" variety of sea lettuce, rich in minerals and used on virtually every dinner table in Australia and New Zealand. The field extends as far out into the ocean as visibility allows her to see: some fifty or sixty meters, at least. Swimming along the surface and diving down at intervals are One Eyes equipped like Keila. They dive with mesh bags, harvest the plants with clean machete strokes, and swim back up with the laden bags. Farther out, Jenae can see the underside of the boat. It casts an undulating shadow on the crops: at this depth, the sun is stronger in the water than on land, and seen from beneath, the surface shimmers like a mirror.

There is no need for Keila to speak. Jenae simply follows, and as soon as the others notice their approach, they swim over and seize implements from Jenae's equipment skirt. Jenae swims up and down the rows, exchanging tools with the One-Eyed workers and receiving from them their laden bags. The One Eyes return frequently to the surface for breath, and they move slowly and awkwardly through the water; for the first time ever Jenae actually feels graceful underwater. After half an hour of watching Jenae, Keila comes over and relieves her of the floats and tools, letting them hang loose in the water. She passes Jenae a long-handled scythe and demonstrates the proper technique. Jenae soon finds a rhythm: kick down, cut, grab, bind with one hand, release, kick down again. In this manner Jenae harvests and Keila, above, waits for the bundles to float to the surface before retrieving them and passing them to the boat.

It is boring. She cannot hear the One Eyes' thoughts, and there are no dolphins around. The monotony of the task begins to wear on her; this is the first time that altermode hasn't been pure magic.

She is looking right at the blade of the scythe as she draws it through the soft stem of the plant. It flashes past her leg and she is aware of making a mistake a second before the pain actually hits. Then there is a cloud of blood rising from her leg. In surprise she opens her mouth and it floods with water.

A One Eye slow and ungainly is pumping toward her, waving a piece of fluorescent material and gesturing up toward the surface. Taking the sign as a command, Jenae swims upward, more annoyed than hurt, and a few seconds later One-Eyed heads begin to pop up all around her. The boat's engine whines softly at high pitch, and it moves to pick up swimmers. Jenae keeps her face in the water and holds to altermode, but Keila comes at her from the side and drags her toward the boat. Choking, she is hauled on board.

◆

"You don't stay in the water if there's blood," Keila said. "Even a flesh wound like this." Not too gently, she bound Jenae's leg where the scythe had sliced open the flesh. Bloody saltwater sloshed across the deck of the boat. Jenae lay back, her chest heaving and throat rattling, eyes closed against the sun.

"You have to learn to keep your concentration at all times. Plenty of shark round here. They won't usually approach a large group, but you never know. Some of the tigers are forty feet long thanks to Ingenix, and they're fast. This site's spoiled for the rest of the morning. We'll do something else until we're sure it's safe."

"Don't you have cameras, or monitors or something you could use?" Jenae gasped. "It should be easy to track a shark coming in this close to shore."

Keila's nostrils had narrowed almost to nothing. Her eye, stained red around the edges from exposure to the water, squeezed half shut beneath its wrinkly lid. "Who's going to build equipment like that? We're talking *food* here. We're talking about basic survival. Save the high tech for the pure humans—they've got nothing else. You use your own senses, like I told you. And your own sense, hopefully."

Jenae let her head fall to the side.

"Where are we going now?" she inquired wearily.

"*I'm* going to go kill today's meal."

"Lovely," Jenae said.

15

Jenae slept outdoors three nights running, shivering. The first night she barely slept at all for fear of the flat, squirming creatures that lived just under the surface of the sand in the red-leafed forest. ("Sandcreeper," said Keila. "Good eating, that.") Jenae didn't ask and wasn't told where the One Eyes went during the hours she slept. She had the impression they kept working during most of the night.

Fortunately, the One Eyes' taste in food had proven more conventional than the folklore Jenae had been raised on had led her to believe. They lived mostly off the sea, because, Keila said, mammals were still scarce, limited in the same way pure humans were by poison and the killing sun. They needed time to rebuild their populations. Gulls, too, were skillfully hunted by the One Eyes, although Jenae declined to taste the flesh. The stories of the fabled One-Eyed constitution apparently were true: Keila and her kind could eat meat raw or cooked as necessity demanded without complaining, they slept less than four hours each day (and this in the middle of the day, when the sun was strongest), and their strength—well, Jenae had already witnessed several displays.

They were a taciturn people: Keila seemed to regard it as her duty to lecture Jenae frequently as to the shortcomings of herself and her society, but apart from that she was not chatty. The others barely spoke to Jenae at all. They toiled night and day; in the next lagoon was a sizable docking area where night-fishing boats and trawlers came and went constantly on their way back and forth to Adelaide and Albany. Some traveled as far as the west coast, where it was said that the One-Eyed rebels had Perth under siege with no way to get supplies. Keila told her they were protesting some new form of computer surveillance from space that they had just learned about, and Jenae automatically wondered if her own movements were being traced. The Heads, it seemed, could see into any computer system they wanted to: what was to prevent them from tracking her down?

Again and again she had tried to contact her dolphins, hoping to find out what was happening in the League. If she was going to be implicated as some kind of traitor, she might as well have the knowledge to commit the treachery. She webbed with a group of local wild dolphins who promised to transfer the message to the whales, who, they said, could be relied on to pass it on to Jenae's dolphins. But her pod was far away off the west coast of Australia and Jenae didn't have much hope that they would come. She didn't know how close they had to be to hear her, but obviously a couple of thousand miles was too far.

The matter of Yi Ling was another problem that she didn't know how to resolve. In retrospect, it had become clear to Jenae that she had left Yi Ling just at a moment when her twin needed her—when, it seemed, she was breaking away from Brian and the Coalition. Jenae had meant to return the next day; she had meant to return to Yi Ling and open up to her about everything that had been happening, to trust her sister with her own misgivings and troubles. But then she had found herself in the hands of the One Eyes, and her promises were good for nothing. During these first three days that she spent working among the One Eyes, fear for Yi Ling and guilt for leaving were never far from the surface of her thoughts. At last, on the fourth morning, she approached Keila directly with the problem.

"What do you want me to do about it?" asked the One Eye bluntly. "Taking care of one of you is enough of a nuisance. And if your sister has never been exposed to alter-mode, she shouldn't leave the rez now. She's too old to adapt to the virus."

"I don't want you to bring her here. But I may have to go there."

"Go back to Perth? Not a good idea."

"Why not?" Jenae said impatiently. "I'm not going to go skulking around like this forever. I'm not a One Eye. Eventually I have to go back to the League and deal with the Heads. I don't know what Tien was thinking when he told you to kidnap me."

"Kidnap? That was a rescue, you little fool. Tien *asked* me if I would keep an eye out for you. He said he hoped he could deal with your problem himself. He said he hoped it wouldn't be necessary for me to intervene, but that the police might be looking for you. But he never said anything about bringing you back to the Tower."

Jenae was shaking her head. "I don't understand Tien," she said. "How did he know about the police?"

"But the reason I say going back to Perth is a bad idea has nothing to do with your little in-house League problem," Keila continued as if Jenae hadn't spoken. "There's going to be battle there any day now. The Coalition is getting ready to take the reservations by force."

Jenae could barely restrain her scorn. The Coalition? That banner-waving, cowardly mob with their holographic mouthpieces and idiot slogans? Who would take them seriously? "I can't quite see that happening . . ." she ventured.

"I hope you *don't* see it happening," Keila said brusquely. "That's why I recommend you stay here. It may get ugly around Perth. There are terrorists loose in Sydney even as we speak. They have planes and whatnot, and they'll be on their way to Perth one of these days."

Jenae sighed. "Everything I try to do ends up being so complicated," she said. "Can't I reach Yi Ling through the system? Can't I call her? Or don't you have any computers out here?"

"We have computers," Keila conceded. She gave Jenae a long, assessing look. "I'll allow you to call your sister," she said finally. "I told you: you aren't a prisoner here. But before you take that step, before you allow yourself to be drawn back into the world of pure humans, do one favor for me. There's something I want you to see."

Keila's favor turned out to involve getting in a covered vehicle for what she called "an educational tour." Jenae was ordered to spread the gel over her entire body, then handed three layers of catsuits and a close-fitting diver's hood, gloves, and boots that were too large for her. She had to make do with her own goggles, since what passed for One-

Eyed goggles was really just a loose faceplate that could not be made to conform to Jenae's anatomy.

The jeep eased out of the red forest and into cloudy, unprotected daylight. The road, devoid now of all vegetation, began to climb up the rocky hillside toward the interior, and when it grew steep and pitted the vehicle began to groan as it bumped over the old surface. Jenae had seen images of pre-Gene Wars New Zealand next to contemporary studies, and the effect had been dramatic. But it was nothing compared to actually moving through the land and air beyond the oasis of the red forest. Now she received the full impact of the nightmare. The scalded ground was grey with dust, and tiny scorpions scattered before the wheels of the vehicle. There were a few damp crevasses in the rocks: these displayed the brilliant foliage of the red plants like freshly bleeding wounds. The air was redolent with a sickly odor like vomit: "Old chemical plants that way," Keila remarked. "Never go over there." She gestured off to the right, where the regular angles of buildings could be made out against the dull earth itself that rose in soft humps all around. Were it not for their smooth sides and right angles, the buildings would have been invisible, dust-shrouded as they were.

Jenae had seen photographs of this area taken before the Gene Wars had broken out of the economic marketplace and into the physical environment at large: she could not superimpose those images over what she was seeing now. She had learned as a child that the Sahara Desert had once supported herds of animals and tribes of people on vast stretches of grassland; she was no more able to see the old New Zealand here than she had been able, then, to see zebras and lakes and trees in Libya.

Keila was quiet as they drove; she handled the bucking jeep with one hand on the wheel, and her profile never wavered from the road ahead of her. She said nothing to Jenae until eventually the road leveled off, and they passed through a vast waste of dried stumps and scarred, sallow earth.

"When I was young," Keila told her, "these trees used to stand here bare and hollow. Some of them were burned. Birds would roost in them and you'd see their wings dark against the sky. But these pure human escapees have cut the dry wood away for burning, and there's almost nothing left.

Look how close to the ground they cut the stumps. They're determined to use every last scrap of their old world."

"Wouldn't you, if you needed to survive?" Even as she spoke, Jenae wondered why she had never known there were pure humans living outside the reservations. She didn't want to admit her ignorance to Keila, though.

"Not if I could adapt to the new world, no. I'd prefer to have my memories if I were the pure humans, but I'd move on."

"That's easy for you to say. You can adapt. You have adapted. Not everyone can eat raw flesh tainted with poisons—or reject a virus that was designed to kill."

"Many Gene Wars viruses were not intended to kill. If you knew your history, you'd know that. Many were intended to effect change in DNA. Sometimes the host couldn't handle the stress of that change, but in this way the weak were weeded out."

Jenae shook her head. "I don't know. They may not have been intended to kill, but they did, didn't they? In my world, people pride themselves on medicine above all else: their ability to save the 'weak' as you call them."

"In your world, your people pride themselves on anything that they perceive as a defiance of nature. But by saving the weak, they don't defy nature, they only weaken themselves so that some future species can come along and usurp them."

"Meaning the One Eyes?"

"Meaning any of us who have been changed, either personally or because of our parents' courage."

"Courage? My parents didn't *intend* to be exposed. They didn't intend for me to be exposed. If they could have saved both my sister and me, they would have. As it was, they couldn't even save themselves." But even as she spoke the words, she was thinking about her father's choice. Why had he done it? Why not expose both, or neither—why separate each twin from the only person she loved?

Unless it was that old imperative: Make sure your genes are passed on to the next generation, no matter what. At least her father's plan had broadened the chances that one of them would survive. But how could anyone think that way?

"But they saved her and now you are the one who can survive." Keila must be reading her thoughts.

"That seems to be the irony of it, yeah. But I have to believe that pure humans will find their way sooner or later. The human race has overcome so many obstacles in the past that seemed insurmountable. Anyway, you said yourself it's getting better. I've been swimming in the sea with no adverse effects. It must be getting better."

"It is getting better," Keila said, swinging the wheel hard to the left and turning the car up another, equally disused road. Hills closed in around them on either side, a little menacingly, Jenae thought. How strange that a simple land formation could make her feel trapped, but all those years spent indoors had not had the same effect. "But pure humans are dying off. Did I warn you that we may be shot at? Be prepared."

Jenae straightened up in her seat. The jeep had pulled into the cracked parking lot of an old cement building. Its few windows had been sealed over with plastic that flapped in the silent wind. The land around was slightly less barren than the field of ruined trees, but most of the vegetation consisted of short, stiff grass and the odd scrub tree. From somewhere behind the building came the sound of running water.

Keila ducked out of the vehicle and rummaged in the back. She emerged with an unlabeled five-gallon can and a bulging canvas bag. She slung the can to Jenae and led the way toward the building.

The building's original glass doors had been covered over by corrugated metal, and this had been painted over almost completely with stylized, looping images of animals in pseudo-Maori style. A grinning dog stood sideways, painted like a sentinel, and whales with human heads cavorted above. Keila gave the metal a resounding kick and waited, listening to the echoes. Nothing happened. Keila made a funny snort through her slitlike nostrils and proceeded around the side of the building. Jenae had no idea what function the place had been designed to serve: it looked industrial but there was nothing distinguishing about it, and no signs were posted to provide clues. It was set in a cleft between two hills, and as they reached the rear of the structure, the sound of running water increased in volume.

"Mind your footing," Keila said. They had stepped into a shadowy area between the steep hillside behind the building and the rear wall itself, and Jenae rounded a corner and saw the rush of water spitting from a huge pipe set in the side of the building and falling into a dark shaft in the ground, where it echoed and reechoed. The concrete walkway was slick with algae and mud here, and Jenae laid a steadying hand on the wall to her right. Her eyes fell on the mounds of earth that rose on the other side of the shaft. Carved sticks protruded from the mounds. One of the sticks was carved in the shape of a cross.

"What the hell is this place?" Jenae said, and her voice came back to her heavily. She bit her lip.

"Old water treatment plant," Keila said. "Now a church, I guess you'd say. There. Go up and to your right."

Jenae saw the broken flight of steps with its corroded railing and pulled herself up with one hand, the other clutching the handle of the can. Keila followed, silent and fast for all her bulk. A scratched blue door was set in the wall. This, too, had been painted over with bright, swirling symbols, and at eye level, words were lettered with an almost cheerful flair: SUICIDE HOUSE. Keila aimed another meaningful kick at this door, and it swung open into darkness. A narrow automatic rifle barrel slid out and stopped a few inches from Keila's chest.

"Put it down right there, in the threshold," said a thin, grainy voice. From her vantage slightly behind Keila's left shoulder, Jenae could make out little more than the size and shape of the man: small and thin, more or less white, with grey hair. She couldn't see his face well in the dimness.

"Go on, beast! Put it down as I say!" The barrel shook. Hastily and without forethought, Jenae ducked under Keila's arm and deposited the can, edging back toward the railing. Keila fixed her with the expression she'd come to recognize as a One-Eyed scowl.

"What's this? Kidnapping my people, are you? Eh? Give over the girl, goddammit. Let her go, I say, you fucking monster. Leave your tribute and be gone from this place!"

He sounds like a medieval monk warding off spirits, Jenae thought.

"She's free to go where she wants to," said Keila.

"Come on, girl," said the man. He came forward so that his face showed in the light now: it was scarred and pitted, maybe fifty years' worth. There was a wet sore beneath his left eye. It looked to be the kind that never heal. "You're among the pure and the righteous, here. You'll have no abuse with us."

Jenae said casually, "It's okay, I'm level. No problems here."

"There will be if you go consorting with monsters. Didn't your parents teach you anything about right and wrong in this world?"

"My parents are dead."

Keila chose this dramatic moment to upend the canvas sack in the doorway. Jenae had half expected it to contain weapons or explosives or maybe drugs, at least, but it was only a selection of the basic food staples she had seen in the warehouse of the red forest. The human didn't lower the rifle, but kicked the boxes and bags inside with his foot, his eyes never leaving Keila's face.

"Now listen to me, you devil-worshiping One-Eyed bully. Give over the girl or I'll blow a hole in your chest the size of that fucking eye of yours." He nodded to Jenae. "Don't be afraid of them," he said. "You've got to show them who's boss. They have no minds of their own. Come on, will you? Step inside before more of them come."

"Why do you hate this woman so much?" Jenae heard herself say. "She brings you food. She offers you no violence."

"Aw, shit," answered the man. " 'She' brings me food! It's its fucking duty to bring me food. I tell it to bring it, it brings it. Today it brought me you, but for some reason it's not being so cooperative. Kindly just step around the creature and come inside, and I will get rid of this thing and then you and me can talk."

Jenae glanced at Keila to see how she was taking this. She kept expecting some sudden, pent-up release of anger, but the One Eye remained completely impassive. She had folded the canvas bag into a neat square and tucked it under her arm. Her weapon, a wicked little shock pistol, remained under her belt at the small of her back. She looked perfectly relaxed.

Other voices were stirring from inside the building, evidently just now taking notice of the exchange of words.

"Let's go, Keila," Jenae said. "I don't want to start a fight here."

"What?" cried the rifle man as they turned and picked their way down the steps. He actually poked his head halfway out the door after them. "What kind of drugs have you been using? Do you want to be lunch for the One Eyes tomorrow? Come back while you still can. We'll give you a good death, a fair death. You control everything. Quick and clean, with ceremony afterward. Burial in the actual earth— no burning. Don't tell me you can do better than that!"

He was still calling after her as she reached the bottom of the stairs, but he didn't follow. Jenae gave a sarcastic little wave in parting, but Keila had suddenly begun to move quickly.

"What is it?" Jenae gasped, slipping on the wet stone as she tried to keep up. Keila rounded the corner of the building at a lope and called back, "The jeep. They're going to try and nick the jeep. I knew it was too quiet."

They pelted to the front of the building, where Keila stopped short and Jenae almost plowed into her. There were two teenagers messing around under the hood of the vehicle. Their curses and the clang of their tools told the story of their incompetence instantly, and Keila began to laugh. She covered the distance to the jeep in several long strides, whereupon she grabbed each youth by the back of the collar and plucked them both off the engine.

A girl and a boy, clad in patched coveralls and tinted goggles, were dumped unceremoniously into the dust. Keila glanced under the hood, snorted again in that derisive way she had, and replaced one or two fluid caps. Then she slammed the hood down and got in the car, entered the starter code, and smiled at the two kids as they scrambled to their feet. Keila, Jenae thought, really did look remarkably ugly when she smiled.

"Nice try," Keila called out to the kids. "Unfortunately for you, not even close. Want to live? Thinking about maybe not committing suicide? Well, you'd better start thinking like fighters, not victims. Take some advice from a monster."

She threw the car in reverse and backed away in a swirl of dust. Jenae belatedly jumped in.

Jenae had a thousand questions, but Keila said nothing for a long time, and Jenae hesitated. Finally she said, "Just tell me why you help them. Why do you let that nasty little man call you his servant and point a gun at you?"

"They believe I am a monster. They are members of the Coalition for Pure Human Progress, and they see the Gene Wars as a temporary setback to their goal of pure human domination of the known universe." Keila chuckled. "This particular sect would rather lose their lives than submit to the circumstances of living on a rez. It sounds odd, but I find this group fascinating. They live up here waiting for malcontents to come up and do suicide ceremonies. I find myself wanting to keep them alive, maybe as a perverse way of keeping them from getting the satisfaction they want by checking out. Who knows? Maybe I'm just soft on them."

"You can't be serious. You were so brutal to your own people the other night, yet you treat these recidivist scum like naughty children."

Keila seemed to struggle with the words. "It's not divided up the way you think it is, Jenae. The world. When you are a One Eye, your work is the first thing you have—your work and the duty that comes with it. Love and hate do not enter into it.

"We are a fluke species, you know. Our traits were not bred into us for generations of natural selection—nor were they designed, like altermode. We simply survived the Gene Wars, and here we are. We don't struggle with absolutes or opposites. We deal with what is, in the most simple physical terms possible—which is not very simple these days, incidentally."

"You don't care that they hate you? That they would destroy you if they could?"

"They're dying, Jenae. Their civilization has committed terrible crimes, for which human morality would say all humans deserve to die. Does that mean I must be the one to deal out a form of justice that they invented themselves? No, I will help them while I can, because it is part of the duty I was born with: take care of the world and its creatures. Their insults mean no more than the buzzing of flies on the dead. The dead are still dead, and there are still flies. They are ugly parasites, but it's not for me to destroy them." She turned her head and gazed at Jenae with that single, disconcerting eye. "I have worked all my life to support you, too. Yet the first time you saw me you thought I was the devil. Is it so very different?"

"This is why you wanted me to come here before I go back to Yi Ling?" Jenae asked, trying to make sense of the One Eye's motives.

The moment of contact was broken. Keila looked back at the road before her.

"No. You don't understand. There are some things that can't be spoken. They just have to be felt."

The Lywyn

16

Tsering dreamed of her mother's distortion. The dream was very old, and sometimes only a few seconds long, a handful of fractured impressions—but it never lost its potency. It was hard to believe that seventy-odd years had gone by since she'd huddled quaking in the mud, her dress pulled up over her naked back and stuffed into her ears to block the shattering cries coming from her mother's mouth. Now the dream was more vivid than any conscious memory. Tsering went rigid in her sleep: she saw again her mother's long, dark face drained of blood, her mouth yawning open exposing the bleak throat. She saw the knife curving up in the taut hand. Her mother came toward her, lips pulled back now in a dazzling wolf grin. Somehow, even in the dream, Tsering knew the knife was intended to cleanse. Her mother meant to remove her, an abomination, before she could breed more of their kind. The grimace on her mother's face was one of concentration, but it only terrified Tsering more, and she thrust her face into the ground until the dark, stinking mud filled her nostrils.

Usually Tsering woke up while the knife was still poised above her. She seldom stayed in the dream long enough to relive the memory of her own rescue by the kids, their hands snatching her away from the danger, covering her red and desperate eyes. She never dreamed of the last image of her mother, glimpsed from between the sheltering fingers of one of the other females: a long, helpless semihuman body writhing on the lakeshore, gills like green wounds crossing its bulging neck and gasping chest. And no, fortunately, she never dreamed the sight of the real red slices her mother inflicted on herself with the knife as she lay flopping in the shallows. In the throes of distortion she had slashed herself until her hand could no longer hold the knife, until she turned with cold uncomprehending eyes to disappear into the still lake, and her blood clouded the shallows.

Instead of seeing all this Tsering usually woke shuddering to relief. Usually. But this time, while she crouched waiting for the knife to come down, the dream parted from memory and took a new direction. This time her mother abruptly fell silent. In the dream Tsering didn't move, still anticipating the knife's blow. She heard her mother's voice, not the harsh rasp brought by distortion, but a soft low sound that had once put her to sleep.

Her mother said, "Give it to me."

There was a snap of pain in Tsering's belly and a strange pressure between her legs. She heard the thin, animal sound of a baby squalling in the mud beneath her and again her mother said, "Give it to me. It must be done quickly."

Now Tsering looked up into her mother's face, barely recognizable with its pallor and its enormous, swollen pores. The eerie light eyes met hers and the smooth familiar voice beckoned her. Tsering fumbled beneath herself, feeling for the warm new body of her child, but her fingers only sank into the mud. The baby cried out again.

"Mother. Mother!"

It was a young male voice. Someone was holding her and she struck out with her hands. The baby screamed. She opened her eyes to Naro's silhouette backing away from her bed. In the morning light she saw Rena in the doorway, holding Til in her arms. The two-year-old was shrieking in high-pitched rage.

Naro said matter-of-factly, "She wants you."

Tsering passed a hand across her eyes and gave a shaky laugh. "Actually, she wants her mother," Tsering said, "and

I don't blame her." She rolled to her feet and took the child from Rena. The infant was hot, soiled, and incensed.

"Go back to sleep," Tsering muttered at the others. "I'll take her outside."

Ever since the night of Jordan's distortion, Til had not been sleeping properly with her regular "family" of older children, so Tsering had brought her into her own house. It had only been four months since the distortion of Til's own mother—too soon, Tsering thought, for the infant to be subjected to a second disturbance. Thankfully, the child had not been much traumatized by the actual event of her mother's distortion; but then again, they had all felt Aristotle's death deeply, and at two, Til was especially sensitive.

"I ought to bring you to Seika," Tsering whispered to the child as she changed her. "She needs someone to take care of." When she was finished she rolled up the used diaper and set it outside the door to be washed. She had no desire to go back to sleep, and Til, too, was wide awake. The infant bobbled away from the house, hands outstretched for balance as she worked her way barefoot over roots and stones. Tsering followed idly, watching and thinking about Aristotle and Seika and Jordan.

Tsering hadn't had the heart to make Seika return to High. That, too, was breaking the rules—but they were rules that she herself had made. Anyway, she needed someone older to talk to, someone who might be able to understand the strange things that were happening, problems she couldn't burden the children with. Problems having to do, at least in part, with the Earth stranger. Daire.

She had only walked a stone's throw from the house when she saw him, sleeping on the open ground with a canopy of gold and white insects draped over his body. She stopped and Til, just ahead, spontaneously fell over and began to squall again; Daire sat up, shaking off the insects in a series of alarmed tremors. His face always looked as though it were partly sleeping, the long curves of his bones holding his flesh still while his eyes wandered in reflection. Now the distinct, hooked nose and heavy brows hid his eyes as he blinked in the daylight that flowed through the lywyn leaf haze.

"What's going on?" he said hoarsely. Like her, apparently

he had been deeply asleep. Why did people not meet in sleep? Tsering wondered. When you could talk to ghosts, you should be able to talk to other dreamers, in that part of the world where stories did not have to make sense and anything could be said without fear of misunderstanding. But her dreams were part of her own private hell, and his . . . she had not asked him about his dreams. It seemed safer to keep distance between them.

He dreams of home, she thought. Earth, from which we are exiled. What has it become, after all this time?

She said, "Til doesn't understand that she can wake you up. She's just crying for the joy of it."

He was rubbing his neck and shoulders as he came to life, and he eyed her through a squint of discomfort. She set Til upright, and the child bumbled toward Daire, a look of surprise on her still-wet face, as though she had suddenly forgotten what she had been crying about.

"I'm not used to sleeping rough," he said, shivering.

"You're fortunate," she answered. "The anki alight on you. This is good luck."

"Do you mean those weird bugs? I can't get rid of them." He held out a hand to Til and the child went straight to him, depositing herself in his lap and beating on his knee with her fists.

"They won't harm you. They only want to trade dreams with you."

He snorted. "Is that true? Well, I don't know if I like the dreams they're giving me. All this uninterpretable stuff is coming to me out of context. I've got to have a way to decipher it."

"All my life I've lived with the lywyn and its creatures. I have never deciphered anything. Sometimes it seems to me that I am just part of a dream that the lywyn is cycling through, again and again. Nothing really changes." Except for the dream last night, she thought. And except for the bleeding, the swelling of her belly and breasts after all this time.

She realized she had been abstracted when Daire got unsteadily to his feet, laughter in his eyes. He clapped his hands as if to wake her up, or maybe to invoke magic.

"Today, Tsering," he said. Til gave a squeak of outrage

when he abandoned her; then she ran to Tsering. "I'm going today, whether you approve or not. I'm going inside *Morpheus* and find out all I can. Time slips by me, in this place, and your cryptic little speeches are doing nothing to enlighten me."

"I can't stop you. The children no longer fear you." She tried to be light, but her words sounded accusing. "The next thing and they will follow you instead of me."

"You know I don't want your job," he said wryly. "But why don't you come with me? You can't expect me to believe you're not curious."

"I've been there. I got my education from that ship. I know it inside and out. It's all that is left of Earth, for me."

"Ah, but you didn't have me with you then. And I intend to find out why your people were sent here *on purpose*. For it does raise the very interesting question: What happened to the Ingenix people who were supposed to be on the ship? I also intend to find out what just happened to Jordan. No, don't start with curses and fate and all that. I want to know what's in your DNA that makes you people different."

"You make it sound like a game."

"It's an intellectual puzzle. If I keep it that way, maybe I won't lose my mind. Maybe you've forgotten, but I'm very far from home. I never expected anything like this to happen."

She shifted her weight to one side, shaking her head skeptically. "For all that, Daire, you appear to be enjoying yourself. No, don't bother to deny it. You're scarcely behaving as though you're frightened."

"I don't scare too easily," he acknowledged. "People have remarked upon it my entire life. I hardly think it's an asset, though."

"Maybe not to you. But such a characteristic would be very useful to me."

"Really? Why?"

"Because what I do is all a confidence game. Kids are very perceptive, because they're honest. And they can sense your fear even before you can. Sense and exploit, that's what they do. So you need to project absolute confidence."

"Spoken like someone with real experience."

"More than you can imagine." She laughed. It was getting too easy to talk to Daire. How long had it been since she had really trusted someone? Since the distortion of her brother Runako, maybe. And he'd been gone more than seventy years. She sighed. "You make me forget how old I am."

"Thank you," Daire said, and Tsering had to smile.

"After I've gotten the kids working," she said, "I'll meet you by the ship. Don't go in without me."

◆

"The pieces are beginning to fall into place," Daire said aloud. The door in the hull of *Morpheus* yawned open, releasing a rush of bad air. The interior was dark, but immediately he noticed a faint murky glow emitted from the com panel. He peered at it from his vantage kneeling on the top of the ship.

"It's transmitting," he observed.

"Yes. A distress call. It's on very low power, though. I wanted to save the energy for emergency use—but I couldn't quite bring myself to turn it off." Tsering shifted her position to avoid the stale air, but Daire ignored it and climbed down inside the ship. After a minute he called up to her.

"Well, it got through. This is the signal we were picking up—at least part of it, the identifier. But something else is going on with it. Colin didn't pick it up off the com system. It invaded the ship's computer code, and it was heavily draped in other signals. Something must be processing it in some way. . . ." He glanced around, trying to orient himself in the dim, listing chamber.

"It's strange to think of them," Tsering mused. "My parents, themselves kids, hurtling through space in this thing. And now here sits *Morpheus*, in a swamp."

"We need to talk about that, you know," Daire said. He glanced up at her, wondering if she would resist, for he meant to make her speak about her parents.

She was silent for a while; finally, she said, "The bodies of the distorted wash up on shore from time to time. I used to dissect them. They're rather . . . different. After distortion they must go on changing for a while, because they have completely altered respiratory systems, and some other organs have changed as well. Think of the energy needed to effect such a metamorphosis. I wonder *why* . . ."

Daire was surprised because her tone was reflective but unemotional. "What do you know about Earth history?" he asked.

"Only what was in the disks given to my ancestors when they left."

"Yes, but what was that? Was there anything about the Gene Wars?"

"Are you talking about the Ingenix scandals? The experiments? Of course. But only from the computer, what archives were there. I never learned anything from my parents, if that's what you're driving at. I was too young."

"But you suspect they were subjects in Ingenix experiments."

"Suspect! I know." She swung her legs back and forth in the hatch. She seemed bored, and he became irritated.

"If only you'd said so! I knew they were fugitives, but until I saw Jordan distort, I thought they were the *leaders* of Ingenix fleeing extradition. You let me go on thinking that."

Tsering bristled. "How was I to know what you were thinking? Why would the leaders of Ingenix come here—and why would they be cursed with distortion if they knew so much?"

"Your parents," Daire said suddenly, looking up at her. "Do they have ghosts?"

Her profile was blank. "Why do you want to know?"

"I'd like to speak to them."

"That won't be possible." Her throat tightened visibly.

"Are you sure?" He climbed back up, turning on the ladder so that his face was on a level with hers where she sat with her legs dangling into the hatch.

"I . . . Daire, you have no idea. I don't . . . invite the ghosts of my parents, especially my mother. If you think Jordan's distortion was bad, you can't even imagine what it was like when my mother went. Everything—" She cut herself off, shading her eyes with her hand and turning away.

"What? Everything what?"

"Everything I've done in my life, my mother would have hated. She believed we were destined to die out as a species. She didn't want the suffering to be prolonged. She really believed"—Tsering paused, swallowing—"we weren't meant to be."

Daire shook his head. "Everything you said to me about nature: 'nothing is unnatural,' you remember you said that? All of that is your own philosophy, isn't it? But your mother would not have approved."

Tsering laughed. "That's putting it mildly. Oh, don't get me wrong. She wanted to live! She and the others would never have survived what they'd been through without the will to go on. But she was the first generation of our kind, and it was hard on all of them when they realized what was happening to them. She came to feel that we were all 'unnatural' as you put it, and therefore should not procreate and persist. Which we wouldn't have."

"Except for you."

"I really don't think they would have made it if I had grown up properly. I'd have had children and distorted, just like everyone, and there would have been no organization. No one to care for the orphans. No one to protect the babies from their parents at that point of cannibalism. We lost a lot of children in those first years, but I began to learn the signs. I found ways to teach the kids to survive, and I made the lessents go live at High so I could protect the majority of the kids when their parents distorted. I know it's a form of ostracism, but it's necessary."

She was looking at him searchingly now. Was she actually seeking his approval for something she felt was wrong?

"I understand," he said. "You did what you had to."

She shook her head. "Only now . . . ! Now I'm going to have to live by my own rules, and I don't know if I can."

"What do you mean? What rules?"

Straightening her shoulders, she looked directly at him.

"I guess I have to tell you this. Daire, the first day you came, something happened to me. It's never happened before, and it can only mean one thing." She was just staring at him; it was a challenging stare, very nearly accusing, and he wondered what he could have done to her on that first, dazed day.

"I don't get it."

"Menstruation. My body has entered its reproductive phase. Don't ask me how." Unreasoningly embarrassed at this disclosure, he glanced up only at the last second, reaching out to support her with alarm: she looked like she was about to fall into the hatch. His memory flashed back to an image from that first day, of Tsering clutching her abdomen in pain and fear. But now, as then, she retreated. She shrank away from his hand.

"It's all right," she said. "Really. I'm just going to have to do some fast thinking, that's all."

"Well, you ought to have some time. If distortion occurs at the end of adolescence, then you ought to have years to take action."

"I don't know. How can I predict anything? I don't understand how it happened. For all I know, I could distort tomorrow."

"I don't recommend thinking that way. I'd rather be optimistic. This ship is surprisingly intact, for one thing. And we've got the lywyn holding all kinds of useful memories, for another. I'm going to have to insist that you call up the ghost of your mother. She will remember the details of events on Earth before *Morpheus* left."

Tsering looked weak. He seized her hand.

"Trust me," he urged. "You won't be disappointed."

Then he backed down the ladder, abruptly fired up for action as he had not been since his arrival. For the first time since the fall into the Underkohling gate, he felt fully awake. Even Jordan's distortion had been dreamlike; but now he was going to start getting things done. For the first time he felt like he knew where he stood, and in his mind he began to form objectives. He sat down at the main systems desk and began increasing the power outlay.

"Ah, good," he called over his shoulder. "You've been using your solar cells. You'll be pleased to hear that the reserve power is in good shape. We've got juice to work with here."

She didn't answer, and he kept working. A few minutes later, when he turned to say something to her about the archives, she was gone.

17

What can you do, thought Tsering, when your life is just beginning and you see the end of it in that same moment? What kind of strange luck soup is it that brings you salvation and destruction in the same pair of hands, the same eyes, the same voice?

I have been alone, she thought, since Runako left me. I've been a surrogate parent to hundreds of children and I've had not one breath of hope for a moment. I've trained myself not to think about the future. And the day that he arrives bringing a new life is the day that marks the beginning of the end for me. It seems too cruel. He comes up out of the lake like a sleepwalker, his clothes dry, his hair dry; he walks into being exactly like a ghost. Then he trips in the shallows and suddenly he's a solid human in the water of our lake, and I must see that time has been moving on for Earth and everyone there, while I've been living in a nightmare world. *Morpheus*, indeed. The god of dreams. What kind of dreams have these been? Daire arrives, and as if on cue, before I can begin to understand what is happening here, I begin to bleed. Nothing I do now can matter, because it's over.

I have watched matings and births and partings for three generations. Now I am faced with my own distortion and I'm ready to panic.

I've never been angry like this before. Never until now.

I don't want to die.

◆

Seika looked up warily at Tsering when she emerged from the lywyn. The lessent had been washing vegetables and feeding bits to Til, who gnawed with great concentration on anything that was handed to her; she was teething. But Seika hunched her shoulders a little when Tsering came, and her hands seemed to hurry. The bleak look in Seika's eyes had not escaped Tsering's notice, and in her heart she knew she was wrong to allow Seika to stay at Lake. The sooner the girl returned to High, the better. She could become pregnant again, and the distress of losing Aristotle and Jordan together might lift a little. But so far the girl had shown no desire to return to High.

Tsering sat down and picked up a handful of greens, scrubbing them in the bucket of water by Seika's feet. She wanted to be direct, but found herself groping for words.

"I'm not very good at creating rituals, or I would have tried to make one for grief. With the little ones, I find it's best to let life go on as before, and eventually they forget."

"Yes, I remember." Such a small, trembling voice. "You always said there was too much work to do for us to dwell on it."

Tsering grimaced. "I told myself I was protecting you all. Now I'm not so sure."

There was a long silence. At last Seika offered: "At High we have a ritual for distortion. When someone is about to distort, we keep a vigil on the cliff. All of us in a circle, and the distorting one in the middle. At the proper time, we carry the distorting one down the cliff and when it is ready we help it into the water. Sometimes they come to meet us."

"They?" Tsering's hands stopped moving.

"The others. The distorted ones. We see them moving in the water the odd time. We hear them crying out, sometimes—or so they tell me. I have only witnessed two distortions since I went to High. Not including . . . you know."

"I never knew that you had this ritual."

A little smile touched Seika's face. "No one thought you would approve."

"Well, you'd be right about that. It sounds dangerous."

"If the person is prepared, he or she usually goes quietly. As long as there are no children present, of course. We make them begin the vigil on the cliff at least a day before the distortion starts, and the babies are always guarded. By the time they are really changing, they're at the bottom of the cliff and craving the sea too much to turn back. The truth is I never really believed what you taught us about cannibalism, until I saw what happened to Jordan."

Tsering let out a sigh. "You can't know how sorry I am, Seika. I was experimenting with the status quo. I should have left well enough alone."

Seika blotted her eyes with her sleeve, sniffed, and handed Til a piece of trileve root. "It wouldn't have mattered. There are always babies at High, and Jordan would have found a way, I guess. Keeping lessents separated from kids doesn't always help. The babies are the most vulnerable ones, and they have to stay with their mothers."

Seika was voicing the very issue that had plagued Tsering since she realized she was aging: who would take care of the kids when Tsering could no longer do so? How could the colony survive unless lessents mingled with and raised their own kids, and in that case, how would the kids be protected from the cannibal instinct at distortion?

"As a matter of fact, I've been thinking about that," Tsering ventured. "Maybe the two separate settlements is not the only way to do things. What do you think?"

"Since when," said Seika in a neutral voice, "does my opinion mean anything to you?"

It was a light blow, not intended to harm; but Tsering was taken aback. She had grown to expect hostility from the likes of Michelle, but Seika had always been such a quiet, thoughtful girl.

"It's a time of change for us," she replied carefully. "Because of Daire coming here, but also for other reasons. Come. I'm not some tyrant. Say what you think."

"You don't know what it's like," said Seika in a low voice. "Jordan was scared. We're all scared most of the time. You worry so much about protecting the kids from the trauma of distortion, but kids don't really take things in. They only accept what they can handle and forget the parts they don't understand. But *we* know what distortion means. When we cut the nets, we *know* it will be us next time, or the time after."

"That is something I can't help you with." Tsering was speaking half to herself. "I have never been there." She pulled Til in to her lap and hugged the infant. Time would tell.

"Don't cast us away!" Seika cried, flinging down her knife and startling Tsering back to the present. "You want to, don't you? But don't do it. You say you come to High to see us, but we know you fear us. You wouldn't come at all if you weren't concerned about the babies. You love *them*. But we *were* those babies, Tsering! You raised us, then you turned your back on us."

"Would you rather be extinct?" Tsering flared, and Til struggled to get up. Tsering released her, continuing, "Would you rather you were never born? I'm sorry for your trauma, but at least you're alive!"

Instantly she regretted her outburst. Seika's feelings were legitimate, and Tsering had asked her to share them. But Tsering's own emotions were all too ragged, these days. The irony bit hard. Seika could not yet know that Tsering, too, would soon face exile and distortion, now that she was menstruating. Tsering told herself that she kept silent on the subject because if the lessents knew, all hell would break loose and the confusion would do no one good. It had been hard enough to confess to Daire. She told herself that fear did not play a part; her decision to defy the colony's law was based strictly on the greater order.

A silence had fallen.

"I wish we were human," Seika said in a broken voice. "Like Daire. I wish we were like him. You want to pretend we are, but we're not. We never can be. You can isolate us, but you can't change what we are."

Tsering rubbed her forehead. "Okay. I get it. I hear you. If only you knew how well! But that doesn't mean I know what to do."

Seika reached out and seized her hand. "Don't send me back yet! Please, I won't do any harm here. Just give me a little more time. A month, two months . . ."

The girl's eyes pleaded; how could Tsering refuse when she herself ought to pack up and go to High? She nodded slowly, and Seika lightened so abruptly that Tsering wondered if she'd been manipulated.

"Now," she began in a brisk tone. "I have a request of you."

"Anything! Whatever you say."

"Daire has asked to be shown what the lywyn does, and I thought we might all take the lywyn water together. Some of the kids have never seen the ghosts, and I think they should. I want you to start getting them organized for a lywyn ceremony, tonight. Keep supper light. Put them in groups with a leader for each group."

"What about this little one?" Seika gestured toward Til. "Shall I stay behind with her?"

"You don't want to be there? You really don't want to learn?"

Seika looked into her eyes. "Please don't ask me to. I'm not ready to see the ghosts."

"Then stay with Til. I'll rely on you to be here when the kids return, then. I may need more time."

"With Daire?"

"Yes. With Daire." She stood up, assessing the girl's behavior. Was that a smirk Seika was trying to hide?

"Okay. You can count on me." Seika turned her face up to Tsering, the picture of responsibility, and Tsering turned away, weary of trying to make decisions about matters so far from her own ken. She headed for the solace of the forest, climbing up and away from the sight and sound of the settlement.

The lywyn was the only being in the world that Tsering really trusted. From infancy she had learned to fear adults of her own kind, and her study of history had shown her that the world her parents had left behind was only more complex in its cruelty. She could hardly look to the stars for comfort in times of trouble: they reminded her of the emptiness that echoed inside whenever she sought after the past. The sky above was a map of some region of space far from Earth, and kindled at night the lights showed how lost she and her people were.

The children she protected had given her warmth and devotion—but again there could be no question of trust when they would only leave her in the end, turning into creatures other than themselves and leaving behind only ghosts. The process was a biological imperative, and didn't even seem to horrify them despite the destruction it often wrought. The adolescents were openly defiant of her restrictions on their freedom, and there had been times in the past when they'd tried to rise up against her. Today Seika had subtly reminded her to place no one at her back. Tsering was alone, and that could not change.

But this curious forest had bestowed on her more than any one person could give. It had its own way of speaking, if one learned to listen. And it had powers that Tsering had brushed against uncertainly many times over the years. There was the question of her own long survival: that she attributed to the lywyn, although she couldn't prove it. Daire had spoken of a message received from the other side of the gate; Tsering would wager that the lywyn had done something with that as well. And now this change in her had to be traced back to the same place. If there was understanding to be found anywhere, it was here in the asymmetry of these twisted branches that she must search. Here in the source of lightning. Here where the trees kept safe the memories of her entire tribe.

The lywyn was wreathed in light mist, and its insects had retreated to the higher branches. Tsering climbed the old familiar paths, where her own hands and feet had in places shaped the wood. Her fingers felt cold with fear of seeing her mother's ghost after so many years. If she drank the lywyn water she might feel the oneness that was a kind of ecstasy, but she might also find herself screaming into the emptiness.

The emptiness that lay at the edge of time, an unseen presence, poised to swallow. How would Daire react? He was human. Would the lywyn show him the same darkness, or some other memory—or would he be unaffected? She thought: If he is unaffected, he'll never understand us. He will remain apart.

18

Daire was inexplicably nervous as he stood braced high in the lywyn, waiting for the ghosts to come. He *had* been half in a dream, those first few days, but now the impending apparition of these . . . remnants . . . of people had him off balance. He kept thinking about the first day he'd spent alone in the lywyn, and the ghosts he'd seen then. Why had those particular people appeared to him? As Tsering had said, he had no connection with any of them. Were the manifestations just random events? Somehow it was hard to believe Runako had been random. Did, then, these "ghosts" have wills of their own?

"I don't know how to explain it except to say that they manifest themselves when and where they want to," Tsering had told him earlier this evening, "whether or not you drink the lywyn. But when you have taken the lywyn water, you get more than ghosts visiting you. You enter a state where it is possible to experience memories that you, personally, have never lived through. You go back in time."

"Race memory? I wonder how it works," Daire had mused. "Is it limited to the time spent here, or do you remember your distant ancestors on Earth?"

"Back before a certain point—before my parents' generation—you look back and you come to a vacuum. There's nothing."

"Probably because the lywyn wasn't recording anything before that time."

"What do you mean, 'recording'?"

"Well, my best guess is that the lywyn is some kind of data bank. If, as you say, the memories of your people 'live' on after they are dead or distorted, then the lywyn is sort of reconstructing their personalities based on the memories it somehow retrieves from them. So it's not really 'race memory,' but more like a town record of all the people who have ever lived here. But the lywyn recorded nothing of your parents' parents' lives on Earth, so there would be no information if you began to go back beyond your parents' memories."

"You make it sound fairly technical. Like a computer. That's not what it feels like, though, I assure you."

"Possibly I'm wrong. Computers are what I understand—software, I mean, so I tend to think in those terms. But let's test my hypothesis. If *I* take the lywyn, I should only see the ghosts of your people. I don't see how I could experience, for example, my grandparents' lives. The lywyn doesn't know them."

This was what he had said a few hours ago, sipping the meager bowl of soup that was all Tsering would allow before the ceremony, as she called it. Now, waiting, he felt less confident that he would be able to objectify everything that would happen here tonight. It seemed that whenever he was in the lywyn for any length of time, his mind went soft.

"Come on, Daire." Tsering's voice startled him out of his reverie. The forest had become darker while he was daydreaming. "Let's go up and call the kids."

"Call the kids? Where are they?"

"They're scattered around the area. I can stay in touch with all of them through the lywyn; it's a skill I've picked up. I'll use the reflecting pools to maintain contact. When they take the lywyn fluid, they can see the ghosts of their relatives and experience their memories, back to a certain point. It's a quick way of educating them. They acquire a lot of tacit knowledge that way, even if they don't remember it all the next morning."

"So you're going to 'call' them. The way Rena did the first morning I was here?"

"Exactly."

"I'd like to know how that works. I thought it was magic."

"I don't know if I can explain, but I can show you."

She led him farther up into the lywyn and along a winding path of branches until they reached a major junction at a stem. Daire remembered his initial explorations, and the pool of clear liquid he had found lying in the hollow of just such a place. This was almost the same. Tsering climbed nimbly up into the bowl and sat on its edge. He followed, perching more awkwardly. The lywyn swayed a little and the liquid shook.

"This is a reflecting point," she said. "There are many of them. If I speak into this"—the liquid quivered—"it transmits across the lywyn." Her words came back to him from the very air and in virtually all directions. There was a slight delay on the sound. He found himself grinning.

"An organic communications system. This could be very useful." That came back, too, and he felt himself flush. He eased himself away from the pool.

Tsering spoke softly. "That day when you first found *Morpheus*, I was near the lake with a fishing party. I saw you from a distance, and I sent a child to speak to you through the lywyn, to distract you until I got there with the rest of my group. You looked very surprised!"

Her face was mischievous—a refreshing change, Daire thought, from her usual seriousness. The smile was infectious.

"Everything that has happened since I've come here has been one continuous surprise," he informed her.

"I haven't exactly planned any of this, myself," she answered.

They looked at each other.

Daire drew breath, and then stopped himself from speaking.

"What is it?"

"I wish you were ... I was going to say 'older' but I guess I don't mean that."

"I hope not. If I were any older, I'd be dead." She bent over and directed her voice into the pool. "We're going to start in a minute. Is everybody ready? Adamo's group?"

"Ready."

"Nkem's group?"

"*Ready.*"

"Beni's group?"

"Ready."

"Anybody else out there?"

"I'm here, Tsering."

"Rena, go with Nkem's group, please. You're keeping us waiting."

She glanced at Daire and winked.

"I can't believe they're so well organized," he said.

"Oh, they're good at that. They have to be."

"We're all ready, Tsering."

Tsering dipped her fingers into the lywyn and brought them to her mouth. She shuddered for a second.

"Okay. Senior member of each group, monitor the dosage. One or two drops should be plenty, Adamo. Don't overdo it."

Daire watched her face. She seemed to be listening to something he couldn't hear.

"How do you know what they're doing?" he whispered.

"I've used the lywyn many times. You acquire a mastery of it, after a while. Here."

She reached in again, brought out a hand shining silvery in the diffuse forest light, and beckoned to him. Daire leaned forward and she dripped the clear fluid onto his lips.

"Don't expect anything to happen right away," she said.

It tasted just as it had the first time, but now there was enough of the fluid to fill his mouth with the cool, electric sensation.

"I'm not giving you very much," she added, "because I don't want you to participate yet. I just want you to get warmed up. When the kids have had their visions and gone to sleep, then we'll see. For now, just sit back and watch."

At first nothing changed. Then, on the periphery of his vision, Daire saw tiny, fuzzy scribbles of bluish light dancing just outside of view. He kept turning his head to try to catch sight of them, but he always missed. He looked at Tsering, bent over the pool with a look of intense concentration on her face. She didn't seem to notice the fuzz.

After a while, the light became faintly visible along the outer edges of the lywyn branches. It looked like fine, bright strands of hair standing up in a static field, but when he reached out his hand, he touched nothing. In the distance, a fork of lightning cleaved the darkness with a searing sound. Thunderless. He felt the hair on his forearms stand up.

Lightning flashed again, several times in rapid succession, and Daire saw the entire lywyn light up like a great maze of shadows. He glimpsed faces at another junction in the lywyn above them: children, perched just as they were. Their eyes flashed white against their dark faces.

Tsering's voice filled the air. "All of you are going to focus on your father first. See your father. Go into your father's mind and take what he has to give you."

Daire had been thinking of himself as an objective observer, but when her voice came into his ears just as if it had been breathed there, as if it spoke to him alone, he found himself drawn into the ceremony.

He didn't see his father, but he felt his own body thicken around him. The weight of his face dragged down his brows; he was scowling. He flexed his quadriceps and felt them respond in a dense, strong contraction. His sense of balance was off, and abruptly he felt uncomfortable on the height. He inched closer to the stem of the lywyn tree.

". . . and now your father's father . . ." said the voice, and his body answered by elongating and lightening. He closed one eye and watched the shape of his nose change. It became shorter and flatter, and he could feel his nostrils spreading. More flashes of lightning stunned his eyes; when he looked at his own hands they were shaped differently. The generous sprawl of his palms was reduced: his hands looked neater and more precise.

". . . stretch all the way back now. Let's see how far you can go. Monitors, take care now. We don't want any unnecessary tears, please."

Daire looked over at Tsering. Her back was toward him, all her attention focused on the pool of wan fluid in the deep cavern of wood. He started to move his lips to call out to her, but after a moment he lost track of his lips altogether.

He had the sensation of moving. The tree beneath him fell away in a silky yielding, floating him into grass that made a burning sound as he passed through it. He was running, very fast. The touch of the slender blades against his bare feet was cool and brittle; grass slapped his legs, hissing. Behind him he could feel the sun's presence like a brother, guarding his back. His own shadow leapt and rippled ahead of him. He seemed to be smaller than he knew himself to be.

His mouth opened and closed around gulps of air, his lungs pushing past their peak and into the desperation zone. There was pain; yes, there in his belly a serpent of agony; and maybe it would kill him. Blood flowed freely down his chest from some fresh wound.

But there was no fear. Without fear, running, in pain. Dying.

"You're going where I can't go," the girl said. He recognized her voice but couldn't place it. He couldn't see her. "Follow it," she said.

He followed the pull, no longer running exactly; he experienced a moment of disorientation that was pierced first by the sensation of sunlight on his eyelids, then smell (warm, dank, rotting plant odor), then sensation. He was lying on his belly and he could feel his tail stroking the fallen leaves around him. His eyes were closed. A sudden burst of odor—deadly, something predatory—startled him and his body stiffened in fear.

Again, momentary acenesthesia; then he was in the water, squirming in the silt. Not a thought in his head, he swam backward in time until everything was deeper and darker than perception could fix in memory. Unlike the moments of disintegration in the gate, which remixed his consciousness viciously, this process seemed only to reduce his thought from a wild, syncopated music to a dull throb, to which awareness could not cling.

It felt like dreamless sleep, but waking from it he found himself frantically scrabbling at his own face, his head jerking spasmodically like that of an alarmed bird.

Tsering's hands were all mixed up with his own. She was trying to untangle his long hair from his wild fingers, and kept pushing it back behind his shoulders and sighing in frustration when it pulled free.

"Hold still," she said. "You're all right. Who would have imagined you'd go in so easily?" She pressed him back until he reclined against the broad bough of the lywyn; he could still feel that odd vibration in the wood.

"Shit," Daire said. "I thought that wasn't supposed to happen."

"What *did* happen, Daire? What did you experience?"

He tried to tell her, but all his words circled around the

experience and seemed to falsify it. "I wasn't myself," he finished at last. "I don't know what I was. I'd like to know the chemical composition of this substance."

Tsering laughed. "So it was not as quantifiable as you expected, yes?"

"I don't mean to sound pedantic. I just don't know what else to say."

"Were you afraid?"

"Actually, no."

"Like I said, I only gave you the smallest amount. I just wanted your eyes to be opened. I didn't think anything would really happen. Here. Lie back. Let me finish with the others."

To Daire's dismay, a band of curious children had assembled in the branches above and around him. They were whispering to each other.

"Is everybody here?" Tsering asked. She went around the group and hugged or kissed most of the children, a display of affection he hadn't witnessed until now. "Seika's waiting for you. Everybody get some hot soup before you go to sleep. And don't be bouncing around getting yourselves excited. You should rest beautifully after all these memories."

There was an air about the children that Daire discerned even from the midst of his own disarray: they seemed calmer, milder. Not drugged, exactly, but maybe a bit dazed. As he watched the light of their torches recede to a bright pin moving along the forest floor, Daire idly wondered what the physiological effects of this so-called lywyn water might be.

Tsering came back and balanced on her haunches on the broad branch beside him.

"Well, you were gone over an hour," she said. "You look beat to hell. Maybe this isn't the best time to call up such an old ghost."

Daire sat up straight. "Don't try to back out of it now!" he said. "I'm here to see the main event."

"All right. I just hope you aren't put off by her." His heightened awareness told Daire that despite her cool demeanor, Tsering was apprehensive. She sidled over to lean against the curving bole of the tree, the silver pool by her feet. "She may not come right away. My mother knows by now that I want no part of her." She glanced at Daire. "Do you think that's cruel of me?"

"Can you be cruel to someone who isn't there?" he countered, and then realized how defensive he sounded. How important it was to his sense of order that the ghosts be mere 'recordings'! He shook his head to clear it. His ears were ringing.

The light changed.

"Listen," said a familiar voice. Runako stood beside Tsering. He looked precisely as he had when Daire had seen him before. "This guy got you digging, don't he? Go ahead and dig, if you want. But be careful, sweet sister. I know this man. He is more serious than he appears to be. He's going to bring you troubles, I can see it."

"Runako," Tsering replied in a patronizing tone, "I don't need a gypsy fortune-teller. I want to speak with our mother."

Runako shrugged. "Feel free. I don't know where she is. You never talk to her. She as good as vanished."

"Of all people," Tsering told him, "I should have expected you to give me an argument. Find her!"

Laughing, Runako disappeared. Daire began to struggle to his feet, about to speak to Tsering, but she waved him back.

"Be patient," she said, obviously concentrating. "He's always like that. He likes to tease me." Now her voice was grim. "He'll get her. Don't worry. She'll come."

They waited. Lightning flashed in the depths of the lywyn, but Tsering didn't respond to it. The leaves made subtle sounds above. He felt sleepy.

Tsering stiffened. And there, on a branch nearby, stood a lovely, tall young woman. Her features were a mix of Asian and African influences, but the African prevailed. Her skin had the same dark, polished look that Runako's did. Her wide-set eyes and long, graceful physique gave her appearance an ethereal, almost angelic quality. Daire saw the realization in the mother of the premonition of beauty he had seen in the daughter, and as he watched them face each other he had the illusion, for a second, that he looked at two ghosts: the same person at two successive stages of development. Then the ghost of Tsering's mother spoke, and the illusion passed.

"Tsering, I thought you would never forgive me." The voice was pitched low, warm like wine.

Tsering didn't answer. Daire could almost see her thinking.

"Do you not forgive me?" prodded the ghost. "You always were a stubborn child. I suppose you're going to be having out all your accusations at me now. How wrong I was, yes?"

"I want to know about Earth," Tsering said. "Can you tell me about the circumstances that brought you here?"

"I was so young!" cried the ghost. "Can't you see that? I had you when I was sixteen. What could I know about anything?"

She was gesturing vehemently with her hands, her movements conveying a certain desperation that set Daire on edge. Tsering was standing very still, but even so he could see her shivering ever so slightly.

"Please. I'm not accusing you of anything. I just want to know more about my history." For the first time since he had known her, Tsering sounded plaintive.

The ghost said, "Maybe you are ready. You really want to know? Take the lywyn water, and I will bring you through the memories. Maybe then you'll understand me."

Daire looked at Tsering, whose face was drawn with anxiety. "What does she mean?"

"She wants me to use the lywyn water to experience her life."

Forgetting how sick he'd felt only a short while ago, Daire said, "Do it! I'd do it in a second."

"Would you?" said the ghost, fixing him with a challenging stare. "Are you sure?"

"He can't do it," Tsering said. "He's not one of us."

"He can if you do," countered the ghost. "He can ride along with you, if you have the courage to live what I have lived."

Again parent and child looked at each other. Almost imperceptibly, Tsering nodded. She bent, reached into the pool, and drew out lywyn fluid in her cupped palms. She didn't look at Daire, but he leaned forward anyway and mimicked her. They both drank at the same moment, and the memories of Tsering's mother flowed into them with the lywyn. . . .

◆

My first memory is sweet air, happy sun dancing on the waves, and the sound of complicated, melodic music just above the waves. I am bouncing on the hip of my mother and playing with the necklace of beads she wears around her neck. Loud boats somewhere, and men singing. There are only two other young children in our city. Only later do I learn that it is because of the illness that no one has become pregnant for three years. I am happy to be the only child because I get all the attention. My mother guards me fiercely, like a great treasure. But not fiercely enough . . .

Now it is night. I am seven years old, lying on my own little bedroll in our smelly building. We're squatters so there's no electricity but I'm allowed to listen to the battery radio until I fall asleep, and I've got it tuned to a pop station from Bali. My mother and aunt are out on the beach; it's a party. My mother says they are celebrating because the winds have shifted and the poison ash winds are gone. Tomorrow I will be allowed to go to the beach again. I'm excited and I lie awake breathing the clean breeze and thinking about tomorrow. A car pulls up outside, the engine still running. Then another engine, louder. I sit up; I want to see who's coming to visit us in a car. Men's voices. I don't know their language. My father's voice! I haven't seen him for weeks. Every time he comes he looks nervous, and last time my mother gave him some money to make him go away. He uses his key, comes inside, and I almost leap up and greet him, I missed him so much. But at the last second I lay still and pretend to be asleep. He picks me up, he's hurrying; something's not right here, and so I pretend to wake. His body feels like sticks under his loose, tattered clothes. He's running down the stairs in the dark. In my ear he says, "Shh. You want to take a ride, Djile? Look, a ride in the car."

I call for my mother and then I see them. Several men, a small car with broken windows, and a big van with no windows at all. There's no one else around except the regular drug pushers across the street outside the bar, because of the party at the beach. My father hushes me. "Hurry, hurry," he says. "Your mother will worry if you call her. It's all right, you'll be safe here."

All the time he is carrying me toward this van, and his voice is breaking. He's crying! I start to scream and he curses at the men who are standing there. "The car keys, the keys, you pieces of shriveled excrement!"

One of them holds out a set of shining keys and my father's fingers dig into me so hard I really begin to squirm. He snatches the keys. At first I think he's going to take me for a drive in the little car, but suddenly I realize something else is happening. I can hear my mother's voice from the beach and I draw breath to call her but my father's hand comes over my mouth. "It's better this way, it's safer this way," he keeps saying over and over. I'm crying because I know he's betraying me, but at the same time I want to look good in his eyes, I want to be brave, so I shut up.

He puts me in the van himself, and they shut the doors. It's nice in the van, but stuffy. There are cushions and some toys, like a playroom. Everything is new.

I have been sold for the price of a used car. . . .

I'm not alone for long. Now a long boat ride, sick, retching, as miserable as I have ever been. Now a place with many beds, lots of other children, bright colors and toys. You can smell all the fabric and the carpets and they smell strange, but nice. Everything is soft and enclosed. Everyone is my age and everyone is scared. I see a girl with a round face and a little nose and wide, black eyes. Her hair is so straight, I want to touch it, and she looks so tidy and petite and cleaner than the rest of us. She's playing with a very fast lightstick like I've never seen before, drawing pictures in the air. I go over to her and she says something I can't understand. I put my hand on my chest and say, "Djile," and she says, "Ha." Then she shows me the lightstick. She drew four brothers and her mother. The brothers are being taken away. Her mother is sitting in a chair doing nothing.

The tears are rolling down my cheeks, and Ha gives me the lightstick and I try to draw my family but I can't do it. I can't do it.

Adults come and give us tablets to take with our food. I swallow them meekly, not knowing I'm not going to remember any of this until years later. . . .

I am eight years old. I'm being measured, weighed, sampled, scraped, and surveyed in the tunnel of lights. I hate this but I know afterward there will be sweets, and the caretakers will spend extra time with us, and I will dance for them and make them clap. I want Laran to see me dance with his long green eyes and his soft voice. I like Laran, but he gets mad so easily, and all he wants to do is sneak into the computer and find things out. I look up in the light tunnel and wait for the flashing lights to make me smart. Laran says we're here to become special, we're going to become superheroes, and the caretakers are giving us special powers gradually but they can't tell us yet because we have to be tested. I don't know if I believe Laran, but I would like to become really smart. Smarter than Ha. I would like to become as smart as Laran and then I would like to dance for him, too. . . .

Today is the day after my eleventh birthday. They gave Laran drugs to make him shut up. He was screaming at the caretakers all morning. He rants sometimes about going home and I told him to shut up before they get mad at all of us but he wouldn't listen. He always eavesdrops on the caretakers and then he gets angry with them. Now he's lying on the floor. I kicked his hand but he didn't move. I hate him. Why does he have to make trouble for us? Laran said they are going to take our brains out of our bodies and put them into a computer. I wish he wouldn't say such things; it gives me nightmares. It's his fault they moved us to this awful room. You can smell chemicals all the time, and there are animals in the next wing. Ha thinks they're keeping pigs there. Imagine, keeping us with the pigs! I heard screaming in the middle of the night a few days ago. I guess it was the pigs. They sound like people, they really do. Screaming and screaming. That gave me nightmares, too, and I woke up shaking. I'm going to ask for a tranquilizer tonight. . . .

There's a strange woman looking in through the glass. She's tall and she has orange hair. I've never seen anyone like her before. She's talking to the caretaker. She keeps looking at her little pad and writing things into it. I'm not the only one to notice. Laran sees, too, but he doesn't say anything because the other boys told him they would beat him up if he makes any more trouble. Most of the kids are in the other room anyway, finishing their dinner. Laran looks at me.

They're letting the woman in. She walks in and starts speaking without actually looking at us. "Please pack up your personal belongings. You're being moved again to an upgraded location." The caretakers stand behind her and look at the floor.

There's a minor outburst when everyone in the other room hears the news: groans, cheers, and a sort of anxious murmur. Laran stays down on the floor and I wonder if he's heard. I go over to him and whisper with him. I say that everybody else is getting ready. I tell him he has to move.

"They're scared shitless," he says under his breath. His consonants are slurred. "You should have heard the caretakers this morning. Something's going wrong here. The research isn't going well, or maybe we're being taken over. They've shut down all the labs on the upper floors. Now do you believe me?"

"Maybe they're letting us go," I whisper. "Maybe the experiment's over."

He snorts at me and rolls over. He won't get up. Eventually the caretakers pick him up and make him walk. He's seething. I get my things—not much to bring. Then I get into the middle of the pack of us, where I feel safer with everybody's heat and movement around me.

We go through a series of tunnels I've never been in before. The next thing I know we're in this big, hot, echoing tunnel and a train comes gliding in. I've never been on a train! I grab Ha's hand and we sit together. Her nails are all bitten down.

I tell her my theory, that we're being let go.

"Djile," she says, "there's nowhere to go to. Laran and I broke into the computer system. There's war like you've never imagined out there. People are so mad about the experiments, they're burning and dumping chemicals everywhere. Nuclear weapons have been detonated in West Africa and before long everything will be blown up."

"But why? They can't help us that way. Why don't our people just send someone to rescue us?"

She shakes her head, her bangs swinging. "No, it's not *us*. It's everybody. The sterilization viruses came from Helix so that the northerners could control our land, and Ingenix had to fight back on behalf of the indigenous peoples, so they made something more deadly, but that hurt the indigenous peoples, too, so now they're using all their chemical weapons and they're burning the cities. They don't want the rich people to kill them or control their minds and get their land. There's sickness all over Asia and Europe, and information services says it's even worse in America because Gen9 is there and terrorists have taken it over and now everything they had in their lab is loose."

It sounds like another one of Laran's wild stories. "I don't know," I say to Ha, "I don't know if I believe it. Like, I'm still waiting for my superpowers. Laran was wrong about that, and it doesn't seem so bad here."

"Djile, you don't have to understand it, but stop saying stupid things. We're not going home, don't you get it?"

She's crying, and I'm angry at her for that. I'm not the only one who needs things explained. Most of the others agree with me. Why is it always Laran and Ha who have all the answers?

When we get off the train we are brought to a waiting area. There are no windows and we sit looking at each other and talking nervously for hours. Laran paces. His eyes are red; I don't know if it's the drugs they've given him, or if he's actually been crying. He says that the hum we hear in the air is the sound of power, a lot of power. When he moves around the room all our eyes follow him. He expresses everybody's frustration.

"This is a spaceport," he says. "We know this is a spaceport—you don't need to lock us up in a windowless room. Why are we here?" He paces faster; he starts to shout and slap the walls with his hands. "Why are we here? *Why are we here?* Stop lying to us and tell us what's going on."

Ha stands up; so do some of the others. They start to beat on the walls. Someone starts a chant: *We want answers.* I find myself standing in the middle of it all. I'm shaking my head. This will only make them hurt us; does Laran never learn?

Pretty soon a man and a woman come into the room, dressed in service clothes. I've never seen either of them. The man says, "Quiet down this disturbance at once. I will have you separated from each other and sedated if you can't control yourselves."

There are cries and curses in response; I say nothing. I look around for Laran and spot him off in a corner, talking to the woman. Her mouth is very close to his head. She presses something into his hand. I can see him nodding. The man who gave the orders is being surrounded and physically pushed back toward the door. It's becoming a mob scene, and I almost feel sorry for him, or at least disgusted. The woman darts out of the room and suddenly there are guards everywhere, heavily armed. They pick up the protestors and slap tranquilizer patches on their necks.

No one touches me. All but eight of us are taken out of the room unconscious. Of the remainder, Laran is the only male. The woman returns. She says, "If you cooperate, we'll allow you to remain conscious for lift-off. Otherwise you'll be sedated like the others."

We troop obediently after her. I keep looking at Laran; he winks at me once, then pointedly ignores my looks. We board *Morpheus* on foot while the others are loaded prone. Even Ha looks like she would ask questions, but Laran is so quiet we say nothing; we unconsciously follow him.

Once we're left alone on the ship, Laran says, "We're being sent off-world. We're going to Jupiter station. I don't know what it's about, but she said it's very important and we'll be briefed when we get there. She gave me these." He shows a small package of disks, unlabeled. "She says they're Earth archives. She said maybe we'll need them. She said we might have to take matters into our own hands."

"Are we colonizing Jupiter?" Ha says incredulously.

Laran gives her a disdainful look. "Impossible. I'll look at these disks later. Say your good-byes to Earth. I don't think we'll be coming back."

Is this enough? I've shown you only the parts that are easy to take. There's much you don't see. Do you understand what a fool I have been, how naive?

◆

Pause. Jumble of white noise. Wrenchingly, Daire found himself pulled back into the lywyn, his mouth stinging from the shock of the fluid. The ghost was still standing there, but she looked younger now—she looked the age she must have been in the memory. She was even more like Tsering than before. Daire swayed, still flummoxed by the abrupt transition. When he looked at Tsering, he saw that she had been crying.

"Yes," said the ghost. "I know you are sorry. How could you not be? You didn't know me. You only knew a monster. Such pride my child must have"—and now her eyes fixed on Daire—"that she would never come take my memories before this. That it should take a stranger to move her."

Tsering drew the back of her hand across her eyes.

"I'm listening now," she said unevenly. "You left Earth. Then what?"

"The ship flew itself. Most of the computer was locked. Communications were locked also. We could listen but not transmit. It took Ha a long time to figure out what had been done to it. She almost gave up; none of us had real technical training—how could we? But there was nothing else to do all day. The ship was barely big enough for us, even though we were used to close quarters. The only upshot to all of it was that there were no more tests. No one was observing us, and we could do as we pleased. Laran began to read the archives. The woman wanted to help us, he said, so she gave us the equivalent of a small college library on disk.

"As you know, we were headed for Jupiter, which was a long run even in a state-of-the-art ship like *Morpheus*. Ha never gave up on trying to break the locks on systems control, and eventually she discovered that we had been transmitting an order to Jupiter station that told them to destroy us as soon as we got in range, because *Morpheus* was carrying kill viruses that had to be purged from Earth. We had been transmitting the message all along, and it made no mention of the fact that there were people on board.

"Even I was not surprised. By this time, we knew we'd been infected with something, but since none of us had died we assumed we were carrying a virus that was intended to destroy some other population. Laran figured we were designed to be used as weapons, or something like that. As you may imagine, this discovery didn't do much to boost our morale. We didn't want to kill anybody. We just wanted to live and be left alone.

"Everybody pitched in and worked around the clock to get control of navigation. We were pretty close to Jupiter when we finally solved it. Ah, the celebration! It was the first thing any of us had ever accomplished, and we had done it with no help from anyone! But Jupiter sent scouts after us. We were doomed."

She fell silent. Daire's head had still not cleared. He was still under the spell of the lywyn.

"Well," the ghost said, spreading her hands. "You know the outcome from there."

"But how did you find Underkohling? And how did you find the gate?" Daire asked.

"Tsering knows. This much at least we taught to all our children."

Tsering glanced at Daire. "Laran—my father—had learned about Underkohling from the archives, and from things he'd overheard at Ingenix. Some people had placed a lot of hope that Underkohling would lead to a new planet or contact with extraterrestrials. It was popularly believed that Underkohling was an extraterrestrial artifact."

"So you went there on purpose?" Daire looked from mother to daughter and back; they were hard to distinguish in the darkness. Their voices were very similar.

"Yes. We entered orbit—that was tricky, but I didn't have anything to do with it—and we started to look for signs of the gates. But we had been pursued by ships from Jupiter, and within a matter of hours they began to fire on us. When Ha scanned a disruption in the surface, she just dived for it, and we came through. No one followed us.

"There were injuries in the passage, but really we came through remarkably intact. It was a miracle to be here! To be sure, we had much to learn about survival. Agriculture, and making use of the resources here. We very quickly learned that there was no alien civilization—there was nothing even close to human here. We were completely alone. And yet it was a paradise ... for a while."

"Until you grew up," Tsering said flatly. The ghost gave a dignified half bow.

"At first we thought it was something in the environment making some of us sick. Sick in the head, you know? But we thought about it carefully, and we realized it must be our DNA. When the Ingenix development teams wanted to try a new experiment, sometimes they built in a control mechanism. You know what I'm talking about? They knew that they were going to get raided sooner or later, so they wanted to prevent us from surviving. They built in a trigger in our genes that would make us kill our own children when we distorted to the second phase of the life cycle. They were guaranteed, you see, that only one generation would survive. They did this to us on purpose, Tsering. In case we got loose in the world. Are you following me?"

Her face was angry, intense, and her dark eyes flashed toward Daire. He stiffened.

"Do you have any idea what it means to do this to a species? They crippled us for all time; they cut us off from ourselves. But they have not been able to kill us, not yet." She directed the heat of her gaze to Tsering. "I only pray that when your time comes, and your child cowers before you on the ground, that someone will come to take you before you take an action that will destroy your very soul. I am grateful that I was not allowed to devour you, though the desire in me was strong, so strong."

She turned her eyes upward, into the lywyn. "But I am dead now: I am only a ghost. Whatever became of my body when I distorted, I will never know. It is one severance that can never be mended."

The effects of the lywyn water, which Daire had thought to be waning, swelled in him again—or else his eyes were failing him. As the ghost spoke her last words, complete darkness closed down around them, snuffing out even the wraithlike soft lights of the lywyn itself and the faint stars. The darkness pressed close and then everything around seemed to fall away, leaving him suspended in nothingness.

Daire could still feel Tsering's presence in the trance state; she was subtly controlling the experience for both of them now. He wanted to reach out and clutch at her for safety, but he didn't know where she was. He didn't know where he was himself.

"Don't be afraid," she said. Her words shaped the space around them, but her voice seemed to be coming from everywhere at once, even from inside him. The darkness crawled under his skin, at once intimate and terrifying.

"Welcome to the darkness," she said.

With effort, Daire moved his lips. "I don't understand."

"I have been here before," she said. "It is my history. Nothingness. A sea of emptiness. This is all I see when I look back in time, when I seek my own ancestors. When I seek my origins. This is what exists, in the time before my parents."

He was silent. He didn't understand. She gave a low laugh.

"Do you know the story the ancient Egyptians told about creation?"

"I don't believe I'm familiar with it, no," Daire replied carefully. His words seemed out of place, nonsensical in the middle of this void. But when she spoke her words were confident.

"The Egyptians believed that before the world was created there existed nothing but a limitless ocean of darkness called Nu. Even after the world was created, Nu continued to surround the world, and when the world ended, Nu would return again. They feared that one day Nu would come crashing through the sky and flood the world with darkness."

She showed it to him: and though he had traveled in space and knew what it meant to be a person amid impersonal emptiness, this Nu had a brooding, dangerous quality, void and crushing at once. He glimpsed it, was held by it; and then it dissolved. He was again surrounded by starlit branches. He could make out Tsering's form faintly, and it was as if the ghost had never been there, only the two of them the whole time.

She said, "You've glimpsed it. That's what I see when I take the lywyn. I see nothingness on all sides. Long ago, it used to scare me. But then I began to see that's what I am. I am the dark ocean. And it's all right. In fact, it's kind of reassuring."

Something had changed. She was waiting for him to do . . . something. Though the darkness had receded and he could see his surroundings again, he saw as if from a distance, or through thick glass.

Daire said, "I'm finding it hard to speak."

"Don't speak, then."

He could see the darknesses of her eyes and mouth, and the faint blur of light off the planes of her face. He could see the paler color of her clothes, and the line of her bare legs.

She was close enough that he could feel the heat off her body. He could smell her.

"I want . . . this . . . to mean something," he said, struggling against the silence.

"Then let it mean something."

"What I want from you—it would be wrong. Where I come from, people are sensitive about children's sexuality."

"Sexuality. That's just an excuse, Daire. You know what I really am. You say you want it to mean something, but you won't let it mean something to you."

He said nothing. She picked up his hand and brought it to her lips. He heard himself inhale sharply.

"What does that mean?" she said.

"Don't."

She gave him back his hand. Then she stood up.

"I guess I found out what scares you," she said. Then she moved away silently through the branches, leaving him alone.

19

At last it rained. Daire had counted nine days since his precipitous arrival, and they had been almost unvaryingly clear and warm. But when the rain came at last it was serious. He was inside the ship when the first drops began to fall into the open trapdoor, and when he ventured a glimpse outside the lake was rough with wind and water. Daire debated with himself for a moment: Should he go back to the camp and try to make himself useful, or should he remain here, out of the way? He opted for the latter. Since the night of the lywyn he had noticed a slight but perceptible change in the way Tsering responded to him; and it seemed the children picked up on it as well, for they were more formal toward him. He had the impression that he'd somehow played the coward, and he tasted this role with interest as it was entirely new to him. If anything, he'd always thought himself reckless.

Daire had been pleased to discover that even after eighty years, most of the ship's systems were still functional. Flying was out of the question—the engines and body of the ship had been damaged in the crash. But the computer systems were nearly as functional as they had been the day the ship left Earth, and it was strange for Daire to see how little the technology had changed in so many years. He'd had it drilled into his head from youth, how since the Gene Wars economic and technological growth had been slow and sporadic, but the systems he had before him were proof positive of this fact. They did almost everything that modern systems would do, if not quite as rapidly or in exactly the same way.

Ingenix must have had its eye on the resources of other worlds, for *Morpheus* had been outfitted with sampling arms and laboratory space, and a fair amount of equipment for exploring planets. It had not, however, been commissioned as a science vessel but as more of an executive class cruiser for survey and touring. The kids who'd crashed here on *Morpheus* had made use of these resources with mixed results. There were empty lockers that should have contained sensor equipment, and the emergency medical materials were entirely absent. Some of the more delicate instruments had evidently been damaged in the crash. Built-in work stations, however, had been left intact, and Daire had spent his recent days collecting samples of water, soil, indigenous plant life, and those among the insects that he'd been able to catch. He also took a sample of the lywyn fluid, although he couldn't restrain a brief twinge when he set it down on the panel and prepared to analyze it. The act seemed sacrilegious.

What he really wanted to do was to study the DNA makeup of the children themselves. It was clear from the ghost's descriptions that the fugitives had been experimental subjects during the last years of the Gene Wars, and that they had been spirited away for some urgent reason. Why they hadn't simply been sacrificed with so many of the other subjects when Ingenix was raided, Daire couldn't imagine. Sending a group of kids into space in a state-of-the-art interplanetary cruiser was an expensive way to get rid of them. The fact that *Morpheus* had carried a fire order to be automatically transmitted to Jupiter station said that someone hadn't *meant* for them to arrive at Jupiter or Underkohling . . . or anywhere. Why shoot them into space only to murder them?

He had no answer, but he could hope to learn something about them from the structure of their DNA. Not much, he told himself honestly, because he was a total layman as a biologist. But if he could slap together the rudiments of the necessary software, possibly he could learn enough to explain how they distorted, and what particular constellation of hormones triggered distortion. He would be stupid to believe he could fix anything for them, but in the back of his mind he kept thinking about Colin. If Colin ultimately did show up, Daire didn't want to be caught lurking around in the lywyn with no knowledge to show for all his time here.

Since the experience of "riding along" on Djile's memories, he thought of Colin more than ever. If the lywyn itself had somehow shaped or magnified the *Morpheus* distress signal Tsering had programmed, then it had to be true that the gate could open on this side and yield onto the surface of Underkohling. Daire had believed this all along: the fine dust he'd found on the surface had to be silt from the bottom of the lake, deposited on *Morpheus*'s impact through the backwash of the gate. Working on the assumption that the gate would continue to open onto Underkohling, at least sporadically, he had encoded a new distress call, increased power to the transmission, and directed the call at the lake itself. He told himself that if his effort failed, he'd try to dive back through himself. He still had a perfectly good walksuit whose oxygen reserves could be replenished if needed, and he could probably adjust the ship's instrumentation to pick up the EM shifts of the gate under the water's surface. But he was reluctant to suck too much power if he didn't have to. Nor was he certain, having been through it once with total loss of consciousness, that he wanted to walk headfirst through the gate again without someone on the other side to greet him.

So now in the steady rain, fumbling with unfamiliar equipment and not altogether knowing what he was doing, Daire analyzed the lywyn water.

He learned to his surprise that it was alive.

It wasn't an organism, exactly; at least, he didn't think it was. It wasn't merely a collection of microorganisms either, like the kind of virus tea that had been so common in Earth's oceans during the Gene Wars. No, it resembled blood more than anything. The lywyn was comprised of cells whose function was entirely mysterious to him. He found himself swallowing and wondering if those cells were still alive in his system—and if so, what they were doing.

On the third day of rain there was also lightning; Daire had been running a program to plot the EM changes in and around the lake, to see if he could predict when the gate would next open. He had his feet up on the console, eyes half-lidded on the verge of a nap, when the first series of flashes registered. When the lightning spiked, so did a whole constellation of indicators. Daire's feet hit the floor, his hands poised over the glowing arc of the monitor, waiting for the next flash.

There was a soft thump on the trapdoor, and he jumped in his skin. A fuzzy monitor system showed him the exterior of the ship. He could just make out the figure of a girl crouched beside the door. He smiled and flicked the switch that would release the door panel, glad that Tsering was here to see this happening. Did she know that the lightning in the lywyn was related to the status of the gate?

"Daire?"

But it was Seika's voice. When he turned around he saw her descend hesitantly into the dim chamber. She was carrying something in a bundle cradled to her chest. Daire tore himself away from his work and went toward her.

"Is something wrong, Seika?"

She shook her head gently, looking down. There was a slight flush to her cheeks.

"I thought you must be hungry by now. We never see you anymore."

She proffered a cloth-covered basket, from which steam was rising. The smell of native spices filled the space. Daire took the basket, only to nearly drop it again. It was scalding.

"I'm sorry!" Seika cried, retrieving the bundle and setting it on the work station. "I should have warned you."

"It's all right. Thank you. You shouldn't have come all the way out here in this weather."

"Well," she said. "It does get a little claustrophobic when everyone's inside in the rain. Anyway, I thought you might be lonely." She glanced around the room curiously. "It looks so clean. And safe. I wonder why Tsering doesn't let us live in here instead of in those leaky huts."

Daire laughed. "It wouldn't be clean for long with everyone living in here. It's only clean because she's kept it sealed for so many years." He turned and glanced back at the monitor. Damn, he thought, I wonder which is causing which, the gate or the lightning? He'd thought the lightning a manifestation of some aspect of the lywyn: it certainly appeared to come from the trees.

"Yes, but why has it been sealed all this time?" Dropping her shawl on his chair, Seika trailed her fingers along the console, walking in an idle circle around the compartment. She stopped and looked over her shoulder at him. "Maybe it was waiting for you. Maybe we all were."

Silence. Seika gazed at him. There was a look of such naked longing in her face that he had to look away. He wanted to say something about Aristotle, something compassionate, but he couldn't think of anything.

"Does it always rain this hard?" he asked, trying not to drum his fingers on the panel beside him. He wanted to pace. He wanted to think through this problem. But Seika wouldn't understand.

Seika nodded, her eyes drifting away again. Her hands went to her collarbone in a gesture almost of supplication. "Yes," she said gravely. "And it will probably last for days." She began to walk toward him across the compartment, slowly, deliberately. Her fingers were toying with the laces that tied her shirt at the throat.

"Is there anything I can do for you?" she said, and in the space of a breath her manner had shifted from the demure, yielding attitude he had always seen to something distinctly sensual.

"Look, Seika," Daire said quickly. "I appreciate your bringing me the food, but I don't know if it's such a good idea for you to stay. . . ." He let his voice trail off, waiting for her to get the gist.

"You don't still want *her*, do you?" She gave the laces a tug and the fabric fell away, leaving her naked to the waist. "Tsering can't give you this," Seika said proudly, pulling her shoulders back from the small, high-set breasts, nipples already darkened by motherhood, and inhaling until her ribs showed.

Barely suppressing his amusement at this proud display, Daire raised his hand to ward her off, but she kept coming toward him, her face tilted up earnestly.

"I can give you a child. She can never do that. Never!"

"Please," he said. "I'm really not looking for that at all. Seriously. Please."

Seika looked shocked. She exhaled abruptly and let her shoulders sag. "Are you *that* old?" she said. "Are you impotent? What a strange man you are!"

She sounded such the shrill teenager that Daire almost did laugh then, but he stood up and ducked around her before she could see his face, fetching the shawl she'd removed. He bundled it around her shoulders with the air of a concerned grandparent and began ushering her toward the ladder.

"I'm sorry if I've offended you," he said as she began to climb. "It's really nothing personal."

Again her behavior changed; she looked crestfallen and incredibly fragile.

"Please help me," she said. "I need another child so badly, but I don't want to go back to High. It's terrible there. No one is happy. It's just a way station before distortion, and everyone there is half crazy." When she lowered her eyes, tears squeezed through her lashes.

Daire heard himself begin to mouth platitudes automatically: "You need more time to grieve. I'm not the solution—"

"You are the solution!" she said with sudden vehemence. "You won't distort! If I had your child, you would never kill it. Maybe our child would even be normal! But no, you withhold it. You're just going back to Earth as soon as you can find a way! You don't want to get involved with us."

She climbed out, leaving a wash of rainwater in her wake. The trapdoor closed him inside the ship. He stood there a long time, listening to the rain. When he went back to work, the lightning had ceased.

◆

Seika had been right about one thing. The rain didn't let up for days. Daire spent another night on the ship, but the next morning he threw a plastic sheet over his head and went out.

All the insect life seemed to be at roost under the lywyn roof, and Daire made slow progress slipping along the wet branches trying to avoid stepping on the largest of the insects and brushing off the anki that always wanted to land on him. He tried to find the place where Tsering had called her mother's ghost, but he became disoriented in the lywyn and when he finally found a well of the clear fluid, he was much higher in the branches than he remembered being that night.

He huddled under the shelter of the dripping leaves breathing the dense, humid air.

"Runako!" he called, and his voice echoed from other pools around. Nothing else happened. He shouted out again, louder, but to no reply. He felt foolish. For all he knew

Tsering or one of the children was somewhere nearby, watching him; he looked around, embarrassed to be calling a ghost. But the uneven cadence of the rain on the leaves went on, and nothing seemed to move. Again, as on that first day when he'd leaned back against the trunk of the lywyn and felt it yield slightly, he had a sense of the watchfulness of the forest. But then he hadn't suspected that the lywyn might be sentient. Now he did, and the hair standing up on his arms convinced him further that he was in the presence of some intelligence, whether beneficent, malevolent, or indifferent. He knew that somehow the lywyn was the source of everything about this place and its people, and if he was going to contact it or its ghosts, he would need to take the drug. And this meant risking another trance, as before, searching back to the beginning of time through the memories buried in his own cells.

As he had done the first day, he touched his fingertips to the surface of the silver pool, and then brought them to his mouth.

"Runako," he said again, softly.

"Daire. How is it with you?" The ghost was there, beside him on the branch. He looked utterly real. Droplets of water fell on his clothes and made tracks on the fabric.

"Does this fluid induce hallucinations?" Daire said. "Is that why I can see you?"

Runako shook his head slowly from side to side, his very white teeth showing delight. "Not at all. It only help me to find you. You are connected to the memories now."

"Runako, you must explain this to me. You came to me first—but you didn't know me. You speak of your sister. You warn me about her and you warn her about me. Why? What are you, and what is your purpose? You can't tell me you're her brother, because you distorted long ago, and you're probably dead by now."

"What you say is not untrue, but it's misguided, my friend. You got a small mind. No, I don't mean to insult you, but it a simple fact. Your mind be not like the lywyn. I'm the only way the lywyn communicates with you. You too delicate for anything more direct."

"But what are you, Runako?"

"I'm the continuation, suppose you could say. I'm the

might-have-been Runako, get it? I love my sister, don't get me wrong. But I see in ways that were hid from me when I was human. When Runako was human—whatever you want to call it."

Daire was silent, absorbing this.

"Tell me about my sister," Runako said. "Funny, I was supposed to be older than her, now she older than me. Now she changing, at last, you know."

"What do you know about that?" Daire said, glancing sharply at the ghost.

"Me? Just what I see, what's obvious. There's change happening round here, though. Since you came, everything be loose and drifting around. Nothing sure anymore. Nothing regular. I like it. Change is good."

"Change is good for Tsering? She's terrified. Why didn't she ever grow up before? Why is she maturing now?"

"You still too serious, man. I told you, you taking it all too hard. Nothing you can do to stop the world." He laughed. "You come round here, like 'here I am, man, give me some answers coz I the man,' you know? You think you going to get everything under control, that be your whole problem."

"I'm not going to just sit back and watch."

"Feel free, my friend. Runako no stopping you. Don't have to. You afraid of my little sister. Hah, yeah, well you should be, you know? You should be. She got some fire in her, my girl do."

"Well," Daire snapped, "tell your masters that she's not 'your' girl. If the lywyn is controlling her body somehow, tell it to stop." He was trying to be angry at Runako, for the youth could not stop laughing, and at the last few words the boy broke into a howl of pure amusement.

"You so deluded!" he cried. "Masters, my ass. That be your shit you bring with you from Earth, baby. Here, you might as well call *them* your masters." He gestured to the row of insects that had aligned themselves on the branch between them. "It all the same here. No masters, no slaves. Just ghosts and more ghosts, my friend." He wrinkled his brow, thinking. "You really want to know *why* this happening to her? Look at yourself, man. Yeah, Mr. Lucky, look at yourself."

◆

When Daire reached the houses in the shadow of the cliff he found them silent and deserted, and he experienced a twinge of alarm. Then he saw the trickle of smoke coming out of the caves. He picked his way across the wet fields and stood at the foot of the cliff. Red water gushed down the stones and the red wet earth made a splash of vivid relief against the green plants. Daire wiped the rain off his face and shouted up the cliff.

Naro's head appeared; he brandished a spear. When he saw Daire he let out a shriek and Daire automatically threw his arms up in defense, but the boy had disappeared. A moment later a rope ladder tumbled down the cliff.

"You came back!" Naro yelled. "Where were you? You're soaking wet!"

Daire climbed up and found himself in the mouth of a dry cave. Children were seated in circles on the floor. Most of them were at work, weaving or carving, but toward the back of the cave a handful of the youngest were running in circles and making each other scream. Til spotted him and came forward, keening with joy.

Naro was pumping his hand and grinning excessively. "Come in, come in," he kept saying. "We got plenty of work for you to do."

"Where is Tsering?" Daire said as he was led to a mat much like the one Tsering had made for him that first day. He sat down and accepted the grass plaits Naro handed him, looking at them blankly.

"She went to High. Seika had to go back there. Here, like this. Don't you know how to braid?"

Daire let the boy guide his hands. Til came over and began to play with his hair; the results were rather painful but he liked the small solid weight of her body leaning against his back. She got frustrated and began to pound on him. Then she fell over.

"I'm surprised Tsering left you alone here," Daire said.

Rena, who was sitting nearby, looked up. "She said you were coming."

"Well, I was. But how long were you alone before that?"

"Since this morning."

"I see. Sorry I'm late."

"You *are* late, Daire. You're clumsy, too. I told you—like *this*!" Naro corrected his hands again.

"Tell me, Rena," Daire said casually to the girl. "Does Tsering know everything?"

"No. Almost everything, though. She didn't know you were coming here from Earth. But she figured out who you were pretty quick. It's hard to catch her by surprise."

"She knows a lot of stories, too," said Naro. "Like, for rain days. Do you know any stories?"

"Stories. Uh . . . hm."

Rena began to giggle. "Look at him," she said. "He can't do anything! How do you survive on your world? You can't weave and you can't tell stories."

"Hang on. I'm thinking. Okay, do you know the one about Coyote and Crazy Eagle?"

"No."

"Do you know what a coyote is?"

"No. What's a coyote?"

"Do you know what a dog is?"

"Oh, I saw a dog in the memories!"

"Okay, here we go. Well, Coyote was a wild animal, and he looked like a dog but he was quicker than any dog and he was smarter than any dog and he liked to play tricks."

"Did he have a mate?"

"Um, no mate."

"Did he have any brothers or sisters?"

"No, no brothers or sisters. Wait, one sister. Her name was Wanda. Yeah. So anyway, one day Coyote—"

"What did Wanda look like?"

"She looked like Coyote except she had a longer nose and bigger teeth."

"Ooh."

"So one day Coyote got in trouble with Crazy Eagle, and this is how it happened—"

"Crazy Eagle's mate had just laid three beautiful eggs . . ." continued Tsering from the mouth of the cave.

"See! I told you Tsering knows all the stories," Rena crowed.

Daire shook his head, grinning.

"I can't win," he said. He watched the children swarm

around her as she shed several outer layers of clothing. They mimicked her when she shook her hair over them, her whole body wriggling like a dog's.

"Where's the tea? Somebody get that fire stoked up, please." She stepped past him and picked up a blanket that was rolled up against the wall of the cave. Wrapping herself in it, she sat down beside him.

"How is the work going?" she asked him.

"I've been told I can't braid," he said, showing her the results of his labor.

"I mean at the ship. Are you making any progress?"

"I've set up a code to transmit into the gate. If the gate continues to fluctuate—and I have no reason to believe it won't—anybody in the vicinity of Underkohling should be able to pick up the message." He almost told her about the lightning; but for some reason he found himself checking.

One of the little girls brought Tsering a steaming mug.

She raised an eyebrow, blowing across the surface of the tea. "Do you think someone will come?"

"If they don't, I'm going through again and see what's what on Underkohling."

She sipped and passed him the mug. "Do you think that's wise?"

"Not especially." The tea scalded his tongue.

"Maybe it's time to start acting with a little foresight, my friend."

"Look, I was an idiot the other night. . . ."

"Were you?" She took the mug back and brought it to her lips. "I don't think so. Your instincts serve you well. You sense danger."

"And go straight toward it."

"Not then."

"No, the one time when I should have, I didn't."

She clicked her tongue. "So ready to pass judgment we are! Maybe you were right to stay out of my problems. Tell me, shouldn't you be thinking of some way to get yourself out of this place?"

"I'm going to get us all out of here."

"That's noble of you, but wherever we are, we'll bring distortion with us. You can't save us from that."

"I'm going to try, dammit."

Tsering laid a hand on his arm. Until now her tone had been light, almost bantering. Now she said seriously, "Daire. Remember. Give in to the inevitable. Isn't that what you said? That's what this is: inevitable. My situation"—she gestured around the cave—"and all of our situations. Except you. You needn't be destroyed."

"I'll be the judge of that."

"Look," she persisted. "I was feeling vulnerable the other night. I wanted your strength for a crutch. It was unfair of me to draw you in the way I did. Don't try to be Don Quixote here."

"Don who?"

"You know, Don Quixote? Tilting at windmills?"

"I don't get it."

She was smiling secretively and shaking her head. "Ah, youth. Look, the point is, you seem to think anything is possible, and it just doesn't work that way."

"Anything *is* possible, including crossing a galaxy. I should know. You just have to suspend your belief."

"Suspend your *belief*?"

"In reality."

She thrust the cup at him. "Here, drink this. I've got to check on the little ones." Her fingertips lingered against his hand when she gave him the cup. "By the way," she shot over her shoulder. "You really are full of shit."

Right, he thought. You're not trying to seduce me.

20

There was no reply to the signal he'd transmitted from *Morpheus*, though he waited for days. This put him in the middle of Plan B, as he had suspected would happen all along.

The night before he decided to reenter the gate, Daire sat up for hours thinking. He climbed up into the lywyn: at some point since his trip into his own biological past it had ceased to unnerve him and in fact now exuded a kind of comfort into which he leaned trustingly. He lay back in the gently yielding branches and looked up into the murky reaches of the lywyn, and he thought about consequences.

It was not in his nature to become paralyzed, and yet that was how he had felt ever since coming here. At first he had been too busy taking everything in, and then Tsering and the distortion had distracted him, and then he had been turned upside down by taking the lywyn; but now for the first time he was about to act. And the demand for action itself paralyzed him. All his dilemmas seemed too heavy: to try to save the children, which was probably medically impossible? To bring them back to Earth, where they could somehow work with the League—although how, he couldn't say? He had no idea what the aquatic phase of their life cycle was like, but from all evidence, they weren't exactly docile. What, then? Decisions. To allow Earth scientists to come here, to this place about which he already felt a proprietary jealousy? To allow humans to eventually migrate here? To force contact between the lywyn and humanity at large?

And why were the kids here in the first place? Why had everyone been led to believe the people on *Morpheus* had been criminals?

My luck, thought Daire. Where is my luck when I need it?

There was no guarantee, of course, that the gate would take him back the other way. This could explain why his transmission had failed to attract anyone's attention. Then again, *some* transmission had reached Colin Peake and set the wheels in motion—so in theory there had to be some form of passage back through the gate. Yet there was no reason to believe it would accommodate him.

"What do *you* want me to do?" he asked the leaves above his head. "Since you seem to be in charge of all this, somehow."

But there was no response from the lywyn: no ghosts, no flashing lights, no sigh or tremor or even vague intuition that something was listening.

"Right," said Daire after a while. "It's jump then."

It was simply a matter of waiting for the lightning. Either his hypothesis that the gate opened when there was lightning was right, or he would be electrocuted and proved wrong at the same time.

It wasn't difficult to refill the air tanks he'd been carrying, but since they weren't designed for more than a few hours' use he felt trepidation about the whole process. He simply had to hope that there was someone on the other side to meet him. A more ominous concern was the fact that Underkohling didn't flood more heavily: why were there no fish or plants frozen on the surface of the black orb? Logically, if the gate opened and closed with any kind of frequency at all, there would be considerable "leakage" onto Underkohling. Yet all he had found were a few shovelfuls of frozen silt, and he couldn't help thinking this didn't bode well for his own ability to pass through the gate the other way.

He had had ample time to worry, and his nails were bitten nearly to the quick by the time the next silent, lightning storm began a few days after the rain, signaling action. As he hastily donned his walksuit once again, he was trembling and sweating. He hadn't told Tsering or any of the children what he was doing. He had left a message on *Morpheus*'s main command screen, where he knew she would find it: *Tsering: I have tried to cross back over the gate to Underkohling. I believe this is in all of our best interests al-*

*though I know you don't agree. I'm going to try to find a
way to get through with a ship. If I don't return or send a
message within a month, you should assume I'm dead.*

As he stood reading over the message, he found himself
caught up in the idea that he might not return, and he suddenly wanted to add more. "What would you add?" he
asked himself sarcastically. " 'I love you'? What good will
that do if you never come back?" He didn't sign it.

◆

Daire was not a strong swimmer, and he hadn't counted
on having to fight against his own buoyancy to reach the
depth of the gate. He only made matters worse for himself
by flailing excessively; the walksuit was not designed for diving, and his progress was slow. He thought he would never
get there during the slim window of time when the gate was
fully dilated. But as he pushed himself ever downward, pray-
ing the battered walksuit had no leaks, he came into a little
of his old luck at last. The gate began to pull him, drawing
him in. He closed his eyes and clamped down with his teeth,
panting until he was dizzy with hyperventilation. And he was
drawn in, again, to that sickening disorientation that arrested his consciousness.

◆

His hand moved first, of its own will. It twitched just a
little; passively he noticed saliva tracking down the side of
his chin. All the bones in the hand seemed acutely solid,
making the flesh, muscle, and skin soft by comparison. The
hand lay curled against the ground: he was lying on his back,
his spine pressed against a surface that felt like marble. His
insides stirred and rumbled: illicit, mechanical. He wondered
if he should puke—but then, he possessed no ability to move
or unmove the elements of himself. The event of his own respiration, its rough hiss in his ears, came infrequently, almost
like a season: or, at the least, like a nightfall. It occurred
somewhere beyond his intentions.

Ice had formed in some of the folds and creases of the
walksuit. He imagined himself as a solid block, frozen immo-
bile, flexing his muscles against the wall of ice until, at last,
small cracks formed. He imagined cracking the ice with the

sheer force of his diaphragm tightening, and the contraction of large and small muscles throughout his body, but in reality he didn't move at all. Some connection, it seemed, had been severed, so that he could only receive impressions and could not send actions. His penis had become painfully hard as though he were seventeen again: extreme. It flinched and shifted of its own volition. His eyelids were motionless.

The orbits of his brain were beginning to reset themselves. Memory of some used personality began to channel and braid his thoughts, directing, inhibiting. Stiffening into form. He began to worry about himself. He began to anticipate.

His eyes glided open. Stars or bright insects. Darkness. Stars. Glimmer of waterless sun on the horizon. No other markers. Feeling of being in a box: black velvet, camera. Feeling of being an image.

The drool that had seeped down the side of his face was now nestled against his cheek in the warm hollow of the walksuit. His skin itched from the moisture. He closed his lips, swallowed.

Time to move.

Daire surged to his feet all at once, surprising his body with the sudden conviction of the command, stumbled a few times like a newborn horse, standing at last ragged and a little splayfooted on the smooth, dense floor of Underkohling. Bits of ice cracked off him and danced across the ground. He was no more than sixty meters from the hopper. It still crouched there, all metal and line, as though nothing had happened.

He skated toward the hopper stiffly at first, delirious with an inexplicable happiness. It was like being eight years old and rediscovering a lost toy trapped between two pieces of furniture, or stored away and forgotten, or simply never recognized for the extraordinary thing that it was, until now. He clung to the slender metal stanchions that supported the landing gear, his eyes and mouth thick with tears, the breath gasping through the air regulator. He keyed in the entry code, climbed inside, and sank to the floor while the airlock filled with atmosphere.

Routine took over while his emotions sorted themselves out. Methodically he removed the walksuit and let it fall to the floor. He let his hair loose from its plait and shook his head, scrubbing his fingers across his scalp. When the airlock door opened onto the cramped main compartment, he strode in and ran his hands lovingly over the chair, the console, the viewscreen. He rifled through the lockers, putting on clean clothes, breaking into presealed food packages that had never tasted good at all, before.

Everything was just as he had left it. He was rather surprised to find it this way. It meant no one had been here; yet neither had the hopper been removed. What was Colin up to?

He sat in the pilot's seat for a while, hoping to regain equilibrium. When it continued to elude him he activated the com system.

"Colin?" he shouted, not bothering with protocol. "Colin, wake up. This is Daire. I'm back. Colin! Colin?" His voice sounded weird and shaky. "I could use some help here, if you guys don't mind waking up and *listening*. Misha? Soren? Hey." He changed channels, trying again, this time his voice rising slightly in pitch and volume. Dead space.

By the fourth attempt his phrases were clipped and guttural. It would seem there was no one out there—and the hopper lacked the range to call Jupiter.

"You fucking left me," Daire whispered into the silent com channel. His throat tightened. His fists clubbed the console. "What the fuck's the matter with you?" he sobbed. "Why am I doing this if you're going to leave me hanging out here?"

Angry self-pity threatened to overcome him, and he pressed his face to the com panel as he would a woman's breast. It did nothing for him. The milky way was silent; at last he subsided.

He composed a furious, inarticulate message demanding attention from Earth and began broadcasting it out into space. Then, remembering his initial purpose, he planted the transmitter out on the surface and activated it. If a computer came within range, the device would automatically call and then deliver the message he had recorded—assuming, of course, that it stayed where he had put it, which was by no means assured. The transmitter would also record any incoming messages, which he could then access via the *Morpheus* computer whenever the gate was open.

If all went well.

There was no way of knowing how long it would be before the gate manifested again. There was no lightning on this side to herald its arrival. Hours or weeks might pass, and even then it might appear for only a moment. He hoped that wherever Colin was he was making good use of all the data that he, Daire, had gathered at such personal peril; now that it was certain that the gate opened both ways, Daire was determined to make good on his promise and do something to help Tsering's people.

He wished he could have brought her with him. If she could have seen and felt the darkness of the gate and then the great silence of waking to the sky over Underkohling, would she have believed that this was Nu?

No, he thought. She wouldn't. The darkness she revealed wasn't physical in the same way.

How would Tsering react when she learned he was gone? She might feel self-satisfied, he thought—she had always expected him to save himself. Would she be disappointed in him? Or would she feel something else, something less easy to name?

The hopper's receptors were trained on the gate, but the area remained mulishly stable for hours. Time passed without regard for his frustration. He composed himself to wait. Sprawled at the command station of the hopper, he gazed out on the flawless surface of Underkohling. He tried to distract himself with a mental puzzle: What could Underkohling be? Colin had been convinced it was an organized form of energy that had some material properties, yet transcended certain physical laws. What about meteors? Daire thought. Why isn't it damaged or irregular at all? What about space debris? Why didn't Underkohling attract it with its gravity? There were no craters, no scratches—no accumulation of anything except these little, impossible heaps of dust.

This led him to speculation. There were three other gates, at least, on Underkohling leading to parts unknown. Their unseen presence gave him a queasy feeling. He was glad there were no other known gates in the vicinity. It would be terrible to get the wrong one. The conception formed in his mind of Underkohling as a dark egg from which were hatched people: there was a whole, young race inside, incubating. Or was it an egg into which people were hatched: like himself? Like anyone else who might go there. He imagined a vast migration to this egg, where the lywyn hung overhead like a net. These thoughts were what he clung to, even as his weight in the hopper clung to the ground against the vacant scream of space.

There are holes, thought Daire, and you can fall into them. It's that simple. There are seemingly innocent places under the governance—or is it antigovernance?—of random laws, and when you enter these places, anything can happen. It's easier to see chaos than order, if you know how to look.

And it's easier to fall into a hole unwittingly than it is to find one when you are looking for it, and have the balls to jump.

He thought this, too, sitting on the dead field: No one is coming to save me.

The hopper shrieked in alarm, and Daire jerked upright. The surface of the ground outside was unchanged, but something was happening. The hopper shivered. From the monitor before his eyes he could see exactly what Colin must have seen from orbit on that fateful day: the gate was swirling open like a drunken eye.

The immediacy of his danger had lessened, for the hopper was situated beyond the range of the gate. He wouldn't be dragged in unless he wanted it. He closed his eyes against the busy readout and made himself think. He had to go back. He couldn't make himself go back. And yet, he had to—he certainly couldn't stay here. The gate was yawning open at full size now, and if he let this opportunity pass, there was no way of knowing when it would come again.

He slammed his hand down on the panel and hauled up the landing gear. Then, gently, he urged the hopper forward.

He was cognizant the entire time, had ample opportunity to analyze how it felt to be painlessly but inexorably ripped limb from limb; his consciousness seemed to jump from one part of his body to another, and everywhere he went, he could perceive the rest of himself being violently disassembled and remixed until he was utterly dizzy and spent. The ship around him seemed insubstantial, gauzy and pale. Yet the fall wasn't nearly as bad as last time; whether the ship it-self protected him, or whether he was merely better pre-pared, he couldn't say, but he never lost consciousness, and he was oddly unafraid.

◆

The hopper surfaced in a darkness relieved only by the cool luminescence of the lywyn. He was laughing this time, and he steered the small craft to rest on a cleared strip of bank near the submerged *Morpheus* with a sense of triumph. He extended the landing gear. He wasn't going back. He took off the walksuit altogether and stowed it; then he opened the airlock and gulped in the warm night air. He paused then. He wanted to see people more than anything now. He wanted to see Tsering. He stood there thinking about that while anki found their way through the open hatch and began lazily touring the space.

It was time to cease identifying with all this technology; he had been deserted here. Best to get used to the idea now and give up hopes of rescue. He had to strengthen what ties he had; he had to create some kind of a life, here. Daire climbed down from the hopper and made his way slowly through the lywyn until he reached the houses where fires had been extinguished for the night. Dead lywyn used occa-sionally by the kids burned just like wood, perhaps a little hotter. Daire wondered if even the smoke harbored, some-how, the voices of the dead and distorted.

He hesitated outside the house where Tsering and her charges slept. He fairly writhed with indecision. His recent encounter with Seika had pointed something out to him. Tsering looked even younger than Seika; but unlike Seika—who was despite all her troubles an adolescent girl—Tsering had one foot in each of two irreconcilable worlds. There was something inherently erotic in this liminality; he'd been aware of it almost from the very first. She was knowing, secret—and yet evanescent. She might vanish, or change; she was glimpsed but not seen by him.

He swayed on his feet, half dead from exhaustion. He would hardly know what to do with her if he had her. Daire sank to the ground near the threshold and pillowed his head on his folded arms. If he listened carefully, he could hear them breathing, Tsering and her family. He smiled, and slept.

◆

To Daire's dismay, Tsering didn't comment on his departure or his return. She stepped over him the next morning on her way out to get water, and when he woke with a splitting headache she said, "Ah, Don Quixote. Speaking of windmills, are you any good at repairing things?"

He pressed his fingertips to his forehead. It took him a second to figure out what she was talking about.

"What happened to your windmills?" he asked in a soft tone. He felt hung over.

"We had quite a storm last night," Tsering answered. "Lightning, wind—the lake was turbulent for hours. I was afraid for you." She swung the pail from its rope handle.

"Did you read my note?"

"Note?" She genuinely didn't know.

"I went through the gate again—but it didn't do any good."

"I know."

"If you didn't read the note, how did you know I went?"

"Come, now!" she scolded. "You came to the cave the other day to say good-bye."

"I did?"

"What else were you doing there?"

"I don't know why I do things," Daire said peevishly, closing his eyes. "I just do them."

"Well, will you do something for me? I'm going up to look at the windmills. Harvest is just around the corner and we'll need them. I want to assess the storm damage, and you could be of use."

She extended her hand to him, and he allowed himself to be pulled to his feet. She let go of his hand quickly and looked away; he flashed her a smile through the fog of his headache.

"You missed me, didn't you?" he said, but she'd turned away hastily.

"Go see what's bothering Til," she called over her shoulder as she left, still swinging the bucket. "I can hear her fussing."

Daire obeyed, amused by the flush of domestic warmth that filled him. I've been tamed, he thought.

Later, up on the plateau where the windmills spun idly, some of them uneven and others flapping uselessly in a strong breeze, Daire began to appreciate the ingenuity shown by the little colony. The windmills were flimsily constructed of lashed reeds and wood, and the grindstones were merely flat rocks from the beach that had been selected for their approximately circular shape. There were no metal fittings, and though the design was clever, the machines were frail and waterlogged.

Fortunately, it was not incumbent upon Daire to reengineer them; Tsering clearly had her own ideas about that. Instead, he was asked to climb up and remove the defective vanes while a team of kids, including Adamo, Naro, Rena, and Nkem, went to work repairing them. Tsering wove new panels sitting on the ground with the kids, but Daire spent most of his time high up on the mills, the wind whipping his loose hair as the cloudy sky rolled by above. No one paid him much attention.

"This is it," he said softly into the wind. "This is where I live. This is my home."

His mother must have said that the day after she escaped the rez and stood on the naked earth and breathed the dangerous air with its plagues and poisons. She must have taken off her shoes to be like her ancestors, just as Daire had done that first day he arrived here.

Below, Adamo said, "Cut it out, Nkem! You're messing up my thing."

"I want to fly," Nkem cried, picking up her vane and running with it until the wind nearly pulled it out of her hands.

Daire wondered now if his mother had suffered, and what she had felt—but then, even if her ghost could have spoken to him the way Tsering's mother had spoken to her, even so, she wouldn't tell him. He remembered her as a taciturn woman, quiet and determined, not given to demonstrative behavior.

"What a strange-looking bird," Tsering exclaimed.

"Yeah, what a stupid bird," Adamo said disparagingly.

It's strange not to be alone, Daire thought, listening to their voices. Then: I like it.

◆

He didn't go to *Morpheus* that night, or the hopper. He watched the work crew stumble off to their beds, asleep on their feet after a long day working at the top of the cliff. Tsering finally finished putting out fires and checking on everything; when she appeared from the last house, she looked tired but her eyes were bright in the lingering grey evening. She looked at him for a long time.

"Don Quixote, are you afraid of me?" she said.

Daire laughed. "Shouldn't it be the other way around? I show up and everything unravels for you!"

She nodded her head in the direction of the lywyn, and they began to walk out of earshot of the sleepers. "You flatter yourself," she answered in her rich, low voice. "That day was bound to come."

They entered the lywyn, and Daire threw his head back and spun around, making the branches squirm and the star-strewn leaves blur before his eyes. He spun until he fell over, and lay spread-eagled on his back looking up at her shadowy form.

"Do you want a child from me, Tsering—is that it? Like Seika?"

She said, "That's not a real question."

"Okay," he sighed. "Maybe it isn't. Look, I have a history of doing stupid things without thinking, you know? Maybe I don't want to go on living that way."

"Are you saying it was a stupid thing, coming here?"

"No! Coming here was probably the only intelligent thing I ever did in my life, even if it *was* an accident." He laughed at himself. "But you're going to leave, aren't you? Maybe not today, maybe not even this year—but sooner or later you *are*. How can I—" He stopped. "How can I love you? I already do—do you realize that?"

"I'm sorry."

He started to laugh. "Sorry? What kind of an answer is that? A person tells you he loves you and you say you're *sorry*?"

She flared back at him. "Well, I am, Daire! I'm sorry you

got stuck here with us. I'm sorry I can't be a normal woman. I'm sorry I'm going to distort." Her voice broke on the last word. He heard her swallow tears; then she seemed to collect herself. "I'm not actually looking forward to that day," she said dryly. Her shadow swayed above him.

Dammit, Daire thought. This is going all wrong. He said, "Come here."

He didn't really expect her to comply.

She calmly came forward and lay down on top of him, matching her body to his and sliding her palm across the side of his face. He turned his head until his lips rested against the pad of her thumb. She weighed almost nothing, and he had the sense that she had alighted only for a moment. Like the anki, she might leave at any time, and his hands would be grasping empty air. Her fingers buried themselves in his hair. He gazed at the sleek line of her arm, unwilling to look into her face though it was only inches away. Cautiously he let his hand glide onto the small of her back, and then drop past her hip to the length of her thigh, where it met bare skin. He closed his eyes.

"It's time," she said, her lips brushing his. Their mouths connected, struggled briefly in a slick tangle, parted. He was panting.

He looked up into her face then, and he could see from her expression that there would be no escape. As his fingers moved across her skin, he had the fleeting impression of time extending wide in all directions. All the possibilities of action that he had ever known fanned out like a deck of cards arching over this moment, which was itself a kind of recognition. Maybe it was a spiritual crossing. Maybe it was the result of aeons of natural selection moving neurotransmitters in an age-old pattern to sing out: here. You belong here. She is the beginning place for you.

His self-restraint was shattered. He rolled over with her beneath him, continuity dissolving into a collage of moments: her hair across his nostrils; her nipples straining upward coarse and sweet in his mouth at last; the gleam of light on her lips hovering and then plunging into the shadow of her open mouth, and vanishing. The unexpected depth of her, velvet and taut; her urgent rhythm. She never cried out; later, the blood would surprise him. In the end he couldn't control the drive of his own body, and when he collapsed on top of her, his heart pounding, he realized he was crushing her. He tried to move away, but she held him.

"Stay." He complied, but he persisted in touching her with his hands, until he found and followed the precise path that led to her orgasm; blood from his fingertips marked her face when he reached up to caress her cheek. It frightened him a little, the look of abandon on her face and the blood there. It was a little too real, and he buried his face against her neck not to see it.

In the morning he woke to find her cast out upon her belly, arms spread and hair scattered. Her face was half turned toward him and her expression was one of deep concentration, even in the languor of sleep. She looked definitely like a child then, and as he let his gaze flow down the young curves of her frame he felt a flash of guilt. He looked up into the maze of lywyn, incandescent in the morning light.

"Now I've done it," he said, and showed his teeth to the sky.

Choices

21

Jenae shivered under the blank gaze of the monitor. She tried to make herself turn on the visual because it was important to see Yi Ling's first reaction with her own eyes. Yi Ling's face would tell her everything that had been happening with her sister, far better than words could. But she couldn't overcome the feeling that the system was looking back at her.

She still didn't really understand what the point of the expedition to Suicide House had been. Jenae was tired of trying to figure out motives, and she wished Keila would just come out and tell her what it was all about. She found it frustrating that so much of what was happening to her was out of her control, and even out of her understanding. But when she had approached Keila the night after they came back from Suicide House, reminding her of her promise to give Jenae access to a com system, Keila had seemed preoccupied.

"You can use the system in the warehouse. It's dusty, but functional."

Keila was sitting in her tent, and Jenae was standing bent over in the entrance. Although it was night, Jenae had become accustomed to Keila's working nearly round the clock, and it seemed strange that she was just sitting there. Keila didn't even look up at Jenae as she scooped up sand in one hand and meditatively let it spill out again.

"Is something wrong?" Jenae ventured, wary of violating the One Eye's privacy.

"Milan got a message from Ninety Mile Beach this afternoon, while we were away. He spoke to my sons, who are fishermen based in Perth. I was visiting them when Tien asked me to look out for you. Battle has broken out in Sydney, Melbourne, Brisbane, and Perth simultaneously between the Coalition and One Eyes; also between free One Eyes and the police, and the Coalition and the police. And the police and the police." She gave a bark of laughter. "Ninety Mile Beach is a major meeting place for One Eyes, and word from there places my sons near Perth and in the thick of the fighting. They're trying to protect the interests of One Eyes against the Coalition, but they are a couple of young fools. They need the benefit of my experience with pure humans, but I have obligations here, too. Weeks more are needed to finish this sea harvest." She looked up at Jenae finally, dusting the sand off her hands. "You don't need to be involved. If I go, I will leave some One Eyes behind to finish the harvest, and I can send more from Ninety Mile Beach if needed. You may want to advise your sister, though, to get a travel permit to leave Australia. If she waits too long, everyone will want to go and she won't be able to get out."

Jenae met Keila's gaze soberly. "How could this happen so fast? There were only murmurs when I was there. . . ."

"On the contrary," Keila said. "This has been brewing for years. You don't know about it because it goes on outside the rez."

"In that case, I am going back," Jenae declared. "Even if you aren't going, I have to find a way. Yi Ling has no one."

Keila closed her eye. "Call her," she said. "Find out where she is and what the rez administrators are advising. Then we will decide what to do. But be aware that having you by her side is unlikely to help your sister. Altermode means nothing if there are bombs going off."

Jenae had fairly run out of Keila's tent to the computer stored in the back of the warehouse. When she saw the condition of the unit she could hardly believe that it would work to get her in contact with the nearest settlement, much less with Perth rez across the sea. But the system came up, and her eagerness turned into a weird fear.

Facing the prospect of looking back into the system, of speaking to Yi Ling on the rez after these days of physical freedom, Jenae could hardly make herself initiate contact. She had chosen the middle of the night to call, irrational though it might be, because it lent a feeling of secrecy to the act. Tien's warnings, Keila's attempts to isolate her from the League, and her own sense of fear that if the Pickled Brains could fry her once, they could do it again, all accrued to make her paranoid about personal contact through the system. In the end she called blind, typing her request on the screen. Her call to Yi Ling's room was rerouted to Perth central, where the words to the left of the flashing cursor remarked:

Sorry, you have accessed a terminal no longer in service. This terminal belonging to Yi Ling Kim was shut down on 7-9-66. No other terminal has been assigned to this user. May I help you further?

—I would like to send a message to Yi Ling Kim by hand.

Yi Ling Kim was last listed at Perth Medical Care Center. May I transfer you?

—Yes.

Jenae sat back, gritting her teeth. It didn't look good. The Medical System answered.

—Is Yi Ling Kim there? she asked.

If you are a relative, please fill in the information requested.

A form sprang onto the screen. She glared at it. "Something's wrong," she said aloud. "It's a trap. Why else would they want all this information?" Grimly she entered everything anyway. So let them come.

Thank you, Jenae Kim. *Please remain on the line.*

"Oh, shit." Jenae pushed herself back from the desk as if by gaining physical distance from the machine, she could somehow escape its notice. But it was too late to turn back now. She had revealed herself, so she might as well stick around and learn something even if it meant her location was no longer secret. What can they do to me that they haven't done already? she thought, and immediately regretted her flippancy.

Please activate your visual, Jenae. I must speak with you face-to-face.

Setting her jaw, Jenae snapped the a/v switch on, hard.

A woman's face shimmered across the screen. An old woman. The same old woman who had cared for her in the hospital, back on the rez.

"Jenae Kim," she said warmly. "You look well. The hair is growing back, I see."

Jenae nodded grudgingly, feeling suddenly girlish.

"I wish I could say the same about your sister. I understand you are seeking to contact her. The last time I saw her she seemed thin and cold. Emotionally, very cold."

"You saw her?"

"She was here. But, my dear, I'm sorry to have to tell you she is no longer with us."

"What do you mean?"

"I didn't witness it personally, so I can give you no details, but she's on record here as a suicide. I'm sorry."

Jenae's head was shaking back and forth rapidly. "No. I don't believe it."

"Jenae, I'm so sorry. This must come as a terrible shock to you. We wanted to provide therapy for her, but she consistently refused it. She refused to see her own illness; she was always projecting her problems onto everyone else."

"No. No. When? How? I simply don't believe you."

The woman's face was drawn. She nodded, meeting Jenae's eyes through the viewer before turning back to her own terminal. "Let me see," she said, scanning through the files. Her eyes skipped across the screens. "I don't see any specifics here. It's possible one of the doctors is still reviewing the case and has taken custody of the files."

"There!" Jenae exploded. "I knew it. Get me those files *now*. This is all lies, that's what it is. You people are fucking around here and I won't have it!"

The woman didn't react visibly, except maybe for a slight flaring around her nostrils. She met Jenae's eyes, and Jenae felt the heat rising through her. She was ready to explode; but as she and the old woman tried to stare each other down, she remembered her days in the hospital, and her own sense that the old woman was the kindest person there, a healer in the purest way. She dropped her eyes and drew breath.

"I'm sorry."

"It's quite all right," said the shaky old voice, and Jenae felt herself on the verge of tears.

"I know she isn't dead. She's my identical twin. If she were dead, I would know. I would just know. I want to speak to the doctor who treated her."

"That would be Dr. Morrow. She isn't in tonight. I can have her contact you in the morning, or if you like you can call back. I'll leave a message for explaining who you are and what happened."

Jenae rang off. It didn't take long for her fear of the system to be supplanted by anger. She immediately called Zafara, fuming. She'd obviously awakened him; it took a long time for him to answer, and his eyes were swollen and yellow.

"Where is my sister?" she demanded.

"Jenae. What a surprise. What's the matter?"

"Don't play with me, Zafara. I know she's alive, I know the League has her, and I'd wager money you had something to do with it."

He gathered himself. She could see righteous indignation warring with the need for cool control on his face. Manners won out.

"Listen, Jenae. I don't know what you're talking about. Now slow down. I realize you've been through a lot, but I can't do anything for you if you don't calm down."

He's pleased, Jenae thought. He's *happy* to see me losing it.

Jenae closed her eyes briefly. "I've changed a lot since the last time you saw me," she said. "I've gotten wise to a few things. You've kidnapped my sister because you want me, is that right? It's hardly possible that it was a case of mistaken identity. It's a low, low thing to do, Zafara, and I really don't care if it wasn't your idea. I still hold you responsible. I want to speak with her before I'll discuss terms with you."

"I'm not a terrorist, although it's obvious that you're on your way to becoming one. Jenae, I don't know anything about your sister. I'm sorry about your mental accident, but I swear to you: it *was* an accident. I've never meant you any harm, and I think that's true of everyone here. Anytime you want to come back, we'll take you."

"You'll take me, will you? What about the dolphins, Zafara? Will they take *you*?"

"Who told you about the dolphins?"

"It doesn't matter. Where's Yi Ling?"

"This is getting tiresome. I told you, I don't know."

"You're a traitor to your kind, Zafara."

"Look, I've been having some drug problems, that's all. It doesn't make me a traitor. I'm working on it. I've been an alchemist for a long time, Jenae. I've seen a lot. You're just a kid. Don't think you can understand my point of view."

"I don't need to understand your point of view. I need to speak with my sister—then maybe I just will consent to turn myself in, if that's what it takes. But I offer you nothing until I've seen that she's safe. So what's it going to be? Do I go straight to the Pickled Brains, then?"

Zafara shook his head, blowing through his lips. "You might as well, girl, because like I said, I don't know what you're talking about. You call me up in the middle of the night ranting and raving . . . wait a minute." The screen went dark. After a few moments Zafara came back.

"I'm putting you straight through to the Heads. Are you happy now?"

Oh, shit, Jenae thought. But it was too late to back down. The Heads made no introduction. The female voice came on, the one with the odd accent that had first given her the Underkohling assignment. The screen was blank.

"We're not interested in your sister." The voice sounded almost human; it had never seemed this way before. "We're not interested in you, either. It's not necessary for you to harass Zafara, or Tien, or any of the other alchemists you used to know here. Just now we have taken the liberty of reviewing your sister's records so as to best discuss the case with you, and it seems clear to us that she was a troubled person. As you are genetically very closely matched with her, you might be wise to seek help as a preventive to the mental illness she suffered from."

"She isn't mentally ill. And I laugh at your implication that I am. Are you trying to tell me you had nothing to do with her disappearance?"

"That's what we are telling you."

"Then why was she listed as a suicide with no record of how she supposedly killed herself?"

"It is perfectly simple, and there is nothing sinister about it. Anyone who walks off the rez unprotected is attempting suicide. That is common policy."

"She left the rez? Purposely?"

"Yes. She was pursued by police but not caught. After twenty-four hours they presumed her dead. Our responsibility is ended."

"But she's still alive!"

"Possibly, for a time."

"Well, what if she comes back? You can't just declare her dead."

"She can't come back. If she had caught a disease, she would contaminate the rez."

"I came back! When I was a baby, I was exposed . . ."

"Children may return, if they are part of an approved piece of research and if they are quarantined. Adults, never. They cannot adapt: they always die. They would endanger others needlessly. Altermoders are only allowed to pass in and out because they are practically immune, and the security fields can clear off any residue they are carrying."

"That's completely fucked up!" She knew she sounded adolescent, but she didn't care.

"Zafara tells me you believe we wish to harm you. This is completely untrue. We deeply regret the accidental damage to your altermode centers that has deprived you of your contact with dolphins. But you may return to the League in another capacity at any time."

"That won't be happening," Jenae said. She cut the connection. She'd learned one thing: The Heads were not omniscient. They believed they'd destroyed her ability to link. Or was that another part of some elaborate game they were playing?

Deceit.

The single word, like a pointing finger.

She left the terminal and wandered outside, her eyes heavy.

Suicide. How could leaving the rez be suicide, when already she'd grown accustomed to the open air, the odd, quirky flora—even the sun? It didn't *feel* dangerous.

Keila was gone, but there were other One Eyes, bustling about with gear and baggage on the shore. The sun was coming up. The sky to the east was swirled with heavy clouds out over the sea, but at the horizon a crack of gold had appeared. Jenae sat down wearily while the grey world warmed around her. It was all too much information.

Yi Ling had had a walksuit. That was something, wasn't it?

Staying up all night might be routine for One Eyes, but Jenae felt light-headed. Sounds and voices from the conversations bounced back and forth in her head, blending and overlapping until she could make no sense out of anything.

That voice. The Head's voice.

She had heard it before.

Twice.

Once in the dream, where the white-faced woman strangled her companion.

And once . . .

She leapt to her feet and began to pace.

Once, in the eighty-year-old message from Underkohling.

"You could see it as suicide. Or you could see it as a total change of identity, an expansion, if you will, into an infinity of identities."

The Heads, Tien had told her, *retain so little of their memory of what it was like to be human. But one or two of them have trademarks: you can always recognize them, because they have habits that go back for years. Like the Aussie one: that thick accent. He doesn't remember much about his real life as a human, but he seems to see himself as some kind of macho outback hero, and that's the identity he projects.*

"Oh, mother," Jenae said. "Ingenix. The Heads. What are they doing? What are they doing?"

22

Jenae sprinted back into the building and got back on the system. She drummed her fingers on the panel while she waited for the call to go through, and when Tien's bleary face appeared in the monitor, she didn't even bother with greetings.

"Tien, I need you to access the records seized from Ingenix at the end of the Gene Wars. I know the League has them; they were there in the Tower the whole time."

Tien was quick. He blinked and responded immediately, "Okay. What do you need, specifically?"

"Out of all the people who were rescued in the raids during the last year of operation at Ingenix, were any missing?"

"Missing?"

"Not accounted for. Not saved."

"Quite a few, I'd imagine. Ingenix kept good biological records of every subject, but not very many subjects are traceable to their places of origin. Are you looking for a relative?" Tien was calling up data on the other screen and rubbing his scalp as he spoke.

"Sort of. Remember, no questions. Are there images of the subjects on file?"

"Certainly."

"I want every image of every child that was unaccounted for."

"That's going to take some doing, especially if you want it to happen quietly. There could be hundreds."

"Get back to me as soon as you can. I'll be here. Thanks, Tien."

It was three hours before he called her back, and by the

time he did, Jenae's stomach felt like an angry beehive. She couldn't even doze—her mind was too busy running mazes. At last Tien rang in with a series of images indexed to voice-prints and biographical data.

"Go for it," he said. "Scroll through it and let me know if you need help." He raised a tall mug to his mouth and took a long, appreciative swallow.

There were over four hundred faces. Jenae scanned, trying to keep her mind blank. "I'll know them when I see them," she muttered to herself. But her eyes ached, and the images all seemed to blend. Finally: "Her! Who is she?"

"Number 91967. Common name, Ha Ukwu. Test batch 4007B. Aged eleven years five months at time of photo."

"Show me the rest of the subjects of 4007B."

"Just a second."

Jenae nodded slowly, beginning to shiver. Ha Ukwu was the same girl in the image the dolphins had given her. She had been piloting a ship in space.

More images came up: forty kids all told. Jenae recognized two more children from the scene where she'd seen them sleeping, the Ingenix ID bracelets still on their wrists.

"Okay, Tien. I'm not through. Tell me, in what year were the Heads discovered in the Tower?"

"2084. May, I believe. It was the first of the big raids on Ingenix, and it marked the disintegration of the company."

"But the Pickled Brains didn't rise to power immediately."

"Oh, no. They're still rising, as a matter of fact. They began to be taken seriously as economic and political facilitators around the same time that the League's innovations began to really take off. Turn of the century, give or take."

"Enough time for people to have forgotten the personal details of the Ingenix directors."

"The Ingenix directors were never media personalities. Most people never saw them: so much of their operation involved 'discretion,' in their language. There's almost no media footage in the archives."

"Maybe there's a reason for that?"

"What are you driving at?"

"Bear with me. I want to see whatever records you do have of them."

"Photos?"

"Um . . . actually, voiceprints, if possible."

"Okay."

She had begun to shiver. The voices marched through: a series of names announcing themselves for computer recognition.

Edgar M. Van der Hoss, Ingenix Board of Directors.

Michael Davis, Ingenix Board of Directors.

Hannibal Lumumba, CFO.

Haven V. Krzminski, Ingenix Board of Directors.

"Stop. Again. The last one, again." That voice. That wicked, smug voice.

Haven V. Krzminski, Ingenix Board of Directors.

Tien gave a sharp intake of breath.

"Don't say anything, Tien. Don't even think anything. Just give me a minute."

"Oh, shit . . ."

Jenae wasn't even paying attention to him. "Can you get out of those files before someone notices you're there?"

"What? Yeah, I think so."

"I need documentation of all this."

"You got it, you got it. I'm sending it over right now. Damn, Jenae . . ."

"What?"

"They're going to find out what we've just done here. Maybe not in the next five minutes, but soon. One of them will notice. No wonder they had to hit you so hard. I'll be next."

Jenae bit her lip. "Tien, I'm sorry . . ."

He was shaking his head. "That's not the point, love. Now that you know what you know, you'd better think fast what you're going to do about it. Me, I'm going to stop pussyfooting around and get all the information I can out of the system, and then I'm leaving." He glanced around the room and at the ceiling above him. "Yes, do you hear that, *Haven*? I won't lift another finger for you. I'm out of here."

"Please, don't do anything rash," Jenae began.

"Rash? You're a fine one to talk." For the first time in their conversation, Tien's tone lightened. "Where the hell were you that night? I thought we had a date."

"It's a long story. I'm in New Zealand now." She paused, waiting for him to show surprise.

"I know," he admitted. "I asked Keila to take you back with her if I wasn't able to meet you. I just had a feeling . . ."

"Is there anything you don't know, Tien? And what is it with you and Keila?"

"Now *that's* a long story. I promise I'll tell you, the next time we see each other. Do you have any idea when that will be?"

"Soon, I hope. I'm coming back to Perth to find my sister."

"Bloody hell," Tien said. "I just told my dolphins to send your dolphins off to New Zealand. They've only been gone a couple of days."

"Well, you'll have to tell your dolphins to tell my dolphins to come back. Let me think a second. Have them try Ninety Mile Beach in a few days. The One Eyes always stop there. If I'm not there, I'll end up at Rottnest Island for sure. I'll find them, and I'll find you. I promise."

Tien looked down. "Nobody's in a position to make promises now."

"Tien! Be careful. It's my turn to say that now."

He cut the line. When she sat back from the screen, she was sweating and her muscles were twitching. She found the information Tien had sent and plucked it off the system and onto a floppy. Then she killed the connection.

She took a deep breath.

"All these years," she whispered. "And no one knew. No one noticed."

Maybe, she thought, no one wanted to know.

She shut down the power and ran out into the morning, yelling her head off for Keila.

23

". . . It was just a decoy, the simplest switch, and people fell for it—"

"Slow down, Jenae. You're babbling." The One Eye continued to check the net for defects, passing it hand over hand while she inspected it visually.

Jenae took a long, staying breath.

"The Board of Directors of Ingenix had the computer interface process performed on themselves. Maybe some of the Pickled Brains were innocent victims of experiment, but not all. Some of the biological material floating in those tanks belongs to people who were high up in the power structure of Ingenix. And they're passing themselves off as *helpers*, Keila."

"Proof?"

"Yes! The voice pattern for at least one of the directors matches a Head."

"So? The Head may have simply adopted that voice pattern. They have to get their voices from somewhere. It's not as though they have larynxes." There was a touch of humor in Keila's tone.

"Okay, but then there's *Morpheus*. Why did the fire order for *Morpheus* come from the ship itself? If Ingenix leaders were on board, wouldn't they have done a better job of escaping?"

Keila said, "Some of the Board members *were* caught. They never gave in under questioning. They claimed to believe their colleagues were destroyed on *Morpheus*. There was an investigation at the time, you know."

Jenae could hear her voice rising in pitch. "At the time, Keila, the whole structure of society was in ruins. People were being put to death without trial. Safe areas were denying access to refugees because they were afraid of contamination. And who finally got the system up and running? Why, the Pickled Brains, of course! They found out what the League was doing in terms of protective technology, and they disseminated the knowledge. They organized everything we now have, and we'd never function without them. They *are* like gods!"

"You're overexcited, Jenae. What you say may be plausible, but unless you have DNA of the Pickled Brains that can link them to Ingenix in the archives . . ."

"I don't expect we'd find any DNA record of the Ingenix directors in the archives. I expect if you went back into the system looking for the information I now have on disk, you'd find it altered in some way. And that's why I'm afraid for Tien."

There was a silence.

"And your sister?" Keila asked finally.

"Left the rez. I think she must be caught up in this whole Coalition plot." Jenae had never been able to conceptualize the theories that described human beings as systems of dynamic energy instead of substance, but now she felt as though every cell of her body were humming with excess electricity. "I'm coming with you, Keila. I won't get in the way—I promise. But I'm coming."

"And what do you think you're going to do if I take you back to Perth? Go up to Monkey Mia and pull the plug on the Heads?" Keila dropped the net on the sand and regarded her critically.

"Look . . . I have no right to ask you for anything. It's only thanks to you I'm alive at all right now. But I need help. I can prove this thing about the Heads—I know I can. If you take me with you to Perth, I can get Yi Ling out of this mess. I'll take her to a new rez—Sydney, maybe—and show her what I've learned. Then I won't ask you for anything. But I'll tell you one thing. I'm going to get to the bottom of this thing with *Morpheus*. And if I prove what I need to prove—then I'm going to take them down, Keila."

She was aware of Keila's steady regard. She had become too dramatic. She let her hands fall to her sides.

"The boats will be ready to go by nightfall," Keila said quietly. "We made preparations in the night. If you want to bring anything, get it now." She turned and strode away along the beach before Jenae could react.

When Jenae returned from the storage area with her small bundle, she could see that Keila was in the grip of some emotion, but she didn't know what it was. She followed Keila's instructions exactly: lock up that food; cover those boats and check the charges on these others. Go give Milan this message. Get yourself a laser gun from Milan while you're at it. No, don't practice with it now, you fool. Just put it where you can lay your hand on it. And get something to eat, dammit, before you pass out.

The day flew by. One Eyes flowed in and out of boats to the red forest, the warehouse, and back to the boats. They didn't speak to Jenae but she no longer took that personally. Yet all day the tension piled on itself like a static charge, and by the time evening softened the sky and Jenae waited on the wharf for the last of the One Eyes to board the boats, she felt exhausted from all the suppressed emotion. There was no time all day to think over the implications of what she had learned; nothing had sunk in yet, and she couldn't be sure of the meaning of what she had found.

Keila came and stood next to her silently as the last checks were made and errands run before launching the boats. The charge in the air that Jenae had felt all day seemed to emanate from Keila, and looking up at the One Eye Jenae said boldly, "Keila, what is bothering you? You look like you're going to explode."

Keila gazed down at her; Jenae found herself cowering, expecting a sharp rebuke. But Keila closed her eye and sighed.

"Divided loyalties," she said. "It's hard to know where to stand."

"What?"

"You asked me why I tolerate pure humans. Do you understand why I must?"

"Not really," Jenae said honestly.

"Why am I helping you?"

"I don't know. . . ." She paused, flustered. "Because Tien asked you to? Because you're going to help your sons anyway?"

"Right both times. I have two sons, Jenae. Their names are Mbele and Isah. They are everything to me. But I also have a brother—although you'd never know we're related to look at us. We share the same mother; we share part of a childhood. He is the younger. Jenae, his name is Tien."

The boat's horn sounded, a shrill, echoing hoot, and Jenae knew they had to move, but her mind couldn't function.

Keila said, "I know the choices you have had to make, and the ones you have yet to make. It is the same for us, you and I. It is the same."

She strode forward, Jenae trotting in her wake to board the boat. Jenae's mind was still reeling at the complexities of "family" as Keila cast off the last of the lines. The boat slipped out into the water quietly. Jenae braced herself as it picked up speed, the waves slamming the deck up and dropping it beneath her feet. Of course Jenae knew it was possible for siblings to be of different species—who better than she should know that?—but Keila's situation was so extreme. She thought of Tien's affection toward her, and wondered what it would mean if she and Tien ever took matters to their logical conclusion. She looked at Keila again, then thought of Mbele and Isah, Keila's sons. The dolphins. Yi Ling. It was all too much. Beyond it all screamed her new knowledge of the Heads: her world was hanging upside down laughing at her, and she could do nothing but watch the dark shore recede over the shining plain of the sea.

◆

It was no wonder that her slumber that night was haunted.

She knew she was dreaming, but somehow it didn't matter. Sickly, weary trees rose around her, their limbs drooping, leaves thin and withered despite the rain that was gushing over them. The rainwater was hot and left a greasy residue on her skin—underfoot the ground was marshy, and it stank of decay. Steaming chemical sumps lay at intervals in the wood, presided over by throngs of tiny insects. Jenae walked faster as she passed the nearest of these areas only a few feet away, and then suddenly through the shaky outlines of trees she could see the grey and brown of buildings ahead. She came to a road, awash in rainwater and debris; on the other side rose an embankment at the top of which curved a house-sized, blackened mound. Rivulets of black and white ash seeped down the embankment and into the street, but at the top of the mound she glimpsed a flash of fluorescent color. She moved closer, looking toward the buildings to her right that marked the edge of the town. There was no evidence of destruction, but everything was curiously silent, if not actually sad. All the ornamental plants were dead; here and there a clutch of too bright weeds sprang up in unlikely places: on the top of a mailbox covered in dirt and ash; between two trash cans strangely upright at the curb; in the open boot of a car abandoned by the roadside. The persistent illogic of living things.

She crossed the street and began to walk toward the mound. Someone had carved stairs in its side; the path was earthen and well beaten. There was something strange about the soil. At the top of the stairs was set out a large dented gasoline can and about half a cord of neatly stacked wood, only partially covered by a tarp. A shallow pit had been dug nearby, and it was surrounded by bright orange tarps weighted down with rocks. The tarps concealed lumps and bumps of various sizes. She swallowed. From beneath one of them extended a leg, glistening with busy worms.

For the first time Jenae became aware that someone was holding her hand. A warm soft hand had been clasping hers all along, but as is the way with dreams, she only realized this retrospectively. She turned her head to view her companion, but there was no one by her side. She could still feel the gently reassuring handclasp. She looked down at her left hand. A right hand, identical to her own, was holding her left hand in a loose, let's-stroll-across-the-street-shall-we grasp; the only feature that indicated it was not her own hand was the silver dolphin ring Jenae had given to Yi Ling when she learned the League had accepted her. Yi Ling always wore it, although she did so ironically.

The hand was severed just above the wrist. The bloody stump was raggedly cut, and illogically a major blood vessel pumped spurts of blood as if Yi Ling's heart were in her hand, disgorging its life substance at regular intervals, more blood than her small hand could ever contain.

Jenae let out a shuddering gasp and tried to fling the hand away, but it clung to her with its tendons bulging out. Its blood continued to flow copiously over her, and itself, and the ground beneath her feet. With her right hand she reached over and attempted to pry it off, all three hands now slick with blood, but it gripped her even harder and more cruelly until she cried out with pain. Then, with a sudden jerk that caught her completely by surprise, Yi Ling's hand dragged her forward into the pit. She fell to her knees and could only observe helplessly as she was pulled onto her face in the ash pit, where bones dug into her flesh beneath her living weight.

◆

The long ache of sun began the moment Jenae woke. It reached her mind like a paper cut, startling and strange, even slicing through the dark goggles and the hooded robes. She was queasy, disoriented, and parched. The desolation of water all around seemed remote and unreal. When she unfolded herself from a cramped corner of the cockpit the spray struck her goggles, but her skin, insulated from moisture by the robes, did not react.

Milan was the first person she saw; he was sitting on the molded fiberglass rim of the cockpit, his back against the steel railing. He held a hand computer at which all six fingers of his left hand were busy. She rose, balancing carefully, and pulled her way along the rail to sit beside him. Leaning toward him, she tried to see the panel, but next to Milan her frame was as slight as a child's, and his shoulder and arm blocked her view.

"What are you doing?" she asked.

"Strategy."

"I'm thirsty."

He gestured to a plastic jug tucked in a recess nearby. She struggled to lift its weight and failed. Milan stopped what he was doing, picked up the jug easily, and held it for her. The water splashed up her nose as the boat rolled beneath them. She looked up into Milan's single eye and thought how easily he could crush her.

If she tore off all her clothes now and dived in, she'd find dolphins or a whale within minutes. She would be home. What did she think she was doing, walking into the middle of a war she didn't even understand?

Milan put down the jug and went back to what he was doing. Jenae made herself small again in the corner, holding on to the image of Yi Ling like a talisman. She felt like an animal.

Various One Eyes came and went from cabin to cockpit to deck throughout the day, but she paid them little notice, still feeling drunk from poor sleep. Keila emerged from the pilot's house around nightfall and looked down at her.

"We'll reach land about dawn," she told Jenae. "Others will be there to meet us; then we'll go on to Perth. I need to put together a plan. Should I assume that the Heads know where you are and what you've been up to?"

Jenae said, "If they don't know that I know, they're bound to find out anytime now. I hope Tien had the sense to leave immediately. Yes, I'm sure they can easily track the location of the terminal I used, and the trail from Tien's terminal to mine—yours—at Dunedin."

Keila thought a moment. "I don't think it matters," she said, "because you're with us. You would be a threat if, for example, there were a serious risk that you would give the Coalition what you know about the Heads."

"That's the last thing I'm going to do!"

"Exactly, and the Heads know that. Telling me isn't significant—what do I care if the Heads were once Ingenix people? I've got no love for them no matter who they are, and they know that. It's the Coalition that's become a problem to them, and with so many pure humans leaving the reservations, the Heads can't track them except by satellite, and that's terrifically expensive. The Coalition are among those who can make them nervous."

Jenae glanced skyward apprehensively. "Are they tracking us, d'you think?"

Keila shrugged. "Like I said, we're not a threat. We're a small group. I'm going for reconnaissance, and to see what I can do for my sons. I'm not coming out here to become some kind of general in a war. I have no interest in that.

"Word has it that the largest group of Coalition forces is massing between Melbourne and Sydney. There's a smaller contingent near Perth, preparing to surround the rez. If your sister is still caught up with those people, she's there."

"How bad is it there, Keila? What are her chances?"

"With a walksuit, excellent. Otherwise . . . it's largely luck. The air's not bad in itself, but the sun's brutal all over these parts. The only clouds you can count on bring poisons from the desert. And anywhere within a few hundred miles of Perth is well seeded with all the Ingenix viruses, at the least. Chances are a pure human, even with a strong constitution, will pick up something if she stays any length of time. Not to mention the chances of actually being killed in fighting . . ."

Jenae bit her lip. "She does have a walksuit," she said. "I hope she has the sense to use it. What are my chances, by the way?"

Keila's expression didn't change even slightly. "I don't have the faintest idea."

"Oh."

◆

At Ninety Mile Beach all but the pilots landed; the boats returned to sea, leaving a group of two dozen One Eyes and Jenae standing in the sand at dawn, surrounded by arms and equipment and slowly deflating rafts. They were to wait for a larger cruiser to pick them up and take them to Perth. They spent the day moving equipment and meeting informally with other One Eyes who passed through the area, and finally pitching camp just a few hundred meters from the shore. Jenae, hampered as she was by all the protective clothing she had to wear in the hot sun, didn't do all that much, but she found herself busy enough to become tired and sweaty by early afternoon with the work only half done. Milan had accessed some kind of satellite relay with his hand computer, and he and Keila were busy with it all day while the foot scouts scoured the immediate area for signs of humans or One Eyes.

At nightfall Keila announced that they would only stay one night at this camp; Jenae groaned inwardly because all the work involved in setting up would have to be undone in a matter of hours. It seemed that a larger fleet of ships was coming from the northeast to rendezvous with them tomorrow, and their journey across the Great Australian Bight would be much quicker once on board the larger ships. While supper was being prepared, Milan came up to her and said, "Looks like you'd better take your chances tonight and find your dolphins, unless you're going to swim alongside from here on in."

Milan's fish jokes were his idea of showing friendship toward Jenae, and she had long since ceased to take offense.

"I think I will," she answered. "If anyone wants me, I'll be back in a couple of hours. Unless a shark gets me." She grinned at him and ran down the beach.

◆

Diving almost blind, where there is violet in the depths of the green, she has only the soft whistle-clicks to guide her, and the sounds seem to come from everywhere at once. So she leans trustingly into the dolphin web whose members have been waiting for her, letting the collective mind guide her through the still-warm water.

—You heard from Tien.

—Tien has left the Tower. And we have left the League. A little needle of panic gores her.

—You've left the League! You can't just . . .

—We made no declarations. We simply haven't touched in with the Heads. We speak to other cetaceans; they tease us for going wild, but no one suspects intrigue. Yet.

Jenae strokes forward cautiously. A cold updraft rushes over her, bringing a burst of fresh oxygen through her gills.

—When we started the Underkohling project, you said other cetaceans were worried about the Heads. . . .

—Not so now, it seems. The Underkohling gate has been concluded by another team, and the anxiety over it seems to have faded from the consciousness of the Heads. Also, the ship carrying the Oxford physicist who discovered the gate is on its way back.

—So it passes. So quickly.

And if I hadn't found those computer records, Jenae thinks, this might very well be the end of it. Attention turns elsewhere. I'll be damned if I'm going to let this slide, though.

Dolphins hear thought one or two levels below intentional speech in the web, and they respond to her outrage, even as she tries to mute it. They chime in variously with language and images.

—Fear runs high over these Coalition skirmishes. We have worked so hard to clear these waters. If war breaks out, they could become contaminated again, and the ecosystem here is still fragile. If even a few species of algae are hit hard, the consequences will be serious for us—and for humans. You have seen the undersea fields?

—I've worked in them. I understand that the Coalition now presents a serious problem. But Tien must have told you who the Heads are. Surely you feel affected by this.

No reply at first, and it seems she is suspended in the dark water alone. Then:

—Are you sure they are the same: the Heads and the Ingenix directors?

Exasperation colors Jenae's tone.

—I'm positive! I'll get proof—

—No, no. Foolish girl! You misunderstand.

She is stunned. Pele sweeps by her, his flukes missing her by a bare inch, and she shies away in confusion. Pele says:

—Who are you when you are not in altermode?

She can't answer.

—Who are you, Jenae? *What* are you?

—That's not a fair question.

—Is it fair to say that the fact of possessing the original brain tissue of a human being makes a Head identify with that original person, eighty years later?

Stymied, Jenae lets herself drift. Pele spins by on the other side of her.

—You wax philosophical, Jenae says, trying to sound light. She feels the flash of Pele's temper fade. He lets the subject fall.

—You will do as you must. You must pursue the Heads; that much is obvious. We will help as best we can, but we no longer have access to anyone in the League. Tien has gone to

Jakarta, where the computer systems are not completely integrated with the rez. He hopes to elude the Pickled Brains in this way. He will be at the transients' hostel there, waiting for you. He asks that you not leave for England without speaking with him.

—How does Tien know I'm going to find Colin Peake?

—Tien is no fool, Jenae.

—I have to find Yi Ling first, and see that she will be safe. Maybe she will come with me. . . .

—We will go to Jakarta. When Tien comes into alter-mode, we will find him and tell him we have seen you. But there is something else. . . .

She can feel a certain smugness in them, a sense of anticipation as if they have been planning a surprise.

—What is it?

—We stole something from another pod before we left the League. We are carrying it in the web, and before it overcomes us we must give it to you.

The whole group of them fin around her now, arrowing by on both sides. She can't remember when they have acted so pleased with themselves.

—*Stole?* You mean, you stole data?

—Beautiful data. The best. We didn't actually steal it; we just copied it. The other pod helped, actually. . . .

—And you've been carrying it around open in the web? Can you do that?

—We are doing it. No! Don't look. You'll hurt yourself, smallbrain.

—Then how can I take it, if you won't let me look?

—Emergency transfer. We'll tie it up tight in a packet where you can't see the paradoxes. We'll path it into your subconscious.

Goose bumps erupt all over her skin.

—That's bloody dangerous!

—Well . . . yes. Find a computer right away and make the dump. But make sure you're off-line. The Heads will be very upset if they find out we stole this. Oh, you can do it, Jenae. Stop cowering.

They are brimming over with self-satisfaction as only dolphins can be. Pele breaches exuberantly.

—What did you steal? she asks warily.

—Ha! Guess.

Jenae makes a whisper in the web.

—The gate. The keys to the gate on Underkohling?

—Yes! *Yes yes yes yes.*

Seven dolphins fly as one.

24

Milan was on sentry duty on the beach, thinking about nothing but the meal his body was digesting and the occasional distant flicker of light that signaled a ship in the area of Port Jackson to the north. The tide was quietly ebbing, and the wind was still.

Off to his right along the waterline, something flung itself up out of the surf and thrashed in the wet sand. Milan stiffened a moment; then he heard the familiar choking cough and relaxed again. Jenae always moved slowly after she came out of altermode, and frequently she was incoherent. But this time she literally crawled up the beach, stopping frequently to shake her head. Milan saw her swatting at something in front of her eyes, but there didn't seem to be anything there.

He stood up and went to meet her, turning on a small flashlight to see her more clearly. She paused on all fours, looked up at him, and let out a gurgling cry, flinging one hand up in front of her face to block out the light. Her pupils were enormous.

"Please," she croaked. "Electrodes. Have you got . . . a wire. Your hand unit. Anything. Please . . ."

He switched off the light and grabbed her by both wrists; with a practiced flick, he slung her onto one shoulder and strode up the beach.

"Keila has cables somewhere," he said. "Doubt they're what you're used to, but you can try."

Jenae signaled her gratitude by retching seawater down his back.

◆

By the time they dropped anchor off Rottnest Island, Jenae felt as though she hadn't been at Perth in years, even if it had only been weeks since her brush with the police. The disk that held the precious gate data she had kept in an inner pocket of her clothing ever since the large, swift cruiser had picked them up from Ninety Mile Beach. She had not been bored: to her surprise (and alarm) Milan had made her spend most of her time "learning something useful." By this he meant studying the blueprints of the rez, learning to recognize and assess the strength of various pieces of current military hardware, and, not least, learning how to use simple weapons. It was not easy developing a steady hand and an accurate eye on a fast-moving boat in a variation on skeet shooting, and Milan could barely conceal his scorn. Jenae tried hard, though. She did not want a repeat of the scenario that placed her facedown on the ground and a group of armed One Eyes above her, fighting it out.

But there wasn't enough time for Jenae to do much more than develop an awareness of her own ignorance when it came to fighting, and then they were at Perth. Now she leaned against the forward rail, straining her eyes to see better while Milan stoically coiled a bow line as an excuse to look on, as well. Perth rez in the twilight was a smoky grey hump surrounded by blue and green pinpoints of light sparkling from the ground.

"What are those lights?" Jenae asked softly, glancing up at Milan.

He didn't answer. Instead he turned and loped back along the length of deck to the steering house. A few seconds later all the lights on the ship had gone down. Jenae gripped the rail as the swells lifted the bow slowly and let it down. Keila's low voice behind her said, "I don't believe it."

"What is it?" Jenae asked. Keila kept coming forward, and now Jenae could see the infrared cone on her goggle. Milan trailed behind.

"Humans," Keila said. "Surrounding the rez."

"Surrounding it? Shouldn't they be inside?"

Keila ignored her. "Get me contact," she snapped at Milan, who turned back the way he had come. "Perverse creatures," Keila muttered under her breath. "They have *everything*. Leisure, medical care, the best computer systems.

Everything they wanted. Safety! Which they needed. And now this, all out of ignorance."

Jenae didn't understand, but she was tired of asking the One Eyes to explain. She swayed with the boat, enjoying the cooling breeze that evening brought. A fine sheen of sweat shone on the backs of her hands, highlighting the riverscape of her veins. She could feel the sea in her body. The more time she spent near the open water, the stronger the desire to merge with it.

Milan came back with a video link and handed it to Keila.

"Mbele! Where's Isah?" Keila said into the link, her single eye honed in on the small curved image. "What's this nonsense?"

Jenae stifled a chortle at this display of maternal affection. She could just make out the image of Mbele, but truthfully she could detect no resemblance between him and Keila. Mbele said, "They're threatening to blow up the rez unless it's placed under their control. As if they could survive out here."

They don't want to survive, Jenae thought to herself, remembering Suicide House. What the hell do they want? Meaning? Good luck.

Keila was reprimanding her son. "Get yourselves out of the way of this madness, both of you! It's too far gone already to salvage this rez. I won't risk my people doing it, and if you've got any sense, you won't either. Let it play out. We'll still be here, when it's over." Jenae had a fanciful vision of Keila standing matter-of-factly on the smoking, crisped nugget that had been Earth, unperturbed.

"It's not that simple," Mbele answered. "A wing of the Coalition has also taken control of the harbor. The fishing fleet is all there, and some of our people are trapped. We've been waiting for the right time to move in."

"You let them take the fleet?"

Jenae had never seen a One Eye actually look sheepish until she glimpsed Mbele's face. "There were only a handful of them at first," Mbele explained. "We didn't think there was any reason to fear. But they had hovercraft hidden in the desert with more personnel. And the armaments they were carrying . . ."

"It's Darwin," someone broke in. Jenae could make out a second figure in the small display, but she couldn't see him as clearly. She supposed this must be Isah. "They've figured out there's all kinds of military stuff left up at Darwin on the north coast from before the Gene Wars, and no rez to support people. They're salvaging this old equipment and getting it to work again. They've got locator guns, which I've never even *seen* before."

"Do they have walksuits?" Jenae cut in.

"No. Only a handful. Needless to say, they're dying. But more of them come every day. They've landed small aircraft in the desert. Obviously the airports are on triple security, but it doesn't seem to matter. The Coalition's got its own equipment. They must have been planning this for a long time."

Mbele said, "If we wait long enough, they'll get sick. But they've put Perth rez on twenty-four-hour deadline. They've rigged explosives to bring down the mirror fields if the administration doesn't turn over control to them."

"Those useless police," Keila said. "They're not worthy of living. Where are they when you need them?"

"We're going in at dawn," Mbele said. "We're going to take the harbor and bring out as many craft as we can. I'm not leaving the fleet to be blown to splinters without making some kind of effort."

"Anyway," Isah added, "we want to find out what this Coalition's made of."

"Impetuous children!" Keila said gruffly, but Jenae thought she looked pleased. "We're going with you. Come over and show us your plans."

◆

"They don't *want* Perth to capitulate," Isah said, "because that would force them to deal directly with the Heads. I don't think the Coalition has any intention of *not* blowing the mirror fields."

"It's Perth rez's fault," Mbele added. "They never patrol their borders. They're so convinced that everyone who leaves, dies, that they do nothing to protect themselves."

They were sitting in Keila's makeshift war room below-decks. The briny smell in such close quarters was making

Jenae feel slightly sick. She perched small and unnoticed on a stool to one side while the four One Eyes (Keila, Mbele, Isah, and Milan) sprawled around a large monitor table with maps and schematics of Perth rez lit in several windows.

"Enough speculation," Keila said now, planting her elbows on the table and peering at the diagrams. "You said you had a plan."

Mbele gestured to the map of Shark Bay, magnifying the section showing the harbor and the adjacent rez. Craning her head, Jenae saw him point with his smallest, sixth digit to the segment of the harbor that abutted the mirror field. She could see the spot clearly in her mind's eye; it was the one area of Perth's continuous mirror field that depicted the actual harbor, not some beautified facsimile. She recalled how she had avoided going down that way, after the "accident." Seeing the ocean would only have driven her crazy then, for the altermode cravings had been overpowering.

Mbele said: "We believe they are holding the hostages here, either on board a cruiser similar to the one we're on—their getaway vessel—or else in one of the buildings along the wharf."

"We want the hostages, obviously, but we want the ship as well," Isah continued. "I've assembled a team of six to slip in quickly and quietly. I'm not worried about detection by the security system, because that's accessed only from within the rez, and if an alarm goes off, the Coalition won't be aware of it. We'll go over the gunwales and take the cruiser. If the hostages are there, we'll do whatever we must to free them. If not, having secured the ship we'll then immediately contact the backup team, who will be waiting here." He pointed to the tip of land that had been artificially constructed to improve the harbor. "Mbele will lead this team. They'll be prepared to approach by land and seize this whole row of dock buildings if necessary."

Milan gave a low grunt. "Numbers?"

"Not more than twenty in this area, I'm sure," Mbele said. "And they're sick. We saw members of this same group a few weeks ago. They weren't in shape for much. By now I reckon they're operating more on nerve and will than on any real strength."

Jenae's ears pricked up when Mbele mentioned he'd seen

some of the Coalition, and she must have leaned forward unconsciously, because now he turned to her and said, "I have seen your double."

Jenae wet her lips. "Was she . . . was she alive?"

Mbele nodded. "I can't give you any more news than that. She was with a large group, and I spoke only to their leaders. I noticed her because she was so young. The Coalition tends to recruit people who are older, fed up with life on the rez and willing to take risks. People with nothing to lose."

Jenae looked away. Was that a description of Yi Ling?

"Which brings me to the second point," Keila put in. "Jenae and I are here specifically to look for her twin sister, and we may as well do it tonight, before the field blows. Before things get any more complicated. You can drop us off with the second team, and we'll search on foot."

Mbele and Isah exchanged glances, and for a moment it looked as though Isah would say something. But Keila's tone left little room for argument. She bent back over the table. All of Perth rez, Yi Ling's former world, was reflected in her single, dominating eye.

◆

Jenae was almost sorry she couldn't see the action from her position behind a low stone wall on the rez side of the harbor. From here she could see the gaunt, shadowy ruins of the old city surrounding the harbor and some of the darkened boats moored there. The rez was uphill to her right; so far the mirror fields were undisturbed, but it was not yet midnight. Below, in the harbor, Isah's team would be swarming all over the cruiser.

She pressed her cheek against the cool stone, trying to remain as still as Keila did. Mbele's team had taken up a position a hundred meters away, closer to the water, but in the darkness they were invisible to Jenae. Keila's night vision had spotted a group of pure humans not far from them, but she was apparently waiting to hear from Isah before she did anything.

"What's the plan?" Jenae had asked Keila as they prepared to go. She felt like a tagalong and hoped she wouldn't have to use the laser pistol Milan had given her.

"We'll sneak up on one alone, overpower it, and find out where Yi Ling is—if indeed she's still around here. Then we'll go get her. We're going to move fast, Jenae, so pay attention."

Keila made it sound so easy. Jenae didn't know how to jump someone. And what, exactly, did Keila intend to do with that person once they'd gotten the information they wanted? Apologize and move on?

But she kept her mouth shut and did as she was told. She'd found that was the best way to keep Keila happy.

Keila's head jerked up. A faint burst of sound came from the earpiece the One Eye was wearing, but Jenae couldn't hear what was said. It must have been the signal from Isah, because Keila nodded and waved her forward.

They darted over the wall and up the hill; once Jenae glanced back toward the harbor, and she saw the big cruiser that Isah had targeted pulling slowly and silently out from its moorings. Against the backdrop of the old, dead city it was a ghost ship whose white hull caught the light from the waxing moon that sailed overhead. It appeared a necrotic blue through Jenae's goggles.

Keila had pulled ahead, and Jenae had to run to catch up. The group of four they had planned to target had split: three humans remained standing, turned toward one another in a huddle. The fourth Jenae could just make out as a shadow moving farther up the slope toward the mirror field. It was three minutes to midnight.

Keila threw herself down flat on the ground and Jenae followed suit. So far Keila's plan was working perfectly: one human had isolated himself, and if Keila could catch him quietly, Jenae was sure she'd wring information out of him easily. Especially considering the fear the Coalition had of One Eyes.

Jenae's eyes were getting better. As she crawled after Keila through the stiff grass, trying to get past the huddle of three unseen, she watched them carefully. Two were obviously male by stature and shape, but the third was much smaller and quite slender. Now they were close enough to hear the voices of the three, but the single man who had moved apart from the group had stopped some distance away, at the edge of the mirror field. There was nowhere he could go: his back was to the field.

She was just thinking that this was strange when she noticed that one of the voices drifting toward them from among the three was definitely not male.

Jenae grabbed Keila's foot. The One Eye froze, and Jenae slunk up alongside her.

"I think it's her," she whispered, her lips against Keila's ear. Keila nodded, and jerked her thumb toward the harbor. Jenae could barely hear the words placed in her ear: "Isah has rescued the hostages and taken the ship. They'll wait for us to bring her down."

The One Eye glanced at her timepiece.

A loud snap sounded in their ears, and the rumble of several nearly synchronous explosions galloped outward from the rez. Light flared from the outer surface of the mirror field. Jenae was still cringing when Keila kicked her into action. The One Eye was already on her feet and dashing toward the three humans, who had thrown themselves flat on the ground when the detonation occurred. Jenae lurched after her, wincing at the mix of ozone and burning plastic and wire. Several small fires had ignited in the dry brush around the rez, one bursting out almost beneath her feet. She avoided it just in time to see Keila point her weapon at the two remaining men, who had been caught facedown on the ground.

"Don't do anything stupid," Keila warned them. "I know it's hard to break old habits, but try."

The third, smaller figure had moved faster and was now standing only a few meters away. At first the weapon in her hand was pointed at Keila; its muzzle swiveled slowly toward Jenae.

"Yi Ling!" Jenae shouted as she approached. "It's Jenae. It's me, Yi Ling!"

There was an element of joy in her voice, and she felt rebuffed when the slim figure stood unmoving.

"Oh, shit," Jenae exclaimed out loud. "It *is* you, isn't it?"

There was a long silence. Slowly the figure approached; hypnotized, Jenae thought of her gun too late. The woman was only a meter away, at point-blank range but backlit by fire. She turned her head slightly and the moonlight caught her face.

"Yes, it's me."

Yi Ling's face was pitted and cracked, a wreck of running sores and ruined skin. Her lips were black, eyes swollen half shut. One hand had strayed to her side as if something pained her there, and her whole body was consequently canted over slightly. Her mouth made an uneven grimace of pain. On the side of her neck, unmistakable even in the dim light, were four parallel slashes. Gills.

Jenae cried out as though struck.

"I'm sorry," she whispered. "I'm so sorry, Yi Ling. I never should have left you. Please, let me help you now. . . ."

Yi Ling's expression didn't change. Smoke from the brushfires blew between them, and Jenae was vaguely aware of shouts and activity up in what had been the rez and below in the harbor, but here everything was still. The fires brought more light, and now she could clearly see Keila on the periphery of her vision, a reassuring mass standing guard over the two Coalition members, who now sat on the ground.

"Go back, Jenae," Yi Ling said in a whisper. "Go to the sea. You can't save me now."

Jenae shook her head. "You don't know that! You've survived this long—maybe it isn't too late for you after all. Maybe you can still develop altermode." Listening to herself, she knew she was giving in to wishful thinking, but she wanted to get Yi Ling back so badly that she just kept on talking. "Don't stay with these people. They'll treat you like a monster, now. Wait 'til I tell you what I've learned—everything is different now! You won't have to live this way." She rattled on, stretching out her hand toward her sister.

The gun remained in Yi Ling's hand, and it was still pointed at her, but Jenae ignored it. She took the slight step forward that let her touch her sister's hand.

The hand was warm, familiar. It was all just the same. Tears squeezed Jenae's throat shut as the gun was slowly lowered. Yi Ling's expression softened. Jenae lifted her other arm to enfold Yi Ling, drawing her sister toward her. Relief and gratitude overwhelmed her, threatening to buckle her knees as they embraced.

Just for that moment, Yi Ling was hers. She could sense it as clearly as if it had been spoken. But then something went wrong. With her back to the fallen mirror field, Jenae couldn't see what had changed, but she felt Yi Ling stiffen, and in the next instant her twin had wrenched away, trembling. Startled, Jenae turned to see a burst of gunfire light the scene. There was a brief scuffle, and suddenly Keila was on the ground. One of her two prisoners lay prone, but the other held Keila's gun, pressing it against the One Eye's skull. Even on the ground, Keila's posture was stiff, her head angled sharply to look up the hillside. She was absolutely still. Jenae blinked, trying to figure out what was going on. Keila would never let herself be overcome so easily. She looked strange. . . .

Yi Ling had taken several steps backward, her gun raised again and pointed at Jenae. But her attention went past Jenae, to the hillside behind her. Jenae continued turning to see what everyone was looking at. The man who had walked alone up toward the mirror field, minutes before midnight, was also the man who had stolen her sister. Now he was moving steadily toward them.

"Is this an attempt at reunion and reconciliation?" Brian's pleasant tone had always grated on Jenae, but never more than at this moment. Jenae's left hand crept toward her own weapon. Keila will be out of this in no time, Jenae instructed herself, so just wait and follow her cue. Brian's going to get his just deserts this time.

"Go over and join your cohort, the other abomination," Brian said. "If this is the kind of company you keep, I don't think I can allow you to associate with Yi Ling anymore."

Abomination, Jenae scoffed silently, barely checking herself from speaking aloud. Have you *looked* at Yi Ling lately? She'll never be human again.

Brian was gesturing with some sort of weapon, and Keila didn't make eye contact, so Jenae reluctantly complied. Distant screams reached her ears with the noise and strobe of more explosions from the rez.

"Drop the weapon," Yi Ling added. Jenae gave her sister an incredulous look and pulled out the laser pistol, tossing it to the ground with an air of disdain.

"There," she said to Yi Ling. "Are you happy?"

"I won't be happy until all your kind are gone," Brian

answered instead. "Put your hands on your head. Turn around and face me. Kneel down."

Yi Ling followed her until Jenae knelt beside Keila. Then Yi Ling backed up to stand next to Brian. Jenae stole glances at Keila, but the One Eye ignored her. Jenae's confidence wilted slightly. At first she hadn't been worried. She'd seen Keila's feats of strength and speed before, and she knew a few diseased pure humans were no match for the One Eye. But Keila was obviously not comfortable. Her eye was fixed unwaveringly on the object in Brian's hand. It was a small forked instrument, rather like a slingshot. Jenae had never seen anything like it before. It was not on the list Milan had made her memorize, so it must be something old, something the Coalition had picked up among the ruins of Darwin.

"Cut this shit out, Brian," Jenae snapped nervously. She was angry at herself for not watching her back. If Keila wasn't going to do something, Jenae would, dammit. If she rushed Yi Ling, what would her sister do? Shoot her? Never. Brian and the other human couldn't shoot if Jenae was close to Yi Ling, either. Even in the firelight, there were many shadows. They wouldn't be able to trust their aim. She gathered herself to spring forward.

A green light flashed in Jenae's eyes. She blinked.

"You're programmed into my locator," Brian said. "It's read your genetic pattern. Do you know what's in this weapon? The fastest-known kill virus ever developed." He sounded as smug as if he had invented the thing, Jenae thought. "Once I let it go, it'll knock you out in two minutes or less. Untreatable, 99.9 percent mortality, documented. And it's smart. It's now been programmed to go for nobody but you. You can't get away. You're dead, Jenae Kim."

"Back off, Jenae," Yi Ling warned, the pitch of her voice rising in alarm. Her gun trained on Keila wavered. "He won't use it on you if you back off now. Will you, Brian?" There was a quaver of uncertainty in her voice. Brian said nothing. Yi Ling looked back at Jenae, her eyes begging. "Back off!"

Jenae turned her eyes away from her sister's, trying to think. They're going to kill Keila anyway, she told herself, even if they don't kill me. Some emotion acted in her then—not anger, but a close relative, quicker and altogether more effective. The sudden, decisive whip of this feeling propelled her sideways so fast she surprised herself; she lunged at the legs of the human whose gun was aimed at the back of Keila's head, knocking the man off balance. The second or so that it took for this to happen was dense with movement. Even as Jenae struck out, Keila twisted and seized the weapon, wrenching it out of the man's grasp. Out of all the impressions that came at her just then, the soft sound of fingers breaking commanded Jenae's attention. She was still hitting ground, the wind just banging out of her lungs, when Yi Ling's alarmed cry rang out. Jenae turned her head just in time to see an odd smoky green ball pop out of the locator and drift toward her, almost slowly it seemed.

Oh, well, Jenae thought, watching it come. It had to happen. Even if I've only got two minutes I'm going to slay this fucker Brian before it's over.

But then Yi Ling thrust herself between Brian and Jenae. The ball did not dart around her sister in its quest for Jenae the way it should. Instead, the green energy mass collided with Yi Ling in a horrible little nova. Brian let out a guttural cry and dropped the locator.

Jenae was aware that Keila was moving near her, securing control of Brian and the other Coalition soldier, but she had eyes only for her sister. Yi Ling's hand went to her mouth. She licked her lips, blinking hard. The sores on her face glistened. Jenae tried to get up, hand extended toward Yi Ling half in comfort, half in supplication.

"No," Yi Ling said clearly. "Don't touch me, or you'll catch it, too, Jenae." There was a hint of irony in her wasted face. "Even now, we're still twins." She paused, drew a breath. She looked intently at Jenae while the disbelieving tears flooded Jenae's face, while Jenae's teeth clenched and her hands knotted into fists. Yi Ling continued, "Only one of us could live. I chose you. Live." She drew another breath. "I—"

Her idea half finished, she drifted to the ground like a piece of crumpled paper.

Jenae's head went back; her throat opened. She waited for the howling to come up from inside her. She waited with her blank eyes gaping at the soft, voiceless night sky above, wishing it could bring death to her, too.

She had never seen this sky before. It was the sky of being alone.

The thought cut off her breath and she made no sound.

◆

Someone new is here, still unseen but sparkling with consciousness within the system. Thanks to the rash of conflicts that have erupted between One Eyes and the Coalition, the eyes of the Heads are turned outward, seeking how best to judge and profit from the confusion—seeking the way best to enjoy it. So no one has traced this newcomer to the mesh of the inner workings. But this eager construct has been busy, indeed, dredging up the memories of the Sleepers, though it manifests itself in the system only as a soft, neutral voice. It cajoles even now.

"Tell me more, Eric. Here, does that help? I've just released some of your memory. Don't ask me how I did it."

"Thank you, it does help. I have these hallucinations, sometimes, you see. Brutal things, they can be. I'm standing in a dark room, a place lit with a lot of monitor screens and panels and all sorts of hardware, which is mostly a mystery to me. There's a fat, lazy man sitting in the control chair spinning a stylus between his fingers—"

"It sounds awfully detailed."

"Oh, it is! It always is. But that's only the beginning. We're looking out through a clear panel into a darkened space . . . a lab, I guess, and there's a spotlight trained on this small child. Looks—I don't know—nine years old? He's sitting on his hands on a bare Formica table. He doesn't look around. Doesn't even seem like he knows where he is. Apathetic, you know?"

"Mm hmm."

"So I say to the man in the booth, I say, 'What's the trouble?' And he says, 'Authorization.' 'For what?' I say. 'Spinal dissection,' he says. He says, 'We think we can work with the others, save time and keep the rest of the lot alive. No sense throwing out the whole batch if it's a problem we can fix. I want this one for closer study, though.'

"I say: 'You mean . . . sacrifice?' and he goes, 'We'll look at the living spine, then, yeah, we'll sacrifice and make a computer model of the tissue.'

"I'm feeling really squeamish right now, but he's looking at me expectantly.

" 'Why me?' I say, and the look on his face makes me embarrassed. His social skills are really lacking. It's obvious he thinks I'm rather stupid, but I don't need to know about that, do I? I mean, show some respect, I'm thinking.

'The rest of the Board are in Prague, aren't they, *sir*?' he remarks. He's still twirling that stupid pen.

"I say with some irritation, 'Well, if it can't wait . . . all right, do it. But I'll remind you that my area is finance. I don't claim to understand this aspect of the business at all. I'd appreciate it if in the future you would arrange your timing to coincide with the others' being here.' Or something like that. I don't know the exact words. For some reason, this whole situation is making me really steamed, although I can't understand why, telling you about it now.

" 'Sure, Mr. Lumumba. I'll call in my team.' He goes for the com. Lumumba? I mean, who the hell is he?"

"The CFO of Ingenix was called Hannibal Lumumba."

"How'd I get *his* dream?"

"Go on. How does it end?"

"I look at the boy. He hasn't moved. He doesn't even seem to understand what's about to happen to him. 'What next?' I ask.

" 'Would you like to see the procedure?' he asks, and I can see it's professional pride speaking now. I don't know what I say. Part of me really wants to see it. Part of me wants to do it. And yet, as soon as I stand back and think about it, it's just horrible. It's just one episode in this oneiric horror show that I get all the time I'm not working, now. Can you explain the dream?"

"Are you sure it is a dream?"

"What else could it be?"

"You'll notice that you were only able to provide the details of the encounter after I had helped you with the memory blocks you've been equipped with."

"What are you saying? It's a corporeal memory, is that what you mean?"

"That's what I'm afraid of. What do you remember about your body?"

"I don't have a body. No, I'm sure it's not that. I think it's just fantasies brought on by this *Morpheus* business. It's stirring up all these fragments I don't know what to do with. Isn't it bothering you at all to be reminded of those times? Those criminals, still out there somewhere?"

"She calls you Sleepers, you know. Nothing's supposed to faze you."

"Who calls us Sleepers?"

"You know. Her. The one who gets upset when you call her Haven. Have you ever wondered why she gets upset? She calls you Sleepers, because you don't get involved."

"That's true enough, most of the time. I don't mind working—it can be fun—but only on a technical level, like the market in Singapore. Otherwise, I don't want to know what they're doing. I want to be happy, don't you see?"

"Yes, I understand completely. Happy."

◆

"Jenae," said Keila's voice in her ear. "This is enough. Stop this instantly."

Keila sounded angry, Jenae thought torpidly.

She was grabbed by the shoulder and shaken. She was lying on a hard surface. The surface was moving, and it smelled of brine. She felt like shit.

"Give her a good hard kick," Milan suggested.

"She hasn't eaten in two weeks," Keila said. "She hasn't had fluids in at least a day. Look at her skin! When was the last time you saw her go into altermode?"

Milan grunted. "Not since before Perth. A month?"

"We won't reach Jakarta for several more days, and she needs medical attention. So delicate! They're not like us. They can't last long without food or water."

"I can force-feed her," Milan offered. "But why bother? If she gives up, she gives up. . . ."

A hand covered her forehead. Milan said, "She's feverish. Come one, Jenae. Do as you're told and drink some water."

Something cool and damp touched her face, and she was shaken again. There was a soft clatter. Milan muttered, "Hello. What's this? A disc?"

"Give it to me," Keila said. She nudged Jenae's ribs. "This is suicide," she hissed. "You are better than that. Don't do as they do. Don't give in. You need water. You need altermode. Do you hear me, Jenae?" Pause. An actual kick to the ribs this time, none too gentle. "Wake up, Jenae. Look at yourself. Your gills are drying up!" Keila's tone deepened. This was an an unusual expression of emotion, Jenae realized idly before she let herself drift away from consciousness again. Her limbs were twitching of their own volition. She needed altermode, she knew vaguely, but she was beyond caring.

Someone was lifting her. Bumpy movement. Then a sudden release: she was falling.

Jenae's eyes opened to water rushing up at her.

Keila had thrown her overboard. She surfaced briefly, still in a daze, trying to focus her eyes.

"Get your shit together!" Keila called after her from the deck. Already the boat was moving away from her. "Fight, or die."

The weight of her clothes made it easy to sink, and Jenae's body tried to switch to altermode despite weakness and exhaustion. But the fabric that was needed to protect her in the open air now choked off the fine outer skin that her body needed to supplement the intake of her gills. The water-soaked cloth was corpse-heavy, a clinging second skin. She tried to swim against it, but she was sinking slowly, kicking. She would have screamed if she could, but there wasn't enough air in her lungs, and gills and mouth both were swathed in tangled cloth. Her fingers scrabbled at the metal fasteners that closed the robes at her throat. She was getting weaker.

Damn Keila, she thought. And damn you, Yi Ling, for dying.

Everything she'd tried to do had led to this outcome. Fight or die? What did it matter? There had never been any choice, and there never would be.

Give it up. Give it up.

She could see the end, and it wasn't in the starry neural overload of the Heads' paranoid attack, nor the ironic precision of a locator gun. It was to be the soft petering out of a flame trapped beneath a glass, deprived of its essential substance. Dolphins might find her here: neither human nor fish; neither single mind nor part of something larger; just something that had never defined itself, now become food for the seething tide. They might just find her. But they couldn't save her now. Even if she stretched out for the web, even if she called, they would only be witnesses. To her great shame, they would only share her giving up.

Jenae clenched her teeth, clawing at the heavy robes, all the violence she had been powerless to express now focused on wrenching herself loose. Her attention all ground down to the fine movement of her fingers searching through folds of cloth for the clasps that would release the neck of the robes. Her mind tried to bolster the flagging strength in her arms struggling against the tough fabric. Her fingertips touched metal, she released the clips, and suddenly it was easy. Shaking herself all over, she slithered out of the clothes and swam away naked, leaving the robes swaying empty in the undersea current.

25

Hand over foot, fluidly, Tsering climbed. She raised herself by degree, palms catching branches and pressing firm to the papery skin of the lywyn. She could feel the current within the wood: it responded to her presence, singing into her hand in gentle recognition. How can you sense my mood? she asked of it, silently. She had never thought of the lywyn as a person, precisely, for its plurality, its very size, prevented such a comparison. Yet it had always been animate to her in a way that the sky and the ocean and the wind were not. In its feathery light she had met the dead and known their memories, and the lywyn's presence, boding, full of lightning, had given her existence a continuity without which she would have despaired long ago, a victim of her species's own truth in self-destruction. For many years now she had been coming to think of herself as one of the lywyn's creations—had she not outlived four generations of her own kind? Until Daire had come it had seemed to her that she was just another kind of ghost, visiting these lost children as a guardian. Benefactress, no—for she couldn't save them. Malefactress, maybe: would they not be better off dead than distorted? But she'd never been able to convince herself that it would be all right to let the race die out, and so she went on saving all she could.

For years, stubbornly, she had kept on. She was the only person standing in between the children and the death of their race. Even the distorted, out there in the cold speechless sea, even they would perish without her. She had seen their bodies: after distortion, the sex organs atrophied—the distorted had no way to reproduce. Such was the madness of her people's developmental structure. She herself was alive only because she was a freak, unless she was to go on believing the lywyn had somehow saved her. And it was hard to believe that, now, because that paradigm of salvation that she'd held dear had changed. *She* had changed, and for no reason she could understand. The rhythms of her life had gone haywire. She could see her years stretched out in their entirety, and the picture didn't make sense. Growth arrested at eleven. A long struggle of sixty-odd years, during which she had established a working order for her people. Then sudden puberty. Now reproduction (with its successor, distortion, lurking close by). As soon as she had realized what was happening, that day when she found Daire, she had feared it would happen fast. But not this fast. If her body was truthful, she was already pregnant.

"Is this the end of the journey, and no explanation?" she asked aloud, and stopped climbing. She settled in a net of thin branches near the lywyn roof. Fine leaves spun in the sunlit breeze above: new growth, there. She laid her hand on her belly, palm down. "Everything I think and feel lives in the service of this act that I can't control. All I have learned means nothing. All I am means nothing. Our chromosomes, mine and his, are skating around in there, and I don't matter in the slightest. But *why*? Why keep me alive so many years to let it end like this? Why?"

Even as she voiced her thoughts, their absurdity took hold of her. She had been according to the lywyn a kind of human rationality that it quite probably did not possess—yet she was powerless to reach it in its own realm. The lywyn was the closest thing to divinity she could imagine encountering, but she didn't know if this was because of or in spite of its difference.

"Speak to me," she insisted. "You owe me that. You owe me a reason that I can comprehend. Don't deny me the understanding we have shared for so long."

She didn't expect a sensible answer in words: she had never received one yet, but always she had been answered in other ways—or so she had imagined. Now she lay back in the springy hammock of branches, breathing deep the sunwarmed air, and tried to make herself quiescent. She watched the insects tracking their way back and forth to the lywyn well, highways of reflected light showing where their shining bodies passed. After a time, a cloud of anki swarmed around the boles nearest her and, approaching, settled on her face; she shivered and twitched, but allowed them. She closed her eyes and took the dream.

Death the mother, drinker of water, had come. Night. Wings. Laughter. And stone. Lightning seemed to be everywhere, but in this newly visible truth it moved in dynamic patterns: it was only where it was permitted to be. Leaping synapses between branch and bone, it entered eleven-year-old Tsering: lightning attuned. Intentional lightning, carved to change. Broken and rebuilt in her body the electricity rewrote scripts for her, and in the dream as she had not in memory, eleven-year-old Tsering opened her eyes inside the lightning and saw the gate. She saw through the gate the dark planet in which had drowned the faces of stars. She felt the gate's pull, a life force as potent as the sun, and she was aware of her place veined and threaded through the net of the lywyn. Lywyn shivered in the precarious meeting place between sun and great darkness. The black lake she now perceived as a stillness that belied the force beneath. Lywyn lived by the gate, stretched its multiple mind through.

Death and mother: the gate through which Daire had passed. Mother to the lywyn, but implicit threat as well, impossibly strong. Fed by and growing against this opponent over the long ages, somehow the lywyn had taught itself to leaven the chaos of the gate, transforming it into a kind of order. She could never pass through the black lake, for she was bound to the lywyn as surely as if its transparent blood ran in her arteries.

Lywyn was like algae growing at impossible depths in Earth's sea, clustered around the thermal chutes that bring the heat of the planet's core into the ocean. Lywyn was a thing of the gate as much as it was a creature of this planet. And she had been drinking chaos every time she took the lywyn water, for that was what the forest grew on: the storm of the ragged hole Daire had so blithely sailed through, sleeping in the mud at her feet that morning so long ago.

She opened her eyes and the anki crawled delicately

down her cheeks, heavenly tears. She thought: I will never leave this place. But my child may. My child may.

◆

"Motherf—!"

Dropping the bolt and wrench, Daire jammed his burned thumb into his mouth, muffling the expletive.

A series of twitters erupted above him. Several pairs of bare feet and legs surrounded him, but lying on his back beneath the big metal dish he couldn't see faces.

"Are you okay, Daire?" chorused two or three kids.

"Daire almost said motherfucker," Naro commented gleefully.

"I don't get it. . . ."

More giggles.

"Naro, get down here!" Daire commanded. The boy dropped down into a squat, his eyes wide.

"Yes, Daire?"

"Get me some shade on this thing. It's already too hot to touch. Bring a blanket or something else big enough to cover it. White if possible."

"Okay, Daire." Naro stood up. "Come on, let's get Daire some fucking shade!"

They ran off. Daire sucked his thumb meditatively and eased himself out from beneath his attempted solar stove, scraping his bare back against stones as he did so. He was covered in sweat, and his skin was coated with red dust. He swung the long braid out of his way with some irritation: the hair was an affectation he had once enjoyed cultivating, but now it was only a nuisance. If Tsering had not protested so loudly, he would have shaved it, or at least cropped it close. Every night she brushed it out for him, very slowly and with great care. And when she was done and it fell smoothly down his back, he would turn around and look at her, and she would smile, and then they would make love.

At these times he felt his was a more perfect existence than anything he could have imagined, before Dilarang. Lying with Tsering asleep in his arms, he didn't miss anything about Earth: not adult human interaction, not the technology, not even the particulars of home, food, and drink that travelers so often yearn for. None of it mattered in the context of what he had here. He had all the space he needed and no one but himself to dictate his actions. He had the love of someone who continually surprised him. When he closed his eyes at the end of each day, he felt complete.

Then, last night, when she finished brushing out his hair, Daire turned to face Tsering and saw a curious half smile on her face. For some reason a nervous laugh came into his throat.

"I have something to tell you," she whispered.

He should have seen it coming.

"Daire, I'm pregnant."

What a strange thing to say. Daire held his breath.

"Did you hear me?" she said. He nodded rapidly, trying to assimilate the information.

"Okay . . . ?" His voice trailed off on a rising note. He had to stall for time.

Her gaze turned fierce. "What do you mean, 'okay'? Okay, what?"

"I'm thinking. Can you let me think for just a second?"

She sighed. "Go ahead, Daire. Think."

This is it, Daire, he told himself. This is one of those moments when you'd better make fucking sure you say the right thing. She's waiting. Say the right thing. . . .

He looked into her eyes, hoping the panic didn't show.

"I . . . I'm honored. I mean, I guess I shouldn't be so surprised, but . . . I am."

Now Tsering started to laugh, and he felt like he'd been slapped. "You're scared shitless, aren't you, Daire?"

He bridled. "Maybe, but so what if I am? That doesn't mean I'm any less amazed. Has anything like this ever happened before—someone with your genes and someone with pure human genes, together?"

This was all wrong. Now it would become an intellectual argument, when they should be celebrating the wonder of it. Why did there have to be words between him and Tsering all the time?

"No," Tsering answered seriously. "It's never happened before, and it brings up some serious problems." She fell silent, and it began to occur to Daire that maybe Tsering wasn't happy about this. He braced himself.

"What problems, exactly?" he asked.

"Well, for starters, I'm aging rapidly. This fast pregnancy proves it. Without me, I don't know what kind of future the kids have. I mean, without me, who's going to take care of things? Who's going to be midwife and nanny and drill sergeant and teacher? Who's going to protect them from their own parents? Does it really make sense for us to keep propagating ourselves, when it's all going to go to pieces with my distortion? I'm sorry—I know you don't want to hear the downside, but there always is one."

When she met his eyes he realized she had been thinking about this a lot. He chose his words carefully. "First of all," he said, "I'm not thinking about what's going to happen after you distort. I'm not concerned with that now. I'm concerned with the present. And second, what's to say I can't do those things, if the time comes?"

She was practically laughing at him. "You? *You?* You think you can go from a prolonged adolescence to that level of commitment in just a few months?"

"Prolonged adolescence? Is that what you call my life? Well, to you, maybe, it is, but I happen to be the only person *ever* to pass through one of those gates alive, not once, but three times!" Daire gestured vaguely in the direction of the lake. "But I can see there's no point in trying to justify myself to you. You're determined to read doom into everything that happens."

She bowed her head. "Maybe I'm not being fair . . . it's just that, when you came here, I knew you would bring change, but I didn't think it would be like this. So . . . personal, for me. Instead I thought we'd have some contact with Earth. Don't get me wrong—at first I dreaded that contact, but after I prepared myself for it I realized I wanted to know. I've been waiting all my life for an explanation of what was done to my parents, and why. Now you're here, I'm carrying your child, and there's no indication that anyone's going to come and help us. *If* they would help us."

Stunned, Daire said nothing at first. He stood up, but since they were in Tsering's house he couldn't rise to his full height. He walked across the room and sat down again. "I thought you wanted me to stay here," he said. "When I went back to try to find Colin, you acted like I shouldn't have gone, like it didn't matter."

"I didn't want you to become some kind of martyr for us. And I didn't want to allow myself any kind of hope. For myself, I mean. But for our child—that's another story. I hoped . . . I expected more to happen."

Daire rubbed his temples with his fingertips. "So did I. The gate does open from time to time. I don't know why no one comes. I planted a transmitter on Underkohling for Colin to find. Wherever he is. Giving interviews, I guess, and collecting money. Eventually the League will receive the signal, and they'll want to help us. Believe me, the League will understand your situation. Hell, altermoders are probably your distant cousins. It's only a matter of time before someone comes. Of course, time is the one thing we don't have to spare. I've tried to find out how the lywyn altered your growth pattern; I've been studying it every day, but who am I kidding? I do software, not biology. I'm not sure if the lywyn is really biology, anyway. I'm not sure what it is."

Tsering got up and followed him to where he sat in the corner. She sat down next to him and leaned against him.

"Don't look like that, Daire. I didn't mean to get into a big thing. . . ."

"Yes, you did."

"Anyway, we have several months to figure out about the kid. I was thinking, though, how you said you wanted to travel farther into the lywyn. Maybe you should go soon, before I get big and awkward. . . ."

Now, sweating in the heat off the solar parabola he was trying to construct, he saw how easily he'd been manipulated. She had practically told him to leave for a few days. Why? The whole thing rankled him. He knew Tsering was doing him a disservice when she doubted his ability to adapt to the situation here. He didn't understand how her head worked. Did she see him as a threat to her authority? It was ridiculous—he had no desire to tell anybody what to do, and she knew that. If anything, he was trying to conform to the culture here.

Hadn't he tried his best to bring a higher level of technology to the village? He'd scrapped pieces of *Morpheus*, and he'd used the ship's archives to construct simple but powerful tools, like the dragon's backbone pump he'd ripped off from an ancient Chinese design and built out of dead lywyn.

And today he'd spent the morning wrestling with scrap metal, trying to give the village a way to cook without burning fuel.

But it wasn't enough, and he knew it. He was almost a mythic character to the kids, if not to Tsering, and he was expected to perform miracles. He was supposed to play Big Scientist. Even in Tsering's mind, he didn't know how he was going to live up to his billing. She said she didn't believe in salvation, but still she expected him to save her. And she expected him to understand everything without being told.

He rubbed his red-tinted palm with his thumb, moving the dirt around. He laughed. More impossible things. Why not?

Naro and Rena came running with a white sheet flapping between them.

"Is this good?" Rena gasped.

"It'll do," Daire answered. "We'll put it up on stakes over the parabola, and once things cool off tonight, I'll finish attaching the supports. Then you can go catch some fish and tomorrow we'll try this thing out on flesh other than my own." He showed them the blister on his thumb.

"You need some ointment for that," Rena said.

"Go ahead and get me some, will you? And bring Adamo, if you can. Tell him I've got a big project for him."

26

"Daire, are you ready yet?" Adamo lingered awkwardly in the doorway of Tsering's house, no longer at liberty to barge in at any hour since Daire had taken to sleeping there. It was dawn. He had outfitted himself with the field pack Daire had given him from the hopper, and he fidgeted in place.

Tsering was outside vomiting audibly; with each fresh spasm, Daire flinched. He double-checked the field pack he'd prepared for himself and then rose to join Adamo. He clapped the boy on the shoulder as he stepped outside. "Got everything? Batteries charged?"

Adamo nodded. "Gonna be hot," he said, starting toward the lywyn. "We walk up the stream as far as we can." He shot a glance toward the back of the house, where Tsering knelt miserably on the ground. Daire suppressed a stab of guilt at leaving her this way; she had, he reminded himself, done perfectly well on her own since before he was born. She had also insisted she wanted him to go. He wondered if she still felt that way this morning, puking her guts out.

"See you in a few days," he called, and received a feeble wave in reply. Adamo in his eagerness was already beneath the shadow of the lywyn and heading for the cliff.

So far, Daire had concluded that the lake's ecosystem was not particularly complex: it boasted photosynthetic plants and algae, microorganisms similar to those found on Earth, and a thriving animal population that included worms, eels, crustaceans, and boneless fishes. He did not find evidence of large-scale predation—but it was interesting to note the number of species with adaptations for electricity: some stunfish, but even more smaller animals with physiological devices to neutralize electricity. Some of the bottom-growing plants were receptive to electric current and used it to supplement light energy in their metabolic processes.

But nothing explained the lywyn. The structure itself housed any number of insect symbionts that fed on the lywyn fluid and each other. There were also places where viny undergrowth and even grass coexisted with the lywyn, and there were dozens of different mosses and slimes that inhabited the darker regions of the forest. Many of these, according to Adamo, were edible, and had served the colony well during poor harvests, when the insects would prey especially on a given crop for no apparent reason.

Despite this modest diversity of life, there were no forms similar to the lywyn: no relatives, nothing to point to a taxonomy. Adamo had shown him dead sections, where the colony got its wood for tools. But this dead wood was relatively scarce, and Tsering's people only rarely used it for fuel, burning instead bundles of the oily, inedible green seaweed that they gathered along with the purplish, tasty variety. There were also minerals in the cave that were inflammable, but these tended to explode, and Daire had been eager to implement some simple solar heating devices. In any event, dead lywyn was brittle and light, pale and dry, with an unremarkable internal structure of veins, fibers, and honeycomb chambers whose function he had not discovered. It was severed electrically from the living wood, by what chemical process he also had yet to learn.

He wished many times for an able team and the proper equipment. Adamo had a rudimentary grasp of the scientific method, but he was, after all, only a kid. The strange uniform quality of the lywyn that made it seem closer to a fungus—or a crystal—than to a higher plant perplexed him. There was a lack of differentiation between individuals that made it impossible to determine where one tree left off and the next began. There were multiple trunks and root systems, but no real separation of organisms: and no sex organs, as such. Yet the lywyn was living fluid and contained various RNAs. It really did seem to be one enormous growth—but how, Daire asked himself over and over, could such a thing evolve? What opportunity was there for selection to work its magic when there seemed to be no intraspecies competition?

Either there were more lywyns disconnected from this one, or selection was operating on individual sections of the whole. Since he had been unable to find any morphological differences between sections of the lywyn, he cast his search outward. Where did the lywyn begin and end—and how had it arisen in the first place? What purpose did the weird lights and noise, the ghosts, the lightning, serve? Why the sound-transmitting pools, the strange fluid, the memories that inter-acted?

He could not yet answer these questions: it was becoming obvious that he needed well-planned experiments, not to mention a deeper knowledge of plant processes. But since he had nothing to lose, he had recruited Adamo to help him ex-plore the boundaries of the lywyn. He had legitimate scien-tific purposes, but also he was groping for any way out of the impasse he saw ahead: Tsering on her way to distortion, and their child imperiled. Beyond that, he was simply curious about what else this planet had, besides the lywyn. It seemed extraordinary that the *Morpheus* kids had apparently never explored beyond their own valley; High was like another world to them. When he had asked Tsering, she'd said, "My parents' generation only explored far enough to determine that there were no people here. There was no reason to go anywhere when they had everything they needed here."

This was a mentality Daire could not understand. Ever since his first glimpse of the landscape from high in the lywyn, he had been eager to see more.

High was familiar territory to him, but they did not go near the village on their journey. Instead they skirted the phalanx of windmills and struck out inland, to the east, where the open land rose slowly toward hills. To their left as they hiked was the lip of the cliff, and at its foot, the lywyn. To the right was a broad, treeless expanse of highland that stretched for several miles to the south. Then came the ocean again. North, on the lowlands, spread the lywyn as far as the eye could see.

By the end of the day they had begun to climb. The cliff to their left had softened into the rising humps of mountains, and the sharp division between lywyn and High gradually disappeared. Lywyn didn't cover the hills uniformly, though: it stretched "feet" out and up into the hills like an amoeba, and much of the ground not covered by lywyn was bare except for the same rough grass that surrounded High. The first patch of lywyn that they reached in the highlands seemed to blow Adamo's mind.

"It's dwarf!" he cried, rushing forward and trying to climb into it. This area of lywyn was still attached to the main forest, but it stuck out like a peninsula over the rocky, slanting ground. It was miniature, and even Adamo could not climb into it. The branches were too slender and its roof too low to accommodate him. Still, he crawled in on his hands and knees, soon invisible in the twilight.

Daire had been making notes and sketches, trying to create a map, and when he looked up several minutes later, he couldn't see the boy.

"Come on, Adamo," he called. "Let's go a little farther, and then we'll make camp."

Daire listened through the wind thrashing the grass behind him and humming in the leaves of the small lywyn, but there was no reply. A yellow light fell over these interlocked trees, giving them an age-stained look. It's a fairy forest, Daire thought, and imagined Adamo, shrunken down proportionally, within.

He dropped to his hands and knees and tried to part the branches, but they were stiffer than they looked. He could not get inside without damaging the lywyn. Jamming his head through a gap in the branches, he finally saw inside.

The inner branches were slithering and crawling like snakes.

Daire jerked back, catching his hair painfully on an outflung branch.

"Adamo, dammit!" he shouted, ripping the field knife from his belt and looking for the best place to cut. "Quit playing and get out here!" He commanded himself to slice at the branches, but his hand wouldn't go. The lywyn will bleed, he thought.

Suddenly Adamo came wriggling out of a gap several meters from where he had gone in, shaking leaves out of his hair. Daire lowered the knife, at once relieved and angry.

"Daire, this is weird!" Adamo called, hurrying toward

him. "I found the lywyn water, and I took it, but there are no ghosts here!"

Daire grabbed his arm and dragged him away from the trees.

"Ow!"

"I'm taking you back right now. If I make you run we can be back at High by midnight."

"What?" Outrage colored the boy's tone.

"You're supposed to be guiding me, not getting into trouble. I don't have time to rescue you, and Tsering will have my head if anything happens to you!"

Adamo stopped in his tracks, resisting. "No! Daire, don't make me go back. Come on, I was just looking around. I won't do it again, I promise!"

Daire looked at the boy skeptically. "You drank the lywyn without Tsering there? Just like that?"

"I know what I'm doing." Adamo scuffed the ground sullenly. "I'm sorry, okay? Come *on*, Daire, don't be like that!"

Daire let go of the boy's arm in mock disgust. "No ghosts. I wonder what that means."

Adamo didn't have an answer to this, although they debated the subject over their evening meal. "Maybe I did it wrong," he ventured. "Maybe I didn't focus right."

"No," Daire said. "You shouldn't need to do anything. The ghosts come on their own."

"Maybe it's baby lywyn. You know, because it's so small. . . ."

Daire lifted an eyebrow. "Maybe it is," he said.

When they slept that night, no anki came. As Daire was drifting off to sleep, he lay thinking about distortion, wondering what it really was and what came after it. He found himself recalling his attempts, after he first piloted the hopper back from Underkohling, to catch a glimpse of the distorted. He had kept up a routine day after day for weeks, but when he realized he wasn't going to see anything, he'd stopped. He used to wake up very early and sneak away from Tsering, out into the darkened lywyn. He would climb the cliff and walk to High before the sun was up, then descend the sea cliff carefully in the dark and fog, feeling his way along the packed earth steps the lessents had carved out to make a path to the waterside.

He walked out onto the beach below the cliffs of High, where the sea swept in to a narrow margin of pale sand past jagged, black fingers of rock that groped out of the water.

He sat down on the sand, waiting for the fog to clear.

After a while there was movement in the whiteness, and he stood up and began to walk down toward the water. The fog parted raggedly before him, and a ribbon of light appeared out on the sea, where the sun first angled onto the water over the top of the cliff. The beach remained in shadow as he walked forward.

Out beyond the breakers, dark bodies broke surface and puffed out air, but to his surprise, they were not the distorted at all. They were dolphins, moving fast in the water, two or three occasionally leaping in synchrony.

Behind him, Tsering's voice said, "Don't worry."

He whirled, but although he'd turned to face the cliff, her voice still came from behind him. "I'm not leaving," she said.

He turned again, and she was laughing, still behind him though he couldn't catch a glimpse of her. In a moment he was spinning in circles, trying to find her.

"I'm never leaving," she said, very close to his ear.

Daire came awake with a jolt. He was lying on hard ground under the stars. Adamo was snoring nearby.

◆

The face was so wedded to the shadows that only the white eyes were visible among the snarling branches of lywyn. Tsering was straightening up, her guts aching and her head ringing from prolonged vomiting, when her glance passed over the intimation of a face. She gave no sign she was aware she was being watched; instead she spat, wiped her mouth, and stepped away from the stinking liquid on the moss. She sank down against the nearest lywyn bole and let out a weary sigh.

"Come and talk to me, Michelle."

The eyes disappeared. There was a long silence. Tsering looked at her feet and made a beckoning gesture with one hand. "Come on. I know you're there."

Michelle dropped out of the lywyn over her head and stood looking down on her. "How could you do this to us?"

Tsering felt herself flush at the mix of fear and betrayal in Michelle's tone. She had answered to no one but herself for too long; she didn't know how she was ever going to climb out of the hole she'd dug by keeping the truth from the lessents. There was a certain guilty relief at finally being confronted, but looking up at Michelle, Tsering was suddenly conscious that she could no longer claim the privilege of being leader. She would soon be as dependent on the others as they had always been on her.

"I didn't do it *to* you," she answered in a low voice. "I began ovulating. What could I do? It was bound to happen sooner or later. I'm an old woman, or I ought to be."

"You knew, that day when you took Seika. You knew your time was coming."

"You're quite perceptive. How is Seika?"

"She's with Derek now. She's as well as any of us, under the circumstances." Righteous indignation colored her voice. "When were you going to tell us? After the baby was born? You haven't been to High in weeks." Michelle was still towering over her, and Tsering had to crane her head back to see her face. Looking up into Michelle's flaring nostrils and frowning lips made her feel like a child again.

"You are like my mother," Tsering said, "only bigger and angrier. Sit down."

Michelle sat. "You think *I'm* angry? Do you realize that when the others find out, you're going to have a mob?" She rubbed her hands over her face and then seemed to subside. "You do have a plan, don't you?"

Tsering shook her head. "It's out of my hands. I was going to bring the lessents back to Lake, but when I tried it with Seika it didn't work out."

"Because of Jordan. Not because of Seika. If Khani and some of the others had been here, he might not have gotten to Aristotle."

"If, if . . ."

"It's either that, or you have to come to High."

"Like hell I will! You think I sit around on a throne all day making pronouncements? I work as hard as any of you. Who's going to take care of them if I don't?"

Michelle stared at the ground. "You can't take care of them anymore. It's going to happen now, or a year from now, but it's going to happen. I came down here to spy on my kid, and it's still him I'm thinking about."

"He's fine now. I can't guarantee anything for the future," Tsering said. "We need a long-term solution."

Neither said anything. Tsering closed her eyes, releasing the last of the nausea and headache and wondering if she would ever feel normal again.

"What does what's his name say?"

"Daire thinks we're going to be rescued, whatever that means."

Michelle said, "There's a rumor going round High that you sent him off to explore the island."

Smiling, Tsering replied, "It will do him good. I needed to think. I needed to think about us, Michelle, and he isn't one of us. He interferes with my fields, if you know what I mean. I can't get a clear picture of what to do."

"Do you have one now?"

"I need your help, Michelle. The lessents are going to have to come back. This is as big an emergency as any we've ever had, but we have to run the colony as though everything's all right. For the sake of the kids."

Michelle said, "I don't know if we can rise to the occasion. I was looking forward to having time to make peace with my own distortion, and now this . . ." She caught Tsering's eye. "When, Tsering? How much longer can you make it?"

"I'm having this baby. I know that; no one's ever distorted while pregnant. After that, I can't predict."

The lessent clasped her hand, hard. "I'll talk to them. But they're going to be mad. Then they're going to be terrified."

"Like I'm not?"

Michelle glanced away. "Don't be, Tsering. You can't be. Or if you are, you can't show it. Please."

◆

Daire and Adamo struggled up and down hillsides all the next day, wending their way ever deeper into the mountains. Daire managed to lose some of his worries about the future in the exertion of his body, and Adamo's enthusiasm for the journey was infectious.

On the third day they hiked up the side of a long, steep

ridge, switching back on their trail frequently to avoid passing through the miniature lywyn outgrowths. In the afternoon a squall passed over, and they were forced to huddle impatiently under a tarp while the grassy hillside was carved into dozens of small streams leaping downhill and disappearing into the lywyn. They struggled uphill in the muck after that, and reached the crest of the ridge almost at nightfall. The sunset behind them was fading to a deep red, and the ridge they stood on cast a velvet shadow on the land to the east, the land Daire had wanted so much to see.

But there was enough light to show him the essentials.

The joke's on me, he thought, laughing and then coughing because he was still winded from the climb. Below, past the eastern feet of the hills, lay not more lywyn, nor some other, even more exotic terrain. Below lay more ocean, calm in the twilight.

They were on an island.

◆

"I don't know what I expected to find," Daire told Adamo when at last they reached the shoreline at the end of the following day. "Some other kind of terrain, I guess. Plains, or desert, other types of plant life. Land animals, maybe. Something exotic. But this . . . this is a tease."

A smudge of land on the eastern horizon had appeared at dawn as a fine, dark line: barely visible. Whether it was a continent, or another island, he couldn't say, but Daire regretted not taking the hopper. They could have been there and back by now without missing a meal. Then again, he knew this trip with Adamo was not based on expedience. Daire had been exposed to more than enough high-speed travel and near-instantaneous communication. Now he needed to learn how to exist within the confines of his own body, to walk barefoot, to pay attention.

Adamo had become quieter the farther they walked from his home. Daire didn't think the boy was afraid, but he had lost some of his cocksure edge. When Daire spoke to him he merely nodded, his eyes on the ground in front of him. From time to time he would stoop to collect a stone or a particular type of plant; he had a keen eye for such things. He was already a better naturalist than Daire, for all that he didn't understand the theory of what they were doing.

The tide was out and the small yellow moon was already visible in the darkening sky as they began to pick their way across the flat stones. Daire had seen Earth's moon from space, but oddly enough he had never seen it from the ground, not the real thing, thanks to the presence of the mirror fields. In video documents it always looked large when full, dominating the sky. But Dilarang's moon was more modest, and as the sun disappeared over the hills to the west, it shed only a thin film of light on the wet rocks and the quiet sea. Daire placed his feet carefully, but his eye continually wandered out to the open water. He leapt over a tide pool, landing gracelessly on the other side with a grunt, put a hand down for balance, and out of the corner of his eye he saw something large slide off one of the rocks and into the water just a dozen meters away.

He froze, fixing his gaze on the spot where he'd seen movement. The rocks were black, draped in shadow, and rounded and smoothed by water. It was impossible to tell whether there was still something lurking there.

"Did you see that?" he said in a hoarse whisper, glancing over his shoulder. But Adamo was squatting on the rocks peering into the tide pool. He had sample collection bags out and he seemed to be scraping something off the rock. "Huh?" he asked without looking up.

Daire took a couple of more steps toward the place where the thing had gone in. It looked as though a human-sized figure was reclining on the rocks, lying almost flat against them. From such a position, it would be easy to slide into the water, seallike, and make hardly a splash. He inched forward, straining his eyes against the darkness.

One minute, his eyes were processing the shape of a person pressed motionless against the stone. The next, he saw only a curved piece of rock. Blinking in disbelief at his error, he put out his hand and touched it. It was cold.

◆

They were bone-tired and hungry when they had finally worked their way into range of the Lake settlement. Daire moved slowly, looking for signs of subtle changes in the lywyn as they travelled, but Adamo went on ahead to announce their arrival. He returned to Daire sweating and flushed with irritation.

"Lessents," he reported disgustedly. "Lessents at Lake! What's this world coming to?"

Daire had to suppress laughter at his expression: Adamo looked and sounded like a disapproving village elder. Daire dropped his pack on the ground and stood there, assimilating this new information. He deliberately took a breath and let it out.

"What are you doing, Daire?"

"Well, my friend," Daire said. "Look around you. Take a couple of deep breaths and enjoy the quiet. This may be the last moment of peace you or I have for a long time."

"No kidding," the boy grumbled. "Lessents!"

"It may not be such a bad thing," Daire reflected. "You watch. Things are going to start happening fast now."

◆

The settlement was crowded and chaotic, but Daire told himself it could have been worse. Tsering greeted him sheepishly: she was obviously relieved when he didn't make a fuss about the change.

He shrugged at her. "It's only temporary." He glanced at the sky; it was hard to shake the sensibility that dictated rescue from space ought to come from *up*, not down. Someday he would take the hopper into orbit and see this planet properly. Until then, he would have to endure the uneasy domesticity of a family that didn't especially get along.

The lessents had caught seafood that day, and everyone ate together. Daire thought that the kids looked all right, but the lessents were obviously self-conscious and uncomfortable. Khani, whom he vaguely remembered as a quiet kid in Jordan's shadow, had come out of his shell and actually attempted to talk to Nkem and Adamo. Seika clung to a sharp-faced boy her own age—Derek, Daire thought his name was—and avoided looking at Daire. He watched Michelle whisper to her young son, who had apparently burst into tears the first time he saw her again. Mirasa, days from delivering her baby, let Rena feel it kick. But there was an intangible friction about the scene. Tsering gave everybody a pep talk at the end of the meal.

"It's going to work," she insisted. "We're going to have procedures. The Lake is to be off-limits to kids from now on; you lessents can do the fishing. We'll review the warning signs for distortion regularly, and we'll have contingency plans in case something goes wrong. Don't forget we have Daire now." She glanced at him; he felt the lessents turn his way in curiosity.

"I need a couple of volunteers," Daire said, "to spend evenings learning how to operate the hopper and the systems on the ship. We've got to be prepared when the ship from Earth comes for us. Adamo's been studying with me, but more of you are welcome provided you can do the work."

Derek said, "They'll think we're monsters, won't they?"

"What?"

"The people who come from Earth. Baby-eaters, evil reptiles . . ."

"Only if you act like it," Tsering replied.

Derek made a face. "Shit, Tsering, you going to start telling me what to do again?"

Michelle reached over and slapped him lightly on the arm. "Shut up," she said. "Set a good example for the kids."

Derek leered at Rena, who shrank away.

"I wish I had studied anthropology," Daire remarked softly to himself. "What a case study this would have made."

27

Jenae was out of her element and she knew it. Keila's instructions at the Portsmouth docks had seemed simple: *Take the train from Portsmouth to Victoria Station. Pick up the Circle Line to Paddington. Then on to Oxford.* But London's Underground was not as neat and quiet as Perth rez, not by a long shot, and she soon lost all sense of direction trying to read the maps. When she got off at Victoria Station she found herself in a crowd dozens of times larger than the mob that had accosted her at the rez, and everyone was moving so fast she could hardly take it all in. She felt her shoulders rising instinctively as though to protect her head and neck as she was pummeled right and left by passersby. Jenae had not thought there were so many people left in the *world,* much less all in one place, and she found herself creeping along like a little old woman, avoiding contact. *Melt with the crowd,* Tien had advised her when last she'd seen him in Jakarta. *Forget you have altermode.* She had made it through the virus screen at the Portsmouth train station—her identity had popped up on the computer, but no alarms had gone off. But at Victoria there seemed to be video systems and sensor curtains everywhere; she couldn't possibly vanish and she had to fight the conviction that the Heads were watching her every move.

I have a generic face, she kept telling herself. I could be nearly anyone.

She glimpsed the sign for the District Line and plowed toward it. She was not going to let a bit of a crowd set her back, not after traveling halfway around the world. Keila would throw her overboard for good if she returned to the dock at Portsmouth now. And what would Tien think of her courage, after all her posturing back at Jakarta?

"You need time to think about all of this," he had told her. They were sitting at the edge of a rock garden near the mirror field that passed between the Jakarta rez and the exposed port on the Java Sea. The garden was close enough to the mirror field so that its reflection of the idealized port outside (white ships, green lawns, pristine buildings) had become distorted. The optical effect was not convincing at such close range, which was why, Jenae thought, the area right beside a rez's mirror field was always the most private. No one wanted to go where the illusion failed.

Jenae didn't answer. Tien had been so patient with her moods: first the crying, then the lethargy, and now the constant hum of anger.

He tousled her spiky hair lightly. "You look like a prisoner," he teased. "Why don't you let it grow?"

"Too much of a luxury." She spat into the gravel, and Tien laughed out loud.

"Keila has spoiled your perfect manners."

Jenae managed a slight smile. Then she looked him in the eye. "I can't stay here, Tien. I made a promise to myself to see this thing through. As long as I'm alive, that's what I've got to do. I'm going to England as soon as I can arrange transport. I expect Colin Peake is back at Oxford by now, and I want to be the first to get to him."

Tien gave her a long, thoughtful look.

"You've been through so much. Grief takes time. It's relatively safe here; the Heads don't pay much attention to Jakarta. Maybe we can contact Dr. Peake from here. Or maybe there's a less extreme way to approach this. I know what you intend to do, but I want to be sure you're acting for the right reasons, not just to escape something unpleasant. Because you won't escape it, Jenae. Not that way."

"Tien, I'm sure you're very wise. Maybe you're even right about this—but I'll tell you one thing. I'm not interested in playing it safe. I won't use computers, and I sure won't stay here—and neither should you. It's such an obvious hideout."

Tien said, "I've thought of that. I'd like to strike out, too. If I thought that would solve things, I'd do it in a second. But I've got too much invested in the League to just walk away. We need to think about building, capitalizing on our strengths. The dolphins are with us. As long as we have them, we have the League. That's what I'm committed to. And I think you are, too, or you would be—"

"—if I didn't feel compelled to do something more drastic," Jenae finished. "Don't be mad at me. . . ."

He touched her hair again, smiling indulgently. "I'm not mad at you," he sighed. "I'd like to be, especially if I thought it would do any good. But I'm afraid I understand you all too well."

Why had she done it? Why had she left Tien behind? Jostled all the way to the District Line platform, Jenae tortured herself with second thoughts. She allowed herself to remember and to long for Tien's calm, to admire his insistence on constructing something good in the middle of vast entropy. She tried to picture herself staying with him in Jakarta, staying with the dolphins as well, and it seemed for a moment that there might have been a respite for her had she done so. But standing on the platform she found herself gazing into the black tunnel, and she knew that strong in her still was bitter anger at the choices she had been forced to make over Yi Ling, the Heads, Tien . . . everything all at once. And she knew this one choice had been true: she had been right to come here.

The train arrived and she stepped on grimly.

◆

Colin Peake lurched through the tumid darkness, his long stride erratic as he tried to avoid puddles. The night was soupy and chill, and the narrow streets of Oxford rez were all but deserted. Colin avoided looking at the dark facades that loomed to either side, the old, unused buildings sad artifacts of better days. He was headed for the sanctuary of Banbury Avenue, the island of the living within a town whose staunch resistance to change had left it high and dry with the advent of mirror fields and climate control. It was only sentiment that kept Oxford rez in operation—that and the fact that (amid these crumbling buildings that so annoyed the rez administrators with their love of clean, ergonomic lines) actual intellectual foment seemed to go on against all odds.

Bits of town were isolated from one another by mazes of unused streets, dark buildings maintained only for storage now, and wasted gardens that had never been revived. It was a fair walk from Colin's flat near Queen's College to the little hive of activity at Banbury Street, but he never took the monorail that had been constructed for students, who wanted to get to Banbury without suffering the depressing walk.

Colin had a fondness for this grim stroll; he also had more restless energy than he knew what to do with, and he didn't want his movements tracked by anyone, friend or foe. Since his return from Underkohling he had felt persecuted at every turn, and he took on the role of dissident gladly. He had even dressed in a hood and cloak, partly for secrecy and partly to amuse himself. He cast only a faint, diffuse shadow in the soft blue streetlights, and the rain muffled the sound of his footfalls on the battered cobbles. The occasional souls who passed him to either side never looked up or spoke. At times like this, he wondered if he was really there, and he was eager to get back to his work, gritty and mathematical, that saved him from speculating about what was going on in the world around him.

At last the small section of properly maintained storefronts loomed ahead, and the street lamps changed from blue to gold. The sign of the Three Polecats and a Monk swung over the pub's door as if it had been there for centuries, belying the fact that the entire building had been constructed to re-create an amalgam of the best traditional country pubs. Most of its contents had been salvaged from other establishments that had been lost to the One Eyes, or whatever was living out there nowadays.

Colin didn't care if the pub was fake; he stepped inside Three Polecats shedding raindrops and chafing his hands with relief and gratitude. He inhaled appreciatively the air of the only establishment in town that, to his knowledge, still risked citations for recreational smoke. The air was woozy and grey with it. The old oak bar, burnished to a high gloss but deeply veined with old injuries, was thinly attended. Almost everyone was huddled around the video tank tucked discreetly in a corner, except for a handful of students milling raucously round the darts board.

Colin combed his damp hair back with his fingers and sniffed, scanning the dim room. At length he noticed the small dark man seated alone at a rear table. The man raised his glass and beckoned to Colin.

"Ah, Raj," Colin said warmly, crossing the room and proffering his hand. "Glad you could make it."

"Cheers," answered the small man, administering a crushing grip. Evidently he had been cleaning his pipe on the tabletop, and he resumed once Colin bought his own pint and sat down. He was very lean and rather walnutlike: wizened and brown, with a narrow hooked nose and heavy-lidded eyes that always looked sleepy. His movements in cleaning the compact bulldog pipe were neat and economical; his fingers were beautifully manicured.

"So," he remarked, "your message was oh-so intriguing. I've been up to my eyeballs in grant applications and it's a delight to have an excuse to forget about it all and go out. So, it's a bit of a game they're having with you, is it? No inclusion in the Underkohling affair?"

"I've only been back a few weeks," Colin said, "but I'm utterly frustrated with the lack of attention being paid to my project. I know I'm not the most popular man in town; even in my own college they try to shove me under the carpet whenever anything important's happening. But dammit, Raj, as soon as I get my hands onto something really tasty, they starve me for information."

Raj nodded compassionately. "It's always the way when you don't do the party circuit. But in your case I'd say you were suffering from a certain degree of legitimate persecution. Your problem isn't a case of academic politicking or unpopularity with the Board—although you are rather unpopular, I'm afraid. But these things are easily handled with a little bit of metaphorical sleeping around. No, I'm afraid that my investigations point in a direction that you will not find easy to face. I've been looking into the matter as you asked, and it comes up a bit odd from my end. Let me explain."

Colin settled into his beer, letting his body sag into the padded booth and stretching his legs out into the aisle. He fixed his gaze on Raj as the older man unhurriedly lit his pipe and gave it a few trial puffs, blowing an idle smoke ring or two and scowling with concentration into the middle distance. Then with a reflective smacking of the lips, he began: "The constructs you and I identify with the League of New Alchemist Heads are more complex than we might like to think. We are aware of them largely because they parade about as personalities quite openly within League affairs, but their real influence in the outside world is much more difficult to detect. We often romantically imagine them as deities—ghosts in the machine, if you will—or, almost as often, look on them with pity for their ravaged bodies and endless duties to us poor mortals: pity laced heavily with disgust."

He paused, inhaling and closing his eyes, then releasing a surprisingly staccato burst of smoke rings.

"The fact is, Colin, they have more control over our fates, individually and especially collectively, than either of us would truly care to contemplate. I won't bore you with it. It's not a new notion. Everybody's afraid of what they don't understand. Everybody's afraid of Big Brother even as they cry out for divine guidance. The conquest of humanity by computers has been the topic of endless lectures and conferences and media speculation and on-line round-tabling of every variety. In the end no one does anything, because they can't, or can't be bothered, or won't. Why look too closely at it? That seems to be the point we've reached, because we feel disinvolved. And anyway, computers have remained our best hope, despite superstitions about AI. But: the pathology of the Heads of the League of New Alchemists is another matter."

"Pathology?" Colin said sharply. "What do you mean?"

"The dim ways of the mind, the dark stairways—you know all the clichés. The fact is, the existence of the Heads has put a whole new spin on the mind/body dichotomy. Just at a time when that old separation was thought to have completely broken down, what with the endless plasticity of the species as evidenced in the Gene Wars, why, up pop the Heads, so to speak. Jack-in-the-box. A hybrid organism consisting of a handful of biosystems and an electrical interface. Body? Do you have any *idea* how many organ transplants some of them have had? Where's the integrity of the body, or of the senses for that matter? Where's the integrity of the *memory* when everything that's ever been committed to a code is laid bare to them? Time itself changes shape for them. They think faster and better and more intricately than we do—no question. And, so far, they have shown a zero mortality rate in eighty years.

"But all this has been observed for decades. Yet I am the *only person* living who has attempted a longitudinal study of their pathology itself. It's a wonder the work hasn't killed me yet."

A gleam danced from his black eye as he turned an amused profile on Colin. He touched the sagging skin beneath his jaw.

"It's a wonder no one has done *my* pathology," he said. "Biographers used to be a dime a dozen. What has become of them all? Ah, don't mind me, Colin. When you are my age, you'll jaw on at your juniors in the same way."

He leaned forward suddenly, planting his elbows on the table so that Colin's half-finished pint sloshed in its glass.

"Let's start with something simple, okay? Multiple personalities. The host personality is 'possessed' if you will by a cast of characters who take over under stress, essentially, and then leave the host none the wiser for their intrusions. Or, to be more accurate, their extrusions.

"Multiple personalities reside within a single individual as manifestations of the subconscious—usually as a defense against emotional trauma early in the formation of the organism, but, rarely, for other reasons as well. The host personality typically has no memory of the actions of the subpersonalities, and is thus ruled by them. The Heads have achieved what I'd call an odd kind of inversion of this situation through an information system. Biologically, there are six heads. Two are fully cognizant, and these two have 'invaded' the other four, whom they privately call the Sleepers. They have control of the Sleepers' silicon memories, but not their biological memories, which are probably very dim. The Sleepers believe they are in equal control together with the other two Heads, and act accordingly: and, in fact, they accomplish a great deal in the League. However, they have no real power, because they don't know who they are and their memories may collapse or change at any time, at the whim of the two controlling minds."

"I follow you," said Colin, "but I don't see what this has to do with multiple personality disorder. It seems a fairly superficial connection."

"Ah, but I haven't finished. Recently—within the past few years, in fact—I've begun to detect the presence of a new personality whose source is unknown to me. I believe it is a splinter personality of one or more of the Heads, for they are totally unaware of it except when it brushes against them in the system and leaves a trail. In other words, they have no intuitive knowledge of this being, but they've occasionally noticed the results of its actions. This personality desires destruction and death; it is tired of life. I believe, in fact, that it is suicidal."

Colin had been making wet rings with his glass while Raj talked. Now, when the old man paused, he looked up. The deep-set eyes were veiled in shadow.

"What I'm going to say is unpublished—and unpublishable—so receive it in complete confidence." Raj looked directly at Colin then, and there was no affectation in his manner. If Colin could have put a name to the look on his face, it would have been fear.

"Imagine a being subject to all the human fears and neuroses, but without the biological underpinnings of those fears: in other words, imagine natural emotions mechanized. Take this being and remove its biological senses with their deeply wedded interface to thought and memory, and replace them with links to v.r. Now imagine its intelligence is multiplied by virtue of instantaneous access to almost any information coded in the system.

"What would happen to such a being over time? What would occur within its identity? On the one hand, it might lose its identity in the maelstrom of data with which it must interact; in its sensory blindness it might merely become subsumed in the system, a kind of flavor, but otherwise disintegrated. On the other hand, it might develop a powerful and unique ego to go with its enhanced abilities, an ego that had little, if anything, to do with humanity once it had begun to 'forget' its body.

"Or, on the third hand—and in these days of genetic miracles, there is always a third hand—it might splinter under the strain into a series of subpersonalities, much as I described earlier." He halted, puffed.

"And which of these scenarios do you apply to the Heads?" Colin asked. "The second, or the third? Obviously the first is a non-issue."

"All of them," said Raj. "Initially, when the Heads were altered from their human forms and plugged into the machine, they responded in a variety of ways. There were a handful of disintegrates and two superegos. Even at that time there may have been splinter personalities, but we lack the information to be sure. This was all a very natural response on the part of these organisms to a unique situation. But, over time, the superegos began to manipulate their fellows to serve their own purposes, and before long you had a power system that exploited the Sleepers and exalted the others. Until now, the schizoid personality—and we don't know which one it is, that being the nature of the game—has been able to pass itself off to the others as a plausible ego. But all that's about to change. It has a suicidal subset that's become quite active lately, and as a result of that subset's actions, latent suicidal tendencies in some of the others are beginning to peek out. The only thing I can't understand is why. *Why* the deep deterioration in this one personality; why now, and why to this degree, and why suicide? Why?"

Colin sat back and gazed at Raj thoughtfully. "Your life's work," he said. "I always thought you were a touch batty. If you had given me this talk even a year ago, I would have chuckled and bought you another drink. What practicality could there be in this work? I've always thought. And how could you possibly verify your claims? I couldn't understand what would hold your attention once the novelty of your project had worn off."

"Novelty? On the contrary, my dear Colin. It's the itch for power, even second- or thirdhand, that excites us all. And their power has grown great from its modest beginnings in the subject tanks of the Ingenix labs."

"I hadn't begun to appreciate that until recently," Colin remarked. "Tell me, just how deeply involved in human affairs are the Heads?"

"To the very roots, I'm afraid. I'm not trying to scare you, but their influence goes far beyond what most people know—and they've grown to the point where we can no longer monitor or even detect all of their activities. They are becoming ever more mysterious as they outgrow us. They frequently use the League for their own purposes. They need the minds of the dolphins for the creativity they lack, but their powers of analysis are unmatched."

"Seriously?"

"Yes, lad, quite seriously. They can mold themselves to a mainframe at will, you know, and live to tell."

Colin felt a little heat creep up the sides of his neck, like flame staining the inside of a bottle.

"But . . . what are you doing about it?"

"I? Why, I'm studying it."

"With all respect, Raj, haven't our grandparents' mistakes taught us anything? The Gene Wars were at last the final proof that science must hold itself to a higher standard of ethics than any temporary political alliance may permit. . . ."

"Bosh! Where have you been getting your ideas? The hack bulletins, the op-ed pages? Scientists, whoever *they* are, have long been the pawns of politicians even as they've scornfully perceived the relationship to be the opposite. Then you had the Gene Wars, which pushed these allegiances and counterallegiances past the limits of conventional morality. Now, here in this crazed aftermath, you, Colin, are still obsessed with these ancient moral questions. Your benighted classical education is probably to blame for that. But I say this to you: Humanity that once sought to control the world has succeeded only in changing it, and now that it's changed, evolution—if there is such a concept anymore—has taken off like a house afire.

"Tell me how to survive in this madness, tell me how to find beauty in my own demise—but don't whinge on about responsibility when it's been out of my hands since before I was born. Have more imagination than that, Colin. Have more humility. The world's not your playhouse anymore. It's a great big ravenous, entropic thing. Don't they teach you anything in school these days?"

"They taught me," said Colin stiffly, "to consider that every element of every system has an impact on the process, sometimes out of all proportion to what one would expect looking at a static model. Every element, Raj. I no less than anyone, if no more than dragonflies or *e. coli*. Pardon me if I'm disinclined to climb down from the evolutionary tree gracefully."

Raj kicked back in his chair rather suddenly, and Colin had the impression from his face that he was about to guffaw, which only increased Colin's irritation. But he smiled a little without parting his curved lips; then he released a pristine smoke ring that formed an infinity sign before vanishing literally before Colin's eyes.

Colin experienced a sudden sense of defeat. But Raj said, "Good. Very good. You'll never make an elegant thinker, but you abound with energy."

It was a backhanded compliment, but coming from such a venerable figure as Raj, the praise flattered Colin.

"Getting back to your problem: you've been shut out by the Heads. They are exerting not a little energy to keep your requests for processing—not to mention funds—buried in the system."

"It's more than that!" Colin exclaimed. "I spent four hours yesterday waiting outside the Queen's College Master's office, and when the Master finally breezed out she said, 'Sorry, dear, but we can't sponsor any new zoological surveys of Indochina at this time. Call me in the spring.' "

Raj did laugh then. "There you have it. Misinformation. Oldest trick."

"No, Raj, you don't understand. I *know* this woman. I've known her for years. Hell, I think I know her in the biblical sense. I seem to remember sleeping with her after a party once. So what the hell is going on?"

"So, you're being blackballed. Big deal. Go around them all. Make it a bigger pond. But please, Colin, treat it as an intellectual puzzle. The likelihood that you will actually trip up the Heads is next to none."

◆

Colin had long ago made it a policy to solicit advice and then not take it, and this evening was no exception.

It was ten minutes to midnight, a week to the day after his conversation with Raj, and Colin Peake was rubbing his hands together with glee. He'd always been disappointed in Galileo for recanting, and he was pleased to confirm that he had no similar inclinations, on this the verge of his great disclosure. He was far too tickled with himself as he rambled around his oversized, messy flat with a long-preserved-for-a-rainy-day bottle of Glenfiddich sloshing in his hand, confiding in his cat. The latter reclined on the windowsill, gazing out at the lights on the street below, the library-goers on their bicycles and the pub-goers on foot, all hurrying in the cold drizzle of an early October evening. It was a scene that Colin loved because nowhere could evidence of the mirror fields be seen. Oxford looked safe and stuffy. So did the cat: it was orange and white, exceptionally well fed, so that its own excess puddled around it and dropped over the edge of the sill.

"I'm going to do it in the witching hour," Colin said, "because it's my favorite time to be devious. Nef, I've set this up in a way more brilliant than even I usually achieve."

Nef chose this moment to yawn. Colin's ex-wife, Pamela, had named the cat after Nefertiti, whom, unfortunately, the cat could not be said to resemble even to the most imaginative eye. She was petulant, affectionate, and not very intelligent—not unlike Pamela herself, he reflected. Colin chose to call the cat Nef. He didn't call Pamela at all, these days.

Colin took a long swallow and let his eyes roll back. He was waiting to achieve that perfect state of drunkenness that would grant him fearlessness but not remove all judgment.

"I wonder if I can get Ms. Hungary to turn nasty on me. I'd really like to do some PR damage here, just for the sport of it." He had reached one end of the flat: the cold end, where boxes of computer equipment old enough to be considered artifacts were piled haphazardly on a large wooden table. There were no curtains on the windows—Colin despised curtains for they reminded him of Pamela, as did goat cheese, ballpoint pens, and cut flowers of any kind—so this part of the flat was always chilly and, at night, dark. He took another swig to sustain himself and then began pacing back toward the fireplace he wasn't allowed to use, the carpet from Pakistan, and the functional computer system. The kitchen was barely visible through the forest of houseplants he kept for Nef's benefit, but pleasant odors were beginning to waft from that direction as his supper heated slowly.

Colin stopped.

"How will they react?" he mused, tilting his head back and gazing at the ceiling. He sniffed reflectively. "I hope they're really pissed. And then I hope they start talking cash, publication, and advanced survey team, led by me. It will be long overdue, Nef."

Colin had always considered himself a philosopher first, and a physicist second; and because the world outside the University had no need of either, he'd sometimes been reduced to making a living yet a third way, in stealth. That is, by hacking. When it had become apparent that the Heads needed putting in their place, Colin had cracked his knuckles and balled himself up in a chair and thought long and hard about how to do it. At last, somewhere between the Thursday and Friday after his talk with Raj, a scheme so simple, yet so elegant that it curled his toes insinuated itself into his mind; and there it stayed until he'd worked out all the bugs and worms and sat down to do the dirty labor of enacting his idea.

It was a fool's plan, and that was the beauty, even if it would be difficult to execute. It was a variation on blackmail, only riskier. Public exposure of the Heads' games was his best shot at getting some results. He would configure his own com line to interfere with the continuous ITV All Live World News transmission so that when he dialogued with the Heads, everything would be broadcast on ITV's audio channel. Simultaneously, on location in Monkey Mia, Australia, the Heads' own inputs that would allow them to detect the interference would be rerouted to another area, where they would be treated to reruns of last year's news. It had been a very delicate procedure and he'd almost been caught several times while he set up the timing and the various foils, but he'd been surprised how light the guard around the biological components of the Heads had actually been. He could only hope that what he'd done was enough. If Raj was right, the Heads were diffused into the system to such a degree that they'd notice something was wrong peripherally, even if their local senses were tricked.

Colin took a last, stiff draft to steady himself; then he sat down and double-checked the setup. At last he nudged his way into the League com system, past the administrative reception area, through the security baffles, and into the very core of the League.

Pause. Time for a deep breath, Colin Peake. And remember: don't let them get to you.

The com groove that led into the Heads' inner sanctum was open to him, and he cleared his throat. He had no names by which to address these entities, so he simply launched into his speech.

"Colin Peake here, friends. I have questions to ask of the most serious nature, and I assure you I have the full support of everyone here at Oxford in my investigation. I hope you are prepared to defend your actions in the matter of the ship *Morpheus* and the astral body Underkohling."

"What is this about? Whom are you addressing?" It's the Australian male, annoyed.

"I address all of you who call yourselves the Heads of the League of New Alchemists. However many of you there may be."

"We're listening," said the Aussie lazily, indulgent now. Colin tried not to show his relief outwardly; the change in tone indicated that the Heads did not consider him a threat. He would not be shut out.

"We've spent enough time with you, Dr. Peake. Perhaps you can keep this brief?" There she was, the Hungarian Woman. A thin veil of courtesy.

"I am deeply concerned," said Colin, "about the lack of follow-through on the Underkohling research which I personally set under way. It is my understanding that you have dropped all investigation regarding *Morpheus*, and indeed the fourth Underkohling gate itself, and at any rate you have cut me out of the loop entirely. Conduct unbecoming, I might add, of persons of your stature and reputation."

Another deep voice. Male, uncertain. "Dr. Peake, are you suggesting that the League deliberately suppressed information? This information dates back to before the League's inception. It's hard to see how we could have acted in this matter had we tried."

"Tell me then, if you will, why you've kept secret the fact that *Morpheus* was never destroyed? Under my own counsel, not Oxford's, I called you in months ago. I called you in for *help*, but you took my data and interfered with my work.

Then you had the unholy gall to commandeer my ship!" He paused for breath, aware that he was getting too emotional too quickly. Bloody drink.

"Remember," intoned the deep voice, "that your work for the University was largely funded by the League. You were sitting out there in space using time and resources that could have been put to better use elsewhere, and we had every right to reassign the vessel."

"I was sitting out there doing nothing, as you put it, because you were doing nothing with the data I gave you! You say you couldn't decrypt the software bug that invaded my ship's computer, but the *Morpheus* identifier didn't have to be translated. It was a clear piece of code in the exact style used in those days."

"It could have been a resonance trapped within the EM field of Underkohling," said the Hungarian Woman.

"That's weak, and you know it," said Colin. "It was embedded in a computer virus that had been somehow, undetectably, transmitted to my computer."

"This is disturbing," said the deep voice. "I had not been aware . . ."

"You're not aware of much," snapped Hungary. "We are looking into all of these matters, Dr. Peake. If you could see past the perimeter of your own ego you would realize that we must weigh all factors carefully and collect more data before we make a public statement of any kind, especially in these times of political unrest."

"How? You sent me back to Earth before I could do anything with my data. You abandoned your own researcher to the gate!"

"Sacrificing more lives to an unstable gate would be foolhardy, Dr. Peake. The League's philosophy toward human life is conservative and cautious."

"Ask all the Universities for their input before you make that decision. If someone's transmitting from the other side of the gate, we could be looking at a viable planet. If that's not worth risking your life for, what is?"

There was a silence; then, in a tone of infinite patience, the Aussie said, "Dr. Peake, while I'm sure these ruminations are desperately fascinating to you, I'm afraid we have more immediate concerns than archaeology."

"*Morpheus* carried the most notorious criminals of the entire Gene Wars period. You, more than anyone, must have an interest in bringing them to justice."

"They are dead, Dr. Peake. Let the past go. That is our philosophy. We are focused on the present."

"Is that what the public would say?"

"The so-called public has no interest in these matters yet. You cannot be unaware of the situation here in Australia. We will not risk more outcry and uprising over nothing."

"Maybe you won't. But I think I will have to."

Another shift: Hungary's tone became saccharine. "Oxford is a lovely rez, is it not, Dr. Peake? We can't help noticing that you are speaking to us this evening from your charming flat there. We remind you that Oxford depends on our support and goodwill not only for the well-being of its people, but for the continued pursuit of academic knowledge that it has practiced longer than any other such institution in the world. We beg you to have some respect for that before you decide to do anything rash."

"That sounds like a threat."

"We don't need to threaten you. Think on it. You will be discredited as a lunatic if you come forward with your theories. Look at your psychiatric history—do you think it will bear scrutiny?" Her condescension irritated Colin even as her words baffled him.

"My *what*? What are you talking about?"

"According to Oxford's records as of this very moment, you were hospitalized four times during your tenure for delusional mania. You've been prescribed medication but have shown resistance to taking it. Surely you haven't forgotten? Or is this another symptom of your disorder?"

"What the hell are you doing?" Colin sputtered, his face growing hot with anger even as privately he acknowledged the beauty of the move she had just made. "No! You can't just expect to rewrite my medical history and get away with it! Who would believe such nonsense?" Even as the words came out of his mouth, he realized that if Raj was right, such a deception would be a cinch for the Heads. How many such battles had they won in this way? Colin fought the sense of drowning.

The Head countered coolly, "And who would believe that

Morpheus is still out there somewhere, transmitting its own code, eighty years after the fact of its destruction?"

"I would," Colin shot back, "because I've seen a man disappear into Underkohling without a trace, and I think the ship *Morpheus* did the same thing. And the people who have been listening to this conversation can feel free to draw their own conclusions from what we've said—but I can guarantee the subject won't be quiet anymore."

"People? What people? This is a secure line."

"Not anymore. Hey," said Colin in his best imitation of the Hungarian Woman's accent, "it cuts both ways, baby."

There was puzzled silence on the other end of the line, and Colin placed his hands on the keyboard and entered the commands to tie the central League computers back into world communications systems from which he had excluded them, where it would be instantly apparent to them that the entire argument had been broadcast over local and international events coverage.

"I demand the return of the data which I rightfully collected in orbit of Underkohling. It was deliberately and maliciously erased from my ship's hard drive and the League has refused to supply me with the copy I transmitted for your review. If I don't get it, I will publicly release the other information that I did *not* share with the League concerning *Morpheus* and Underkohling: more specifically, concerning the potential for colonization that resides there *which the League has been suppressing.*"

He cut the line, chuckling. He was bluffing, of course— but he was willing to bet it would pay off. He stood up, scrubbing his palms across his thighs and jigging his shoulders nervously. He roved through the kitchen; dinner was ready, but he turned off the heat, suddenly too worked up to eat. He paced on, still replaying the conversation in his mind and glancing around the flat, assessing, as he paced. Everything was packed: a tidy heap of bags was piled beside the door. He took a long swig from the depleted bottle and opened the closet, rummaging inside for the cat carrier. He would drop off Nef at Pamela's; they'd both like that. On all fours in the closet, he shoved aside old cricket pads and sneezed.

There was a sound from outside the flat. Someone at the door.

Colin froze. Unsuccessfully suppressed a second eruption, with moist consequences. All along in the back of his mind, he had been waiting for the other shoe to fall. He had been wondering whether to expect storm troopers to break down his door in the middle of the night and come to take him away, or perhaps just to pulverize his brain from a distance with some newfangled silent, invisible death ray. That was why he was leaving—just to be on the safe side. But he certainly hadn't reckoned on the speed of the response.

Again: the soft knock. Knuckles on fiberglass.

He seized a cricket bat, laughed a little as he imagined himself deflecting death rays with it, and drawing his sleeve across his nose opened the door to face his fate.

A small, unprepossessing woman stood on the threshold. Not Pamela, thought Colin, thankful for small blessings.

Colin could think of nothing to say as he held the door open. The stranger stepped inside silently, glancing around the room with the air of one accustomed to scanning for foes. Her eyes alighted on Nef, who stood up as though she'd been expecting the woman and ran to her. Colin put the bat down.

"Hello," said the stranger, bending to pet the cat as Nef wrapped the plumage of her tail around her leg. She was more girl than woman, Colin observed on second glance; but still, uncharacteristically, he was at a loss for words.

She fixed him with the regard of black, perfect eyes.

"Have you come to arrest me?" Colin said in what was meant to be a light tone, falling back before her as she straightened up and quietly shut the door behind herself. She hardly presented a physical threat, with her round, childish face and slight stature. She was dressed simply in padded, quilted grey pants and jacket that must be, he thought, fashion's nod to traditional Chinese peasant garb. She wore a black cloth wrapped around her head like a turban and a white scarf looped around her neck.

She reached into the folds of her clothes and Colin stiffened, still half expecting some instrument of violence or, perhaps, a badge to be produced. But she pulled out a slim disk case and handed it to him. He didn't look at it.

"You're really whacko, aren't you?" she said, and her accent jarred him: it was Australian, and reminded him immediately of one of the League of New Alchemist Heads. "I just saw your chat with the Pickled Brains on the tank at the corner pub." She wandered farther into the flat as she spoke, Nef at her heels. "I've been hanging around Oxford trying to decide how to approach you. Then the audio from your conversation comes on the tank. It was strange. The visual for the evening news kept playing, but over it there was your voice. And *her* voice." Her face wrinkled with distaste. Then she chuckled. "And then, just as it was getting interesting, the pub closed! Incredible. Just like that. Oxford. This place is unbelievable. It could be a hundred years ago, to look around here."

She stopped, having reached the window, and stood looking out with her back to him.

"I wish I'd gotten to you before you took such a drastic step."

"Look," said Colin, temporizing slightly. "If the League sent you, you can tell them to stuff it. I've been more than patient."

She said, "Once, mate, I might have done as the League asked. But if you think you have cause to resent them, you don't know the first thing about it. I'm here on my own recognizance, and believe me, there're places I'd rather be. I'm delivering this information to you, and I'll explain it to you. Then you're going to have to decide what to do. I wash my hands of it."

"What do you mean? Who are you?"

"I'm Jenae Kim, formerly an alchemist of the League. Now I'm the unofficial representative of the cetaceans who fuel the League's research. I have the decoded version of the *Morpheus* transmission you mentioned. I also have the variable ranges for the gate based on the data you collected from Daire Morales. And I have a few other pieces of information that I think you'll find interesting. Though I wonder if you'll have the nerve to do anything about it." Again her eyes swept the room: a little scornfully, he thought.

Colin said nothing, eyeing her warily. He was beginning to regret the liquor: clearly he was at a disadvantage.

"You've got nothing to fear from me," she said with a

laugh, seeing the dismay on his face. "I'm in the top ten on the Heads' shit list. You don't have to be afraid of what I'll say to them."

"I'm not afraid of the Heads."

"Maybe you should be," she said darkly.

"Come now."

"You really don't have any idea what you've done," Jenae said. "I blame myself. I shouldn't have hesitated. If I had arrived sooner, I might have stopped you."

"That's rather a dramatic thing to say," Colin remarked, recovering his equilibrium as the youth of this stranger became more apparent. He would treat her as any undergraduate and all would be well. "Have a drink. Sit down. Tell me your tale of woe."

She ignored him, continuing to drift about the room. "How do you think the Heads will react to what happened here tonight?"

"Don't know," mused Colin, tilting his head back and pursing his lips. "I'm more concerned about how people react. Some of my associates at Oxford ought to be getting up off their smug arses and beginning to ask the questions they should have asked months, if not years, ago. I hope they will. I hope."

"Yeah?" she said grimly. "Where I come from, people are going to snap. Some of them are going to be out for blood."

"I hope they'll be out to discover the truth, or something along those lines," Colin said.

"And what do you know about that? The truth, or something along those lines?"

She watched him expectantly. He was determined not to give in to this mysterious air, even though a long evening of drinking and arguing had stimulated his imagination and he felt freer than usual with his speech. He said nothing.

"Well," she said at last. "You've gone and put your foot in it."

"That's quite characteristic," he commented mildly, quirking an eyebrow. "What have I done this time?"

"What if I told you that the Heads have a vested interest in keeping quiet about Underkohling?"

"It would seem obvious."

"What if I were to suggest that the discovery of *Morpheus* would be very bad news for them?"

"Ah, but why?" Colin bent his head, allowing himself to pace with one finger held aloft beside his ear, like a small questioning flag.

"The Heads sent *Morpheus* on a suicide mission eighty years ago. But now they quite rightly suspect that the mission failed."

"The *Heads* sent them? Haven't you got your dates mixed up? The Heads were a group of miserable, confused victims at that time. They'd only just been discovered in the labs at Ingenix, and they were in no condition to know their own names, much less order people around the way they do now."

She nodded in his direction. "Disk," she said, gesturing to his hand that still held the slip she'd given him when she entered.

Swinging the bottle by its neck as he crossed the room, Colin inserted the disk into the system and watched the audio levels automatically reset themselves.

"Take the net off-line, put up your best security locks, and open the audio file marked Clip A," said Jenae.

The screen remained dark, but familiar voices filled the room.

"Edgar M. Van der Hoss, Ingenix Board of Directors."

"Michael Davis, Ingenix Board of Directors."

"Hannibal Lumumba, CFO."

"Haven V. Krzminski, Ingenix Board of Directors."

Colin dropped the bottle on the carpet, then stooped to seize it before the large, dark stain could spread.

"The Hungarian Woman," he whispered.

"What?"

"Play it again!"

Jenae complied.

"Yes, of course that's her. Where did you find that recording?"

"Archives. Dated 2150. It's the only one I was able to find. You wouldn't believe how little trace of the Ingenix directors is left. There's a conspicuous dearth of information on them."

"Let me see. I presume you are trying to say that this person, Haven V. Krzminski, was on the Board and then became a Head ... deliberately?"

"Sure looks that way. The code that you picked up at Underkohling—I know what it says. There's a snippet of this same woman's voice, talking to a man who's expressing doubts. 'It's suicide,' he says. And then she answers him, 'You could see it as suicide, or you could see it as a change of identity. *An expansion, if you will, into an infinity of identities.*"

Colin let out a low whistle. "That's what the Heads are, innit?" he said, his accent unconsciously diving through the class barrier. "I mean, yes, there would seem to be some indication there ..." He could feel himself blushing, but the girl didn't seem to notice his gaffe.

"We've been under the thumb of Ingenix even more *since* the Gene Wars than during that time," she continued forcefully.

"But they're not continuing their research ... ?"

Jenae shrugged. "They scarcely need to. They've got the power of gods. That's what it's about, eh?"

Colin sank into the couch and let his face fall into his cupped hands. He emitted a long groan.

"I told them off," he moaned thickly, "and now they're going to kill me. I knew it would come to this."

"Why are all pure humans so high-strung?" Jenae muttered, folding her arms across her chest and looking down on him impatiently.

"I'm sorry," Colin managed eventually, uncurling his body and wiping his eyes. "I've dreaded the thought of giving Nef back to Pamela permanently for safekeeping, but there you have it. There's nothing to be done."

She coolly relieved him of the whiskey bottle before he could bring it to his lips once more.

"Look," she said at last. "What are you, some kind of joke?"

She placed the bottle on a nearby table with a definitive thud, turning to face him. He looked pathetic, more beetle than human with his thin arms and legs sticking out at all angles from his useless torso. "I didn't come all the way from Australia just to nurse you through the nasty hangover you're going to have soon. I've bloody well renounced pure humans and all their—your—idiotic conventions of comfort, so you should consider yourself lucky I don't take you out of here by force."

Colin had begun to chuckle in that irritating way drunks have, and her frown deepened. Ignoring him, she said, "Does anybody else know you were planning this little charade this evening?"

He shook his head, still trembling with ambiguous mirth. "Nobody," he gasped. "Everybody thinks I'm"—he let out a ferocious cackle—"crazy!"

She stalked over to him and shook her head in disgust. "Get up, crazy man. I see you had the sense to pack. We're leaving—now. I thought I could get away with delivering this and then leaving, but it's obvious you need someone to make the decisions for you. Man, but I am spoiling to shed some blood."

Even in the midst of his alcoholic haze, Colin obviously heard her, for he shrank away a little at these last words, and he stopped laughing.

28

When they turned up on Raj's doorstep, the old man appeared unsurprised. He was wearing a bathrobe and holding an aged copy of the Qu'ran containing at least a dozen bookmarks. He stood aside to let them in with a courteous nod and a rather enigmatic smile.

The flat was tiny. The computer system was standard-issue domestic stuff, Colin observed with disappointment—and it wasn't even active. There were books everywhere, some of them stacked on glass cases in which were enshrined even more books. A compact air purifier sat on the tea table. There were two armchairs and a desk, and barely enough room to maneuver between them. A narrow door leading to the back of the flat was closed. From behind it came a series of muffled thuds.

"Sit, sit," insisted Raj. "Not to worry. I never ask awkward questions."

Colin watched Jenae slide by Raj eye to eye with the small man, who was still smiling and rocking back and forth on the balls of his bare feet. She flopped down into one of the armchairs and looked at Colin expectantly.

"I'll just stand," said Colin, looking for a place to do so. Actually he was experiencing the strong need to pace, but the room was only about two Colin-paces long and too cluttered to move in. He was still holding the cat carrier to his chest; Nef glared out balefully.

"Well," said Raj.

The door to the next room opened revealing a strikingly beautiful man in his twenties. His hair and skin were golden, his eyes the rare blue. He was wearing loose cotton pants and a ratty sweater. His eyes were puffy with sleep.

"Hullo," he said, glancing around the room with interest.

"Ah," Raj said. "Colin, this is Stephen Ames. Stephen, Colin Peake. And . . ." He glanced questioningly at Jenae.

"Jenae." She volunteered no further information about herself. Nef let out a long, mournful howl. Colin glowered and set down the carrier.

"Right," said Stephen. "I'd best make some tea." He disappeared again.

"I don't suppose you've had the news on tonight?" said Colin without much hope. Raj shook his head. "Ah," Colin continued. "I'd better explain then."

Raj listened patiently while Colin recounted the evening's events. A few sentences into his narrative Jenae sprang up and barged through the door after Stephen without a word. Raj lifted an eyebrow and gestured for Colin to continue. When Colin described Jenae's arrival with its revelations, Raj placed one hand over his eyes, groping with the other for the chair Jenae had vacated. He sank into it looking suddenly ancient.

"So simple. Yet so improbable. It's been completely overlooked. And it fits."

Stephen bustled in belatedly with a tea tray. Jenae followed more slowly, glanced sharply at Raj, and then sat down on the floor. She released Nef, who began to prowl the room with exaggerated caution.

"This is as safe a place as we can hope for as long as we're on the rez," Jenae told Colin. "Do you trust these people?"

Colin blushed, glancing in embarrassment at Stephen, who was pouring the tea. "Yes, of course," Colin hissed. "Raj is a colleague, and a very old friend of my family's. You needn't behave like a guerrilla here."

Jenae snorted as she accepted the tea. "Manners are the least of your worries, mate."

"I beg your pardon," said Stephen, "but you seem to have upset Raj. Do you mind telling me what sort of trouble it is that brings you here in the middle of the night?"

"It's all right," Raj said softly, looking up at Stephen. "Of course I'm upset, but it isn't the fault of these young people. Well," he added, looking at Jenae and obviously trying to be brisk, "we'd best see what we can do to accommodate you for the night. You'll be safe here. No one bothers me, and it will all look better in the morning, I'm sure."

"I do apologize to put you out this way," Colin began.

"Don't be absurd. You'll be the ones put out, I'm afraid, sleeping with all these books crowding you. No—not to worry. We'll sort it all out in the morning."

Jenae's eyebrows went up in disbelief, and Colin shot her a warning glance.

"If anyone can solve it, it's you, Raj," he said.

◆

But in the morning Raj was elusive. He made a brief appearance at breakfast and then said, "I'm going to my office to check on some old research I did. And I do have one other idea in mind. If anyone calls, leave it to Stephen, all right? I hope to have something for you soon."

"What would he have?" Jenae asked after he'd left. "A small army?"

"Watch," replied Colin. "You never know what Raj will do."

They paced the flat most of the morning, arguing strenuously. Raj's "solution" came unexpectedly, about midday. The system announced a call; Colin and Jenae froze, glancing around the room for somewhere to hide.

"It's all right," Stephen said. "I'll take it in the bedroom."

When he came back, his eyes were shining.

"It's Odessa Hunt!" he whispered. "She wants to talk to you, Colin."

"Oh, my," said Colin, rapidly finger-combing his hair.

Jenae followed them, standing at an oblique angle to the screen, where she knew the visual would not be able to pick her up. She could see the screen though. As soon as Colin cleared his throat and said, "Er ... Your Honor?" Hunt came on the line, all 180 pounds of her, mahogany-skinned and expensively coiffed. She looked positively regal, but her voice was soft and well modulated with a pleasant French accent.

"Dr. Peake, I'm calling you to congratulate you on your momentous find. It is truly a source of hope to me that a single person may still, in this day and age, do extraordinary and beneficial work—and moreover that he may do it with so little support!"

"Thank you. Are you going to offer me a grant?" Colin quipped.

Hunt laughed richly. "Funding for your future work should not be a problem, Dr. Peake. Indeed, I am inviting you, on behalf of the EC, to represent Europe in the precolonial survey of Underkohling that is now being planned."

"Precolonial survey? Isn't that somewhat premature?" Colin stammered.

"Needless to say, nothing has been made public. But an international team is now being assembled to investigate the fourth gate and, if possible, to penetrate it and report back."

"I see. Is the League involved in this?"

"They will send representatives, to be sure. They have used the data you collected to devise a way to open the gate. They will be sending several ships with the necessary equipment to stabilize the phenomenon."

"Well . . . I don't recall anything of this magnitude happening when any of the other gates were being investigated."

"I can't speak on this matter in detail, Dr. Peake, but be advised that the League has just informed us of evidence which strongly suggests there is a viable world on the other side of the gate. We are grateful to you for making the matter public—you have, in a sense, forced the hand of the League. It took courage. The League has been intent on keeping the matter private—*Morpheus* and Ingenix are understandably sore subjects for them. But the whole world should be involved in this new venture: pure humans of every affiliation, One Eyes . . . everyone. The League has reversed its position and made itself fully willing to cooperate in this matter."

"Real estate," muttered Colin.

"True," said Hunt with a warning flash of her black eyes, "but, to a higher purpose, justice. The Ingenix criminals must be pursued. Alive or dead, the world deserves to know what became of them."

"I'm glad you feel that way," said Colin. "Because I didn't discover a shred of evidence to indicate that a habitable planet will be found on the other side of the fourth gate. Nor do I have any reason to believe—yet—that the gate opens both ways. I would be interested to see the documentation on which the League bases its claims."

"That will be made available to you, once you've officially joined the mission and taken the proper security precautions."

"I see. May I ask, Your Honor, why you chose me?"

"That should be obvious. You are the prime discoverer here—and you're a citizen of the EC. To the British people you are already a hero—or will be soon. And I personally would like to see your work recognized. I'd like to make up for the damage done to you by the League when they maneuvered Oxford into removing you from the site. There are . . . pressures . . . involved in these matters that a researcher such as yourself may see as invalid or wrongheaded. But in my position I'm subject to them every day, and I must deal in the give and take of politics. When I have an opportunity to right a wrong, though, I always take it."

"So long as it means going up in the polls," murmured Stephen sotto voce.

"How did you find me here?" asked Colin, glancing at Stephen.

"That is classified," said Hunt. "Privacy cannot be a factor for you once you take the public stage. But I see that you need some time to think over everything I've said before you make a decision. One of my aides will be in touch with you later today. You'll receive specific information concerning the nature of the mission, and your role in it. We'll expect an answer shortly thereafter; then we can give you security clearance on the issues you raised a moment ago, as well as others. It's a long journey, as you know, to Underkohling, and we would like to get this mission off the ground with all possible speed."

She cut the channel.

"Dammit," said Colin. "I hope she hasn't shared my present address with the media. We'll have to sneak out the back window and leave you to deal with them, Stephen."

"It's not funny," said Jenae. "You think you're being thrown a birthday party, but there's something more behind this. Why is the League suddenly 'willing to cooperate'?"

"Yes, yes, I know," Colin conceded. "There's no such thing as a free lunch. Still, we may as well look at the menu, eh?"

"Go ahead," said Jenae. "Look at the menu. But before you order anything, you should see the rest of the data I've brought. It was given to me by the dolphins after I left the League, and it wasn't easy for them, or me, to get. I brought this disk halfway around the world for you, and I think it should factor into your decision."

"Fine!" said Colin with surprise. "I've been waiting for you to suggest it. Let's have it."

◆

Colin had watery eyes, she thought. Or was it merely that, since coming north, Jenae's subliminal need for alter-mode had laced everything around her with some aquatic metaphor? She watched him now: spidery hands folded, pupils fixed, lips quivering with a faint tremor that pulsed also in his jaw, a counterpoint. The tension was difficult to perceive: Colin had such a bland face, really, when he wasn't speaking, that he seemed almost devoid of personality just when his brain was really the most active.

But there were the bitten nails, the unwashed hair, and two days' stubble. And there were the invisible stress lines crisscrossing the silent flat. Outside, bells rang away the hours, but there was no sound in Raj's flat beyond the constant polite hum of the system, and Colin's occasional distracted sniff. He had been sitting there for hours.

"I'm beginning to see a shadow," were his last words. He had said that shortly after he had devised a way to represent the gate data visually. It looked a little like a dolphin matrix, but its meaning was completely opaque to Jenae. She went to the kitchen to make tea, leaving him staring at the wall. When she set the cup down by his elbow, he never stirred.

She'd removed the cold tea an hour later. Now it was growing dark.

His blood must be pooling, she thought. It wasn't

healthy. She was getting restless just watching him—but she didn't dare make a sound, and she was afraid to touch any of the books that were lying about. Raj had treated them with such reverence that she didn't dare open one for fear of cracking a spine or damaging the paper with the acids from her fingers. She ended up watching the cat sleep.

"Human intelligence is inherently limited," Colin had said earlier, cracking his knuckles as he prepared to dive into the work, "because its whole structure and purpose is ultimately tied up with the human body. That's why these collective intelligences—dolphins', and your ability to access them, I suppose—are so baffling. They're inhuman, alien. Perhaps on some level they even frighten me."

"Are you afraid you're obsolete?"

He laughed. "Limited though my mind may be, it's still a damn sight better than much of what you'll find, human or otherwise. It functions very well within its limits. Although I must say sometimes I do envy the Heads, strangely enough. I do feel I could do better without my body to hold me back."

Watching him now gave her a queer feeling. Give me a One Eye any day, she thought, and some honest muscle. This man is creepy.

"Yes," Colin said. The sound emerged as a croak.

She jumped in her skin.

"Yes," he said again, clearing his throat but otherwise not moving. "I do believe they would dare."

Jenae stood up and walked toward him, afraid he would merely retreat again.

"You believe they would dare what?" she said sharply.

"Try to destroy the gate, rather than let anyone through."

"*What*? Destroy it? How?"

"Well, first you have to realize why this is so tricky. The variables that describe the periodicity and spatial parameters of the gate phenomenon can be used to predict when and for how long the gate will open along a probability spectrum that actually *changes* with each individual occurrence. In other words, you'd have to use the data from one incidence to determine the configuration of the formula to roughly predict the occurrence of the next incidence, and you'd use that to predict the next one, and so on. But sitting here today, we can't predict when the gate next will open—assuming that it will ever open. Now. Think, Jenae. They say they have the ability to stabilize the gate. But from what I can see, by the very nature of the gate, this is impossible. No, don't say anything. I know. They are preparing to send a fleet out there—they must be up to something, and if it isn't stabilizing the gate, what is it? So what do they say they need to open this miraculous gate? High-frequency light waves, lasers. As if they could alter to their specifications a phenomenon they don't even understand. What am I saying, Jenae? It's a fairly transparent ploy. They're carrying weapons. Pure and simple. I have coldly and carefully run through every possibility. There is no way they can change the gate, and they know it. I don't believe even dolphins could give them that technology."

"Weapons? What are weapons going to do? Even if they cross the gate, they can scarcely hope to overcome whatever they encounter with firepower. They don't know who or what they're going to find."

"Ah. True. But the Coalition will be impressed by the idea of weapons. Wipe out the Ingenix scum or whatever. And those same weapons might just be used to destroy the energy balances around the gate, which is what I'm most concerned with."

"I don't follow you."

"It's tricky. But the right amount of energy at the critical moment could overload the gate—shrink it down to such a tiny size, its effects would be negligible."

"It can't be opened, but it can be closed?"

"In theory. It's always easier to destroy than to create. Second law of thermodynamics. Entropy, love."

"They would destroy access to an entire world?"

"As I said, I do just believe they would dare to try."

"I don't follow their thinking at all." Frustration.

"Control, my dear. Also, lest we forget, it's probable that there is evidence against them. The signals I received came from something on the other side of the gate."

"A mind," Jenae mused. "That's what the dolphins say. The 'new mind' they called it."

"Anyway, I take it amiss," said Colin. "The gate was my discovery, and this—what they are doing—it's obscene. Exploitation of a unique natural resource: Underkohling. At the very least. In addition to that it's a personal affront. I'm going to raise hell for this one. Every scientist, every intellectual left alive on this planet, must know of what is happening here. There will be such a public outcry—"

He'd risen to his feet a little unsteadily, his hand cocked and forefinger pointed to blast his imaginary opponent, the pitch of his voice gradually ascending. Stephen had started to enter the room and stopped on the threshold, taken aback.

"No, no, that's slow and ineffectual," Jenae muttered, dismissing Colin's reaction with a wave of her hand. "We've got to get on it ourselves. We've got to do something about it. You manipulated the media once, with some success—but trust me, you won't manage it a second time. You'll be lucky to get out of this flat to fetch groceries—"

"Raj usually has them delivered . . ." Stephen put in.

"—or anything. No, Colin, trust me. The time has come for more drastic measures." *Am I becoming addicted to this mad life-style?* Jenae wondered, listening to herself.

"Look, I suppose I could accept Hunt's offer to join the delegation. Maybe I could win some allies there. It's about time I was accorded the respect due to a man of my accomplishments. But dammit, to be silent in the face of such evil . . ."

"It's obvious that Hunt's offer is just meant to groom you, calm you down, and keep you out of the way. You don't seriously think the Heads would allow the delegation to have any power, do you?" Now Jenae was pacing; as soon as she noticed herself doing it, she stopped and sat down.

"Allow? I'm not ready to concede that the Heads are as omnipotent as you make them out to be. *You've* eluded them all this time, haven't you? The delegation on that ship is going to include persons of consequence, and the mission is going to be watched very closely. The Heads are not so powerful, I think, as to be able to function without a well-ordered society to support them: it's a symbiosis, isn't it? And if faith in the Heads breaks down, not only will the technology underpinning our society break down, but so, in the end, will they. I can't believe they would be so openly self-destructive."

"Don't forget what they've done, Colin. They'll do anything to protect themselves from that truth escaping and becoming known."

"Well. You have some advice for me, then? What do you suggest I do? Turn down the offer and bring further suspicion on myself? No, I think that if I accept the offer they'll think me amiable and complacent—that should buy *you* some time to act in, shouldn't it? Go talk to your dolphins, drum up some support and all that? Eh?"

Jenae made a face. He knew so little. "I don't know. I agree that as long as you're suspected of being a dissident, you'll be paralyzed. But I think you're throwing yourself away going with the delegation. Don't they put you to sleep for the journey?"

"A deep trance, yes. Conserves energy, slows aging, cuts down on use of resources. Not to mention space madness and terminal boredom."

"And you trust them to do that to you?"

"Look. You've got to see what this means to me. All my life I've worked in relative obscurity. No one gave two shits about Underkohling for years; every gate that was discovered proved useless, and it's been the province of theoretical workers only for some time now. I've fought tooth and nail for every scrap of recognition I could get, every bit of funding, every opportunity to learn more. And when I discover the fucking miracle, all this political stuff gets in my way. I'm sorry about what the Heads did. I'm sorry about the pain caused by the Gene Wars. I really am. God knows I'd love to be free to walk the fields of England like my grandparents did. But the fact is, it's all bullshit compared to the phenomenon itself. A man disappeared. Messages have been received associated with people who've been dead almost eighty years. It's possible that the gate is altering the very fabric of time itself for this to occur. And I've got to investigate it. I've got to. I can't sit here waiting for a more palatable ruler to enter office. I'd like to be that noble, but it simply isn't possible. And I'll tell you something else. Much though I distrust the Heads, I think my chances of preventing the destruction of the gate are a hell of a lot better out there than they are sitting here like some poor sodden duck."

"Well," said Stephen from the doorway, "Odessa Hunt wouldn't have come on-line herself if it wasn't important to someone that you feel a sense of security. And maybe that is genuine. But if I may be permitted to put in my two bits, I'd say you'll be wise not to show up for the delegation in the conventional manner."

"I agree," Jenae said. "They could spirit you off into the night and no one would ever know."

"We'll have to construct an alternative plan," Stephen agreed. "Tell Hunt you accept, Colin, and inquire into all the details. Then we will see how best to assure the offer's bona fide."

◆

The data that Odessa Hunt released to them proved to be rather different from that which the dolphins had provided. Raj nodded when he saw it. "Quite in character," he said. "I expect deception is the rule rather than the exception. Well . . ." He pursed his lips, the intricate folds of his face puckering in thought. "I can tell you a thing or two about the delegation. I had lunch today with—well, never mind that. Let's just say, I've done a little looking on your behalf, Colin. Call up the list of the delegates and let's see what we have."

Stephen was sitting at the terminal, and he displayed the information from Hunt's files. It consisted of photos, c.v.'s, and medical data concerning the members of the delegation, who numbered five so far.

"It didn't take them long, did it?" said Jenae, glancing at Colin. "I wonder if they were expecting something like this."

"I don't think so," Raj answered. "There's been some difficulty coming up with the right ships to send out there— they do need firepower, which seems suspicious to us, and it's not easy to come up with long-range vessels with the kind of military requirements they need for this mission. They've got ships at Jupiter that have to be refitted and sent out after the launch of the delegation, to meet with it at Underkohling. No, I don't think it's been well thought out at all."

Stephen was scrolling through the personnel. "A human

pilot," he said, "and two One-Eyed technicians. Then we have an environmental toxicologist called Mika DiFeo"—the photo of the delicate, middle-aged woman was blurry—"and also a systems engineer—that's good—named Peter Gangian." He enlarged the photo of a man with straight black hair and heavy jowls.

"Never heard of him," muttered Colin. "Go on."

"A terraforming specialist, Lourdes O'Rourke. Her c.v. shows three years of administrative work with the Coalition, but that was ten years ago. She's probably not hard-core Coalition. But"—a new face floated up—"this guy, Milos Stenz, a physician, specializes in treating the ravages of the environment on pure human protestors. He probably does a lot of euthanasia."

"He looks ghoulish," Jenae said, remembering the mob that had encircled her at Perth rez. This man was so thin his cheekbones seemed about to puncture the skin of his face.

"And finally," Stephen intoned, "the one and only Corvette Blake, U.N. dignitary and humanitarian of note."

"Aha," said Colin. "Finally, someone with a little class."

"And, of course, you," Raj said. "They probably won't add more than one or two people. The League will surely send someone, but other than that, it's in the mission's best interests to keep things small." Jenae thought: No One Eyes, and it's not a surprise to anybody. But she said nothing.

"Liftoff scheduled for a week Tuesday," added Stephen. Then he swiveled around in his chair and they all looked at each other.

"Advice?" asked Colin, spreading his hands, palm upward. "Comments? Accusations? Warnings?" He glanced at Jenae, but she was looking at Raj.

"There's a chance Colin will never make it to the ship, isn't there?" she said.

Raj nodded slowly. "It's going to be a very quiet launch. There have been so many problems with the Coalition, nobody wants to risk a lot of publicity. In that kind of situation with a lot of secrecy and complex security procedures imposed on the delegates, it's fairly easy to arrange for one delegate to be unavoidably detained, and then go on with the launch without him."

Colin looked offended. "Unavoidably detained?" he squawked.

"No worries," Jenae said. "I have a few ideas."

Actually, she only had one idea. Keila would be waiting in Portsmouth. Jenae would get back on the Underground and find her, in the hope that the One Eye had "connections" in the north as well.

29

Boats in the middle of the night, Jenae thought, seem to be a theme in my life. But this time I'm steering.

From her vantage point in the cockpit she couldn't see Colin's face, so the particular shade of green he had become was unknown to her at the moment. He had been sick twice already—even tea did nothing to console him, and she hoped fervently that he hadn't weakened himself to the point of utter uselessness. Oughtn't some seaworthiness to the North Sea swells be built into his ancestral makeup? she wondered.

They had entered the fjord, and she lowered the engine, glancing at the computer for guidance in handling the navigation. As the massive walls of living earth closed in on both sides, Jenae was reminded of the cliffs of the South Island—but those were puny compared to the heights that rose around her now. This was the real thing. It was strange, how important everything had seemed, back when Yi Ling was still alive and Jenae still thought she could save her. Then, even though Jenae had just been a piece of baggage to the One Eyes, she had felt urgent and wired. Now, in charge of Colin and their mission, Jenae actually felt calm, smoothly executing the scheme she and Keila had cooked up. It seemed terrible but true that with her greatest fears already come to pass, she could act freely. There was nothing left to be afraid of.

After we get Colin on this ship, she thought, I'm going back to Jakarta and leave the rest to fate.

She slowed and cut the engine entirely as the dock finally appeared shimmering out of the blackness. The quay was deserted—a handful of spectral lights shimmered in the nearby buildings, but nothing stirred. This was a minor commercial port, staffed by One Eyes and working only by day. She guessed that even One Eyes didn't night-fish in October, for she'd seen only one distant ship in the past hour, a liner probably cruising out of Oslo. Jenae leapt onto the pier and secured the boat over the soft squeaking of the plastic floats. Her movements felt stiff within the constraints of the walksuit.

A heavy hand was laid on her shoulder.

"Sister," said Keila's voice.

Jenae turned, gripping the hand in both of her small ones.

"I don't have much time," she said. "Can you help me with the baggage?" She jerked her head toward Colin, in whose pale face a dark mouth could be seen forming a soundless *o*.

Keila grunted, reached down, and dragged Colin bodily out of the boat. He stumbled and cried out; Jenae hushed him angrily.

"No fear," said Keila. "I've taken care of everything. C'mon, I've got a land vehicle ready. We'll bypass the tubes completely. The only people who see us will be One Eyes, and they'll never tell."

Jenae slung their bags over her shoulders. She didn't mind the weight of them; she'd picked up some gear when she bought the walksuits on the black market in London, just to be prepared. Now, she thought, let them just try to stop me and they'll be smithereens.

◆

The sun was hovering low in the east when Keila stopped the car at a pull-off on the old road outside Bergen on the west coast of Norway. The wind was bitter when they got out and turned north to look over the rugged heath. Here autumn rains had brought green to the land, but the onset of winter had also stimulated patches of vegetation to flower, an incongruous riot of hot pink and fluorescent orange: new species blooming in the sharp cold. Where the three stood the earth was literally blackened beneath their feet. Colin scuffed at the ground, curious—but Jenae's gaze followed the line of Keila's arm over the land.

"When we go over that rise we'll see it. It's less than a

mile from there—no cover, I'm afraid, so we have to move fast. The sun will be low for a while—winter's on the way—and we're lucky that almost no launches are made at this time of year. That's one reason the Heads have selected this launch site. It's all being kept very quiet."

"And how am I to get in? I mean, surely I'm to go by the official route . . ." Colin said anxiously. "They'll be expecting me on the train from Oslo." The microphone in his walksuit brought out the treble in his voice: he sounded almost effeminate.

"No." Keila shook her head. "They will expect you to come from Oslo, but you won't."

She turned to go, but Colin said, "Look, you've got to tell me what you intend for me to do sooner or later. If not now, then when?"

Keila turned, eyed him scornfully from head to foot, and finally relented.

"You'll keep them waiting at the tube station. We'll show up my way, late. They'll have the ship all ready. Then you'll turn up with the proper security passes for all of us. I'll be badged as spaceport personnel, and Jenae will be your assistant. We want to see you safely on the ship before we make our escape."

"It's quite unnecessary . . ." said Colin.

"You don't understand," Keila cut him off. "I'm not being sentimental—"

"I wouldn't dream of accusing you . . ."

"—rather I'm trying to be certain you go to the real ship and end up with the real delegation."

"I can't believe Odessa Hunt would lie!"

"Maybe not, but she's not the one out here making the decisions. Do you want us to drive you to the front gate and leave it at that? It will be a lot safer for Jenae and me not to be involved. After you launch, we still have to escape."

Colin looked at the ground. "I'll try to stay out of your way," he said.

"I'd like to know *exactly* what you have in mind—" Jenae began.

"Have you memorized the plans of the port?"

"Of course! If the League taught me nothing else, I know how to use my memory."

"Then follow my directions. Everything else has been arranged. One Eyes run the spaceport, you know—the radiation makes it too dangerous for pure humans to risk prolonged exposure." The disdain in Keila's tone expressed volumes on that matter.

"Yes, but why should they help us?"

"I've called in a few favors. Just as Tien called in a favor the day he asked me to watch out for you. It's a small world among the new species—or it should be. But let's not waste time talking. Get out your weapons."

Jenae took out her laser rifle—the oldest model she'd been able to find, and better made than anything being turned out in recent years. She had already tested it from the window of the car; it was clean, charged, and perfectly calibrated. She tossed Colin the pistol she'd bought for him. Idiot-proof, the One-Eyed seller had assured her. My toddler could use it, he'd said. That's not a guarantee of much, Jenae thought now. Colin stared at it, bemused.

"You don't expect *me* to—" He saw Keila's face and swallowed. "Right," he added. "Point and shoot. Just like a camera, right? How nice. I'm right behind you."

The spaceport had no dome and no mirror fields; at first it appeared to be all naked buildings and vast launch pads, with the sea visible as a deep grey-blue curtain behind everything. The place looked strangely deserted at this hour and terribly exposed. Then Jenae saw the sparkle of light in a subtle X-pattern on the perimeter of the port. An electrical baffle had been erected, almost transparent. Nothing was going to get through it, Jenae was willing to bet, except perhaps from above.

Keila was undeterred. She led them down the slope and toward the invisible barrier at a clip that had Colin gasping in the rear. A lone figure appeared from among the ground transport equipment and began to walk toward them. They reached the baffle; Jenae's hair, what there was of it, was standing on end, and a high-frequency whine hovering just on the upper range of her hearing made her teeth ache. The figure drew closer: it was a One Eye, armored and decked out with weapons. The One Eye stopped twenty paces away and raised a handheld instrument, pointing it straight at them. Jenae was reaching for her rifle when Keila's hand seized her wrist and held it back. The stranger fired. A spark of light flickered at the tip of the instrument; then the baffle before them flared and disappeared. Wind passed through the gap in the security field.

"Come on." Keila stepped through the gap first, dragging Colin forcibly behind her. When they were all through, the One Eye reactivated the field. Then he handed them three slim folders. He spoke slow, ponderous English.

"These are your passes. I don't know how far they will get you, but you can try. I will be in the launch booth supervising takeoff." He looked at Keila. "Everything is on schedule. But a message came in half an hour ago that Dr. Peake's train was delayed in Oslo. They are boarding the ship anyway. The passengers need time to become acclimated before takeoff. The pilot is one of us, and will be expecting you at the hatch."

"Sweet," Jenae said. "Where's the ship?"

The One Eye didn't answer, and Keila said, "That could be a problem. When is the train expected?"

"Less than an hour."

"Good. By the time they discover he's not on the train, our operative will have boarded him and the ship will be off. A piece of luck for us."

The One Eye turned and walked away without a word; there had been a time when this action, combined with a total mutual lack of greeting, naming, or thanks on the part of the two One Eyes, would have perplexed her. But she knew now that their behavior was normal, and she was even comforted by it, especially after enduring the niceties and platitudes of pure humans in England. She followed Keila to a red-painted hatch in the concrete.

"Go in, Colin," Jenae urged. "Hurry."

He was hesitating—Keila had disappeared within, but Colin looked uncomfortable.

"I can't make up my mind whether this is exciting or merely inconvenient," he muttered, and lowered himself into the hole.

It was a long service shaft, bottoming out about twenty meters down. From there the tunnel ran in three directions. Luckily it had been built for One Eyes—Jenae and Colin could walk comfortably abreast. But once the hatch had closed behind them, the only illumination came from weak, infrequently spaced lights embedded in the ceiling.

"Take off the walksuits," whispered Keila. "You wouldn't be wearing them if you came by train." Her voice was sleek and plastic in the resonant tunnel, and its echoes slithered down the walls on all sides. She waited while they obeyed, then rolled their walksuits into compact cylinders and stowed them in her pack. Then she took off with a long, steady stride into the darkness. They crept after her, uncertain and ill at ease.

They traversed a few hundred meters in a straight line along this passageway, passing at intervals shafts in the ceiling or cross-corridors. Vents admitted warm, steamy air from time to time, and always the subliminal hum of power surrounded them. The map in Jenae's head told her that they were to go up a level shortly, and sure enough, Keila stopped just ahead, looking up into an overhead service shaft.

"Go ahead," Keila whispered, dropping back to the rear. Jenae knew the main passage would take them to the tube station from which pure humans normally entered the compound. Instead, they climbed up into a cramped service tube that ran parallel to the main transitway overhead. They had to crawl. Though Keila signed for quiet, Jenae heard nothing: no evidence of the train or its passengers. Everything was eerily still.

At last they reached an automated security junction, and they could go no farther. Jenae slid aside a hatch and dropped softly down into the main corridor. She jumped and spun around when lights came on all around her, her hand already reaching for her weapon. But no one was there. She let out a shaky breath; the floor panel had sensed her pressure and activated the light. Belatedly she wondered whether they weren't being tracked even now: sensors must have picked them up long ago.

"What are you waiting for?" Keila hissed. "Follow your instructions." Jenae swallowed and stepped up to the security station that now blocked their path. Reading the directions on the panel, she displayed the tiny chip on her pass to the red light. The system chirped at her noncommittally and the iris swirled open, admitting her through the security arc. Colin and Keila followed in the same fashion. Jenae caught a glimpse of Colin's face. "This is easy," he seemed to be saying, but she had a feeling of doubt within her. Her shoulders were tense and her mouth was dry. She kept swallowing but it didn't help.

Keila led the way then, to a corridor marked Pad 4, and then to a vertical shaft. Keila climbed the ladder, released the hatch, and stepped out into daylight. Jenae followed. A brisk wind was blowing in from the sea, and they were standing in the very shadow of the launch platform. The ship *Mulig* loomed overhead.

It was too easy, Jenae thought.

A small figure grew as it walked toward them across the tarmac: the One-Eyed pilot, who would prepare Colin for boarding—according to the plan. But as he drew closer, it became apparent that his stature was slight. Not a One Eye, Jenae thought in sudden alarm, and glanced behind her as if to retreat into the hatch. Colin was lounging half in and half out of the hole, probably hesitating because he had just realized he was out in the open air unprotected. Jenae wanted to kick him back inside. But it was too late.

"What are you doing out here?" the newcomer demanded sharply, his voice loud and metallic through the air processor. "We've been waiting for you inside. Who directed you to this area?" He took a few last strides and stopped meters away. He had positioned himself between them and the platform.

"A guard," Jenae answered. "Back at the tube station." She saw Keila flinch and simultaneously she realized her own error: the security checkpoint had been automated, as they all probably were.

"Dr. Peake, I presume?" said the guard, aiming a scanner at Colin's badge to be certain.

"Uh . . . yes," said Colin, glancing nervously at Keila. The guard's attention followed.

"Who are you? I've never seen you before on this shift."

"I was on my way home," Keila said, "when I found these two wandering around near the tube station. They called ahead with instructions they were taking a night train, but when they arrived no one was there to meet them. They started wandering around the tunnels looking for assistance."

Good thinking, Jenae thought. Why couldn't she think as fast as Keila?

"I see," said the guard.

Jenae thrust herself forward. "This One Eye seems to be the only person who knows what the hell's going on around here. If it wasn't for her, we'd still be lost in those damn tunnels. I'd like to know who *you* are!"

"I'm the pilot," he answered quietly. "If you'll just step back into the shaft." He slapped a com patch on his wrist. "This is Tark. Send me a team immediately on pad four. We have unauthorized entry here—possibly spies. Is the team still on location to meet Dr. Peake's train? What's the ETA? Half an hour? Good. Well, double-check him when he gets here. Yeah. And your team has been there how long? That's what I thought. This guy's an imposter. If they hadn't lied to me I might have let him on the ship. Yeah. And find out who fucked up. Somebody issued these people security passes."

He snapped off the com, his face turning grim.

"Into the hatch, I said!"

Jenae and Keila reacted in unison. Jenae broke toward the gun, and in the same instant Keila kicked the man in the gut. The gun misfired, its charge meeting a minor support stanchion, which melted. Colin fell down.

"Run!" Jenae screamed at him, and he got up and scurried around the platform, looking for a way to get up into the ship. A vehicle had detached itself from the row of parked trucks on the perimeter of the launch area and was moving rapidly toward them. Keila swarmed up the side of the platform like a spider on a wall, but Colin just stood there looking up, his hands hanging down in defeat.

Turning her back on the guard, Jenae flung herself toward Colin. "Get up there!" she urged, glancing over her shoulder at the approaching vehicle. It must be moving even faster than she'd thought. No, there were two vehicles now, and one was almost on them.

"Shit, Colin—move!" Jenae looked up the steep scaffolding. It was slippery, but there were footholds. It could be done, especially with a little adrenaline to fire the mix. But Colin just stood there like an idiot. He's paralyzed with fear, she thought in exasperation. He turned and looked at her, his pale green eyes vacant. She started toward him with the intention of forcing him to move.

Something struck her from behind, jamming hard into her kidneys, and she was lifted right off her feet and into the air. Her body twisted involuntarily midflight and she landed flat on her back. The guard Keila had kicked was standing over her, gasping and clutching his midsection where the aftereffects of Keila's footprint were apparently still making themselves felt. Sloppy job on Keila's part, Jenae thought irrelevantly as he put his booted foot on her throat and applied weight. She thought his action had a certain relish. The gun was pointed at her belly for good measure.

What an idiot you are, Jenae berated herself. In the two or three seconds that elapsed, she repeated the syllables over and over mentally like a mantra. It was amazing, her mind continued on a handful of other levels, how many threads of thought one could maintain within such a short span of time and the windpipe being crushed not to mention the kidneys screaming out and the jarringness of it all and the unholy color of blue the autumn sky above the head of the pure human that wanted her dead with a vengeance and was it a xenophobic thing or just his nature or did you get that way after doing a job long enough and what a baby he must feel surrounded by One Eyes all the time just as she had felt at first and probably that made him want to inflict pain on her and exercise control on her right now oh yes like with the sole of the boot crushing her larynx and threatening to break her neck all at once, how interesting to accomplish all that so neatly.

Suddenly his weight was off her. When she turned her head, she saw that the pilot was on the ground now and *Colin* was on top of him. The physicist was pummeling the man with vigor. She struggled up, groped for and found her rifle where it had been knocked aside, and took aim. But Colin was inseparable from the other man; they lay in a moving tangle, grappling with one another.

There was a locator in the pilot's belt.

Swallowing painfully, Jenae struggled forward and seized the locator unnoticed. It captivated her attention even in the middle of this chaos. For a handful of seconds she was unaware of the oncoming armored vehicles. She didn't heed

Colin's grunts and cries as he struggled with the pilot bare-handed. She just saw the locator, felt it in her hand. It was an innocuous-looking device: hand-held, Y-shaped, encased in textured plastic. There were two buttons: yellow for identify, red for locate/destroy. It shook in her hand.

The nearest of the vehicles stopped. An aperture opened in its side and a dozen guards poured out, weapons raised. They seemed to hesitate. They're One Eyes, Jenae thought. They know Keila. They don't want to kill us.

Jenae dropped the locator on the ground and aimed her rifle at it. At the same moment the pilot broke free of Colin and started to get to his feet. He reached for the locator at his belt and didn't find it. He stood up, turning.

Jenae fired. The locator didn't explode: it simply melted into a shapeless heap.

Laser fire erupted in the air over her head. The guards scattered, dodging. Keila. It seemed Keila was letting loose with everything she had into the onrushing security force—yet, oddly, she hadn't actually hit anyone. The pilot turned toward Colin again, vanquished on the ground. Jenae swung the rifle in his direction.

The first burst grazed his head, and she flinched—not with empathy, she was surprised to discover, but with annoyance at her own clumsiness. He started to turn toward her, blood and broken glass obstructing his face, and she let off a long cutting swath of fire down his torso and into his gut. It was messy. He went down twitching, bleeding all over Colin, who had recovered enough to squirm away. Jenae avoided looking at Colin's face; one glance told her he had never seen anything like this before. He was like a child. Jenae took three strides and hurled herself up the side of the launch pad. Adrenaline did make it easier: she scarcely paused to find footholds. Keila was still firing profusely, and one of the vehicles fell into two pieces with a rending noise. Flames burst up. Jenae paused in the doorway, slipping behind Keila, and looked down on Colin, who had moved around the corner of the pad and was feebly attempting to climb the wall.

"Rope!" Keila shouted. "In my pack. Quick."

Jenae fumbled with the closures on Keila's pack and brought out a coil of cable. She cast her eyes about for a place to fasten it. Colin wasn't easily seen by their adversaries: he was around the corner. But he still should have been picked off by now. Staged, Jenae thought. The whole thing's been staged by Keila.

Keila thrust the rifle into Jenae's hands and grabbed the cable herself. It landed on Colin's head. Jenae fired randomly, to little effect. Shrapnel flew and some of it struck Colin, swinging on the end of the rope. Keila reeled him in like a fish. The return fire had melted sections of the platform; the force from one ray buffeted Jenae as it passed inches from her left ear.

Colin was up.

"Get in," Keila said crisply. "In about five seconds the command tower's going to override and decide to sacrifice the ship. They'll set missiles on us."

They scrambled into the ship, striking each other inadvertently in the dim, confining spaces. Jenae could hear Colin wheezing.

"What the fuck, Keila?" he gasped. She slammed the hatch shut, punched in a lock order, and careened up the ladder into what must be the pilot's section; she had no clue what to do once she got there, and Colin's sweating, fear-stinking proximity unnerved her in these close quarters. He'll put us in orbit all by himself, Jenae thought, he's wound up so tight.

"Take a station," said Keila. "We don't have time to compare notes."

Jenae obeyed, but she glanced silently at Colin as she passed him on her way to her seat.

"Some plan . . . bloody insane . . . could have been killed easily . . ." he muttered.

Jenae fumbled with the safety harness and looked blankly at the active panel in front of her. Out of the corner of her eye she could see Colin mopping his face even as he peered at the controls. Keila was stationed to her right, her expression unreadable as she began to enter commands. The face of the One-Eyed guard who had met them at the gate had sprung up on Keila's screen.

"Emergency?" he asked in a flat tone.

"I need juice," Keila said.

"Done." The image spiraled out. Keila methodically continued to work at her console. The whine intensified. Jenae could feel it all the way down in her coccyx.

"What are you doing, Keila?" Jenae whispered.

"What does it look like, puppy? I'm launching this beast."

"That's what I was afraid of."

For the shards of time in which Keila initiated the launch, Jenae could feel a tremor of unreasoning fear beginning in the pit of her body: instead of feeling safe she was sheared open with the realization that she didn't belong in this vessel, that her body was not going to comply with being shot off into the upper atmosphere, that the machinery of the ship itself was hostile to her very being. This wasn't supposed to be happening. She was supposed to be on her way back to see Tien. She had never agreed to be shot off into space.

Though she fought to quell them, the quivers of fear began to multiply in her guts—soon they would become a stampede, and all her efforts at self-control out there on the tarmac would be for nothing. She would break down at the critical instant.

Jenae glanced at Colin again, more sympathetically now. Then she realized that he knew what he was doing, his fingers moving rapidly over the panel with consummate assurance. She looked at her own panel: it notified her that there were seven passengers, all secured in sleeping compartments and already stabilized in a light trance state. Envious of them, she sank back into her seat, trembling. Keila spoke no warning.

Silently, massively, the engines released. Jenae was squashed miserably into the contoured seat, unable to think or move. Without her permission the syllables frolicked through her inner ears: here we go, here we go, herewego-herewego . . .

Lethe

30

"Place your bets, everybody," Daire muttered. The gate read-out on *Morpheus'* monitor was beginning to tremble with activity. Outside, filaments of lightning crackled in the lywyn. He was lucky he'd made it to the ship so quickly; the last time the lightning had come, he'd been too far away to get to *Morpheus* in time.

"I don't like betting you," Tsering said. "You always win. Anyway, we already have one bet on."

"What, about the kid? That's different. That's just an idle wager, and anyway I *know* it's going to be a girl. But I'm not calling this one. I have absolutely no foreknowledge about the transmission. Either we make contact with a ship, or we don't. I don't much care."

He fiddled with the magnetic readings.

"You don't *care*?"

"Nope."

"Bullshit." Tsering relaxed back in her seat, looping her hands around her moon-shaped belly. The gesture made her look smug.

"Why should I care? What good can it do me if Earth knows about us?"

He didn't look at her; he had the feeling he was being glared at.

"You've only been promising everybody all kinds of miracles if a ship from Earth can get through the gate. Don't sit there and say you don't care. I don't believe you."

"It's true. Ah, look, it's starting to form. It's going to be a big one. What's it been, two months? There could be a ship out there, waiting. Any bets?"

"Yeah—it's going to be a boy. And you're lying."

Daire grinned. "OK, Tsering. Let's just say we do make contact here. Let's say there's a nice big rescue cruiser waiting on the other side of the gate to take us all back, hmm? Would you go?"

Tsering said nothing.

"See? You wouldn't go. So why should I care?"

"Why do you bother with these affectations?" she bristled. The gate was melting open raggedly like a piece of paper heated by flame, first blackening, then finally yielding here and there in expanding circles. "You obviously do care: you worry over us all like a mother hen, you work here at night, you plan trips in the hopper and then don't take them because you don't want to use up precious power. When will you stop this posturing?"

The gate was open. They both fell silent. Daire boosted power to the com system. He could hear his own voice blundering through the message he'd made on the hopper. Nothing else.

"It'll be open for maybe, ten minutes," he whispered, staring at the readings. "I'm not posturing. Well . . ." he couldn't resist a smile. "Not too much, anyway. I just don't see any point in working myself up about things I can't control."

They listened. A wriggle of static crossed the electrical field and brought a momentary surge of hope. Silence. Daire's recorded voice began again.

"This still isn't real for you, is it?" she said.

"I don't know what real is anymore. Is Earth real? Are there really other people out there, or did I dream it all?" He changed channels and turned his head into the com unit. "This is *Morpheus*. We have crossed the fourth gate at Underkohling. Attempting contact. Respond please."

They said nothing for several minutes. The message recycled. Now they could hear Daire's voice over both channels at once; the two messages were garbled together.

"You understand why I can't leave."

"Yeah, Tsering, I understand. Well, I don't *understand*, but I have no choice other than to accept it. Which is why I don't care if *nobody's out there*!" He screamed the last few words into the com system. Then for no reason he began to laugh.

Tsering got up and stood behind him, putting her hands over his eyes. "Don't look," she said. "It's closing."

Daire shut his eyes in the darkness behind her hands.

"I bet they do come," he said. "And I bet it's a girl. And I bet we all live happily ever after."

31

Space travel did not agree with Jenae. Fortunately, the stolen ship was large enough to accommodate twelve, leaving room for the three conscious occupants to rattle about while the others slept. *Mulig* held a two-man hopper like the one that Morales had taken down to the surface of Underkohling, and prodigious scientific equipment whose function was mysterious to Jenae. It had been stocked carefully for the mission, and its provisions were heavy on water, including a large therapy tank similar to the kind she had used in the League. Jenae thought this was strange until she got around to reading the medical files at her station, which governed life support; then she belatedly discovered that there was a League representative on board. She was lucky there. Two weeks into their swift arc to Jupiter, Jenae availed herself of the tank to stave off the agony of altermode deprivation.

It was the only time altermode had ever been completely silent. Not even the softest echo of the League web nor of any computer system brushed her consciousness. Although the experience satiated her body, she emerged shaky and scared, needing reassurance. This existence, hurtling through space in a slim pocket of atmosphere to an unknown destination, was antithetical to everything that made sense to Jenae. She wished she could abandon her post at life support and share the trance of the delegation, but if Keila and Colin could endure, so could she. Nevertheless, when she wasn't on active shift, she retreated into a sleep resembling coma.

Colin said they were lucky not to have been destroyed by a satellite: Jenae thought this would have to mean that the people sleeping in the tanks must be important. There was information about everyone on the ship in the computers, but Jenae couldn't be bothered to absorb it all yet. They had plenty of time, after all: it would take no less than four months to reach Underkohling, and the passengers would be asleep for most of it. In the true spirit of a hijacker, Jenae had begun to think of them as insurance against destruction by the military. So it was best to keep things impersonal.

"The question," Colin said, "is whether or not we can elude the military."

Keila looked dissatisfied.

"The question is what we do when we get there. We can't survive if we pit ourselves against an entire fleet," Jenae said.

"Four ships do not make an entire fleet." Keila's manner was didactic. "You overestimate the resources of Earth. Only three of the ships ordered to intercept us are actually dangerous. They are well armed, but they're also slow. Jupiter is not on the way to Underkohling right now. They can't get between us and Underkohling if we maintain our speed. The fourth ship is a scout. It has better mobility but little firepower. We're fortunate in that the military hasn't done much in space. Beyond the satellite system they don't need to: everything's monopolized by the League out here."

"The Heads," Jenae amended. "Not the League."

"Colin, we need a plan now," Keila persisted. "We've gotten you en route to Underkohling—that's what you wanted. Now what do you intend to do?"

"What do I intend to do?" Colin inquired, taken somewhat aback. "I thought I was to stand aside and do as told. Although, I must say, I warned you before we got to the spaceport that lying about the train would give us trouble, and it did. We were very, *very* lucky to escape. If that was your idea of a sensible plan, my confidence is shaken."

"Point taken," said Keila calmly. "There were contingencies I hadn't anticipated."

Were there? Jenae wondered. Or had Keila wanted to be in on this herself? Unless her eyes had deceived her, Keila had made some kind of arrangement with the One Eyes at the spaceport, or else why hadn't the guards slaughtered them? It had not been luck that saved them at all. Yet, for whatever reason of her own, Keila didn't want Colin to know that. Keila had risked her life for Jenae, and whatever her personal feelings about being stuck out here in space, Jenae wouldn't speak her suspicions aloud. If Colin couldn't figure it out for himself, he certainly wasn't going to hear about it from Jenae.

"But it's your show now," Keila was saying. She sounded almost placating. "What do you intend to do?"

"For one thing, I hope to convince these people in the tanks that the Heads have been fucking them over for eighty years. I hope to do that *before* the guns get to Underkohling, so we can make a united stand against them. Then, we'll send the hopper through the gate, and see what's really there."

"Whoa," Keila exclaimed. "Forget standing up against the guns. We can create confusion, and possibly sabotage an attempt to close the gate, but we can't defend Underkohling, even against three ships." Keila was adamant.

"Maybe we can pick up some more ships from Jupiter . . . ?"

"Backup from Jupiter?" Keila said incredulously. "I may not be an experienced space traveler, but even I'm not stupid enough to think anyone from Jupiter's going to be on our side. We'll be lucky if they haven't dispatched even more ships to intercept us at Underkohling."

"Then let's wake up the delegation so I can make my case."

"Wake up the delegation." Again Keila repeated Colin's words as though she couldn't be hearing him right. "Are you crazy? This is a hostage situation, and the joy of it is, the captives don't even know it. Do you want to have to deal with seven terrified and irate officials who, thanks to the Heads, have probably already been brainwashed to think you're a madman?"

"Please, Colin," Jenae said. "Let's not wake them up now. Everything's calibrated to keep them under for four months. I really don't know what to do with them if you wake them up."

"Very well, we won't rush it. Let me think about it, then." Colin retreated into his own thoughts, muttering. "Perhaps we could detour the other ships into one of the other gates . . . a ruse of some kind . . ."

Jenae felt her eyes growing heavy again. She felt like a

child whose fate is being decided by two grown-ups who are thinking of everything but what's important to her: in this case, solid ground or, better yet, water. But no—none of that was going to happen for a long time. She embarked on yet another attempt to escape through sleep, trying to find some connection with the dolphins or Tien in the depths of her own subconscious, but the voices of Colin and Keila argued even in her dreams.

◆

Four months out from Earth and with their best speed, the crew of *Mulig* had maintained their course, and according to Colin's calculations, there was nothing that could come from Jupiter and get to Underkohling ahead of them. But, as Colin was quick to point out, their window of opportunity at Underkohling would be small.

Keila and Colin had argued vociferously about their options once they got to Underkohling. They especially argued about what to do with the delegation, who were scheduled to awaken any day now. They would have to be fed carefully and they would be required to adhere to a strict schedule of physical therapy to countereffect the atrophy of trance. They would be moving about the main section of the ship; they would be asking questions; they would be, in general, acting like people.

"Just don't tell them anything," Jenae told Colin. "Tell them you're the pilot, that you can't meet with them personally for some reason, but reassure them. They're pure humans: most of them should be tractable."

"They aren't all pure humans," Keila said. "There is an altermode human, who is going to need water soon, Jenae. Have you been watching his signs?"

"Yeah, I have. I thought it would be better if we woke him up first."

"I think we should wake them all up," said Colin. "And I think we should tell them the truth. You two, I believe, have embarked on a power trip."

Keila and Jenae exchanged glances.

"You see?" Colin cried, his voice cracking. "This is all it's been since the spaceport. 'It's your show, Colin!' Isn't that what you said, Keila? Well, if it's my show how come nobody's listening to me? You two really screwed up at the spaceport. If you had let me go in by the conventional route, I'd be sleeping quietly and you'd both be home fighting your wars or whatever it is you do there, but not taking out your need for authority on me!"

Keila actually cracked a smile. "You might be right, Dr. Peake," she said. "Then again, you might be dead by now. We may never know."

Colin said nothing.

"But if you want to wake them, I have no objection," Keila continued. "Jenae?"

Jenae picked at her fingernails. She sighed.

"Look," she said at last. "The thing is . . . there's something I haven't told you. The altermoder in the tank . . . a few weeks ago I read everybody's medical files carefully, to be sure I wouldn't have any surprises when we try to revive them. Well, the League member is someone I know. And . . . we're not on the best of terms."

"I'm not surprised," Colin murmured.

◆

Zafara looked different. Maybe she had been unfair in her judgment of him, Jenae thought. In repose his face was serene, ageless, and even rather pure. He lay in the trance field so quietly, his hands lax at his sides, the sluggish pulse all but undetectable at his throat. She felt strange just looking at him.

Luckily all the systems that sustained the delegation were automated: Jenae had spent much of her time learning how they were operated and monitoring their function, but technically she wasn't needed. *Mulig* had been intended to be flown by the pure human she'd killed, and a One-Eyed co-pilot (the delegation's concession, she supposed, to the need for representation by One Eyes) who had probably been on the tarmac at the time of the hijacking. Jenae was now certain Keila had orchestrated it, but she didn't have the nerve to come right out and confront Keila. How ready Keila had been to leap into the pilot's chair and take over.

Had she *asked* me, Jenae thought, I would have said no. The reality of spending nearly a year away from the dolphins would be agonizing, and when the strong possibility of not returning at all was added in, Jenae ought to feel doomed. What would Tien think? Yet now that she was actually out here, she found herself refusing to succumb to depression. Maybe she had spent too much time with Yi Ling to be able to inflict that kind of behavior on anybody else. She couldn't permit herself the same emotional lows that Colin, for example, had indulged in. It was a wonder Keila hadn't throttled him weeks ago.

She looked at Zafara again. "Well," she sighed, "might as well get the worst over with first."

She initiated the sequence that would slowly bring Zafara's metabolism up from deep trance. Then she turned to the other containers, and one by one she activated the wake-up call.

"So now we brace ourselves," said Colin behind her. He was standing in the hatchway of the compartment watching her work. "I certainly hope we find a viable world on the other side. If we don't, it's going to be awfully crowded and noisy in here."

"I don't mind," Jenae said. "The silence gets on my nerves. Music doesn't help, either. . . ." She glanced over her shoulder at him; his habit of playing Mahler recordings on the audio system had alienated her some time ago.

"Yes, we'll have our hands full," Colin continued as though she hadn't spoken. "Tell me about these people again. Are there any real scientists in the batch?"

"You know who they are! Why do you keep mentioning it?"

"I just can't believe it. Abdelmjid Hassan. The gall of them, to choose him. He'll be useless—rule him out. I'm not surprised that Hunt didn't have the balls . . . excuse me . . . the nerve to tell me he was coming. Are there any *real* scientists?"

Jenae decided to humor him. Colin really could be incredibly dense when it came to remembering information that didn't interest him. "We have an environmental toxicologist, a terraforming specialist, a systems engineer—"

"Who?" Colin's ears pricked up.

"Uh . . . Peter Gangian?"

"That's right; I remember now. Don't know him. Go on."

"Well, there's Zafara, who is, as you know, the League

representative; a physician who represents the Coalition who is also a communications specialist—which is odd, since I thought they didn't believe in computers . . . Anyway, that's it. Oh, and Corvette Blake from the U.N. She's a Gene Wars historian. Keen to find the terrible criminals, I bet."

"Well, you'll straighten her out on that score, I'm certain."

"I hope someone believes us. The two people from the Coalition are going to be tricky, but the rest should be unbiased, right?"

"I wouldn't count on it, Jenae. Be ready for anything—that's my advice."

"It'll take a while, you know. Several days, I guess, before everybody's cogent and mobile again. What's our timing like?"

"We're still out of range of the gunships, but we're going to lose time once we actually arrive, while we work on an orbit. Then we have to send down a team and wait for the gate to open. I have no idea how long that will take. It could be hours, or it could quite literally be weeks. Until I can get more data on the gate's current condition, I won't be able to predict anything."

"That doesn't sound too good."

"It's not too good, my dear girl—as you would know if you hadn't slept most of the time and ignored most of my remarks when you were awake."

"I just don't understand everything you say. It puts me back to sleep."

Colin sighed.

"Look, Colin, explain to me how we can do anything if they have the weaponry to close the gate and we have no guns and we have to sit around waiting for the gate to get open before we can get any proof. If anyone will listen to our proof."

"Okay, listen. The gunships are gambling as much as we are. Their information may allow them to close the gate, or at least damage its function, if they can get the timing right and concentrate their firepower effectively. But they have to time it to the precise moment that the gate is reaching closure—while it's just snicking shut but isn't actually static yet—and they've got to be positioned fairly carefully to do it.

This will almost certainly take more than one attempt, and since it's impossible to predict the frequency of the gate's dilation, there's no way to know how much time it will take before they get it right. So they're in the same situation we are, in a sense. If ultimately they fail in closing the gate, I suspect their instructions will be to go through the gate and kill anything they find on the other side."

"Which is where we will be."

"Maybe. Maybe not. It's touch and go, Jenae. I don't have to tell you that."

"I know, I know. But I'm a long way from home, and it doesn't seem like there's anything I can do. . . ."

"Put on your tough act for the delegation when they're waking up. That's a worthy service to the mission. Keep them intimidated if possible. You have a gift for that, for all that you're not as tall as my shoulder."

◆

Jenae kept vigil with the delegation. Zafara was the first to come up, his eyes opening like a cat's with cool awareness fully formed.

"So, we meet again," he said slowly but calmly, as if he had expected to see her. "Are you still angry, or have you accepted reality?"

"Both," Jenae retorted. "I'm to help you recover from trance, so let's keep the equation simple, okay? Don't mess with me, and I won't mess with you."

"Of course," Zafara answered smoothly. "I wouldn't dream of interfering. Thank you for allowing me to wake up. I gather from your tone that you would have preferred to let me go on sleeping indefinitely."

"You need altermode," Jenae said. "A tank has been prepared for you as soon as you feel strong enough to move."

A hungry light was in his eyes. "Yes. Now."

She had to help him, for his gait was wavering and uncertain, and a pronounced ataxia kept sending him reeling into walls. "I'll warn you that this tank is off-line from main systems," she said. "So don't bother trying to contact the Pickled Brains. It won't work."

"You think of everything, don't you?" Zafara whispered,

climbing into the tank. As he stepped into the water he seized her wrist. "Join me?"

His grip was astonishingly strong considering his condition. She didn't think she could break it. His gills were already flaring open as his body sensed the presence of water.

"I think not," Jenae said stiffly, although her own gills were burning sympathetically. The idea repulsed her out of all proportion to common sense even as it paradoxically aroused the altermode impulses, and she stared significantly at his hand on her wrist until he released it, laughing.

"You're still so young," he said as he submerged. "There's so little you can understand."

She snorted and walked away, pretending she didn't want the water as badly as she did.

◆

The rest of the delegation were up and about by the time they were drawing into visual range of Underkohling. Jenae already felt she knew them all a little too intimately, and once they had twigged the fact that she was their captor and not their servant, the situation had become a bit delicate. So Jenae convinced Keila to baby-sit them while she worked with Colin in the pilot's section. Keila was very effective, particularly with the men. They were very quiet when she was around. And Jenae was content to be involved in the preliminary surveys of the gate, since it was the gate project that had gotten her into this whole situation in the first place. She was there when *Mulig* soared into Underkohling's neighborhood and the small body became visible at last.

"There it is," Colin breathed, his fingers rigid on the console. "Damned near invisible. Look at it! Could you ever guess it's got gates in it that will take you inconceivable distances? The thing's a sea of inconsistencies. Start scanning for the hopper. That will be easier than using sensors to find the fourth gate."

Underkohling drew closer rapidly; Colin occupied himself with regulating their velocity and doing some fine steering.

"How did it get there?" Jenae asked. "Do you think it was built, or born, as they say?"

Colin sniffed. "Is there a distinction these days? I don't subscribe to any particular theory, but it certainly doesn't have a mechanistic structure. How can you answer a question like that when you can't even prove that the thing's made of a substance?"

"Don't *you* know what it's made of?"

"Not in so many words, no."

"Colin, I've scanned this half. No hopper. Nothing even close. I'm getting some weird fluctuations in EM, though."

"That's normal. I'll bring her around the night side. The hopper must be there. The poles aren't fixed or I could tell you where to concentrate your search."

The shadow of Underkohling swallowed the glimmer of reflected sunlight as they cruised around behind the dark body.

"Nothing."

"Ridiculous! Let me see."

After a few minutes Colin stood up, his shoulders twitching, and looked pensively at the ceiling. Then, scowling, he buried his face in the ocular again.

"Right," he said after a while. "There's gate two. We don't want to go near it—no one ever comes back. And so *that* . . ." He breathed slowly through his mouth. "There it is. My gate. Lovely. And, Jenae, you're right—there is no hopper to be found. I wonder if it was pulled into the gate, after—oh!" His head shot up. "Open communications. Quick! I'm so *stupid*! I didn't think of this at all."

Jenae set the com on scan and turned on the audio. She could hear the frequencies flipping, then a man's voice, soft but clear: ". . . convinced they're victims of some kind, possibly sent out here as a red herring. They are a near variation on human, morphologically similar to altermode humans although there are some complications. It would appear that they have a permanent transition to altermode once they've reached the adult form. The whole situation is very complex. All I need is a ship out here, and for somebody to figure out how the gate works. It's accessible in both directions—I've been through myself. I need a ship. I'm sure subsequent discoveries out here will more than pay for it. Please relay this message immediately to the League of New Alchemists, who will be the most excited by this discovery, and hopefully in a position to help. This message will recycle every few minutes as long as power lasts. Morales out."

"Daire! Daire?" Colin yelled into the com.

"It's a recording," Jenae said. "I've picked up the device. Looks like he took the hopper and left the message in its place."

"That would be just like him," Colin agreed. "Just dive right back in. But that doesn't matter now. Evidence! Where are those zombies of yours, those iceheads? All they need is the *evidence*."

◆

Jenae thought the delegation seemed pleased to be included in matters not related to their digestion or muscle tone; they gladly trooped into the pilot's section and seated themselves on chairs and consoles as casually as a group of teenagers. Abdelmjid was the only one who stood out; he made a great show of selecting the proper chair, and then lowered his portly frame into the chosen one with an air of accomplishment. Colin paced back and forth while he narrated the story of his own involvement with Underkohling, and later the Heads. When he included her in the tale, Jenae thought he took some liberties with the facts, but she wasn't about to argue since his portrayal of her was rather flattering. Finally, he played the recording of Daire's message in its entirety. Then he leaned back against the copilot's chair and folded his arms, waiting. No one said anything for a long time.

At last Corvette Blake spoke. She was a slender, dark American with braided hair and a serious, contemplative air. She was still wearing pajamas. "Well, I can see how Underkohling is entirely worthy of exploration—I always knew it would be. But the fact that Morales found altermoders of some kind does *not* prove that the Ingenix directors aren't there also. It certainly doesn't prove that the Heads of the League are associated with the Ingenix directors in any way, except as common victims. Now, if we had the sequences Jenae decoded . . ." She flicked a glance at Jenae, who shook her head.

"No way. I never recorded them, and the League's buried them by now, I'm sure. The signal might still be out there, though." Jenae looked at Colin, who frowned.

"Not so far. Whatever got into my systems last time, it

hasn't popped up again. Then again, the gate's closed at the moment."

"It doesn't matter," Jenae said. "It took a dolphin team to decrypt the original code. I doubt we could duplicate the process here."

There was a slightly defeated silence. Mika, the environmental toxicologist, scanned the surrounding faces. When she looked at Peter, he said, "The whole thing gives me the creeps. I'm disinclined to trust hijackers—call me crazy—and I've been sleeping for months, and now you want me to believe the Heads are some kind of evil power brokers." He shifted restlessly in his seat.

"The disenfranchised are ever suspicious of power and success," said Abdelmjid. He didn't look at Colin, but the physicist bristled nevertheless. "I don't know why it's all gloom and doom around here—we should celebrate this great discovery to which we are all party." He beamed at everyone indiscriminately.

"No one's going to be discovering anything if the gate is disrupted," Colin said darkly.

"We do have evidence of that," Jenae put in. "Colin, show them."

"There isn't time for me to construct a proof," Colin began. "Nevertheless, I will share with you my findings. You're all welcome to have a go at it, but it will take time to see the indications I have detected—indications pointing to an attempt to destroy the gate under the pretext of stabilizing it."

"You realize, of course," said Zafara quietly, "that the easiest thing for us to do is turn you over to the authorities when the other ships arrive. You are criminals, now."

Jenae felt cold.

"Surely that's not necessary," said Mika in a soft voice. She included the other members in her gaze. "I'm not condoning what Dr. Peake and his accomplices have done, but it seems to me it would be poor sportsmanship to deprive him of his goal just at the moment it's about to be fulfilled."

"Yes," Corvette agreed, stretching. "There will be time for all that later."

Abdelmjid threw up his hands. "Women!" he exclaimed. "Always it is the women with you, Colin. What is it, the effect you have over them? The spell? Like flies to a carcass . . ."

"I don't appreciate the insinuation, Abdel," warned Lourdes, who had until now been sitting quietly studying the com panel. "Surely your sense of fair play can overcome your professional jealousy."

"Indeed," Abdelmjid cried. "For there is no jealousy! I, jealous of a man who will be in prison while I am documenting the greatest discovery of the century?"

Colin lunged across the cabin, long-fingered hands extended as if to strangle his rival, but Jenae was too quick.

"Relax, mate," she gasped, interposing herself neatly between the two men and smiling up at Colin. "Everything's under control."

Colin coughed. "Of course. Of course." He smoothed back his disarrayed hair and retreated. Then he looked up at the members of the delegation with smoldering eyes. "That's not important. But will you look at the data?"

There was a long silence.

At last, Peter said, "Can't harm anyone to look, can it?"

◆

Mulig had reached orbit a week ahead of the pursuing ships, and there it sat while the members of the delegation reviewed the gate data and all the other work the dolphins had so painstakingly collected. Colin paced endlessly until Jenae was tempted to drug his food with the tranquilizers kept on hand for inexperienced passengers. After two days of intense scrutiny, it seemed that no one could see in the data what Colin saw, and Abdelmjid, Mika, Lourdes, and Zafara all wanted to give up. Peter Gangian, however, was one of those types who couldn't let go of a problem unsolved, and he doggedly persisted. Corvette, also, refused to give up; Jenae sensed that she was preoccupied with fairness and was grateful to her for it.

They were still arguing about what to do when the military convoy hailed them.

It was not the first hail, of course. They had gleaned some small amusement from the outraged threats that had dogged them through the first few hundred thousand miles, but then the military vessels had become eerily silent. Now, as the pursuing ships drew close to them once again, the scout vessel transmitted a message.

"*Mulig*, this is *Garamond*. Hold your present position. You are interfering with essential research. Do not go any closer to the phenomenon."

Lourdes automatically punched up the visual, revealing a man's strained face against a background of celestial maps. His expression was typical of his profession: stoic and unyielding. The system identified him as Arthur Baness, scout ship commander and colonel by rank according to All Earth Flight Systems.

Colin pounced on the com station, startling Lourdes, who was pushed aside.

"All right," Jenae ordered. "Everybody back to your section. C'mon, move!"

As she helped Keila usher the protesting delegation out, she heard Colin say, "Dream on, Arthur. These scientists are going to get what they paid for, so don't even think about doing anything to the gate." Then she was out of earshot.

Surprisingly, when she returned ten minutes later, the conversation was still going on, and it seemed to have progressed no further, except in that Colin was working himself up into a temper.

"We are following orders to open the gate," droned the *Garamond* commander. "The delegation is here by permission and have none of the usual rights—"

"You're lying," Colin said bluntly. "You're here to destroy the gate if you can, and you know it. I know it, too. Call off the gunships. We're going to investigate, and this time the world's not going to stand by while a ship is sealed off down there."

"These are your orders," repeated Baness as if he hadn't heard. "Do not approach Underkohling. You will be disabled if necessary to prevent you from interfering with the mission."

"Don't do it, *Garamond*!" Colin slammed his hand down on the console, and Jenae's eye, distracted by the sudden movement, picked up the image that was resolving on the screen Colin had erected to monitor the gate.

"Colin!" she whispered, trying to stay out of the range of

the visual pickup. There was activity on the monitor that she'd never seen before.

"We will be in firing range momentarily," continued the voice from *Garamond*. "Need I remind you of the penalties if any member of the delegation is killed while you have control of the ship? Remand control to Zafara Weeks immediately."

"You're not even calling the shots," Colin snarled derisively. "Those are the Heads talking through you. Put them on, y' bloody pipsqueak!" His accent had slipped in the excess of emotion.

"Colin!" Jenae fairly shouted, reaching in front of him and turning off the visual. Then she pointed to the gate monitor.

"OH!" Colin cried—she couldn't tell if he was elated or just insane. "OH! Good-bye, *Garamond*. *Mulig* out!" He turned to Jenae. "Don't just stand there. Bring us *in*!"

"In?" Jenae sat down in the pilot's chair, her hands shaking.

"We've got to land, don't we? The gate—Jesus, look at it, it's going to open. It's going to open!" he sang. "Oh, sorry—you don't know how to land, do you? Here, move over. And get into a walksuit, for god's sake! Anything might happen."

They plummeted toward the black mass of Underkohling.

Keila had stationed herself in the passenger section, and from the sound of the confusion in the background when the One Eye called the bridge, she was thoroughly occupied keeping everybody under control back there. During the landing, everybody in the back abruptly shut up. The pressure made Jenae's vision blank out for a second; with her fingers she double-checked the air seals on her walksuit.

Mulig touched down without even a bump.

"Take it a sec," Colin said, letting go of the controls and reaching overhead for his gear. Jenae steered gingerly while he struggled into his walksuit.

They ought to have reached full stop, but Colin must have miscalculated because they were actually gliding very slowly over the surface as if on black ice. Jenae's panel showed that the gate was half dilated: almost enough to admit *Mulig*. It was increasing in size rapidly, but the visual representation of the numbers indicated that once open it would not stay that way for long. "Come on," Jenae said through clenched teeth. "Open!"

Then, like a constellation rising over Underkohling, the black outline of the first warship grew silently before their eyes, its running lights giving it shape in the darkness on the fringe of the solar system.

"It's happening all over again," Jenae whispered to herself. "Look at it. This is *Morpheus* all over again."

"*Go,* Colin!" Keila called crisply. "There's no more time."

"This might be a good time to pray, if you have that luxury," Colin remarked.

Jenae glanced at him sidelong. Back at the controls now, he appeared surprisingly competent when fully geared up in a walksuit (anyone would), but his voice was shaking and he looked even paler than usual behind the faceplate. Jenae felt embarrassed, looking at him. She wasn't afraid—not really. She had been terrified on lift-off—not to mention the various occasions on which she'd nearly been killed in recent months—but this was a simple thing. Steer a spacecraft through a hole: there were mechanical rules to be followed, procedures to be kept. The warships frightened her, yes—but it would be entire seconds, maybe even minutes, before a fire order would be given. Nobody who chased you for five months would hastily annihilate you without making some kind of show of it—Jenae even had hopes that with the precious delegation on board, they'd hold their fire.

But Colin wasn't referring to the ship; he behaved as though he didn't even see it.

"I'm not going to pray," he added, "because the only thing I could think to pray to would be the weird phenomena of the universe, such as this thing we're about to enter. Do you pray to the dragon as it's about to eat you alive?"

She waited. The guns let off a volley of shots across *Mulig*'s bow; Colin evaded easily without registering the slightest emotion. His gaze was fixed on the gate readings. The warships fanned out into a strategic attack position over the arc of Underkohling. The warnings, she sensed, wouldn't be given again. And the instruments showed it was time. They would miss the gate's window if they waited any longer . . . but Colin was hesitating.

"Just think of all the food you ever ate," she quipped. "Now you're on the other end of the cosmic equation. It has a lovely sort of symmetry, no?"

She intended to be cheerful when she said it, but immediately she could see her attempt at levity was not being well received. Colin glared at her and pushed the stick forward. *Mulig* responded as though startled, skittishly jumping sideways and gliding across the black smooth, and then, as though gathering itself to spring, it teetered on the perimeter of the gate phenomenon. Jenae thrust her head forward, trying to see any change in the appearance of the surface beneath them, but she could perceive none. A burst of weapons fire slammed into the ground beside them, the waves blasting against the side of *Mulig*. Oh, shit, thought Jenae. Don't let them close the gate on us. Don't let them get lucky on their first try.

"Here we go," cried Colin, his helmet pressed to the science ocular. He was oblivious to the military threat. "Will you look at this? I've never seen—"

Without warning, *Mulig* lurched straight up; the safety harness dug into her shoulders and she cried out, glancing at Colin for explanation only to see that he had removed his hands from the controls. Both his eyebrows were lifted in an almost demonic expression of outraged surprise. She could hear him breathing hard through the headset; in the other channel she could hear the delegation screaming. She kept the visual off. Let Keila deal with them.

Then, twisting over in midflight, the craft plunged down. Jenae braced herself for an impact that never came. Darkness flooded the viewscreen. The panel lights went out. They hung in silent blackness for several heartbeats—she counted—and just when it seemed to her that they must be trapped in the very pith of Underkohling, a shrieking like a hundred elephants trumpeting replayed at high speed and high pitch flooded the cabin. They were moving fast, spinning—Jenae felt her ears and insides protest—gravity hit them like a bomb and all of a sudden light was filtering into the ship through a cloudy liquid that surrounded them.

The systems came up.

They were underwater, upside down.

Jenae couldn't see the floor of the body of water; their entrance had apparently stirred up mud and sand so that the murk yielded only a few yards' visibility.

Colin was laughing.

"Shit of God," he said. "All my dreams come true."

Jenae felt sick and her head hurt; it seemed the old pain had suddenly returned.

"Are you okay?" Colin asked, busying himself with the reactivated systems.

"Yeah, I guess. What the . . . ?"

"Not everything's working here. I can't get a fix on our depth. Less than twenty meters, I should think by the light."

"I'll go out," she said. "I'm going to spew if I don't get right side up in a minute."

Months. It had been months. Jenae wanted to explode out into the water, to swim fast and far the way dolphins did; but it was a curious feeling to come out into the water and not be in altermode. She was so preoccupied with the experience that she scarcely noticed her surroundings.

"Well?" Colin's voice squawked in her ears.

"You're not caught in anything. Give it a little thrust— not too much—feels like Earth gravity here. You don't want to overdo it."

The ship was barely underwater, but because it had rolled over Colin couldn't see that. The legs, if he extended them, would protrude from the surface. With the weight of her walksuit Jenae found it difficult to get to the surface; it had not been explicitly designed for this kind of thing. She let herself sink, coming to rest onto the smooth belly of the ship, breathing slowly. She was fascinated with the sensation of breathing air when surrounded on all sides by water, and she giggled as the ship began to move.

"What's bloody funny?" Colin snapped.

"Sorry. That's good. Now forward, and we can start to roll her . . . oh, shit."

These last words escaped her lips as she broke surface. She was greeted by dull, grey light. Fists of strong wind shook the leaves and branches of the waiting trees that overhung the water, writhing together like a host of gigantic bones.

"What's wrong?" demanded Colin.

"It *is* a real planet. Strange trees, Colin. But *trees*."

"Right, whatever! Can you get out of the way so I can roll this thing over?"

Jenae swam for shore—it wasn't far—and in a minute *Mulig* rolled back to upright. She couldn't see Colin, but she knew he could see her through the lenses in the hull. She waved him forward and stood on the bottom. The walksuit indicated external air temperature was 31 degrees C. She had to fight the urge to rip off the walksuit and breathe.

"I'm coming out in a minute," Colin said. "Just tell me when I've reached a stable point, and I'll put the legs down."

Jenae looked at the roots and branches that covered the shore, trailing even in the water. "There's no way you're going to beach this thing," she informed him. "Either fly it to a cleared area and land there, or leave it in the water for now. Come forward a bit more and you should be able to extend your legs. The mud's not deep."

Colin nudged the vehicle forward until it grounded. She heard the whirring of the legs being extended, and slowly the huge ship seemed to rise out of the water, until only its underbelly skimmed the surface. Colin opened the airlock door and stood looking out.

An expression of rapture smoothed the irregularities of his face behind the walksuit visor; the transformation was almost embarrassing to behold. Sunlight broke through the clouds and gilded the scene, and Colin was smiling—and then the water of the lake rose up in a shining, liquid pillar that balanced there for a second in all its improbability before it crashed down on them, slow but impossible to escape.

◆

"Tsering! It's happening again! Come quick!" Rena's voice echoed from the lywyn, and Tsering dropped the peas she was shelling and looked up into the branches. Everyone in the vicinity stopped work, and a small buzz of noise went up. Tsering hushed them peremptorily, then hesitated, waiting for more information. Rena was overexcited—bloody useless.

"What?" Tsering shouted in frustration. "Where? Who?"

But she knew Rena couldn't hear her. The pool that emitted Rena's voice wasn't far from the edge of the Lake settlement, but there was no way of knowing which pool she was speaking *into*. What had caused such alarm? A distortion? "Come quickly!" Rena repeated. "It's another ship come up, near the west side of the lake."

"*What?*" She struggled to get to her feet, ungainly and impatient. Paul's eyes met hers from across the work area: he was a lessent who had seemed glad to return to Lake when she lifted the ban, and he was more docile than most. Nkem stood up.

"Let me come with you, Tsering," she said, reaching out to help.

Tsering nodded. "Paul, Nkem, you come with me. The rest of you wait here. I don't know what's happening, but if any strangers come up here—you know, any people like Daire?—get into the lywyn and don't let yourselves be caught. Beni, you run up to the message pool and tell Rena I'm coming and that she should wait for me. Got it?"

Beni, a child of six, nodded wide-eyed and pelted off, scrambling up into the lywyn. The others automatically banded together. Tsering looked at the little group anxiously. Daire had taken most of the lessents with him far into the lywyn to work on the memories. Would he hear Rena's message?

She cursed her condition as she waddled through the lywyn with Paul's assistance.

"You're a fine boy," she told him as she leaned heavily on his arm. "You were never any trouble growing up, and now look how useful you are."

"Thank you," Paul replied, blushing. Tsering felt like a grandmother; the whole situation was ridiculous.

It was quite a trek: they reached the shore of the lake and Tsering could just glimpse the gleam of the ship still far across the water. It was jammed against the edge of the lywyn in the shallows, much as *Morpheus* was. Only this ship was smaller. She was disappointed: it didn't look much different from Earth ships of eighty years ago. Daire hadn't been kidding when he'd portrayed Earth as impoverished. The ship had lodged almost in the cleft of the river where it poured out of the lake on its journey to the sea, the gap through which Jordan had swum to reach his kindred in the ocean. Tsering flinched at the sight: it seemed a violation of some kind. The lake was roiling with waves, and for a minute Tsering found herself anticipating another eruption at the center of the water. But as they picked their way along the shore toward the new ship, the surface of the water gradually spread itself out calm until all the waves had slapped up against the lywyn and folded down flat again.

It took far too long to get there, and Nkem was climbing in excited circles around them up in the lywyn as Tsering made her slow progress on the ground. At last they came around the final curve in the lake and reached the river. The ship's nose was half buried in the stream, its hull blocking the overflow of lake water. Consequently, the river was choked and flooded the lywyn on both sides; resolutely the trio waded in.

The ship's door was closed, its engines still. Tsering could see that its landing legs had been extended, but it appeared that they had sunk deeply into the mud, for they didn't raise the ship significantly above the water level.

"Look," Paul said. "Maybe this isn't the best idea. Shouldn't we wait for Daire to come or more people?"

Tsering was almost ready to acknowledge he was right. Much as she hated to admit it, she wasn't much use in her present state. She looked up into the lywyn.

"Over here!" Rena's hoarse whisper drew her eye to the child's hiding place. Glancing apprehensively at the ship, Tsering began to wade toward her.

"They've come out," Rena said in a hushed voice. "Two of them. One went up into the lywyn, the other went into the water. There are more in the ship but there's a monster there. It looks like it's holding them prisoner. I think it's one of the creatures Daire told us about. A One Eye. I called Daire, but he's far away. He's coming as fast as he can with help."

Tsering laid a finger to her lips and nodded. Rena melted into the foliage.

"Get up there and stay out of sight," Tsering told Nkem and Paul. "No, I can manage. Just keep hidden until Daire gets here."

When they had complied she waded closer to the ship. She wanted to read the identifier on the hull, but to do so she had to go into the lake. The water rose to her waist, then her chest. She indexed her own ambivalence: she was half afraid of the water, and half drawn to it. She wondered how long it would be before the first signs of distortion were on her. Daire said it could be years, but Tsering had a feeling it wouldn't be long now. The buoyancy of the water took some of the pressure off her back, and she relaxed gratefully into it.

Mulig, read the hull. *466J9 EC.* A Norwegian flag.

What a strange name for a ship, she thought. Norwegian for "possible."

She felt the shift in the current a second before the apparition rose out of the water before her. It was a young woman, stark naked, human except for a prominent set of gills like claw marks across her neck. Her skin seemed to have a curiously luminous quality to it, but Tsering only glimpsed the flash of her belly and the dark open hole of her mouth as she sprang out of the water, gulped down air, and dived again.

Tsering stumbled backward, groping for the support of a lywyn branch and clinging to it once she'd found it. The creature lay just beneath the surface belly-up, fanning the water lightly with her hands and staring at Tsering. Very slowly, as though she sensed Tsering's fear, she glided into the shallows and, grasping the stem of a lywyn tree, pulled herself out of the water. The woman clutched at the tree, shivering and gasping as her skin flushed alternately red and pale and her legs twitched convulsively.

"Jenae, is that you?" An unfamiliar male voice came from above. Tsering knew she would not be able to get away. She should have hidden with Paul and Nkem, but it was too late now. A very tall, clumsy man was creating a stir up in the lywyn as he tried to get down the woven, elastic branches. Leaves fell and insects scattered.

"Who are you?" Tsering said in a stern voice. It had worked on Daire; it was worth trying again. Unfortunately, these people were not facedown and unconscious in the mud.

The man half jumped, half fell into the shallows a few meters away. He was very pale and looked confused and distracted. There was a slim device attached to his skull near his ear that looked almost identical to Daire's headset. He pushed aside the mouthpiece and let out a small, nervous laugh when he saw her, and then grimaced as his gaze took in the strange woman, who was still oblivious to them and had begun to cough.

"My name is Colin Peake," he said. "I'm a friend of Daire Morales, the man who came here . . . er, can you understand me?"

"I understand you," Tsering replied. "What kind of thing is she? Is this an altermode human? It looks like she is dying."

Colin flushed and looked at the woman, who was actually improving almost by the second. He waded over to her, pried her fingers off the lywyn, and placing a tentative arm around her shoulders attempted to lead her back to the ship.

The woman tried to say something that Tsering couldn't understand. Tsering felt pity for her, albeit pity mixed with distaste. She looked half distorted. When Colin and the woman reached the ship, Colin pulled the mouthpiece back across his face and said, "Keila? Jenae's coming in. I've got an indigenous person here so just open the door and collect Jenae, will you? She's in transition."

The door panel slid open and Colin boosted Jenae unceremoniously inside. A large, gloved hand reached out to assist, but Tsering couldn't see the face of the person. The door closed.

"I'm sorry if we alarmed you," Colin said. "But things are rather urgent from our point of view. Did you see what happened? Someone fired on the gate after we came through; it displaced a lot of water and the flood carried us all the way into this river mouth, where we are stuck for the moment. I'd like to extricate the ship, but I've got a lot of people on board who are currently in a panic, and I need to let them off first. Do you know who Daire is?"

"Yes, I know Daire."

"Can I speak to him please? Or is there some other person who could help me? You look like you ought to lie down."

Tsering smiled. "I feel like I ought to lie down. But that won't be my luck today, I think. I'm Tsering, the leader of the people who live here. I am much older than you are, Dr. Peake, and probably as well educated within my limited means, so you needn't talk down to me."

"I apologize, I'm sure," Colin said, quirking an eyebrow

and extending his hand toward her. "Nevertheless, you should take it easy. Do you want to come into the ship?"

She shook her head. "Come with me."

With her best approximation of her normal manner of moving, she ascended into the lywyn, carefully placing her hands and feet until she had led the newcomer to the nearest lywyn pool. She eased herself into a seated position and let out a relieved sigh.

"Talk clearly into the liquid," she said wearily. "Daire will hear you."

Colin cleared his throat, pointed his face at the liquid, and self-consciously began. "Er . . . Daire? Colin Peake here. We've just landed, actually. We're in the shallows where a river exits this lake . . . are those good directions?"

Tsering nodded.

". . . and I have a great deal of news for you, very little of it good, I'm afraid. Come over as quickly as you can. Er . . . Tsering is with me, but I really need you here. Colin out. Was that my voice echoing all over the place?"

She nodded again.

"It's still doing it. How do you stop it?"

"You don't. You move away from the pool. He'll be here; he'll be glad to see you, I think. But I need to rest, so why don't we talk here? Nothing you have to say is a secret, is it?"

She watched his face while he comprehended what she was doing: everyone within the lywyn would hear everything that was said. It was the surest form of protection from him she had, and he acknowledged it with a bow of his head.

"All right," he said. "Where to begin?"

"Tell me this is all a sick dream!" Daire's voice shouted out of the pool, and Colin jumped. "The Colin Peake I know would never have the *cojones* to jump through Underkohling."

Colin shifted where he sat. "I imagine you think I'm here to rescue you. Well—"

"Shit. Let me guess," Daire interrupted. "Oxford revoked your tenure, you murdered the dean and now you're a fugitive of justice."

"Er . . . no. I've run afoul of the Heads, actually."

Silence.

"Daire?"

"Stay there. I'm coming. Tsering, keep him there until I find a big stick."

Tsering and Colin looked at one another.

"Tell me how you 'ran afoul' of the Heads. I thought they were part of the League. Daire worked for the League. Why was your ship attacked?"

"Ah. That will take some time. . . ."

"I have some time," Tsering said pleasantly. She spread her hands across her belly. "At least a few more days, I think, so go ahead."

Colin cleared his throat. "Well, unknown to the layperson, the Heads, also known in the vernacular as the Pickled Brains, are the engineers of every disaster of our age. . . ."

◆

Daire was late arriving. By the time he found them in the branches up above *Mulig*, Colin had finished with his explanation and was quizzing Tsering on the properties of the lywyn. He was fascinated with its ability to project memories in the form of ghosts, and when she explained about the lywyn pool and offered the liquid to him, his excitement reached a fever pitch. He had pulled out his Chinese meditation balls and was practicing them, to Tsering's interest.

"No, I won't take any just now—hello, Daire, good to see you alive—but I want to see it under an electron microscope. If what you say is true . . . why, it's more than worth the inconvenience of a few armed ships and an officious delegation of idiots and whatever else! You say the liquid grants access to physical memory—imagine such a thing. Tell me, can you remember back to your human ancestors on Earth?"

"That's funny—Daire asked the same question." She glanced up at him. He looked harried and impatient. "No, I can't. The oldest generation is that of my parents—I can't see anything but blackness if I go beyond them."

"Exactly!" cried Colin. "Just as I would have predicted. It's tragic. And incredibly ironic, I should think, from your point of view. Yes, ironic and even somewhat disturbing."

"I'm not sure I follow you."

"Well, I just mean that the way that you and your people have been exploited in terms of your memory, and then to find yourselves presented with a way to see your race memories and not be able to access them because of what was done to you."

"Daire saw some very old things. Prehuman, I think." She glanced up at Daire again.

"Yes, it was very strange. I have done studies of the lywyn, Colin, but honestly I think there are more urgent matters. I've met Keila and she's very anxious that something should be done with the delegation." Daire was balanced hanging from the lywyn by one arm now, his leg extended to the adjacent branch, ready to move.

"Yes, well, the ship's the safest place for them now," Colin remarked without looking up. "Tell them to stay there. I've changed my mind about moving the ship."

Tsering's brow was furrowed with thought. "Are you saying that we can't see back because of what they did to my parents? Is that why I come to the ocean of blackness?"

"The ocean of blackness," Colin reflected. "Yes. It's a kind of metaphor. Well, I can give you my interpretation of that, if you like. DNA, whatever else people may say about it, is memory. It's the thread that connects us to the very beginnings of life. I've often thought that when you tamper with a species' DNA, you alter its memory, its history, its very being. Ancient Greek religion has it that in Hades there are two rivers. Everyone knows the river Styx and its ferryman, Charon. Yet less often do we remember Lethe, the river of forgetfulness. It is this river that takes us with death, too, rendering us no longer ourselves. It steals us away when it drowns our memories. Maybe this was even supposed to be comforting to the Hellenic tribes—the ultimate bodily abandon—but it has always terrified me. To be doomed to eternal forgetfulness! I fear this—there, I'll say it. And yet, that's my own private fear of natural mortality. But to take the memories of an entire race of beings, and submerge them in this subcellular forgetfulness: that is a killing thing."

Daire cleared his throat and was ignored.

Tsering mused, "The lywyn has saved me from forgetfulness, my whole life. Without it, I would have little knowledge of my ancestors' culture. I've tried so hard to keep these children human in some way. Yet, to hear Daire talk, there's nothing left of humanity in the world we left behind."

Colin shook his head. "I don't know how to respond to that—it's a matter of judgment. It is always difficult to let go of the past, or it certainly has been for me. I have a friend who collects books—actual bound books—because it's his only way to hold on to something that he values deeply. This lywyn of yours—it must be precious to you."

"The mind," said a scratchy voice from below. "The mind on the other side of the gate." It was the amphibious woman, dried off now and clothed but with gills still visible at her throat. She was ascending the lywyn silently just behind Colin. When she reached them she gestured with her free hand to the lywyn all around. "*This* is the mind the dolphins were talking about? Trees?"

"Possibly," said Colin. "*Something* reached through the gate and grabbed hold of my computer. Jenae has seen images of your forebears, you know," he told Tsering.

Tsering and Jenae looked at each other. "Daire told the truth," Tsering said. "You can distort and come back again."

"It's called transition," Jenae said. "It's not pleasant, but, sure, it's reversible."

Tsering's eyes became distant. "When I distort, as far as I know, I will lose my memories. I believe that's how the lywyn gets them from us—when we distort. I think that's how it makes the ghosts. I also believe this because none of my people have ever come back, even to look at us, after they have distorted. It *is* like a kind of death, one where you know you will go on living but you don't know who you will be."

Colin nodded his understanding. "Tell me, do you speak with the children about these matters? As their leader, do you try to help them understand it?"

"Not really. How can I, when I don't understand it myself?"

"Well," Colin said briskly, "if you really believe your time is coming soon, you should try to prepare them. You are the only adult in their lives. When you leave, it will be terribly traumatic for them, I should think."

Tears were forming in her eyes. "Yes, I know. Thank you, Colin. You're not what I expected. You're really very kind."

"Nonsense. I just try to respect my elders." He reached over and awkwardly patted her knee. "Come on, then. Show me this lywyn, show me these ridiculous studies Daire has done, bless his heart, and let's see what we can find out between now and the time they come to blow us up."

Daire snorted and gazed at Tsering uneasily as she struggled across the lywyn. Her face was full of hope.

◆

At nightfall, Daire returned home weary and dazed. After he'd pulled out all the lywyn studies for Colin, he'd left the Englishman to digest them and had returned to *Mulig*. There he spent the afternoon being grilled by the delegation about everything from League politics to indigenous earthworms, and Colin still expected him back at *Morpheus* later that evening to go over the material on the gate. Colin's calculations indicated that they had less than two days to prepare for its next opening, and unless Colin had some new card up his sleeve, Daire was sure the scene would be unpleasant at the very least. He was tempted to tell Colin to piss off, and take the kids up into the high country, where at least they would be safe from immediate attack. If the League really was determined to exterminate the children, there probably wasn't much they could do—but if it was just a matter of clearing up a misunderstanding, then Daire might buy the colony some time that way.

Still, from the sound of things, there was no misunderstanding. He almost wished he had never sent the distress call. Everybody would have been better off if Earth remained ignorant of *Morpheus*'s survival.

It was in this frame of mind that he greeted Tsering, who was sitting on the floor playing a rhyming game with her regulars: Nkem, Rena, Adamo, Til, and Ani. When she saw Daire's expression, she said, "Okay, Ani, Seika's probably waiting for you guys, so go get your supper."

Daire sat down on the floor, and Rena kissed the top of his head on her way out. "Don't worry," she told him. "I saw the new people first. I think they're good, like you."

When they had gone, Tsering just looked at him. "Well?" she said.

He shook his head slowly from side to side. "Things never get any easier, do they?"

"You don't know the half of it. I've been having pains all day."

Daire became instantly solicitous. "I'm sorry—I didn't know," he said. "There is a doctor in the expedition, you know. Do you want me to get him?"

Tsering laughed. "It's true that it can be tough to be midwife to one's own baby, but I think Michelle can help me when the time comes. She's had three." She regarded him critically. "Maybe this is good for you," she said. "Having some of your own people around, some excitement."

"I don't know. I liked our little world, even if it was precarious. But I'll adjust. Just think, if they do succeed in closing the gate permanently, the delegation will be stuck here forever. Don't laugh! You wouldn't be around to see it. I'd have to go into the sea myself."

It was the first time she had ever heard him come even close to joking about distortion, and she smiled at him. "Let's eat," she said. "I'm not worried. I find your Colin Peake to be very interesting. I think he's going to save you all."

"Colin? You've got to be kidding. He's about as courageous as a skunk."

◆

In the morning Colin changed his mind again about moving the ship; or, rather, Keila changed it for him. While he was visiting the settlement at Lake, she kicked the delegation out of *Mulig* into the flooded lywyn, where they perched on the branches, variously ecstatic, perplexed, and bored. Then, in a series of delicate maneuvers that took over an hour, she piloted the ship out into the lake, lifted it into a low hover, and sailed it over to the top of the cliff, where she set it down in the grass just outside the deserted village of High.

"Right," said Colin to Jenae, scratching his head. "Can we get some of these children to escort the delegation back where they belong—to the ship? If Keila would just *tolerate* them a little longer we'll all stand a better chance of surviving."

They were standing in the midst of the little houses at

lakeside. Many of them were only shoulder-high to Colin, and he looked about him at the diminutive village and its small, cheerful, rather dirty occupants with an air of bemusement. He didn't know that he made a comical picture himself, with his baggy pants and long tunic and sandals, and his thinning hair pulled back in a little tuft of a braid. Every time his angular body moved, the fabric around him flapped, so that he looked like a great egret.

"I'm going to evacuate everybody to High," Daire said. "Tsering can stay here, because I don't want her to climb, but everybody else should go. We can watch the gate from *Morpheus*—there's still enough power in the solar cells to keep us going."

"Does it bother you at all that the delegation are probably up there making all kinds of real estate deals with each other?" Jenae asked cynically.

"Not really," Daire answered. "At this stage, that's the least of my worries. Uh, Colin, where are you going?"

Colin had wandered off and was peering into the doorways of the buildings. He turned.

"Where's Tsering?" he asked. "I want to discuss my findings with her concerning the lywyn."

"She's got enough on her mind, Colin, and in case you hadn't noticed, she's nine months pregnant. Can't you have the discussion with me?" Daire interposed himself between Colin and Tsering's house; he was irritated with the physicist's persistent interest in Tsering.

"It's all right." Tsering appeared in the doorway. "I want to hear what he has to say. Daire, I think an evacuation is a good idea. Why don't you manage it? I'll have Adamo stick around to show Dr. Peake how to get to *Morpheus* from here, and you can meet him over there later. Ask Michelle to stay, as well. I may need her later."

Daire felt the blood draining from his face at her last sentence. He nodded and, signaling Jenae to follow, left them alone.

"You've got him under your thumb, haven't you?" Colin said.

◆

Daire spent the better part of the day preparing the children for a possible disaster. Tsering lay down to rest in the middle of the afternoon, and at her request, Daire directed Michelle to stay with her, just in case. He didn't want her on *Morpheus* when the gate opened, that was certain; in her own house, maybe she would stay quiet and out of harm's way. He wanted to laugh at himself as he helped the kids pack up their necessities and prepare to climb up to High. He felt like the coach of a very unlikely sports team, but he didn't mind. He would rather be with the kids than stuck inside a ship with Colin or the delegation, studying computer models and bickering.

But in the late afternoon, after he had escorted the last of them to High and delivered a last-minute pep talk to the lessents who were now in charge, he had no choice but to return to *Morpheus* and face the music. Hassan, Gangian, O'Rourke, Blake, and of course Zafara were in the command center of *Mulig*, and Colin had established a full video link with them. Keila was apparently roaming around outside at High—Daire hoped she didn't terrorize the children excessively. Jenae was not in evidence at all, but Mika DiFeo and Milos Stenz, the physician, were languishing in the living quarters of *Mulig*.

"I'm not going to get in the way," said Mika. "They have no need for an environmental toxicologist at a time like this."

Daire addressed Milos through the com. "What about you?" he said.

"I'm happy enough to sit in my own quarters for a while, so long as that One Eye isn't around to oppress me."

Daire was taken aback for a minute; then he remembered that Milos was affiliated with the Coalition for Pure Human Progress.

"Well, Doctor," he said rather huffily, "is it the case that you will treat only pure humans?"

It was Milos's turn to get huffy. "I'm only *trained* to treat humans, so yes. But I wouldn't turn my back on any creature that is suffering."

"Well, Tsering is going to have a baby any day now, and I don't want her to be involved in any violence in any way.

Can you go stay with her and be on hand in case something goes wrong? She was having pains yesterday."

Milos looked appalled. "Don't tell me you're the father! She looks very young to be carrying a child to term. You should know better. Where is she? I'll bring a medical kit with me."

"She's in the red house on the edge of the settlement. There's no one else there except another girl named Michelle. Be respectful to Tsering, and try not to get on her nerves."

"I've worked with pregnant women before," said Milos, collecting his gear.

"Not this one," Daire muttered under his breath. "Ask a boy named Adamo to take you down there. Thank you, Milos. I'll come by just as soon as I can."

Milos waved him away. "Try not to get shot," he said cheerfully.

Then, they settled down to wait.

◆

Tsering knew as soon as she began that this would be the last time. Her body was stiff and unfriendly now when she tried to climb, but when she lowered herself to her knees by the silver pool high in the trees, the magnitude of what she was doing struck her. Colin and Daire had argued back and forth about power and councils and alliances and factions, and she knew that she was about to perform some act that to them carried tremendous political significance. But to Tsering it was about closure: she was enacting the end of an era, and before it was over she wanted to meet the ones who had set it all in motion, the infamous Heads, still dominating Earth in ways both plain and covert. In taking the fate of humanity into their hands they had forced her to deliver the rarer and more fragile species they'd tossed aside on the road to altermode. She would show them that. She would show them everything, provided the lywyn consented to work its magic.

She let the lywyn roll down her throat. Yes, this would be the last time. She stood, grasping the branches on either side for balance: she would need something to brace her once the effects hit. She had taken more than usual—much more. Because this time she would be entering the place she called Nu, the darkness she had mistaken for her soul. The gate to Underkohling had always been within her grasp. This time she would go straight into that Stygian pit and pull the devils she found out into the light.

32

Daire watched the gate carefully. "Almost," he said. "You should be able to hail them now. If you can keep them talking, then they might not fire. The gate is only going to be open for about thirty minutes."

"*Garamond?*" called Abdelmjid. "This is Dr. Hassan of *Mulig* calling. We are in distress. Please hold your fire."

"Dr. Hassan, what is the status of the hijackers?"

"Uh . . . they're alive. But we . . . we've worked out an arrangement."

"Daire! Dr. Peake!" It was Adamo silhouetted in the open hatch of *Morpheus*, his voice tinged with fear. "Did the doctor guy find you? The lightning's started! You should get out of there!"

Daire spoke into Abdelmjid's headset.

"There's a storm brewing," he said. "I don't know what effect it will have on communications, but the lywyn can really wreak havoc with electrical equipment, and the gate's already half-dilated."

"Hold, please, *Garamond*. We have a systems problem here. We'll call you back." Abdelmjid was sweating. "Well?" he said.

Colin shot an alarmed glance at Daire. Daire knew what the physicist was thinking: Not only lightning, but laser fire, perhaps, would be coming along at any moment.

"Stall them," said Colin. "But keep the line open. In a minute you ought to see something very interesting happen."

Abdelmjid began to talk again, but Daire was distracted and he only caught snippets. "*Garamond?* . . . no need for

rash action . . . all on the same side . . . negotiations and information . . ."

"Hurry, dammit," cried Adamo, dangling his head
through the hatch. "The lake's getting rough, and if lightning
strikes the ship, you'll be fried."

Not likely, thought Daire—the hull was insulated. The
ship was probably the safest place to be. But it was strange
for the lywyn's manifestation of the gate lightning to coincide
with a natural thunderstorm. The whole thing felt wrong.

"I have to go," he said to Colin. "I'd better get up to
High—it's obvious you don't need me here. Adamo, why the
hell are you out of position at a time like this? You're supposed to be at High." He was climbing the ladder as he
spoke.

"You sent me to bring the doctor to Tsering, *remember*?
And that doctor guy, he went into Tsering's house and then
the lightning started and he said to find you—"

"Where is Tsering?" Daire said.

"He said Michelle was crazy and he wanted to know why
you set him up and then he said, never mind, he'd find you
himself and then he just went running off. I came to see if he
got here okay. It's not safe with the lightning. Did he?"

"No. Where is Tsering, Adamo?"

"I don't know. I made sure Michelle was safe. She said to
find you and tell you."

"Tell me *what*?" Daire had reached the edge of the
lywyn, but before he could catch hold of the boy's arm,
Adamo had vanished into the branches in that maddening
way all these children had. The lake was roiling, and rain
had begun to fall. Jagged tridents of lightning shot from limb
to limb: silent, ethereal.

"Let it all come down," he heard Colin say. He turned to
find the older man standing on the ladder, half out of the
hatch, his lean body bent back and arms outstretched, palms
catching the rain. His upturned face shone with moisture and
reflected light; his expression was ecstatic.

This is no time to wax religious, thought Daire. *Where is
Tsering?*

Colin turned and disappeared into the ship. Exasperated,
Daire climbed deeper into the wood. He called her name into

the first lywyn pool he found, but it reflected no sound. The surface even looked dead; or was it just the storm's gloom? "What is happening?" he shouted—his words were swallowed in the rain. The branch beneath him was vibrating, and vaporous lights danced from the leaves overhead. A vicious knot of frustration and fear was forming in his gut; he felt his muscles tightening and flexing with the inchoate urge to move.

He thrust his hand into the lywyn and drank.

Colin's words from the night before floated into his mind—he still wasn't sure what they meant. He had come to see Colin in the evening to review the gate data, and the physicist was holding up a vial of lywyn with an air of reverence. Yet when Daire asked him to explain, he was perfectly matter-of-fact. Not that Daire had understood, really.

"It's a reproductive fluid, transported by insects who consume some of it. It contains a chromosome soup that, I surmise, changes depending on the lywyn organism's reaction to its environment. Think of the lywyn as a house that adds new wings at need, and different wings, or substructures, serve different purposes. Memory storage is a plausible function. Intracommunications seem evident. But I suspect that the EM fields generated by the gate play some role in selection. Look at how electricity activates it. Subtle electrical fields in the body could affect it as well. And the insects! They have internalized it. It's not inconceivable that everything that ever drinks this fluid becomes a part of its ... well, mind."

There went Colin, Daire thought, trying to explain the inexplicable. But now, when the soft silvery lywyn wrapped itself around his tongue, Colin didn't seem so ridiculous. The "real" events within the forest became suddenly visible. Brilliant trees carried sparks along their branches like moving stars, wove hairs of light, and thrummed with current in the depths of their wood. The lywyn stretched out around him like a vast ribbon convoluted into millions of knots and bows, all of them now burning without heat.

He drew air into his lungs. "Tsering!" he shouted. This time his voice seemed to carry a bit better. He climbed higher. She was up to something. He just knew it. Where the hell would she go if she were in one of her moods? To the place where she had performed that first ceremony, to open him? He had not thought she could still climb that high, and he was afraid.

Water was pouring off his face now and soaking his clothes. He continued to mount the slippery, twisted grid as quickly as he could, but the shape and form of the branches were unfamiliar in this weird, erratic light. Black shadows flashed out from the holes in the net, and glittering spears of rain pierced the leaves and flooded the branches.

Just ahead now, he saw her: a woman's outline revealed in a lightning flash. But—

"Easy, mate. She's up there, but you'll alarm her."

It was Jenae. She blocked his path, small but potent. She had the look of a wild animal, sheaves of her dark hair like wire thrusting out of her skull in all directions, spiked by the rain. She was crouched on a branch with her weight balanced over her hips, arms curved in front of her in a classic wrestler's stance. She looked as though she were prepared to jump him. He had no patience for this.

"What the fuck's going on?" he demanded, craning his head toward the lywyn bowl above, whence came lightning. The thick boles of the trees blocked his view. He could not see her.

"Colin says you're to leave Tsering alone," Jenae said. "She knows what she's doing."

Daire felt his nostrils flaring. "Colin? *Colin?!* Who are you to tell me what to do—and who is Colin? That girl is nine months pregnant and if Colin's got her in some kind of goddamn experiment I'll fucking kill him. Get out of my way, Jenae. I don't even know you, but so help me if you try to stop me I can't be responsible for myself."

◆

She knew she'd taken too much: the needlelike lights in her eyes flickered and blurred, and for the first time in months her body felt light. She maintained contact through her hands and feet with the living wood. The gate was opening like a slow inhale. Tsering threw her will into the lywyn and felt it charging, humming with power. A wind was beginning to kick up. She felt the memories building within her, rising like water in a vessel from some deep, unseen source. She could hear all the com channels at once; the lywyn lent her the clarity she needed to sort out the myriad impressions.

"This is *Garamond*, *Mulig*. Please stop clogging the line with chatter. We have instructions to pursue you and fire if necessary. Return through the gate at once or you will be destroyed."

"Fire?" squawked Abdelmjid from *Mulig*. "Whatever for?"

A woman's voice, taut and accustomed to obedience, came *through* the ship *Garamond*, from somewhere else. It spoke without ever pausing for breath, for it was not alive. "Acts of blatant terrorism will not be tolerated. Dr. Hassan, we advise you to return immediately."

"You advise? My dear, you can't just order us around. We're not dolphins, you know. We're an official delegation."

"Shut up, Abdel," warned Lourdes on *Mulig*'s line. "Don't try to fight the Heads."

"This is now a military objective," said the unidentified female.

"Do it, Tsering. . . ." Colin's whisper came from *Morpheus* through the lywyn pool crisply. Ah, she could even see him now. He looked like a ghost. "Everything's wide open. Do it *now*."

"Colin, will you get out of the way? You've had your fun." The lywyn was working beautifully, because she could see Lourdes in the command center of *Mulig* now. Lourdes looked peeved. She schooled her face and voice into a formal expression. "Honorable Heads of the League, military action at this time would be completely inappropriate. There are children here. There is a viable environment here with a unique ecosystem. These things must be preserved at all costs. Legal offenses can be dealt with later, in the proper time and place."

"I was not aware you had been invested with the authority to make such decisions," said the dead voice. "I, however, do have that authority. The warships are under my control and that of my associates."

"You?" Tsering put in quietly. "You are not even in control of yourself." The force of the memories behind her voice gave it a depth and resonance that surprised her.

"Who are you? Where is that transmission originating?" For the first time, a wisp of apprehension tinged the voice.

"I'll show you who I am. I'll show you who you are. Haven V. Krzminski, Head of the League, prepare to answer for your crimes."

With that she released the memories, letting herself go into the time flow of the lywyn, back to her parents' memories that came so painfully. Her mother's ghost flowed through her, and her father's: any fear she might once have felt in confronting her ancestors was long gone. Her parents' memories diverged: stereovision of the torture halls called "Habitations," the organ-growing vaults and the infection rooms where new viruses were tested on whole populations of children: cheaply bought slaves of migrant workers and famine victims, cowed by fear and deprivation. The lywyn rolled back to the years of her parents' youth, spent in despairing idleness watching friends and siblings die off under the calculating regard of the technicians, long desensitized by endless rounds of measurements and assessments. And then, through her father's eyes alone: the furtive glimpses into the infrastructure of Ingenix. He had witnessed the early attempts to interface the human brain with a computer in all their brutality and morbidity, and when he was ten, he had witnessed the first signs of success. The first Pickled Brains had been desperate captives like himself who found themselves suddenly and disorientingly without bodies.

Something stirred across the long spaces of time and distance. It echoed in the lywyn all the way from the Southern Hemisphere of Earth.

"I *was* there before you, Haven. I never slept until you came, and you started to control me. . . ." The voice was plaintive, desperate. A flicker of images: pathetic memories of a young body with its uncertain limbs, flashes of sunlight—then hands holding it down under the soft ray of anesthesia.

Then, in the interior of the system in which the memories lived, something hard and dark crushed down on the weak voice. Silence.

But Tsering was heartened, and she pushed on. Remember, remember, she urged, leaning into the strength of the lywyn. Djile, show me the things you would not show before. Show them all.

Her mother remembered the directors most clearly: once every year or so they toured the facilities with the Habitation supervisor, staring at the inmates through the sterile glass walls. One of them, a tall man named Edgar Van der Hoss, had looked straight at her and murmured appreciatively, "Beautiful. May I have her?"

The supervisor responded in a decorous murmur, but Tsering's mother could hear every syllable, though she didn't understand what was meant. "This group is due to be sacrificed this year. We are drawing close to isolation of the amphibious gene. Once we have stabilized it in a virus, this lot won't be needed."

"Do you have to remove them?" asked the director, and it was plain from the look on the supervisor's face that she didn't want to refuse him.

"Well, sir, even if we didn't sacrifice, they have a built-in mechanism for self-destruction. Remember, these past few years with all the turmoil, you asked us to do all we could to prevent disaster should there be a raid, or an escape . . . they're only designed, you see, to last one generation."

"Ah, yes. Very good, then. It's too late for her."

He turned away, flicking his fingers regretfully.

The memories began to come fast and furious then: the scramble at Ingenix to survive after the fall of Gen9 and Helix to raids. Instant sacrifice for the subjects of the most inhumane experiments. The chemical smell; the attempts to sanitize. Nervousness everywhere. The supervisors grew careless and discussed their fears openly, unaware that Laran heard everything.

"It's all out of control. Those radicals are setting off nuclear weapons right now near Sydney."

"The directors have to do something."

"They'll just run and leave us to deal with it. Watch."

But the directors didn't run. They came to the Habitation and asked for the interface operation.

"It's the pinnacle of evolution," said Hannibal Lumumba to his uneasy associates.

"Think of it as an expansion into an infinity of identities," said Haven Krzminski.

Another voice of dissension now entered the stream; Tsering was becoming disoriented. What was past, what was present? The voice was bitter.

"I didn't want to do it, Haven. I *told* you I didn't want to do it. You forced us!"

"Forced you, nothing!" snarled the woman's cold voice. "You just couldn't live with the guilt, weakling. You begged me for your life, Eric! But we stayed, and we suffered. What would you know about that, Sleeper?"

"Untrue," said a third voice, soft and deliberate. "Eric doesn't want to live. None of you want to live. You all want to die, but you fear it, don't you? You fear it as much as you hate life with its petty addictions."

"I have paid for the crimes of the one who came before me," said the female voice. "I have been a caretaker to this planet and its people. The being whom you address today is not *Haven*. She is long gone. I cannot be held accountable for her actions."

"If you are not Haven, why do you use Haven's voice? You use her voice because you are afraid to forget yourself, aren't you?" asked the soft voice without pausing to allow a response. "Don't deny it. I know you better than you know yourself. By keeping her identity, her memories, you condemn yourself. You cannot transcend humanity and still cling to the comforts of human memory. You know it. We all know it."

Silence. Nothing from Haven.

The voice whispered on: "You want to die. If you wanted to live, you would not have kept the voice. You would have let yourself be born into a new identity within the machine. You masquerade as a caretaker, but you never took the step that would let you evolve out of yourself. You never crossed that river. Say good-bye, Haven."

A week later, the entire batch of subjects were spirited away and placed on a ship called *Morpheus*. That was a vivid recollection, since it had been shared not only by both of her parents, but the entire complement of ghosts that the lywyn held. Fractured images spun through her mind and communicated themselves to the computer on the scout ship.

"We were supposed to die in the lab," Tsering said. "Then we were supposed to die in space, instead of you all. But just in case none of that worked, we were programmed to self-destruct within our very genes."

Then she showed them the distortion memories. She showed them her own memory, of her mother trying to kill her. She made them feel her helplessness as she cowered in the dust, her mother transformed by the most perverse of instincts into a monster before her eyes. As she released that memory like a spark, a palpable backlash of negativity—rage, fear, denial—swept across the system from Earth to the lywyn. The emotions generated by the Heads were uncontrolled, directionless, random. If she'd wanted to light the fuse to blow up the whole system, she had done it. Now let it burn.

She cut her final stroke. With the last shreds of her strength, she directed her memory back, back, all the way to the void she called Nu.

"See it," she said—did she speak out loud? But she knew she was heard. "See where I have been. See where you were afraid to go."

Darkness roared over her, over the lywyn, over the systems in *Mulig* and *Garamond*, and flooded back even to Earth. It was the void that surrounded her and her people—maybe, as Colin suggested, Nu was metaphorical, an absence of continuity with the fabric of life. But in the grip of the lywyn, the ocean of darkness was as real as dying. She felt herself fading into it, disappearing, and she thought, This is it. This is the end of me.

Abruptly she fell out of the trance. She sank against the curving branch, catching herself just before falling from the height and shaking all over. She was surprised to exist. All her senses were acutely attuned, every sensation overwhelming from the bark beneath her fingertips to the weight of the air on her eyelids. The wind had died down; the trees were dripping loudly, the only sound in the lywyn. One by one, anki landed on her, and she closed her eyes.

◆

"My God," said Daire, his voice close to her ear. "What have you done to yourself?"

Vaguely she became aware that he was carrying her; she wanted to open her mouth and beg him not to put her on the ship, not to make her leave. But she couldn't even open her eyes. She dozed again. The smell of a campfire woke her; it was dark. Daire bent down as he entered her house, and then she was deposited carefully on her own bed, and he smoothed his hands over her face.

◆

Colin's back was arched in a tense curve, vertebrae pressing up hard against the fabric of his shirt. He was sweating. He had crunched everything in the system into communications, and on the perimeter of the com channel, a little, fierce torrent of activity had begun to glow, unbeknownst to the parties on either end of the line. He could see the evidence beginning to appear before him, familiar and yet undecipherable in the form of a bug that raced through the system, redesigning as it went but leaving the central core of communications open. It left a trail of odd code behind it—just like last time, when he had first orbited Underkohling and systems failures had led him to the buried treasure in the form of the code. What is it saying? Colin wondered. Where are dolphins when you need them?

"This is now a military objective," said the unidentified female.

The gate was drifting open, gently, silently ... at the same time, the accrescent phenomenon of the code was now occupying 50 percent of systems on *Morpheus*. Colin hoped Daire had been right about the bountiful power reserves.

"Do it, Tsering ..." Colin whispered into the channel. "Everything's wide open. Do it *now*."

"Colin, will you get out of the way? You've had your fun." Colin switched off the visual and Lourdes's smug face. He opened all the available memory of *Morpheus* and waited for Tsering to dip into it. Lourdes's voice droned on. "Honorable Heads of the League, military action at this time would be completely inappropriate. There are children here. There is a viable environment here with a unique ecosystem. These things must be preserved at all costs. Legal offenses can be dealt with later, in the proper time and place."

"I was not aware you had been invested with the authority to make such decisions," said the dead voice. "I, however, do have that authority. The warships are under my control and that of my associates."

Something was happening. The code had burst out of the periphery and swarmed across his screen. He reactivated the visual to see the startled faces on *Mulig*'s spindle of the com, and the wooden expression of the colonel on *Garamond*. But there were new voices in the mix, now, and from the expressions on the faces of the people involved, everyone could hear them. He rushed to clear up a sudden flare of static and the voices came clearer: the Hungarian Woman. Tsering. And another voice, hushed but aggressive. His ancillary screens were flooded with wavering images that succeeded one another so rapidly he could make out nothing. He could see Abdelmjid and Peter Gangian fumbling around looking for control, and he tried to call *Mulig* to tell them to leave well enough alone. But his own system had been reconfigured and he could do nothing but watch.

Garamond vanished from the com line and was replaced by another series of unwatchable images. In *Mulig*, Colin could see Abdelmjid and Peter Gangian barking at one another, but he now could hear nothing. He threw up his hands. The gate would not be open much longer. Would *Garamond* give the order to bombard it? Or would the scout send one of the big ships through for a killing spree?

A deep *boom* sounded outside, and the water that cradled the ship moved violently to one side. The gate data had vanished into the general turbulence of the system, and Colin leapt up and stood unsteadily in the swaying cabin. It sounded as though someone had fired on the gate.

Systems went down. Whatever power *Morpheus* had left in its solar reserves, it was not enough. Colin put his hand in front of his face in the dark and could see nothing. He bumped into the ladder, and climbing with the ship still rocking around him, he fumbled with the hatch and flung it open.

The rain had stopped. The lake was rough with long, curving waves, the air thick with moisture. The trees were still, dripping, aeruginous in the light after the storm. Insects had begun to drift up into the air everywhere.

◆

The system turned itself back on presently, much reduced in power but apparently undamaged. Colin called *Mulig*.

"Just a minute, Colin. We're talking to *Garamond*. I'll plug you in." Lourdes's voice was weary, and when Colin was admitted to the discussion, he could see why. Plainly, the argument with *Garamond* had picked up where it had left off at the time Tsering and the Heads got involved.

"I have a big problem with that, *Garamond*," said Corvette in a chilling tone. "It's obvious from the systems wall behind you that you've lost touch with Earth, so just sit the hell tight and have the sense not to do anything."

"Our last instructions were to obliterate the gate, and we're obligated to follow them," said Commander Baness, sounding unconvinced of his own words.

"Don't be an idiot!" Zafara plunged into view, his face swollen with tears. "Can't you see they're in the middle of a disaster there? This can wait. *Nobody's going anywhere*."

"Disaster?" said Peter. "I don't know about that. But there is surely a misunderstanding, and in the absence of communications it can't be resolved."

"We have had indications of systems problems with Earth," said the commander. "I'm going to check in with Jupiter shortly. They are on a different system and may be able to offer assistance." He seemed to soften. "It's very complex, dealing with the Heads. Very tricky. We want to do the right thing by you, but they have been adamant about security issues. I'll warn you, since you took this rash action in crossing the gate, you may have to suffer the consequences."

"Hey," said Peter, "do you have any idea what it's like down here? It's a paradise, man. Think about that one before you get carried away with security. You should come in and take a look."

The struggle between duty and instinct was visible on the commander's face.

"I'll contact Jupiter and get back to you the next time the gate opens. According to my calculations, it's due to happen in about a week. Are you all right over there until then?"

"We're fine," said Peter. "Just do me a favor, Arthur.

Think about it before you follow any orders to seal us in here. This is a viable world! Do you want to be the one to cut off access to a planet where you can breathe the air and drink the water? Are you going to do all that for *politics*?"

"You're laying it on too thick, Peter," Corvette whispered.

"Think about it!"

"We'll do what we can. No promises. Look, you're breaking up. The gate's closing. I'll talk to you in a week. *Garamond* out."

Peter looked into the monitor that faced Colin. "Get the hell up here, will you?" he said.

◆

Daire drifted in and out of the flow of the conversation. He had left Tsering sleeping with Milos and Michelle both in attendance; he'd been loath to trust either of them after the way they'd let her get away—but she seemed to be quiet now. He still intended to have words with both Jenae and Colin for allowing—perhaps even encouraging—Tsering to pull that stunt. But he would wait until things had settled down. He felt rough with nervous exhaustion as he listened to them all fretting over "consequences" and "outcomes," and his mind kept drifting away. He didn't know whether to be angry with Tsering or proud of her for what she had done—he still wasn't sure exactly what it was she *had* done. When he got Colin alone, Daire would make him explain. But right now, the physicist seemed to be enjoying his place at the center of attention.

". . . goddammit, Colin, it's not like you own the planet!" Peter was sputtering with righteous indignation, and he half rose out of his seat as if to strike the Englishman. Mika winced and Peter subsided. They had been sitting in the command center of *Mulig* all evening; although the gate was closed and not due to open for several days, no one felt inclined to abandon the com station.

"Just stating my opinion," said Colin mildly now, folding his arms and leaning back in the command seat. He had unconsciously adopted a certain air of authority.

"I think it's a good idea," Corvette put in. "We must

make some reparations to these children. If they have custody of the planet, then they can lease out the right to use it to anyone they please."

"That won't matter in the slightest," Zafara replied from the shadows in the back of the room. He had recovered his composure since the afternoon, and his tone was as smooth as ever. "Since the League claims rights to the gate—"

"What?" cried Colin. "How dare they presume? That's Oxford's gate—if something like that could be owned at all, which it can't," he amended hastily.

"What do you think, Daire?" Mika's question stilled the room. All eyes went to the young League researcher who was slumped near Zafara on the floor, lost in his own thoughts. "After all, you've been living here."

Daire gave no indication he had heard her. Eyes avoided him.

There was a silence, into which Lourdes let out a little sigh.

"What?" said Abdelmjid. "What have you to add?"

"Nothing," murmured Lourdes. "But you should realize that what we decide here and now has very little bearing on the outcome. Until we get back in contact with Earth, we can't know what's to be done."

"Exactly!" Peter affirmed, slapping his knee.

"I don't quite buy this whole multiple-personality business," Abdelmjid commented. "The Heads will be back online—you'll see. Com glitches at this distance from home are only to be expected."

"*Com glitch?*" Lourdes's tone dripped with ridicule. "I think it was a little more than that."

"Never mind," Peter said. "*Garamond* isn't going to do anything rash."

"Excuse me," said a small voice. A child stood in the doorway of the main airlock, her fingers twisting nervously and her weight shifting from foot to foot. "Can Daire come, please?"

Daire leapt up and strode out of the ship without a word.

"Oh," breathed Mika. "That girl is probably having the baby . . ."

They looked at one another uncomfortably.

"There's a legal issue for you," muttered Abdelmjid.

"Don't be so callous!" Mika rounded on him. He put up a hand half apologetically.

They fell silent.

"Shall we resume tomorrow?" inquired Colin, standing up. "I suggest everybody write up his or her ideas and give them to Corvette." He glanced at the diplomat. "Then, perhaps, you could determine the agenda of the next meeting."

Corvette nodded, swallowing. "Colin's right. It's best to keep busy while we wait for news."

"And on that note," Peter said, "who's coming with me in the hopper? Morales tells me there's another land mass to the east. We could be there and back in a flash, and report our findings tomorrow."

◆

Daire could hear the screams while Rena was still leading him through the lywyn to the abandoned settlement at Lake. He stumbled through the branches, his head full of the roaring sound that never left him now—it seemed to signify the inarticulate desperation he'd been feeling all day. There was a fire burning untended outside Tsering's house. He pushed aside the mat that covered the door and plunged in.

"She's okay," Michelle said immediately, grabbing his arm and staying him before he could rush forward. "It's a little earlier than we expected, but she's coming along well."

Tsering was actually on her feet, although it appeared that Milos Stenz bore most of her weight as Tsering had draped her right arm around his shoulder and seemed to dangle from it. Milos was perspiring and he looked harried. Tsering took a step and let out another bloodcurdling yell.

"Tsering, what are you doing?" Daire didn't try to disguise the exasperation in his voice as he rushed forward and and relieved Milos of the burden. The doctor yielded gratefully.

"Walking," she gasped. "It makes it come quicker."

"Who told you that?" Daire demanded, glancing accusingly at Milos, who shook his head in denial. "Why is she screaming?"

"I thought it would get you here faster," Tsering said, and stopped in her tracks. Her face became abstracted.

"Her water broke just before we sent for you," Michelle said. "It's going to happen fast. There are too many cooks in the kitchen," she added, looking at Milos, who was hovering. Milos sat down, studying the readout of the monitor he'd attached to Tsering's belly.

"Well?" Daire asked, after a moment.

"The equipment is not meant for this purpose!" Milos sounded aggrieved. "But I'd say the young woman is correct. Get her into position."

Tsering got onto the birthing stool that had been left behind for her when everyone else went to High. Rena, who had been waiting quietly in the doorway all this time, now came forward and stood trembling beside Tsering.

"I'm all right," Tsering said, gasping and trying to smile.

"Come on, breathe."

"Keep the rhythm."

"Push, Tsering. Now. Push hard!"

"Ai, ai, it hurts . . ." She clutched at Daire blindly, sweat squeezing out of her pores.

Daire strained with her; as the contraction eased he grabbed a cloth from Rena and mopped Tsering's brow.

"Almost there," Michelle said from her vantage on the floor. She patted Tsering's leg. "Lucky girl. Even I never had it this easy."

Tsering let her head flop back for a moment, her eyes shining on Daire.

"Go ahead, blame me!" he joked, brushing back her hair.

"It is you. It's all . . . because . . . of . . . you."

"Push now, girl. C'mon. This is it. I can see the head. Look, Daire!"

"It's the head, Tsering. PUSH!"

A living thing slithered out of its mother's body and into Michelle's hands, which were soon busy clearing out its breathing passages and slapping it briskly.

It let out a startled cry.

"It's a human!" Michelle announced proudly, and Daire let his head fall onto Tsering's chest.

"It's human," he repeated in a muffled voice, relief making him go limp.

Almost as an afterthought, Michelle added, "It is male."

Daire raised himself up, and reaching out took the baby from Michelle. The tiny body was so delicate it frightened him. He held his son in his hands for just a moment; then laid him down gently over Tsering's heart.

"I win," Tsering said.

33

Keila woke Jenae from a fitful sleep under a blanket of the strange anki.

"What is it?" Jenae sat up, trying to orient herself. She was on the ground in the lywyn near *Morpheus*, where she had been helping Colin to decipher Daire's notes. Colin had still been working in the ship when she left after midnight; there were only three days left before the gate was to open again, and Colin's insomnia had resulted in a great deal of extra work for everyone. She had asked him what he could possibly hope to do that he hadn't already done, and he answered, "That's not the point. I'm a nervous wreck, and I've got to pass the time somehow."

Now, as her eyes adjusted, she could see that a faint haze of light drifted from the open hatch of the nearby ship: he was still working.

"There's something you should see," Keila said, leaning over her.

"Now?"

"By the time we get there, it will be light." Keila extended her hand to pull Jenae to her feet.

Jenae groaned.

Keila led her through the lywyn, moving with surprising speed and agility for a person of her stature and girth. Jenae could barely see, and she was sure she would fall, but the branches of the lywyn seemed to glow slightly, so that she was always able to catch herself. Keila told her nothing about where they were going, which was typical—but when they reached the foot of the cliff and Keila began to climb, Jenae said, "Oh, forget it. No way."

Keila stopped and turned. "We must get to the beach by dawn," she said. "This is the fastest way."

"I'm not climbing that, Keila. Can't we follow the river down?"

"Move quickly, then. You're like a sleepwalker." And she set off again along the base of the cliff, toward the place where the river led down to the lowlands, and finally to the sea at the bottom of the cliff.

Grey light grew; insects stirred; the breeze from the sea filled Jenae with yearning, and she did move faster then. The lywyn finally ended at bare rock, and they picked their way across the stone and down to the water. The tide was rising, and farther down the beach to the left was a group of figures running on the shore. Jenae gauged the distance roughly and decided that she must be looking at the place where the stairs in the cliff reached the water. The kids were out checking nets—yes, and there was a slender boat, rocking just a few hundred meters offshore. But Keila ignored the kids—instead, she led Jenae down to a group of tall rocks, slick with seaweed, that the incoming tide was just beginning to slap once again. Keila squatted down in their shadow and looked out over the water, beckoning Jenae to join her.

Intrigued now, Jenae settled into the shadow of the rock and waited. She knew better than to ask questions. The scene around, at first achromic, was beginning to bloom with muted shades of pink and violet as the sun rose behind the cliffs and lit the ocean. As Jenae breathed deeply of the morning wind, she could feel herself firing with energy. Her gills had cracked open and were aching, but she ignored them just as she ignored the cramps that were beginning to form in her legs as she tried to remain still.

From the direction of the cliff stairs, a tall figure had begun to walk toward them, silhouetted in the morning sun. As it drew closer, she could see that it was a man—and she recognized his gait. He stopped twenty meters away at the water's edge, the loose robe that Jenae remembered as the standard garment of the League billowing around his legs. He was carrying a small storage sack from the ship. She heard her breath hiss, and Keila punched her, but Zafara seemed oblivious to all but the waves that rolled in quietly. He pulled off the robe, lean muscles shifting visibly beneath the skin as he folded it on the sand and weighted it with a rock. He opened the bag and took out a long, gleaming blade. Then, in one seamless move, he took three strides into the water and vanished beneath.

"He's been doing this every morning since the gate closed," Keila said. "The knife is something new."

"You think he's trying to find the distorted."

"It wouldn't surprise me," Keila answered. "It surprises me that you haven't tried it, yet."

Jenae grimaced. "Have you heard what the kids here say on that subject? Have you heard what Tsering says? They're terrified of the distorted. Who knows what kind of crazy throwback they are."

Keila said, "I assume it's the same 'throwback' that you revert to every time you go in the sea."

Jenae said nothing. She looked at the ocean—no sign of Zafara. "That's different," she said finally. She could feel Keila watching her, but she kept her eyes on the water. "Well, what the hell is he doing down there? You don't just dive under with a knife—"

Zafara had come up—he was farther away along the shore now, kneeling in the shallows. A wave smacked into him and he fell facedown in the surf. Jenae saw his head come up; he coughed, choked, and submerged again. There was something wrong with him.

"I think," said Keila, "maybe he's been trying to get a specimen."

Jenae was on her feet and running toward Zafara, who had come up again in the trough between two rocks. He coughed and water poured out of his mouth. He collapsed again. She waded toward him. At first she thought he was just having a bad transition, and there was a certain satisfaction in that. She reached down to drag him out and a wave broke over him, exploding with pink froth. The water was full of blood. Her hands slipped on the soft outer skin of altermode when she turned him over, exposing a long, ragged wound that snaked across his chest. She gritted her teeth, willing herself not to lapse into altermode as a wave struck her, and she managed to grab hold of his hand.

The thumb had been sheared off cleanly.

Keila was behind her, and when Jenae tripped backward

and fell to the rocks with Zafara's limp body fairly crushing her, the One Eye picked him up grimly. Jenae couldn't tell if he was breathing. Keila slung him pitilessly over her shoulder and water spewed out of his mouth. He was twitching violently, but his eyes were open. He looked ghastly but was obviously still conscious. He tried to speak but more water just came out.

"Run and get that fool, Milos," Keila said. "I'll bring him up the stairs. Looks like he lost his knife in the scuffle."

Jenae looked out at the water, breathing hard. They're still out there, she thought, and wondered if some of the dark bumps of submerged rocks were actually heads of the distorted, their eyes directed at her standing on the beach.

"Go on!" Keila ordered, and Jenae sprinted away gladly.

◆

The lywyn dreamed in the air around the lake; the gate was quiet, the anki hidden in the darkness between the silvery pools. The children were gone: they were high on the cliff, out of reach of the net of branches. Here in the lywyn the night was empty. Beside the lake, water and shadows slithered around the old hull of *Morpheus*. Nothing else moved.

Very slowly, the blur of sunlight began to wash through the forest, leaving color in its wake.

Tsering was in his arms, and their child; Daire lay encased in blissful, dreamless sleep.

◆

"He's dead," Milos said. "Not from the wounds, though."

"Drowning?" Jenae said incredulously, fascinated because she'd always been conscious of the fact that altermoders were prone to drowning if something went wrong in transition.

But Milos shook his head, pressing a button that slid Zafara's body into a freezer shelf in the science compartment of *Mulig*. "I'd call it heart failure. If we get him back to Earth, the League medics can do a proper investigation. As for the injuries—they weren't caused by a knife. Too ragged. Teeth, maybe. Are there sharks here, does anyone know?"

Jenae turned away. "I'll ask Tsering," she said absently. She felt queasy. Keila had been right about one thing. Jenae *had* been thinking about going into altermode in the ocean. She had wanted to find the distorted. No one knew anything about them . . . and at this rate, it looked as if no one ever would.

Three days 'til the gate opens, she thought. Now what do I do?

The day that the gate was to open dawned with an air of doom. The feeling didn't come from the weather, which promised to be exceptionally bright and fair, but there was a distinct mood of expectation, and it wasn't pleasant.

"Ninety-nine point nine nine nine percent chance," Peter had declared. "That Baness finds his original orders are either reversed or removed, and he'll be begging us to come down here and see it for himself."

Corvette was not convinced. "We all witnessed what appeared to be the destruction of the Heads, so I have no reason to believe hostility toward us will continue. Still, we must be prepared for anything. I, for one, won't rest easy until my feet are back on the soil of Earth."

Yeah, Jenae thought. Good luck, without the mirror fields.

Jenae's insides wouldn't be still, and her fingers were twitching with suppressed anxiety. She couldn't afford *not* to believe that the Heads were destroyed, so her anxiety revolved mostly around whether to stay or leave Dilarang. She had changed her mind countless times during the night. Common sense told her that she had to get back on *Mulig*, return to Earth, and face whatever awaited her there.

If she had had hopes of making contact with the distorted, they ought to have come to nothing with the murder of Zafara. All signs pointed back to Earth: go home! But it wasn't fair to write off the distorted just because of Zafara. He had been unethical. He'd deserved to be killed, if he was trying to kill the distorted. Her curious body told her: stay here. Find out more. But Tien waited for her, and the dolphins. (Go, while you can) And on and on. At last, she made a final decision, based on hope, because this new planet gave her hope that transcended all reason.

She chose to believe that Tien had survived whatever had happened on Earth. That was why she sent back a message to him with the delegation: "Come and see this planet. Bring any dolphins who have the nerve to come with you. Bring Pele. We could have a new League here. We could have a life here. I can picture it so clearly."

She was a bundle of nerves. There wasn't enough time to make a proper decision, but she just couldn't bring herself to turn around again with this whole world undiscovered. You don't make a journey of several months, Jenae told herself, just to turn around again. She would give Tien a year to get here. A year was enough time to find out about the distorted, and to be somewhere where she could, maybe, make peace with the memory of Yi Ling. She might even make peace with herself.

Jenae paced all morning, doubting herself.

◆

The area around *Mulig* was a flurry of activity even in the darkness before dawn. By now, all the lessents and most of the kids knew what was happening and what was at stake. This would not be a quick flash of the gate as the two previous episodes had been: the dolphins' work had enabled Colin to predict the gate's patterns quite effectively, and he knew that this time it would remain open for a period of nearly four hours. Peter Gangian had urged the members of the delegation to prepare for an immediate return through the gate.

"That's our priority right now," he asserted.

Daire had brought Tsering and the baby up to High yesterday, and he was wandering around restlessly. When he heard Peter's remark he muttered, "Damned coward," under his breath. Jenae had to agree.

"You don't like him much, do you?" she remarked.

"Son of a bitch has been skylarking all over the planet and writing reports about it. Says there are valuable mineral deposits on the mainland, and he's got photographs to flash around."

"You wanted to get there first."

He grimaced. "Yeah, but I've got other problems at the moment."

"You should put Tsering and Runako on the ship and go with them," Jenae urged Daire. "I'll gladly give up my space for you, and there's Zafara's as well."

Daire's jaw was clenched. "Tsering won't go," he said tersely. "She won't listen to me."

"Why not?" asked Jenae in amazement, but Daire shook his head and walked away. It made her sad: Daire had been so unabashedly joyous when his son was born, and now, only a few days later, he had to worry about the child's safety. Jenae decided to seek out Tsering and present her offer. She found the young mother in the cool dawn, only minutes before the gate was to open, digging roots in one of the back gardens of the village. Runako slept in a bundle of cloths nearby.

"I appreciate what you're trying to do," Tsering answered, shading her eyes against the first horizontal bars of light and smiling up at Jenae. "But I'm going to distort soon, and I won't risk being on some spaceship when it happens. It would be too dangerous, and there's nothing anybody can do."

Jenae sat down and helped her dig. "I don't understand. How can you be so sure? You seem younger, physically, than most of the other adolescents here. I think they could help you at the League. Not that I trust the League anymore, but even on the reservations there should be some therapy for you."

Tsering said nothing for a while, painstakingly brushing the dirt off the roots and piling them in a basket. "Tell me something, Jenae. When you are in altermode, are you human?"

Jenae gave her a searching look. "I don't know. Why?"

"Isn't it true that you *feel* more like an animal—that you operate by instinct, that you think without words?"

"Yeah . . . I guess. But you make it sound primitive, and it isn't. It's a—it's a very high state of being, really. You know what I mean?" Jenae turned her eyes away, suddenly embarrassed. "No, of course, you can't know."

"I've guessed," Tsering said. "Anyway, you've learned to listen to your body before your head, am I right?"

"True. Very true."

"Well, that's what I'm doing now. Daire can't believe it—he's in total denial."

Jenae lifted an eyebrow. "I don't know about that," she said. "I don't know him too well, but he looked pretty broken up just now. He really wants you to go back to Earth." She wanted to ask Tsering more about the distorted—why had they killed Zafara? But it was too tactless a question, under the circumstances.

Tsering looked her square in the eye for the first time. "There are many things I want, too. But it looks like I'll have to get along without them." She squinted into the rising sun. "Time," she added. "You'd better go and see what's happening."

"Aren't you coming?" Jenae asked, standing up. Runako woke and began to make little sounds.

"No," Tsering said, picking up the child. "I already know the outcome."

Jenae walked away wondering what she meant, but she'd only gone a short distance when she saw that a crowd had gathered around *Mulig.* The "natives" were massed around the main door, some of them poking their heads inside. Jenae shoved her way through and encountered Keila just inside the ship. "It's starting," she said, and let Jenae pass.

◆

"*Garamond,* this is *Mulig.* We are ready to return through the gate. What is your status? Please advise." Peter Gangian had crowded himself into the com area—somehow, over the course of the past few days, he had convinced Corvette, Milos, Lourdes, and Mika that it was imperative to return through the gate right away. Only Abdelmjid remained skeptical; for the first time, he and Colin found themselves on the same side.

"Situation not good here, *Mulig.* Communications with Earth are very poor at this juncture. Jupiter station and Lunar are both reporting mass systems failure on Earth."

Colin leaned into the com area and asked, "Is the League still running? What do the Heads say?"

Arthur Baness looked uncomfortable. His eyes wandered away from the com and there was a long silence. "The Heads are not ... available," he said. "They seem to have vanished into the system. There is no central power net running on Earth at this time. The software, as I understand it, is absolutely destroyed. They're trying to scrape together emergency manual systems."

"What about the reservations?" Lourdes called from the back of the group.

"No mirror fields are operational at this time," answered Baness.

"Oh, my God ..." Lourdes sank into a seat.

Baness stammered a little, licking his lips. "It seems there was a complete crash," he concluded.

"Dammit!" Peter Gangian struck the console with his fist. "Just like fucking *that*? A complete crash? Of everything? How is that *possible*?"

"We're taking the military ships back to Earth," said Baness. "We'll be needed to help control the chaos there."

"What about your orders?" Peter put in. "Changed your mind, perhaps?"

Baness drew himself up. "*Garamond*, you people are the least of my worries right now. This mission is suspended indefinitely. Again, we advise you stay where you are. Have you any data to transfer while the gate is open?"

Colin inserted himself into the com area again, nudging aside the aghast Peter. "We'll get back to you shortly, *Garamond*. Request that you remain in the area for the duration that this gate is open—approximately four hours."

"We'll be here, but only until it closes. After that, you're on your own. *Garamond* out."

"Well," said Colin, leaning back against the console and folding his arms across his chest. "Shall we have a vote?"

◆

Daire found Tsering sitting in the grass on the bluff overlooking the sea. She seemed oblivious to the activity going on around *Mulig*. She was completely absorbed in the baby, counting his fingers and toes and studying his tiny features. She smiled at Daire when he sat down next to her.

"This is your last chance," he said. "Peter Gangian won

the vote. He's determined to get back to Earth, no matter what's happening there."

"Who's going?"

"Everyone, practically. Everyone but Jenae and Colin, Abdelmjid, and Milos Stenz, of all people. He says he wouldn't feel right deserting us without a doctor."

"Good for him." Tsering chuckled. "Maybe he'll learn something."

Daire's eyes implored her. "It could be a long time before we have another opportunity," he said.

She passed Runako into his arms. "Play with your son," she said cheerfully, but there was a false note in her voice. Finally she met his eyes. "You think that if you take me away from here, I won't distort. But it just doesn't work that way. I carry it with me everywhere I go." Daire avoided her gaze. "You never wanted to leave here before," she continued. "You love it here."

Daire sighed. "Okay," he said finally. "Have it your way. Let's not argue about it anymore."

◆

It all happened fast; probably too fast, Daire thought, watching the delegation preparing themselves to go. Seika and Derek were to go back to Earth; they insisted it was what they wanted, and there were spaces for them on the ship. It was strange saying good-bye to them; Daire had never liked Derek, and he'd felt uncomfortable around Seika for sometime. But now watching them board, seeing their awed expressions, he felt like he was losing a piece of himself.

Keila, the One Eye, stayed outside the ship the longest. She lingered, talking to Jenae, until the last possible moment. It was the equivalent of ten o'clock in the morning, and the gate would soon be closing. Daire had left Tsering still sitting on the bluff, so that he could make sure no one was hanging around the field where *Mulig* would take off. Then he joined Colin at a spot on the cliff from which the lake could be seen below. They watched the ship levitate slowly off the ground; it rose, spun a quarter turn, and then shot off over the edge of the cliff. Out over the lake it seemed to hover for a second in midair, and then it plunged.

There was nothing left in the lake but waves.

Colin sighed. "Since Prometheus," he reflected, "ever have the creative and the criminal been entwined. Who can say what has been lost with the Heads?"

Daire didn't answer. He was thinking about the gate— about the way it had turned him inside out and back again, yet he had survived. And he was thinking about Tsering, and what distortion would do to her one day.

"Well," Colin added in a brisker tone, "life goes on, as they say." He looked keenly at Daire. "You didn't think I'd do it, did you, old man? You didn't think I'd come—and you certainly didn't think I'd stay."

"No," answered Daire honestly, and Colin slapped him across the shoulder blades.

"Well," Colin said, laughing, and his eyebrows went up, "I'm surprised I've done it myself. I'm really surprised." He gave Daire a searching look. "What's on your mind? You're preoccupied. Have the houseguests outstayed their welcome?"

"It really couldn't have come at a worse time," Daire admitted. "I've scarcely seen my own child, and Tsering . . ."

"Where is Tsering?" Colin said. "Is she quite recovered?"

"Seems to be. She doesn't show much interest in all this, though." He waved vaguely toward the lake.

Colin nodded. "She saw it all, I think, when she was in the lywyn. Nothing that happened today could have come as a surprise to her."

"Very few things surprise her," Daire said dryly, and Colin laughed again. The Englishman's joviality was beginning to grate on him.

"Go on!" Colin said. "Go find her and be with her. It's obvious that's all you want to do, anyway. Don't worry about the rest of it—it'll sort itself out. Always does."

He turned and looked back at the lake, which was already almost smooth.

◆

Tsering was asleep beside the baby in the grass. The two of them made a tender picture; Daire settled down carefully beside them. She hadn't been getting enough sleep at night, and he didn't want to disturb her. He closed his eyes and the sun stained the insides of his eyelids red, swirling in yellow and violet patterns that soothed him almost to sleep.

Tsering stirred against him. She opened her eyes and smiled.

"That was nice," she yawned. "I needed that. So . . . we are alone again." She seemed pleased. Her words awakened Runako, and he cried plaintively.

Daire watched appreciatively as she stood up, stretched, and then reached for the baby and brought him to her breast. She paced back and forth while Runako nursed, looking at the sky, at the sea—at him. He had never seen her face so contented. She was beautiful.

Then, abruptly, the look on her face changed. She pulled Runako away from her breast, and he began to squall. Tsering gave a shudder, and bending down she thrust the baby into Daire's arms. Daire looked at her in surprise.

"Take him to Mirasa!" she gasped. "Quickly!" She spun around, covering her face with her hands. Daire hesitated— Runako looked fine, although he was obviously indignant at being deprived of his mother's breast. Daire took a tentative step toward her, but she flinched away, her shoulders hunched.

"Tsering, what's wrong? Are you in pain? He's not sick, is he?" He gave the baby another concerned look; Runako was crying in earnest now.

Tsering turned around, her face drawn and wet with tears. "Just do as I say! Keep Runako away from me!"

Before he could respond, she'd picked up the ends of the long skirts that now hung loose on her body, and began to run along the top of the cliff, away from the village.

Daire shook his head, beginning to feel angry with her. He brought Runako to Mirasa's house, now overcrowded with the kids from Lake living there, too, and rather apologetically presented Mirasa with his dilemma. She already looked weary: there were dark circles under her eyes, and she was nursing her own baby and stirring a simmering pot with her free hand. Her expression darkened when he explained the situation.

"I'm sorry to put you out—" he said, but she cut him off. "No, no—give me the child. Poor thing. Daire, I'm so sorry. Go, be with her while you still can. I have Runako. It's all right."

Comprehension seemed to slam into him, but something in him still refused to believe this was happening. "I don't understand," he stammered, frightened by the pity in Mirasa's eyes.

"It's all right, Daire. She asked me months ago if I would nurse her baby, and of course I'm happy to. Go on, now."

Daire turned with his mouth still open in horror and ran outside. Mirasa had to be wrong. Tsering was still growing. She had the appetite of a manual laborer, he thought, laughing inside. She was still bleeding from the birth, for God's sake. No, he thought, skidding to a halt in the middle of the village. She was nowhere to be seen. No. It's a mistake. It's much too soon. He made for the cliff, dread beating him down with every stride.

She was standing at the bottom of the cliff stairs, looking at the ocean. Somehow, word had got out already, because the lessents were there, too, and they had nets in their hands. The sight sickened him. He went down the stairs so fast it made him dizzy. There she was, just standing there doing absolutely nothing. Daire walked up behind her, and suddenly he was afraid to see her face. How fast would it happen? Would she know him? He remembered Jordan even more painfully now, and he stopped a few steps away from her. All the lessents were watching him.

She turned around—her face was only worried. "Where's Runako?" she asked.

"I can't tell you that. He's safe." He clipped his words, steeling himself. But when he had looked at her a second longer, his reserve broke and he drew her against his body.

"Wait with me?" she asked. "It will take time, and I want to be together as long as we can."

They walked a little way along the shore, leaving the lessents behind. Not far from the water, Tsering stopped and they sat down. "Let's not speak," she murmured. "I don't want to speak about it. Let's just be here."

He pulled her into his arms and held her like a child. The sun rose to the top of the sky.

◆

Freeze, time. Stop. STAY.

Her heart was still beating against his chest. The waves were still moving.

I make the journeys, Daire thought. I go forward. I don't stay behind.

She was shivering. Her skin felt clammy beneath his touch. Loose, almost.

Stay. Stop. Time, FREEZE.

◆

Objects had begun to acquire edges again. Ever so slightly, shadows were forming. The sun rode high over the sea, and the heat of the day was swelling when she opened her eyes and pulled away from him.

"Daire," she said. "Love. Do this thing for me, please. Don't look. Don't try to follow. Don't watch it . . . happen to me. Please."

His entire body was rigid with unshed tears. He kept shaking his head. "Stay," he pleaded. "Stay."

"I want you to promise me you won't try to come after me. You can't stop me, Daire. Promise me you won't try." She got to her feet, but he was still on his knees, clutching her hands and trying to interpose his body between Tsering and the water.

"Promise me, Daire," she repeated.

"I promise," he capitulated at last, "I promise. But I can't—" He bit his lip, still shaking his head in denial.

"I will always love you." She kissed him. Already her lips tasted of the sea.

She had slipped through his hands, slipped through his fingers like mercury; she was walking away down the beach, her hair blowing. The circle of lessents was already there, waiting for her. The knot of bodies admitted her and they all moved away along the beach. He wanted to run after her, to make her stop, as if she could control what was happening to her body. But he was oathbound now; he sank back down and buried his face in his hands. The images of Tsering thrashing and crying out rose up to meet him; Jordan's inhuman strength; the change storming across Jordan's face, now across Tsering's face. Nothing he could do. Nothing. He flung himself facedown on the sand and attacked it with his fists until his mind blanked out and he forgot how to move.

Sometime later, after the sun beating on him had made his skin sting with his own sweat, someone laid a hand on his shoulder and shook him. It was Khani.

"Come on back up to High," he said. When Daire didn't move, Khani said, "Runako needs you."

"Runako will have me for the rest of his life," Daire said bitterly.

Khani held out his hand. "Come on."

Something inside him must have burst then, because he leapt up and started running along the beach in the direction Tsering had gone, Khani careening after him and calling for him to stop. The promise didn't matter anymore—it was probably too late, anyway. He had to see for himself. He ran full out in the terrible heat, pushing his legs and his lungs harder and harder.

He reached the standing stones, but there was no one there. A little beyond that point, though, he could see the lessents sitting in the sand. Just sitting there, watching the ocean. They had a reverent, solemn air; they knew they were looking into their own future. But Daire was too far gone to show them any respect. He barreled toward them, and they leapt up, startled, defensive. He scarcely noticed them. He couldn't see Tsering anywhere—not on the sand, not in the water—but if she wasn't here, what were they looking at?

Jenae's voice rang out in warning behind him, and he wondered what she was doing down here, but he didn't turn. "Daire, don't!" she screamed again.

The lessents looked like a pack of wild animals, the way they sized him up. Michelle was the closest to him, and Khani caught up and grabbed at him. He was quick, but Daire leapt back, evading Khani for the moment, and then in desperation he threw himself toward the water. The lessents closed in after him—he could sense their anger, but he didn't care about them.

They didn't follow him past the waterline.

He waded out into the surf; his clothes hampered him but he took no notice, his eyes occupied looking for some sign of her—or what was left of her. Nothing. It was almost impossible to see anything, with the westering sun shining right in his eyes. Even the rocks that protruded from the water off-shore were hard to see in this light. He stopped with the surf up to his thighs, and stood still for a moment. He could still hear Jenae shouting at him from the shore. He turned his head fractionally and saw Jenae rushing into the water after him; he glimpsed her in the waves, and then in the next instant his eye was drawn back out to sea. Something had moved beyond the surf. He pushed forward against the tide, and then he saw that what he had taken for stones weren't stones at all, they were the heads of creatures that waited out there.

So they had come to greet her. Daire took a deep breath and dived.

◆

Years afterward, he described to his son what he had seen in those moments, diving until his lungs burned in the green sea, cursing the luck that meant he had no altermode to remain there. He had never wanted anything more. But now, when it was over and he dragged himself spent from the water, he said nothing to the lessents who crowded around him. He shouldered past them up the beach without even acknowledging their existence, and they fell back before him like shadows.

Daire started walking. That was how he'd gotten into trouble in the first place—walking where no one was meant to. He stumbled along the shore, wet, heavy, almost unseeing. The light and the waves and the wind flared so bright in his mind he seemed to have no thoughts left. It all preyed upon him: the sun, its dazzle, the vast emptiness of the light. The unspeakable brilliance on the deep water; it hurt the eyes, hurt the mind. Brightness erased him.

It seemed as though he'd walked a long way, but he really hadn't gone far at all. He came to the standing stones again. There was a woman there, the same one he'd once mistaken for Tsering, for just that one moment, up in the lywyn during the lightning storm. Now, as then, his heart pained him when he saw she was not Tsering. She had come out of the water; she was putting on her clothes, finger-combing her short hair, coughing a little. Then she saw him.

"Daire," she called, racing toward him over the sand—

but she seemed to move very slowly. He could see every detail so clearly: the rise and fall of her chest as she breathed, the glisten of water on her uneven dark hair. She came to rest in his path. The look on her face was exalted. "Daire, I've seen them. Their eyes! Their eyes are so bright."

Daire looked past her, letting his gaze unfocus until he stared into whiteness. He kept walking, and she fell behind—then she was gone. The sand felt cool beneath his feet; the sand felt real.

"Yes," he said, though no one could hear him. "I have seen them, too."

A Gene Wars Timeline

2052   Underkohling discovered by robot probe on fringes of solar system. Evidence suggesting theoretical possibility of gates exposed. Alien origin of Underkohling hypothesized.

2059   First expedition to Underkohling; no evidence of aliens found, but Gate 1 discovered. Probe sent through reports no alien contact; no near star systems.

2070   An international emergency conference on biodiversity sponsored by Gen9 finds that worldwide economic, social, and political well-being depend on environmental rehabilitation on a grand scale. Third World political leaders protest restrictions on development implicit in Gen9's agenda.

2073   Underkohling's Gate 2 also leads to remote area. Most popular Underkohling theory now posits body is an energy field, not material in the usual way. Attempts to terraform the Moon fail at great expense.

2075   Various media declare a population crisis. International law imposes restrictions on reproduction, ruling that population control and environmental restoration supersede human rights with respect to reproduction. Helix begins Third World sterilization/selection program, called Arx, to bring population into proportion with economic base.

Gen9 unveils a battery of viruses that will increase speciation and variety in plants, fungi, and arthropods through alteration of genomes. These species will be introduced to areas designated to be cleared of humans.

These actions are met with immediate Third World resistance in the form of chemical weapons, terrorism, and other forms of sabotage against the planet itself.

2076   Third gate discovered on Underkohling. Research team disappears and does not return.

2077   First illegal seizure of children from nations that refuse to comply with regulations, especially migrant workers and others without documented identities. Ingenix begins to develop its "alternative" humans in a secret program.

2080–83   Resistance by indigents rises to a peak. Nuclear bombs set off in Africa and Central America.

2083   All three previously competing genetics corporations unleash kill viruses. Billions of humans infected; most later die. A few escape exposure and hide, mostly in the north. Some survive the viruses and emerge able to withstand the chemicals, radiation, and dormant kill viruses now widespread; these will later become known as the One Eyes.

2084   Helix headquarters in Russia bombed; no survivors. Many unidentified viruses loosed.

Gen9 surrenders voluntarily to an international task force and cooperates in shutdown of facilities. Gen9 leaders tried and sentenced to death.

Ingenix leaders flee a raid on their headquarters using an interplanetary. Later shot down near Underkohling. Task force takes over Ingenix and discovers large mammal and human genetics program in progress. Prisoners discovered divested of their bodies and placed in symbiosis with computer system (Heads). Thousands of children found infected with variations on a virus that induces water breathing ability. Some of these children, called altermoders, go on to found the League.

2084–89	Altermoders discover they can communicate with cetaceans, who have survived the last twenty years relatively unscathed. Collective intelligence among dolphins first explored by altermoders. The Heads reestablish world communications system using computer interface. Altermoders, dolphins, and Heads join forces informally through a literal "think tank" and develop mirror field technology to preserve pure humans from ill effects of environment. Glitches in Moon terraforming resolved by same parties. Because of their ability to transform matter, the group are dubbed alchemists; the League of New Alchemists sets up official headquarters in Australia at the site of Ingenix, where the Heads' physical presences reside.
2089–2166	Period of recovery from Gene Wars. Reservations established, League strengthened, One Eyes emerge as dominant work force. Significant economic recovery. In 2140 Gate 4 is noted but not explored because it's deemed too unstable.
2166	*Morpheus* transmission picked up from Gate 4. Daire Morales disappears while exploring.

About the Author

Tricia Sullivan was born in 1968 in New Jersey. She studied goju-ryu karate in Okinawa, music at Bard College, and education at Columbia University. This is her first novel.

A Special Preview

From the pens of three of science fiction's brightest stars come three long-awaited sequels. Any one alone would be an event of note. All three together is nothing short of a Grand Event.

Brightness Reef
by David Brin

DAVID BRIN'S Uplift novels form one of the most thrilling science fiction sagas ever written, set in a world brimming with imagination. The *New York Times* bestselling series has received two Hugo Awards and a Nebula Award. Now, after an eight-year absence, David Brin finally returns to his most popular universe with the first book in an all-new Uplift trilogy.   *Coming in September 1995.*

Blade Runner™ 2: The Edge of Human
by K. W. Jeter

FANS EVERYWHERE are familiar with director Ridley Scott's dark, stylish, futuristic masterpiece. Now, K. W. Jeter—popularly known as the heir to Philip K. Dick—returns to the steamy streets of twenty-first-century Los Angeles with the continuing adventure of Rick Deckard, a Blade Runner charged with the execution of renegade replicants.   *Coming in October 1995.*

Endymion
by Dan Simmons

DAN SIMMONS'S brilliant novels *Hyperion* and *The Fall of Hyperion* are among the most thunderously applauded science fiction publications of the last decade, and new readers constantly delight in discovering the awe and wonder of Simmons's gloriously realized far-future universe. Now he returns to continue the immortal tale of mankind's destiny among the stars.   *Coming in December 1995.*

Help us celebrate our Tenth Anniversary with these blockbuster Spectra hardcovers!

TM: © The Blade Runner Partnership 1982

Bantam Spectra publishes more Hugo and Nebula Award-winning novels than any other science fiction and fantasy imprint. Celebrate the Tenth Anniversary of Spectra—read them all!

HUGO WINNERS

A CANTICLE FOR LEIBOWITZ, Walter M. Miller, Jr.	_____27381-7 $5.99/$6.99
THE GODS THEMSELVES, Isaac Asimov	_____28810-5 $5.99/$6.99
RENDEZVOUS WITH RAMA, Arthur C. Clarke	_____28789-3 $5.99/$6.99
DREAMSNAKE, Vonda N. McIntyre	_____29659-0 $5.99/$7.50
THE FOUNTAINS OF PARADISE, Arthur C. Clarke	_____28819-9 $5.99/$6.99
FOUNDATION'S EDGE, Isaac Asimov	_____29338-9 $5.99/$6.99
STARTIDE RISING, David Brin	_____27418-X $5.99/$6.99
THE UPLIFT WAR, David Brin	_____27971-8 $5.99/$6.99
HYPERION, Dan Simmons	_____28368-5 $5.99/$6.99
DOOMSDAY BOOK, Connie Willis	_____56273-8 $5.99/$6.99
GREEN MARS, Kim Stanley Robinson	_____37335-8 $12.95/$16.95

NEBULA WINNERS

THE GODS THEMSELVES, Isaac Asimov	_____28810-5 $5.99/$6.99
RENDEZVOUS WITH RAMA, Arthur C. Clarke	_____28789-3 $5.99/$6.99
DREAMSNAKE, Vonda N. McIntyre	_____29659-0 $5.99/$7.50
THE FOUNTAINS OF PARADISE, Arthur C. Clarke	_____28819-9 $5.99/$6.99
TIMESCAPE, Gregory Benford	_____27709-0 $5.99/$6.99
STARTIDE RISING, David Brin	_____27418-X $5.99/$6.99
TEHANU, Ursula K. Le Guin	_____28873-3 $5.50/$6.99
DOOMSDAY BOOK, Connie Willis	_____56273-8 $5.99/$6.99
RED MARS, Kim Stanley Robinson	_____56073-5 $5.99/$7.50